SVALBARD IS.

40 E

80 E

120 E

60 N

40 N

o Boat
rcelona — Venice
The Yankee

20 N

aga of
naught

RED SEA

Bab el Mandeb

40 N

KENYA

TANZANIA

Mombasa

20 N

The Dreaming Coast

SINGAPORE

0

MADAGASCAR

20 S

40 S

THE WORLD OF TRISTAN JONES

40 E

80 E

chart by Montine Jordan

YARNS

YARNS
Tristan Jones

SAIL BOOKS

Boston, Massachusetts

Copyright © 1983 by SAIL Books
34 Commercial Wharf
Boston, MA 02110

SAIL books are published by
Sail Publications, Inc.

Manufactured in the
United States of America.

Book design by Mel Green

Library of Congress Cataloging
in Publication Data

Jones, Tristan, 1924-
    Yarns.

    1. Sailing—Addresses, essays, lectures.
I. Titles
GV811.J67 1983   797.1'24   83-3114
ISBN 0-914814-41-9

Cardanach yw'r edua'n
gyfrodedd nag yn ungorn

Stronger is the twisted thread
than the single yarn.

OLD WELSH PROVERB

CONTENTS

FOREWORD

Although I have known Tristan Jones for the better part of a decade and believe I have read practically everything he has written, either published or in manuscript form, it wasn't until I was given the opportunity to page through *Yarns* that I understood from whence comes his incredible prolificity. Born the son of a Welsh sea captain aboard his father's ship, he was raised near the sea in west Wales—a land where storytelling is as natural to the inhabitants as going fishing or voyaging throughout the world as crew with the great flag lines of pre–World War Two Britain. Tristan, I understand now, is a true Welsh bard, a natural storyteller, from whose pen has flowed such a quantity of tales of the sea that one is hard put to find his equal. Perhaps Joseph Conrad, whom he admires, comes closest. The measure of Tristan's appreciation of Conrad even appears in this book in a fictional piece called "Breakdown," which is less an imitation than a celebration of Conradian style.

It wasn't always thus. In the early seventies, when I first met Tristan professionally, I had no idea (and I don't believe he did either) that he would end a span of ten years with eleven books or more to his credit. At that time, there was only *The Incredible Voyage*, in bits and pieces of manuscript, accompanied by a package of faded black and white photos, still reeking of the dampness of the sea and of the Andes. I was the editor of *Rudder*, which was then, we thought, still an interesting national journal for boating people. In its eighty-five-year history the magazine had serialized such immortal seafaring books as *The Saga of Cimba* and William A. Robinson's *10,000 Leagues Over the Sea*. *Rudder* was the natural home for Tristan's story of sailing the world's highest and lowest bodies of water and the oceans in between.

But there was one problem, I discovered, after meeting him in St. Thomas and spending a sort of rum-soaked afternoon aboard the Tahiti ketch he was skippering for a charter company. He had appeared in our New York office some eighteen months earlier, a small, tough, driven person, very salty in his turtlenecked sweater and captain's hat, explaining quite passionately his "highest and lowest" plans. My predecessor, thinking him a little crazed, suggested he check in with us when he returned. Quite rightly, having been associated with men's magazines, he knew a lot about the fulfillment of dreams that remained unfulfilled.

But we were wrong about Tristan. He did return from his incredible adventure and he did write about it and as I discovered, to my horror that afternoon aboard his boat, he had received a form letter from a secretary at *Rudder* rejecting the manuscript. I suppose it was the tatteredness of the flimsy paper that put her off. He had, at that time, no money to make copies and no money to finish the book. I suggested that he bring all of the material to our office if he ever came to New York. The rest of the story appears in *Adrift*, Tristan's marvelous book that is a sailor's version of Orwell's *Down and Out in London and Paris*. We bought the *Incredible Voyage* manuscript for serialization, putting Tristan on his feet. Unfortunately, *Rudder* was in the interim sold to CBS. New editorial executives, in their infinite wisdom, cancelled the remainder of the serialization after three chapters, leaving Tristan hanging about the Amazon.

I left *Rudder* and New York for Boston and, eventually, *SAIL*, which also published some of Tristan's work. Tristan moved on, too, out of the Bowery where he had been living to a writing cell in Greenwich Village and from there, unbelievably poured forth the volume of words that have been incorporated into his autobiographical books, two novels, and smaller pieces, some of which are contained in *Yarns*. No one at that time believed this would happen and I remember a conversation with an editorial executive at a major publishing company that did marine books. They had turned down a book contract with Tristan. The executive said, "he'll just take the advance and fade into the sunset and we'll never hear from him again."

The book turned out to be *Ice!*, a classic yarn of survival in the Arctic. Its bittersweet last chapter appears here under the title, "By the Skin of My Teeth." And it truly marked Tristan, I believe, as a writer of importance. Rather than fade into the sunset, Tristan had dedicated his life to the telling of tales.

It is to Stan Grayson of SAIL Books' credit, that he had the acumen to pull Tristan's lesser known stories as well as some of his most important writing into this anthology. What it shows is the author's enormous range, depth of knowledge, and his ability to people his pages with some marvelous seafaring folks, all of whom seemed to like Tristan as he liked them. He has written about the solitude of the single-handed sailor but he is also happy in company with good men (and women) and true as long as they are honest. And the places! Here is Madagascar, Ibiza, Lake Titicaca, the Arctic and the Antarctic, the Pacific, the Red Sea, and the Gulf of Aden. He has voyaged some 345,000 miles in his time and the experiences are all here. Especially significant are pieces rarely seen before like his evocation of the coast of Madagascar ("The Dreaming Coast"), excerpts from his personal journal ("Storm Clouds Off the Andes") and his marvelous invention in the style of Conan Doyle solving the mystery of the *Mary Celeste*.

Tristan's plans to return to the sea were thwarted recently by an unfortunate loss of a leg. Whether he will take to adventure offshore again, only he knows. What is really important is that the yarns keep coming and, if he feels he has to sail again to write them, so be it. As he has written, "I don't love the sea; respect is more the word. But in reality, to most of the ocean voyagers and certainly to me, the questions of 'who, what, when, and how' practically always come before 'why' when we think of the sea and her terrible, beautiful, siren song."

Martin Luray
Boston, Massachusetts
April 1983

INTRODUCTION

When I was first asked to prepare this anthology I wasn't too enthusiastic about it; very few cruising sailors like to plow again back over a course they have already navigated—at least not until some years have passed. For a few weeks I gybed and yawed at the prospect of retelling old yarns, but one day something occurred to me.

I had met two old sailing pals in a pub in Greenwich Village, New York. Over a few beers we spun sailing tales to each other for a couple of hours. Suddenly I found myself wishing that other friends could be with me to enjoy the stories as much as my old shipmates and me. I realized then that many of the accounts to be contained in the proposed anthology were like the yarns we spun that rainy day in Manhattan—some already known to some of my readers, others known to other readers, but not all of them known to all my readers. It was about time that a few selected stories should be brought together, as they would be in good company, to show the development of a sailor-writer.

That is the genesis of this collection of yarns. I hope my readers will enjoy themselves as much as I have during many, many yarns with fellow sailors the world over.

My thanks are to the editors of the following magazines: *East West Journal* (U.S.A.), *Motor Boat and Yachting* (U.K.), *Modern Boating* (Australia), *SAIL* (U.S.A.), *Sailing* (U.S.A.), *Writer's Digest* (U.S.A.), *Yachting Monthly* (U.K.), and to Donna Martin, editorial director of Andrews and McMeel, Inc. (U.S.A.) book publishers, who first published some of the works herein, for their help and encouragement in lean years past and present.

Tristan Jones
New York and Key West, 1983

A HARD SCHOOLING

In 1979 I was asked by the editor of Writer's Digest *to write an account of how I became a writer in the first place. Had I always felt the urgent need to write? Was I impelled by the Muse? Had I ambitions to out-write, perhaps Slocum, Conrad, or Melville? Alas, the answers were much more mundane.*

I have often been asked whether my drive to write came from my voyaging experiences, or whether I went voyaging in order to be able to write about it. It's a bit like the old riddle, "Which came first—the chicken or the egg?" I believe that life is, or at any rate should be, a cycle. I believe that the "straight line" theory of human progress contains in itself its own fallacy. From nothing to nothing seems to me to be too futile. Nature has shown to me that existence is a very well-designed cycle, in all its successful and fulfilled forms. Birth, life, death—who can say which comes first?

So the answer, if there is one, to where my writing drive comes from must be from the tales I heard, and the stories I read, as a child. In other words from my education, elementary though it was.

I don't want to be read as if I'm beating a drum for sailors, but I honestly believe, *I have observed*, that the seaman, as he has been depicted in fiction, is just that—*fiction*. The brawling, boozy, semimoronic character one commonly meets in fiction, stumbling out of some dockside low-dive, has hardly ever shown up in real life—at least not in my lifetime of roaming the world. When he has, he is usually found to be someone who is play-acting. Those types of people rarely last long at sea in all weathers. Nature takes care of herself.

3

Such has been too often the image of sailors ever since, and even before, *Treasure Island*. But I have found the contrary. I have found that the average career seaman, of any grade, is on the whole more well read, and more expressive, than his shore-side counterparts. I would even go so far as to say that the career seaman is probably the best educated of manual workers anywhere, and that probably this has always been so. The nature of his life at sea, alternating long periods of boring inactivity with brief spurts of almost superhuman effort, almost invariably makes the sailor turn to reading. The good writers of the sea—Melville, Conrad, Slocum, Gerbault—recognized the seaman's verbal and other virtues and wrote about them and themselves as sensible and sensitive human beings. The seamen, in their turn, perforce recognized literature for the power it is, and gave writers like Erskine Childers *(The Riddle of the Sands)*, E.M. Forster *(A Passage to India)* and Somerset Maugham, maritime-flavored subjects that greatly added color to those authors' works.

The close relationship between voyaging and writing, which has existed since Homer wrote about Ulysses, is strong indeed, and will continue to be so, no doubt, when our great-grandsons voyage on the far side of the universe.

But back to my own life. I was born at sea, in my father's ship, fifty-eight years ago, to a family whose seafaring records go back to 825 A.D. A *Welsh* seafaring family. The ship I was born in was bound from Australia to Halifax, Nova Scotia. The day after I was born her destination was changed and she was directed to Liverpool, England. So I became a Welshman, and spent the first ten years of my life in west Wales.

West Wales is one of the areas of the British Isles that was very little affected by the Industrial Revolution. Still, only three kinds of men are truly respected in west Wales: a learned man, a man who can tell a story well (they are not necessarily the same thing), and a Master Mariner. My father, though of humble origin, was all three, and when he was at home from sea in our village of Llangareth we were visited by the guiding lights from all Merioneth and Cardigan. Then, with the fire piled up blazing in the hearth and the Aladdin oil lamp at full blast, the cottage was warm and crowded and full of the tales of the old Sail-in-Trade.

There would be Morgan Lewis, harbormaster of now-deserted Barmouth but still a Power-to-be-Reckoned-With, who could reel off the name of every sailing ship known on the coast of Wales for the past fifty years, together with the name of every man-jack onboard; and Mereddyd Philips, a Red Star man who had rounded Cape Horn fifteen times under sail; Rhodri Griffiths and his brother Daffyd, old men now, but merrily pithy-witted, who had been together in Norwegian and American whalers for many years.

Best storyteller of all, as his voice rose and fell with the firelight shadows leaping on the whitewashed wall, was Cadell Rum, a gaunt, lanky sailing-skipper of around fifty, a magical man who could bring to Llangareth the palms of coral islands waving in the trade wind breeze, bring them to moving life, make them weave in the wind like shaggy Highland bulls at the challenge. As Mam poured the tea from the great cosied pot, her head bent, her dark eyes forever glancing, smiling at my father, Cadell talked and took us to where the groaning bergs calve off the glaciers, or up a dark alley rife with skulduggery in Bombay or Madagascar. When Cadell told a tale everyone, even Mister Jeffreys-Geography, the English schoolteacher, stared enchanted as his voice, full of the rolling seas and the call of the petrel, held us nailed to his gestures, lashed to his memories and riding on his laughter. In those moments Cadell Rum held Llangareth in his warm, gentle, hard-calloused hands, such were the power of his words, and a writer was nurtured in the small boy who listened to him in rapt wonder.

I won a scholarship to Aberytswyth College in 1937, but this was in Wales and the times were hard and my family was poor, so instead I went to sea to earn my living as a deckboy on a North Sea sailing barge. I left Llangareth on a fine, sunny day in May. It was four days before my fourteenth birthday and Mam made me promise to eat the meat pie when the train passed through Shrewsbury and to pick a corridor coach so I could go to the lavatory and to make sure to follow the written instructions on how to get across London and be sure not to lose the ten-shilling note she had secured inside my inner pocket with two big safety pins. Then the train puffed through the winding Welsh valleys, and through the spring-green fields of England in 1938, when the stout stationmasters still wore gold watch fobs and walrus mustaches and the fishmongers' box-carts on high wheels waited at the station yards, the horses gybing at the hissing engine, and when we still believed in "peace in our time."

The next two years were—there's only one phrase that will fit—*hard labor*. Try to imagine loading up a sailing ship with bricks, for example, 60,000 bricks a cargo. Just two of us, the mate Bert and me. *All by hand.* And then, once the cargo was loaded and the tide was right, we endured sailing in all weathers. It was a good school, though, and taught me the value of simple comforts so that the war years I spent in Royal Navy destroyers in the Arctic seemed like a blessed relief to me, even though I was in three ships that were sunk.

It was in the navy that I first started to read seriously, as opposed to reading simply for entertainment. The books that were sent to our ship's library varied from stacks of Zane Grey Westerns to *On the Origin of Species* by Charles Darwin. The good Westerns and detective novels were passed around conspiratorially, from friend to friend; the classics languished on the shelves and were much easier to obtain, and so I was lucky.

As well as being natural readers, some of the seamen I knew were also prolific letter writers. Soon I had joined them, having realized the value of being able to channel one's private thoughts, and to express them, in the crowded conditions of a destroyer's mess deck. True, it was like trying to write in the middle of a busy supermarket gangway, but it was a powerful *concentration* trainer, and the experience I gained has served me right well over the years. I have written short stories and articles in conditions that would probably make the average author blanch. (The first half of my first book, *The Incredible Voyage*, was written in the boiler room of Harrods, the great London department store, and the second half was written in the dormitory of a men's shelter in the Bowery of New York.)

The first time I wrote anything for publication was after World War Two had ended. It was a short unpaid piece for our Ship's Book, in which various sailors wrote their own experiences. Everyone else wrote about aspects of life on-board. I wrote about an Egyptian ship cleaner who had come onboard in Port Said and chatted with me. I wrote about his life, a life of unimaginable poverty, about his family and his hovel-home, and about his faith and simplicity. The only payment I had for that story was the satisfaction that I had made some people think twice about the poor souls they hardly noticed whom most of them took completely for granted.

I was invalided from the navy shortly after that episode, and, as I recounted in my second book, *Ice!*, I had great difficulty finding work, until by some guidance, the nature of which I can only guess, I strayed into small craft sailing. And once started on that, nothing—not even a brigade of guards—could drag me away from it, despite the fact that for the first fifteen years my total income was something in the region of, *on average*, a mere ten dollars a week. Most of that time I had, as the old saying goes, "One foot in the gutter and the other one on a bar of soap."

There were three good things about being close to broke for so many years: my pockets didn't get holes in them, I met a lot of very interesting people whom otherwise I would probably have missed, and I was impelled towards the typewriter.

I'd been at sea in small sailing craft, sometimes my own, sometimes other people's, for many years, fifteen in fact, and in bigger ships for fourteen previous years, before I sold my first short story. This was the true (but stumbling) account of how a friend and I had salvaged a wrecked boat on a Spanish island and sailed her, engineless and minus mainmast, to a port 200 miles away, where she was refitted. I sent it in to *Motor Boat and Yachting,* a London magazine, and then more or less forgot it. I had other things to do, such as sail a thirty-eight-foot yawl from the coast of Connecticut to West Africa and then back up to the Mediterranean, heading for the Greek islands.

When I sailed the yawl *Barbara* into Ibiza, the Spanish island, in February 1970, my old friend Rattler Morgan was there on the jetty to catch the mooring lines. *Barbara* had had a good fast run up from Gibraltar, three days of bowling along with a quartering wind, and I was looking forward to having a few beers and seeing my Dutch girlfriend, Marlieka, who ran an infants' school on the island.

"Hey Rattler, howyadoin'?" I sang out as the lines whizzed over to him.

"Wotcher, Tris, good trip?" he replied, hands cupped around his lips to shout against the wind.

"Up and down, up and down, you know . . . " That's the way I would dismiss a 12,000-mile passage in four months in a small sailboat in those days.

"Saw your story in *Motor Boat and Yachting,* mate. How much did they pay you?" Rattler's fair hair—he was ten years younger than I, about thirty-four—blew in the breeze. "Didn't know you could write!" his grinning blue eyes squinted against the bright Spanish sunlight.

For a moment or two I was nonplused. I'd forgotten all about the story I had sent to London. Then it dawned on me what he was talking about. "What . . . where did you see it, Rattler? Did they show the pictures?"

"No, but there was a pretty good drawin' . . . " he finished tying up the lines. "How much did they pay you?"

"I don't know, I haven't collected any mail for four months; it's waiting for me here at the post office..." I rammed an extra fender between the hull and the jetty stones.

Then my sailing mate, Albi (a Portuguese lad of twenty-two), Rattler and I wended our way to the Hotel Montesol for a couple of cool beers on a sidewalk table; I left them to it and went to meet Marlieka and forgot my story.

Next morning though, at nine o'clock, when the post office opened, there was I, waiting, and soon I was settled down again at a hotel table with another beer, sorting through a bunch of letters. Among all the others was an envelope marked *Motor Boat and Yachting*. I tore it open. It was dated three months previously. Inside was a pink slip marked "Please find enclosed check for thirty-five pounds (seventy-five dollars by the rates in those days), payment for article 'Slow Boat to Barcelona.'" Below that the editor had written in pencil "Looking forward to seeing more!" On the strength of that I ordered another beer. It had been the first story I had ever submitted for payment and it had been accepted and published! Now I had found the key to the solution of my problem. For fifteen years I had roamed the world under sail, living solely on my Royal Navy invalid's pension of fifteen to forty dollars a month, at rare intervals earning extra money by delivering other people's boats, usually across the Atlantic. It had been a long, hard slog and I was accustomed to making do on very little food and with not much other comfort; now I had the key to survival in my chosen way of life.

From 1953 to 1968 I had made many remarkable voyages, about which not one word was written during that time. I'd been sunk three times, collided with a whale in midocean and almost thirsted to death, been trapped in arctic ice for just over a year, five months of that under a capsized iceberg with the threat of instant oblivion hanging over me; I'd survived many, many hurricanes and storms, and on one occasion managed to sail a small craft from Cayenne

9

3,000 miles home to France after she had lost her rudder and had her decks stove in. I grinned to myself. Now I would be able to take it easy and live ashore and write these stories. I had enough true adventure memories between my ears to write five hundred stories!

I took another swig of the *San Miguel* beer, then opened the next envelope, from *Barbara's* owner. Together with a group of other people he was interested in *sending* the boat to the Dead Sea (the lowest water in the world) and to Lake Titicaca in Peru, South America (the highest). It was a voyage that had never been made before and was considered by the vast majority of navigators to be impossible. Would I like to skipper the expedition?

Would I? I headed for the telegraph office, all thoughts of writing gone clean out of my head.

I should explain to my nonsailing readers why, after this initial small success, my mind was too preoccupied with other matters to give much further thought to writing at that time.

Also I should make it clear that the explanation of difficulties and problems, to the explorer, is not a matter of complaining. It is merely an *explanation*. No one but a fool would persist in a lifestyle in which he or she did not find fulfillment despite seemingly insuperable obstacles.

A persistent fiction, within the realms of fiction, is the person who sails away into the sunset in his or her sailing boat to live happily ever afterwards without a care in the world. *It ain't necessarily so,* as the songwriter put it. In fact, *it very rarely is so.* Long voyages—any voyages—in small sailing craft are most complex operations when they are carried out properly, in a seamanlike manner. The idea of *escaping* the problems of life by sailing away is a fable. On exploratory voyages, such as those I have undertaken, this is doubly, trebly so. Let us, very briefly, consider the problems encountered by the small boat voyager.

First, the speed of sailing progress. This, to the landsman, must seem excruciatingly slow, but the very nature of a sailing craft dictates that its speed is governed by the waterline length of the hull. If she sails faster than her design allows for, she will overturn and sink: therefore the slow speed, which in a thirty-eight-foot boat is about six miles per hour in ideal weather conditions. However, the weather conditions are very rarely ideal, so the boat's speed suffers, and the average, over a long voyage, is no more than about *four miles per hour*. This is coupled with the boat rising and falling an average of six feet every five seconds while leaning over at an angle of something between fifteen and twenty-five degrees from the vertical. Stop for a minute and realize what this means when you consider that the voyage described in *The Incredible Voyage* was over a total of 62,000 miles, and that my total voyaging, to date, is almost 300,000 miles.

Another preoccupation of a sailor-writer is the weather. This can be anything from halcyon days and balmy nights under a plethora of planets, an upturned stadium of stars, to bashing and banging away in cringing terror before the terrible forces of nature, which make *anything* that man can produce seem like the feeble waving of a baby's fist.

Then the isolation. Even in boats with one or two crewmen this is a great time-stealer, for they must muster from among them their own doctor, dentist, lawyer, engineer, shopkeeper, mechanic, carpenter, restaurant operator, navigator, tailor, sailmaker, linguist, cook; ad infinitum. There are no facilities, no workshop, 'just down the road.' Imagine then, how much time a single-handed sailor, at sea or even in harbor, has for writing during a voyage! But nature has an endearing way of maintaining her balances, and so the very *business* of voyaging leaves little time for introspection or self-doubt and one learns to observe *what matters*.

Next, *space*. In my last vessel, *Sea Dart*, my living cabin was seven feet long by six wide and four feet three inches high. But I managed to write short stories and articles in her. No electricity, no refrigeration . . . no running water at the twist of a tap.

Under those conditions, writing a book is almost impossible. Yet I did it, in 1973. I wrote a 160,000-word book entitled *Indian Ocean Saga*. I sent it to an agent in England . . . and he ran away to Paris with his secretary and I never have heard from him since!

I submitted well over two hundred articles to magazines while on voyages and here I must remind the reader of a very important fact. In the hurly-burly of the Western world, with its seeming relentless pressures, it is easy to be unaware that a good two-fifths of the world's land surface (and almost all its water surface) is exactly the same now as it was a thousand years ago—and, for the most part, so are the people. Sure, we can take pictures of the land by satellite. We can fly from one island of progress to another, swiftly and comfortably, by Jumbo Jet. But the only way we can reach the remote coastal parts of the earth is by small craft or helicopter, and the latter is too problematical from a support point of view. The only efficient self-contained 'terrestrial' coastal exploration vehicle is the small sailing craft. For one man, alone, it is the only vehicle possible. Thus, I have sent off articles to nine different countries from my boat by Eskimo kayak, Polynesian catamaran, Red Sea felucca, jungle river dug-out and Indian balsa reed craft on a lake almost 13,000 feet above sea level. I know there are people out there in the toils of everyday Western life who might wonder if some of the episodes I have written about were not perhaps a little exaggerated—dreams in the night. The simple reply to that is that one does not publish dreams under the scrutiny of the Royal Geographical Society, the world's foremost authority on exploration.

Some of the *dialogue* reported might not be completely accurate, it is true, but conversations reported years after the event very rarely are; and the last thing one thinks of when all hell is let loose is making notes in a diary. But essentially the *sense* of the dialogues is correctly reported.

My coming back into the maw of society in 1976 after a quarter-century almost continually at sea in small craft, was not easy. Many phenomena taken for granted by the average person in the so-called "advanced countries" make no sense at all to someone whose outlook on values can be distilled down to one question—Will it aid survival? I tackled my return into general society as I tackled my exploratory excursions. I tackle my writing in the same way: first—What is the aim? (What do I want to say?); second—Who will it benefit? (Hopefully, everyone who reads it); third—(dependent on the second) Where am I going? (Who am I trying to reach?); fourth—Do I know enough about the area to tackle it properly?

Thus I came to realize that literature, poetry—all art—is an exploration, just as surely as exploration is an art. The process of conceiving, initiating, organizing and writing a book, for example, is very similar to the process of launching and carrying out a voyage.

On the question of luck. I believe deeply that there is a force for good in the world. I believe that if the aim of an excursion, a venture, an effort, is directed to fighting what one believes to be detrimental—evil—then Lady Luck, Fate, the Guiding Spirit, synchronism if you like, will be on one's side. That may appear over simplistic in this day of rampant cynicism (but cynicism itself is a detrimental force and hates simplicity, which withstands it), but to me, in my own experience, it has been proved time and time again.

For instance, the story of how an American publisher came to contract for my first book is a good example of how close reality can be to dreaming. This reality is an example of what I call synchronistic fate: the coming together, as if by design, of evidently unrelated phenomena or persons in order to form a clear pattern. There have been several startling instances of synchronism in my life, and the navigator within me will not allow me to believe that those episodes were mere accidents, nor to believe that these kinds of patterns exist only for me. I can only conclude, therefore, that they are intentional patterns, and that there must be an *Intelligence* behind them, as there must be behind the design of the universe.

After the long six-year voyage, which I described in my first book, *The Incredible Voyage*, was concluded, I was in a parlous state. The many years of mainly single-handed effort, the frequent bouts of starvation, the regular subjection to tropical diseases and insects, the ravages on my intestines caused by a tapeworm, and the lack of income had all brought me to my lowest ebb since my disastrous encounter with a whale in 1967 (this is described in *Saga of a Wayward Sailor*).

To cut a long story sideways, I interrupted my writing of *The Incredible Voyage* amid the roar of a London department store's boilers, to carry out a task toothsome indeed to me: to investigate the infamous so-called Devil's Triangle, to try to ascertain whether or not there were any grounds for the fearful fantasies being written about that area.

I recruited my boat and her crew from New York State. Being short of funds, I took on three eager amateurs. I chose a young pipe-fitter from Long Island, a black ex-U.S. Air Force photographer from Manhattan, and, as cook, a middle-aged restaurant owner from Westchester County. For the purpose of this story I will endow the restaurant owner with the acronym *PP One*.

During the crossings back and forth over the Triangle, for two months in all weathers in the forty-four-foot yawl *Sundowner*, in search of clues to any mysterious occurrences, partly to weld the crew together and partly for entertainment, I encouraged them to tell their stories and I told them some of mine. In case my tales sounded too tall I showed the other three men my logbooks (so strange and incredible is the real world to modern Western man).

The days and nights passed, until eventually, having found nothing but the wonders of nature—no little green men, no things that go bump in the night—we arrived in

Puerto Rico and the crew dispersed. I returned to Manhattan, to my poor lodging in the crowded Bowery men's shelter and carried on writing *The Incredible Voyage*. Living in New York on an income of ten dollars per week is an interesting exercise and should be tried by anyone who is in danger of losing faith in human nature.

After about a month or so of this, I made a trip to *PP One*'s restaurant in Westchester County. There were two reasons why I did this. One was to talk about our sailing trips together, and the other was to get, at long last, a decent meal.

PP One greeted me and made me welcome, and during our lunch together he told me a curious thing. *PP One* had a namesake, who, for the purpose of this story I will call *PP Two*. *PP Two* was a Texas businessman and had recently driven to New York to close a deal. On his way into the city he had seen *PP One*'s sign and his curiosity aroused, decided to eat at *PP One*'s place and introduce himself. While the two men were talking together, *PP One* had recounted stories of his voyages with me and some of the tales I had told him. The Texan was intrigued, for he was also a yachtsman, and had read some of my articles in the yachting press. Even more important, he was a shareholder in Andrews & McMeel, the publishers. Within a week, Jim Andrews, the president of the publishing company was in New York, and shortly thereafter I had a contract for *The Incredible Voyage* and was out of the Bowery. That was in 1976. Since that time I have written a total of eleven books.

A great honor came my way after *The Incredible Voyage* was published in Great Britain in 1978. The book was awarded the first prize for literature, 1978–1979, by the Welsh Arts Council. This is a prize equivalent in cash to the National Book Award here in the U.S.A. Coming as it does from Wales, it is of inestimably far greater value to me, for it is awarded to the work of the small boy who once, long ago, listened so intently to Cadell Rum tell his stories by the light of the flickering fire flames in Llangareth. Another full cycle is completed; Cadell, at last, is rewarded.

SLOW BOAT TO BARCELONA

This is the first story I ever wrote for a magazine. It was published in England in Motor Boat and Yachting *in November 1969. Cresswell is, of course, the boat in which I made my forlorn attempt at the furthest north record in 1959–61, and in which I sailed with the bishop's sister as described in* Saga of a Wayward Sailor. Cresswell *was used by her new owner, an English stage actress, as a floating dog kennel for five Pekingese, from 1969 to 1971. Then she was bought by a Spanish businessman who has restored her lovingly to her former glory. She is still in commission and cruises the Costa del Sol every summer as befits an elderly, indomitable dowager.*

Ronnie Schmidt, my crew for the trip, and his boat, Mari Maris, *both disappeared on a transatlantic voyage in 1969.*

Delivering a 60-year-old converted lifeboat, dismasted, from Ibiza to Barcelona in mid-November, a distance of 200 miles, cannot be considered one of the plum jobs in the Mediterranean, nor would it be advisable for anyone without good local knowledge to even attempt it. However, to get a good refit job done at a reasonable price, and to have the boat ready for the next sailing season, I decided to take a calculated risk and jump into the moderately calm period that records show prevails over the new-moon phase of November. I had religiously kept a record of weather patterns in the western Mediterranean each day I had been there during the past five years, and I recommend this practice to anyone sailing at all seasons in any particular area.

Cresswell was constructed in 1908 by the Thames Iron-works Company for the Royal National Lifeboat Institution

16

as a beach-launched pulling lifeboat. I believe she served in that capacity at Cresswell, Northumberland, and at other stations until 1948, when she was employed for a time by the Trinity House as a supply vessel for lightships in the Channel. She had been extensively refitted in 1958–59 and converted into a gaff ketch on the Medway. She was well known on the Channel coast and in the Channel Islands during the early sixties. I had brought the boat down from the Arctic to Ibiza in 1965. After that she changed hands a couple of times and was used locally as a family excursion boat, visiting the many delightful beaches of Ibiza during the summer months and being laid up at a mooring during the winter at San Antonio.

On November 2, *Cresswell* broke her mooring during a northwesterly gale, which sent her aground on sand, but with minimal damage. The following Monday attempts were made by the owner to drag her out of the sand, using the traditional method of canting her with a hawser bent on to her mast just above the tabernacle, and heaving away with a tractor. This works very well with boats that have a deep keel, but *Cresswell* was flat-bottomed between her twin keels and the suction underneath was far too powerful. Something had to give and sure enough the mast went—into small pieces, being hollow—and the boat was now a sorry sight indeed with shroud cables, halyards, blocks, and bits of mast littering the topside.

Next day it was decided to tackle the job differently, and a strong suction pump was played under the hull to shift the sand and make a channel, while at the same time a tractor was connected by hawser to the forefoot of the bow and slowly but surely she came off and floated.

Next morning the boat was cleaned up and a one-quarter-inch stainless steel wire was rigged from the mizzen hounds down to the old staysail tack fitting on the bow as taut as we could manage, and the staysail was bent on. The luff made an angle of about 55 degrees and I intended to bring the forestay foot back aft a few feet to the winch if the boat sailed to windward too badly, so reducing the angle of the luff. A jib was then bent on, loose-luffed, but by the time this was hauled out to the bowsprit band it was practically horizontal and we found later that it was of some use only when the wind was on the quarter. However, it gave the boat the look of a rather raffish Arab felucca, seen from a distance, and it did help to keep the bow down a little—important in the short, steep "garden wall" seas that develop here during high winds and that take two or three days to die down.

By this time I had been joined by my crew for the trip, Ronnie Schmidt, a Swiss who sails his own 25-foot gaff sloop, *Mari Maris*, single-handed in the Med, and who had only the previous week lost all his sails in the same blow that sent *Cresswell* ashore whilst on passage from Palma to Ibiza. He eventually brought his boat in from south of Formentera using the cockpit awning as a mainsail. Always in good spirits, he is quite fearless and his energy is endless. Also recruited was Jan Van Hoydenk, a young Dutchman who has made several long voyages in motor yachts and one voyage under sail. He is dour and serious, but always ready to carry out what has to be done. Between us we used English and French, usually murdering both languages in the process.

On Monday, November 18, all was ready. The engine had been tested to see that it did in fact churn out the promised eight horsepower, an oil stove of the smelly wick variety had been ceremoniously installed in the galley, Admiralty Chart No.1187 had been turned out, a compass had been installed and checked, a distress band radio transmitter was onboard, and a precious hand-bearing compass had been safely put in Ronnie's pocket.

During the week of preparation a strong northwesterly had been blowing, but this had moderated on Sunday evening and by now it was down to Force 2, though a steep sea was still running. There were three alternative courses. The first was to make for the nearest port on the Spanish mainland, Denia, 55 miles due west and from there coast-hop 220 miles up the coast, a total of 275 miles. The second was to make straight for Barcelona, a run of 150 miles with an engine that could move the boat at only 2.5 knots should we be becalmed. At a time of the year when strong winds from the northeast continually threatened, we stood a good chance of being blown back to Ibiza, or on to the northwest coast of Majorca, not the ideal cruising ground in November. The third alternative was to make for one of a group of three ports, quite close together on the Spanish coast, 90 miles north-northwest of Ibiza: Peniscola, Benicarlo, or Vinaroz.

I knew that *Cresswell* could enter any of these ports easily, and that during November the prevailing winds near the Costa Dorado are northwest to southwest and that we would be in the lee as we approached the coast, all being well. However, the deciding factor in the choice of this third alternative was that two-thirds of the way to the coast, about 60 miles northwest of San Antonio, are the rocky, little-known islands called the Columbretes. These consist of one fairly large island, 500 yards long, and several rocks, spread over an area of five square miles. Smaller fishing vessels sometimes take shelter in the lee of the larger island, and as we only drew three feet, this is what I planned to do should it be necessary. On the chosen course the total mileage was 185 miles, with a break at 90 miles for refueling if needed, and the second half of the trip would be under the lee of the coast if winds should blow as predicted.

We stowed food on board sufficient for five days; mostly easily prepared stuff such as rice, tinned fish, spaghetti, bacon, and of course coffee, bought at the modern super-market in San Antonio. Shortly after dark on November 18 we got under way, with mizzen and staysail hoisted and engine running at three-quarter speed. A short, vicious sea made life uncomfortable during the first night; sleep was impossible, and speed had to be cut right down.

The area to the northwest of San Antonio is notorious for the number of fishing nets laid, and sure enough, in the dark with the boat tossing about like you know how, we managed to get one well and truly tangled in the screw. Not with the greatest of ease was it dislodged, and we plodded steadily on our way, course 330 degrees, taking three-hour watches on the primitive steering gear that had been rigged for the trip—two short lines secured to a metal bar fixed onto the rudder as a tiller.

One of my main concerns at this time was the possibility that the grounding at San Antonio had dislodged the caulking in the garboard strake, and a close watch was kept on the level of water in the bilge. But this proved quite unnecessary and we took on only one inch during the whole of a rough night, with seas up to 10 feet. At about 0500 hr. we were a little disconcerted to find that the violent motion of the boat had shaken the main compass so much that all the distinguishing marks inside the bowl had been completely erased and only flakes of paint were floating about inside. To top this the float had been jerked completely off its pin. The only solution was to stow the main compass and navigate on the small hand-bearing compass. Dawn broke at 0715 hr. and found us 25 miles southwest of the Columbretes lighthouse that, being built of very light colored stone and 279 feet high, showed up well in the early morning sunshine—a cheering sight, but not sufficient to make us forget that in 12 hours we had managed to cover only 35 miles.

We motored up to the Columbretes at 2.5 knots in a dying swell, with no wind at all and brought the lighthouse on the beam in time for supper, which was the first meal we had been able to eat in comfort (with both hands) since leaving port. By this time, surprisingly, the sea was nearly flat calm and we chugged away at 330 degrees until we picked up the bright, easily distinguished light of Peniscola at a distance of 19 miles. We arrived off Peniscola at 0400 hr. on Wednesday after passing through a huge fleet of sardine fishing boats, about five miles off the coast, and sailing across the main steamer track from Barcelona to Gibraltar—definitely not recommended when the navigation lights refuse to function, as ours did, and there are only two small storm lanterns on board. The best plan is to keep well clear of fishing operations, and this we did.

The port of Peniscola is situated immediately below the very picturesque old Moorish town perched high on a hill, and it is well worth a visit by any boat drawing less than four feet. Supplies are easy to obtain and it is the one small fishing port on this coast where one may obtain Calor gas easily. It is full of tourists during the summer, and prices consequently are somewhat higher than at other ports on this coast, but during the winter it is reasonable enough and the harbormaster is very friendly and helpful. However, it is not a port in which to linger, because it is completely open to the south and a very bad swell enters, particularly during the equinoctial periods.

By the time we had arrived off Peniscola, a southwest wind had developed, quite gentle, about Force 4, but as always in this part of the Mediterranean it was not to be trusted. I did not want to be trapped in Peniscola harbor if it should increase and bring a swell along, so I decided to head for the second port on our course, Benicarlo, four miles to the northeast. With a good breeze to push the "goosewinged" mizzen and staysail, we arrived there in no time at all (90 mins.) and entered the port with dawn lighting our way.

We tied up on the shallow end of the fishing jetty and were immediately interrogated by two enormously tough-looking Guardia Civil who were highly suspicious that three foreigners should be sailing about in such a strange craft at such an inopportune time of year. After explanations—plus a glass of brandy—they were friendly and waived all formalities, wishing us *"bien viaje,"* whereupon we all three turned in to sleep soundly for three hours, until 0900 hr., when we were woken by children playing on their way to the local school that, by the way, is run by the local fishermen's syndicate or union and where children from the age of 10 are taught seamanship and fishing techniques.

Midmorning on Wednesday saw a fine sunny day with a slight breeze from the southwest and, in the lee of the land, a fairly calm sea. Because of these exceptional conditions, I decided to push off for Barcelona at midday after refueling at the very conveniently situated diesel pump further along the jetty. Another factor bore on this decision, and this was that 15 miles to the northeast of Benicarlo lies the low, flat delta at the mouth of the River Ebro, one of Spain's few really long rivers.

Navigation thereabouts can be difficult owing to night mists, which can be expected during the winter, and also to the confusion that arises because three lighthouses, each on different sides of the delta, show simultaneously. Two of them, Port Fangar and Cap Bana, show exactly the same light (three flashes white every 15 seconds), and unless one stays well out in the offing or is extremely careful, it is easy to be sitting smartly on the delta mud. So if one can pass this part of the coast in daylight, all the better. We slipped at 1130 hr. after exchanging banter with the friendly fishermen of Benicarlo and taking a quick walk through this untouched town to the telegraph office to notify friends in Ibiza of our safe arrival and imminent departure. Incidentally, the cheapest method of communication in Spain is by telegraph: from Benicarlo to Ibiza, 17 words cost 17 pesetas. (A peseta was worth two cents.) I don't know if my visit was exceptional, but the telegraph office did not have change for a 100-peseta note. This may be the reason, I think, that Benicarlo is one of the unspoilt places on the Spanish Mediterranean coast, together with its next-door neighbor, Vinaroz, with its bullring slap bang on the end of the jetty, and beer at five pesetas a bottle.

We passed Vinaroz on our way northeast from Benicarlo, threading our slow passage through the sardine fleet to the cheers of these hard-working, amiable seamen, towards the low, flat, sometimes highly dangerous Cap Tortosa. But today the sea was like a mill pond with not enough wind to fill even our poor little mizzen. Dusk arrives in these parts very suddenly and we had just got our eyes accustomed to the dark when, with an ominous change of engine beat, the exhaust pipe cracked at a flexible joint just where it passed through the bulkhead between the cockpit and the engine compartment. I throttled down the motor to half-speed and decided to press on as this weather was too good a chance to miss by turning back.

So there we were, chugging away past the River Ebro, pitch-black night with mist obscuring the stars, flat calm sea, Arab felucca rig, exhaust smoke belching into the cockpit, hand-bearing compass lit by a dimmed storm lantern, coffee pot boiling on the smelly stove, jury-rig sails flapping idly in the breeze, and Ronnie Schmidt blowing away at his mouth organ. Jan the Dutchman was busy polishing his shoes in readiness for the expected "run-ashore" in Barcelona, all three happy as the night was black, and perhaps only me wondering what the devil I was doing on this particular venture and trying to dismiss it with the offhand clichés about it being "all in a day's work."

Right through the night we chugged on at a steady 2.5 knots heading for the light of Geltru, a small port 25 miles to the west of Barcelona from where, upon picking up the light, we would turn east along the coast. Unfortunately, owing to the low mist that night, we did not see the Geltru light, but in the early morning picked up the coast at La Trinidad, near Sitges, a well-known resort. From here on it was only a matter of making our way through the hundreds of fishing boats that work this part of the coast and we found ourselves under the shadow of Montjuich at 1600 hr. and berthed at dusk about 200 yards from the statue of Columbus at the very center of the city. We thankfully turned off the by-now-too-noisy single-cylinder diesel, having handed all the hoisted sails in the harbor entrance except the mizzen, which I kept bent in case the engine failed at the last minute. A brisk, five-minute walk saw us at the yacht club looking for a hot shower, but in November this is perhaps a bit too much to ask and we contented ourselves with welcome, cold fresh water. After a meal of kidneys in sherry sauce, salad, and wine in one of the hundreds of small restaurants off the *ramblas*, the main street of Barcelona, we all turned in at midnight, tired but satisfied.

Morning at 0500 hr. brought first a thick pea-souper fog and secondly a Guardia Civil, demanding to know what we were, where we had come from, and where we were going. Again, after explanations about our rather piratical appearance he was quite happy to stay long enough to wave us on our way a half-hour later. Steering through the Barcelona fog in company with about 300 fishing boats, all doing over six knots, is, to say the least, an interesting experience. But when the engine starts pouring forth steam from the exhaust halfway out, you could wish yourself in a better situation.

This trouble was found to be caused by our old friend the plastic bag, stuck in the water intake, but which was soon cleared. At 0800 hr. we were off to Badalona and a fresh southwest breeze sprang up at noon, which pushed us at a great rate towards our final destination of Arenys de Mar about 24 miles northeast of Barcelona, where we arrived at 1300 hr. on Friday, November 22. Our client had arrived at Arenys only one hour before us, and was there to welcome us with a pint of beer and a celebration lunch.

REWARDS AND REMEMBRANCES

*This is a true story from the days when I was a delivery skipper,
taking sailboats for their owners to most parts of the North and
South Atlantic. It was first published in* East West Journal *as
"The Sailor and the Saint" in 1980. The last I heard of Pete
Kelly—I have changed his name—was late in 1982. He was in the
Manhattan Correctional Center languishing under an apparently
trumped up drug-smuggling charge. He expected to be deported
after a year or so in jail.*

Albino Manuel DaCosta Ferreira was, at eighteen
years of age, one of the clumsiest deckhands I
ever came across—or so it seemed to me when I
first knew him.

Back in 1967 I had been engaged to deliver the eighty-foot
marconi ketch *St. Louis* from her builder's yard in L'Orient,
on the French Biscay coast, to Dakar, in Senegal, West
Africa. She was built for the president of recently independent Mauritania, West Africa, and consequently no expense had been spared on her. Her costs had been met by
UNESCO and a French automobile manufacturer. 'Nuff
said—such is the way of the world, and anyway, at the time
I needed the money I would earn on the delivery. Who paid
was my least concern.

St. Louis was the largest fiberglass vessel built in France to
that date. Topsides she was a first class display of all the
latest developments in stainless steel, cordage, sails and
navigational aids. Below she was fitted out like a palace—
even to the proverbial (but very seldom seen) gold bath
taps. Her owner's cabin was fitted out in black lacquer

panels decorated by Chinese craftsmen in inlaid gold drag-
ons. It was like a scene from a James Bond film.

I had taken my regular delivery mate with me to pick up
the boat. This was Pete Kelly, a real hard-nosed tough nut if
there ever was one. He was a Manxman, about twenty-
eight at the time, and he could sink a whole bottle of Scotch
at one sitting, without batting an eyelid, then go back
onboard and splice a two-inch wire cable as quietly, quickly
and easily as his old granny could darn a sock. Pete was a
good lad at spinning a yarn, too, like most of his ilk on that
storm-bound rock in the Irish Sea. He was of average
height, yet stocky, and Leif Ericson or Harald Fairhair
would have recognized their offspring alright. Eyes like a
southwest gale in the Solway Firth, except when he
laughed, which was most of the time.

Because of the size of *St. Louis* I had to send for my back-
up man, Jean-Pierre Berton, a Breton from Brest: another
child of the storm, another hard case. He was also twenty-
eight and was built like an agile bullock. We—Jean-Pierre
and I—together had made the worst transatlantic small
boat voyage ever, in *Quiberon*, some years earlier.

Jean-Pierre, at my behest, had brought along two other
Bretons, Astrol and Dure, both also fishermen in their early
twenties, who supplemented their wages and voyaging
instincts by taking off on yacht deliveries from time to time.
So, you see, by the time we'd put *St. Louis* through her
paces in the offing of L'Orient and took off for Dakar there
were onboard ten arms, ten legs and five Celtic dreams to
drive her—and drive her we did; you may be sure of that.
So much so that by the time we fetched Gibraltar she and
we were showing dire signs of wear, tear and grudging
haste. We also had aching noses, a bequest of four storms in
the Bay of Biscay and the Portuguese offing. December is
not the ideal time for frigging around in those waters.

In Gibraltar, that haven of decency, that bastion of *habeas
corpus*, we, descendants all of the Druids, held an eistedd-
fod of our own in the shrimp shell and lass-littered cool

shade of the Cafe Suisse and decided that what we needed for the hazardous passage down the west coast of Morocco was a sixth hand. Despite the pelf and power that had been so liberally bestowed on *St. Louis*, by UNESCO and the French car industry, our pay for her delivery three thousand-odd miles was meager indeed. A total of approximately 1,000 dollars in all, so the extra hand would have to be paid out of our own pockets—100 dollars and fare back to Gib was the remuneration decided upon; Jean-Pierre volunteered to cull from the alleys of Gibraltar a suitable candidate for the position of sixth hand of the good ship *St. Louis*. He left us to our chores in the early afternoon and returned in the gloaming as the sun disappeared behind the great looming Rock of Jeb El Tarik and the houses turned from silver to gold to pink to grey. The apes slept on the high ledges and the necklace of lights reflected on gleaming Algeciras Bay.

Jean-Pierre turned up with a stocky, dark, little lad in tow. The boy was dressed in the baggy canvas pants, sandals and blue shirt of a Portuguese fisherman. On his head he wore a straw hat, and on his face a down of incipient beard. His face was handsome in the Portuguese manner, and his eyes were fiery with goodwill.

Jean-Pierre grinned as he came onboard. *"Alors, Capitaine. We have a good catch here—a fisherboy from the Algarve."*

I put on my best skipper's stance, looking the Portuguese lad straight in the eye as I spoke to Jean-Pierre. "What's he doing in Gibraltar?" I could tell by the slight change of expression in the boy's eyes that he understood me.

"He has come here as deckhand on an English yacht, but they do not treat him well . . . and there is no pay . . . only his food . . ."

Both Astrol and Dure, standing behind me, muttered *"merde."*

I turned to the boy and asked his name.

"Albino Manuel DaCosta Ferreira" he replied, *"Senhor Capitan."*

Kelly, who was sitting on the bulwark behind the boy, piped up, "Sounds more like a bloody parliament, Tris."

"Good," said I, "then we will call you Albi, *bueno?*"

"*Si, senhor.*" A wide grin broke over the lad's face, for he knew he had one foot firmly on the deck of *St. Louis* already.

"Been at sea long?" I asked him.

"Two years, *senhor.*"

"Under sail?"

"With my father, he works for Dom Enrique Manuel Da Sousa..."

"Alright, lad... alright..." I looked at Pete and Jean-Pierre, who were both grinning widely at the conversation going on in my Spanish and Albi's Portuguese. I tried to keep my face straight at the thought of Portuguese names, which sound more like a football crowd than one person. "Where's your gear?" I asked him.

"Onboard the English yacht, *senhor.*"

"Well, *machito*, go and fetch it, and get your sailing papers."

"But the *Capitan Ingles* will not give them to me; he wishes me to stay and sail with him to Greece..."

I turned to Kelly. "Pete, you go over with Albi, put a toggle or two on that *pyeso* ("stingy") Saxon bastard and tell him that if he does not release this lad's gear and papers it's your man himself that'll be over the harbormaster's office as fast as Christ will let me and I'll swear out a warrant against his bloody boat for back-wages for Albi. Throw the Board of Trade Regulations at him, Pete... scare the living lights out of him, Pete. Tell the son of a whore that slavery is..." I stumbled for words.

"*Pas d'etiquette*" said Jean-Pierre, quietly.

"*Touché, mon ami*," I said to Jean-Pierre, then turning to Pete, "Simply not on, old chap" I said, in English.

"*Pas encore*" murmured Dure, whose old man was a leading light in the Aberwrach fisherman's union.

Pete grinned. "And if he refuses?... give him the..."

"Nothing, Pete. If he refuses, come back here and it's ourselves who'll sort the sod out."

"Right, Skip" said Pete, which was about as near to nautical formality as a Manxman can ever get. Pete touched Albi's shoulder and they disappeared over the stern plank and across the jetty, to return a few minutes later with a duffle bag and Albi's papers, leaving behind them a fuming, irate, indignant, but silent English colonel (retired).

It didn't take long for us to discover how "clack-handed" Albi was. His first job, the following morning, after breakfast was cleared away, was to fill the fresh water tanks. He put about fifty gallons of fresh water into the *diesel oil tanks*! With the cloud mounting over the peak of the Rock it was obvious to every mariner within fifty miles that a sharp westerly gale was in the offing. There was no time to clear out the fuel tanks. Only time to curse and swear in English, Manx, Welsh, Breton and French, and to fume against ourselves that we had overestimated Albi's understanding of English and our lack of realization that he could neither read nor write.

"I should have known . . . I should have bloody-well known . . . " I ranted at Pete.

"Not his fault, Skip . . . though he could have asked us . . . "

"Well, too late now, mate. We've got to get the hell out of here and make westing as fast as we can, so we can use this flamin' blow to make southing down the Moroccan coast. It'll be sail all way, mate."

"Don't trust the engines, anyway, Skip . . . never did" said Pete.

"Right. Well, get the hands mustered and let's slip. It's me that'll nip over and clear our souls for Dakar" I said, heading for the gangway.

"Hang on, Skip" shouted Pete, as I stepped onto the jetty.

"Wassup?"

"The laddie . . . what's his pay?"

"Five dollars a day, payable on arrival, a packet of fags a day, and his air fare back to Sagres when we fetch Dakar. Help in the galley, on deck, keep watch with Astrol, sluice himself off every day, and same grub as the rest of us, right?"

Pete grinned. "Right" he said and turned to go below to roust the hands, "there's the man."

Some people are, at sea, to the manner born. Some people just are not. Like poets and pianists, I suppose. Albi simply was not. For a start, he was left-handed. Then we found out he was long-sighted and could hardly see the compass at three-feet range. He was the exact reverse of Midas. Everything he touched turned to quivering crap. For example, one morning it was his turn to make breakfast. Kippers poached in milk. What did he do? Laid seven kippers in a tray and poured *condensed* milk over them and *baked* them in the oven. When he appeared with the tray I caught hold of one burned tail in the corner of the blackened tray and lifted it. What came out of the tray could have been hung on the walls of the Metropolitan Museum of Art and validly scrutinized. Imagine it, seven burned, blackened kippers cemented together with umber brown condensed milk toffee!

By the time we had worn our weary way into Safi, three days later, everyone, although quiet about it under my warning eyes, was thoroughly fed up with watching Albi over his shoulder, correcting Albi's mistakes, holding Albi's hand, wet-nursing Albi. We'd a severe weather forecast and I decided to cower in the safety of Safi, for the desert-bound coast of the Sherifian Empire is no place to be in a westerly storm with no engine and no sea room, and prudence is the key to long life in those waters (and ashore thereabouts, too, come to that).

"Right, lads," I said when we'd made fast to the fishing wharf. "We hang on here until this blow's over. Should take about three days, then, with God's grace we'll have a wind-swing to the northeast and be able to make Cape

Timiris as direct as a Liverpool tramcar, and none of your worrisome offshore clawing."

"Bien" said Jean-Pierre. The rest said nothing, all glum, like a glowering morning in Glasgow, eyes searching for wraith ringbolts at their feet.

"What's up, Pete?" I asked, after a moment's awkward nothing.

"This bloke Albi," said Pete, speaking English for his troubles.

"?" I looked at Pete.

"Well, he's getting on everyone's tits. We have to watch every bloody move he makes..." All three Bretons and Pete looked at me with weariness in their eyes.

I ordered "Let him stay on the jetty while we're here. Give him simple jobs to do...he can paint the anchor-chain fathom marks... lay it out for him. Allow him on-board, on deck, for his meals, and to sleep. Work him from 8 A.M. until noon only, then let him wander off if he wishes. That's all. If he's on the jetty he can't do too much damage, right?"

"Right" said Pete. *"Bon idee"* said the Bretons. And so it was made so.

For three days I hated myself for having sent Albi to Coventry, for keeping out of his own harm's way. For three days I struggled with my own sense and firmness, and all the while Albi carefully and patiently painted the fathom marks on the fifty-fathom-long anchor chain, thinking to himself that he was carrying out a vital job, and happy at last that he was out of range of correction and criticism; but we needed not the marks (we would never need to use them) and cared not how he painted them. Anything to keep him off the ship was our only selfish thought.

All the forenoons Albi would work under the ever-heightening hot Sahara sun, then at noon he would come onboard, collect his lunch and cigarettes and disappear over the dusty jetty toward the town, which was now shimmering in the distance, the minarets and fortress walls quivering in the heat like a mirage.

On the third day, as we sat under the awning eating our pilchards and olives, Pete said "funny bloke, Albi. Had no pay yet, but off he goes to town every day, with his grub and fags . . . comes back grinning all over his face . . ." He thought for a minute, as we watched him. "D'you know what I reckon, Skip?"

"Wazzat?" I asked between mouthfuls of pilchard and bread.

"I reckon he's either got a bit of crumpet up there and he's paying her in grub . . . 'cus, look, he don't get any fatter, and God knows he gets enough food to feed a bloody horse . . . and when he gets back he's got no cigarettes left either . . . bums one or two off Jean-Pierre and me. So what's he doing with his victuals is what I'd like to know?"

"Eets true, Treestan," observed Jean-Pierre, breaking into rare English. "Everee day 'e come back wiz nozzing."

There was silence for a minute, then I said, "Right . . . tomorrow its meself'll keep my eye on him. He's only eighteen . . . if anything happens to him it's my responsibility."

"An' if there's a lass involved and he gets some local mad . . . we're all going to be up the creek," said Pete. Jean-Pierre passed his open palm across his throat, turning his eyes up to heaven in the French way. Dure made a gesture as if he were cocking a submachine gun. Astrol threw his hands out, then slapped his knees.

And so it was decided that an eye must be kept on Albi, even ashore.

I trailed Albi when he wandered away with his food and cigarettes the next day. I followed him at a discreet distance and saw him walk under the long tunneled archway that was the gate into the town under the old fortress. I saw him stop and start to put his food and cigarettes into little bags hanging on strings dangling down the mildewed walls of the fortress. I saw the strings pulled up by unseen hands and the bags disappear one by one as Albi filled them. Then, as I drew closer to the gateway, trying to keep out of Albi's sight, I heard muted voices shouting in Arabic. Then I watched as Albi sat down in the shade of the tunnel and closed his eyes to sleep away the afternoon, a slight grin on his dark face. I watched him for a moment, then I sat down in the long esparto at the side of the sandy track, hardly able to stop tears of shame and humility. Then, as the sun lowered itself into the ocean, I walked back to the ship and explained to my crew that Albi, this simple fisherlad working for a pittance, had taken upon his great heart to comfort the lost souls in the Emperor of Morocco's prison—souls abandoned, bodies cast away to starve, spirits left to desiccate. The Bretons and the Manxman listened, silent, as the wild Welsh words rolled out of me into the gently cooling Saharan night sky with its million trembling stars and the horizon, pale grey and crystal all around our sad eyes, set to shatter into a billion cries of silent rage.

We sailed next day with a nor'easter, and fetched Dakar four days later, as kindly as a feather landing. We didn't send Albi home to the poor coast of Algarve. Instead, by a unanimous vote, we took him to Brest with us and bought him a new blue suit and a pair of spectacles, and then Jean-Pierre and I took Albi with us as third hand on our next delivery—a spanking new Italian yawl from Genoa to Martinique. We taught him to read and write and the rudiments of navigation, and sent him home, in the end, with close to 500 dollars to solve his family's poverty and salve his mother's aching heart.

Albi had to join the Portuguese Army upon his return home. He was shipped out to Angola in 1969, as he wrote to me in fair English.

Albino Manuel DaCosta Ferreira was killed in a stupid firefight in the Angolan jungle on September 23, 1970. It was his twenty-first birthday.

PEOPLE ON PASSAGE

This is the body of a speech I was invited to give to The Explorer's Club in New York in March 1977. The title of the speech was "The Psychology of the Ocean Sailor: The Reasons Why." I showed this to Bernard Moitessier, of Joshua fame, when we met in California in 1981. Bernard and I were riding in the back of a pick-up from Ventura to San Francisco. As he read it, tears came to Bernard's eyes. It must have been the wind. But he did say, when he handed it back to me, that it was the clearest exposition on the subject he had ever seen. With words like that from a man like Moitessier, who needs a Pulitzer Prize?

There's an old saying in Wales, where I come from... "There's nowt so queer as folks." One of the biggest wonders of human nature is its infinite variety. At one end of the scale you have the shy, introverted wallflower, and at the other end there's the blustering, swashbuckling extrovert, and in between an array of natures marvelous to behold. And so it is with sailing folk. They're no special type. Shakespeare himself would have found it hard beating to delineate the spectrum of different characters that can be found in any good-sized yacht club or marina.

One of the more obvious results of going sailing is to form or strengthen some traits in one's psyche. Among these, I would put (in *my* order of importance) patience, compromise, ability to get down to brass tacks (i.e., clarity of thought on immediate problems and swiftly calculating priorities), humor, even at your own expense, fairness, precision when it is necessary, generosity when it's not, physical fitness, determination, and the understanding not only of your own weaknesses, but also of other people's.

If anyone asked me why I think people take off single-handed on long voyages in small craft, I would answer that they were probably seeking any or all of the above virtues in their own nature; and if they continue to sail alone, then it is either because they are content with what they found inside themselves, or they're still looking.

The question of the psychology of the average single-hander is impossible to define in general terms, because each person is different (thank God) and so each one must be taken separately.

In my case it was purely and simply a matter of logistics. In other words I either could not afford to feed a crew, my vessel and itinerary were so risky that no one else would come, my vessel was too small to carry the stores and water needed for more than one person on the voyage, or the extra weight would impede progress. I have, on other occasions, probably sailed with as many other people as any other man alive, and yet I can think of only two of those hundreds of people that I would not sail with again on a voyage of any duration. The reason I would not sail with the two exceptions was that they consciously, and against orders, put other men's lives in jeopardy, and even after the danger was over adamantly refused to admit that they had been wrong. Stupidity in an intelligent person is unforgivable and, especially at sea, downright dangerous.

My own attitude towards the sea is basically very practical. I want to go somewhere; my home and my vehicle is a boat, which sails on the sea and leads to wherever I want to go. I have had people come up and direct some very loaded questions at me; that is they are loaded with the implication that I am some special kind of creature who, like a hermit, only wants to get away from his fellow men and the problems inherent in modern life. That's complete and utter bull. There's nothing I like better than good company and telling and listening to yarns; there's nothing I admire more than man's achievements in every field in the tremendous struggle to reach the stage that civilization is now at. Sure we've got our problems, but then, if we'd no problems, there wouldn't be the challenge of finding the solutions, would there? I've seen the so-called idyllic existence of the so-called "Noble Savage" . . . no thanks, give me Piccadilly Circus or Times Square any day, not to mention the Louvre, the Sistine Chapel, running water that comes out of taps, miraculously, and is safe to drink, and television and automobiles and telephones and all the rest of the paraphernalia of modern life that a whole generation of misguided and certainly inexperienced people have been so busily criticizing for the last twenty years or so. No, if the sea is good to me, which it is often, then I love it; if it's not, then I hate it with a bastardry that would make Genghis Khan himself look like Tiny Tim. But no matter how it is, I always respect it; in other words, as much as I can I load the dice on my side. And so should you, and for that reason you must be careful about choosing a crew. They don't only have to fit the boat; they have to fit you and you them.

But let's get back to the single-handers I have known. What would I say was their general trait? First and foremost—and I'm talking about after they have completed long voyages, not necessarily before— they all have a great courtesy to others; it wasn't forced on them as it often is with landlubbers, which is immediately clear to the single-hander or any ocean small-boat voyager with his sharpened perceptions and instincts. These perceptions reach a stage where one knows what another person is going to say before he says it, once one is back in company. In my experience *déjà vu* has been very common, and I have known what was coming long before it appeared, or before I rounded a point, even when I had no prior information on whatever it was that eventually did turn up. I think it is possible that everyone has this "sixth sense," only alone at sea it is highly pronounced once developed. Other single-handers have remarked to me on the same thing.

Being alone is not the same thing as being lonely. I can feel more lonely on the New York subway than I ever would in mid-Atlantic. In fact, after being alone, awareness of other people, not only loved ones and friends but even the slightest acquaintances, is very pronounced. I have felt closer to people while alone in midocean than I sometimes have felt whilst being in the same room with them. Love and friendship have nothing whatsoever to do with geographical position or distance, or, as my old skipper Tansy Lee used to say when we were sitting in some *estaminet* in Cherbourg, France, waiting for cargo, "Absinthe makes the heart grow fonder." I remember being in mid-Atlantic when the news came over the radio about the U.S. astronauts landing on the moon, and I sat in the cockpit and stared at the great round thing in the night sky in stupefied wonder, for I felt as if I was with them, and that each time my boat lurched to the sea she was stirring up moondust.

Of course, anyone contemplating single-handing the ocean should at least like some of his or her own traits, and be able to generously forgive the ones he or she doesn't like, or at least make allowances for them and not let them interfere with the well-being of the boat and her skipper. If the voyager tends to be lazy, then he or she should be lazy about the right things. (I direct my own tendencies to laziness towards varnishwork and small things like peeling potatoes; I just pop them in the pot, skin and all.) It pays to be sloppy in a few, comparatively unimportant ways, because a perfectionist would be hell to live with, even if it was yourself. Also very boring. And if you bore yourself, don't single-hand. Always make sure you've got someone else to bore, as long as it's not yourself.

Single-handers tend to be monotheists. I have for years thought that if I were formally religious I would probably become a Moslem, or even better a Jew, because I found that in Israel they at least have a good old booze-up in the synagogue at some ceremonies. That would suit me fine, and I don't at all mean that in a disparaging way. On the other hand, if I were a Moslem I might wind up with an oil well . . . if I did I'd charge special low rates to the stink-pot lads and lasses, and good luck to them if they enjoy it. With respect to religion, I have found that it has mostly been very difficult to converse with single-handers about this, as they nearly always shy off the subject. Then I realized, looking back on my own experience, that the reason is because they shy off about it even with themselves; and I consider this the healthiest thing to do. One could very soon go mad if a Creator is dwelt on too long. Of course, once the crossing is completed then it's gratifying to send a little thanks skyward, especially if it's been a hairy trip.

As for goblins and ghosties and things that go bump in the night, if you believe at all in that claptrap, for your own sake don't go to sea alone. I twice hallucinated, though, and saw a little man, but I'm pretty certain it was the effect in both cases of lack of certain essential contents in my diet that, at both times, was pretty poor.

In my own case I have never had the so-called "racing spirit." I never felt that I wanted to outdo anyone else and, apart from food and water running out, fast passages never meant much to me. True, I went for the "vertical record" where I seemed to wind up being first at a number of things, but the underlying motive behind that was merely to point out the ridiculousness of racing round and round, faster and faster; in this day and age, it seems that very few people will take notice of you unless you break some ridiculous record, so I set out to break the most ridiculous one of all.

Anyone who single-hands to achieve anything but a passage and his own satisfaction, unless it is a race against other single-handers over a reasonable distance, is wasting his time and should take up goldfish swallowing or doughnut eating. He will achieve the same result in much more comfortable surroundings. This seems to be the attitude of a number of solo artists I have met. They are more concerned with making a good passage, not so much with outdoing anyone else. Of course, I realize that there is a great sport in racing under sail and I appreciate the techno-logical advances that racing has brought about. I don't want to knock racing. I'm saying that no single-hander should take off on a transatlantic passage with the idea of beating Jimmy Blogg's time in a smaller boat because he did it in a twelve footer in X number of days. And there we come again to the old stumbling block in any argument about ocean cruising, "One man's meat . . . " But I know my own inclinations in this respect: above all, a *good* passage and *to hell with heroics.*

Fear is probably the single-hander's greatest hazard, and it can lie in wait to ambush him at the times when he can least welcome it. It's only nature's way of overcoming man's inherent intelligence. Nature is a wily old bitch when she wants to be, and the way to deal with fear is to remember that it interferes with man's place in the scheme of things as a logical, crafty, scheming, calculating son of a bitch who should not allow nature to take his mind over. Fear is a nuisance—it clogs up the brain, it doesn't do a damned thing for the boat or for the successful conclusion of the passage. It belongs with all the other vices that nature seems to have thrust at us to prevent our reaching the infinity that is our right and that we are going to reach for anyway, unless we let that scruffy old whore—fear—foul up the winch-sheets.

Concern is another thing altogether. That is facing up to the reality of any given situation. Worry, often confused with concern, is nature's way of getting her foot in the door so that fear can come traipsing in, bringing her second cousin, a real dangerous doxy, panic, with her. Concern is the hallmark of a good seaman. About himself, his ship, other people, and the situation with which he is confronted. It is the harbinger of solutions, the defeater of fear.

J.R.L. Anderson, in his excellent summing up of solo voyagers in the book *The Ulysses Factor* says that the common denominators of single-handers is an instinct that derives from the need to explore alone. I agree, but each man has his own areas of exploration, both within himself and in the world at large. Some people do it to prove themselves (a few do), some for nationalistic reasons, some for material gain (the racing people, in the main, but by no means always), some do it to escape a "humdrum" life, whatever that is, some to sort themselves out (though I cannot imagine why anyone would go to sea to do that), and some for the pure poetry of it, and these I'm with, all the way. Because it's there—that's the most human reason of all.

When Donald Crowhurst of the trimaran *Teighnmouth Electron* went mad during the single-handed round-the-world race in 1969, I was out looking for him in mid-Atlantic, in *Barbara*, for it was well known that he had been faking his positions. He had made the mistake of undertaking a voyage for all the wrong reasons. When he set out he trusted neither himself nor his craft—that is plain from his logs; and the whole thing had deteriorated into a lunatic playing at God, even though, of itself, his voyage was quite an achievement for a man with his slight experience. It reinforced, though, my intense disdain for all these highly publicized, commercially sponsored stunts, and made me even more determined to cast as strong a light as I could on the rapidly developing rat race by going for the *vertical* record, which would confound the hucksters and sponsorship mongers by being unbeatable.

Above all, a single-hander should be a good seaman. He should try to get as much experience as he can with other boats and people before setting off alone. I know that there have been some very lucky beginners, but there have also been a vast number of unlucky ones. I myself sailed for five years as crew before taking off alone for the Arctic. During those five years I learned to handle a small craft under all conditions, and to be my own carpenter, plumber, mechanic, sailmaker, cook, navigator, wiresplicer and general dog's body. I also learned a lot about human nature, including my own. Quite a few of the single-handers I have known, when transferred to another craft other than their own, would be utterly lost as far as running the unfamiliar vessel was concerned. The best training, I think, is to gain experience in various craft, preferably without engines. This instills a wariness about lee shores, for example, which one would find it difficult—almost impossible—to obtain in powered craft. There are some single-handers who take great pride in the fact that everything they have done they have done completely on their own. That's erroneous, for we are all part of the whole, and I consider myself to be part of a vast company of sailors who stretch back to the dawn of time; and on their patiently gained knowledge I have perhaps added a few meager scraps.

Some people are natural, born seamen. You can tell that by the way they move onboard a small craft. Others are clodhoppers, and I have nothing but admiration when they eventually, patiently, turn themselves into sailors. A good seaman, when he boards another vessel, has his eyes everywhere but on the comfort—or lack of it—below, or on the gadgets and fancy gear. He is watching the rigging, the deck fittings, the way the gear is stowed, the way the wires are spliced, and the way lines are coiled. Whatever he does, he is always learning.

Age is a touchy subject in Western countries, and especially in the U.S.A. Here youth, because of its affluence and purchasing ability, is put on a pedestal. At sea, forget it. There has been at least one case of someone under twenty making a very long voyage alone; but as I understand it, Daddy's check was waiting at each port of call and there were frequent flights back home whilst en route. There was no lack of money for shore-side repairs. In the particular case I recall, it was a case of the father sailing vicariously through his boy and the lad was subjected to inordinate pressures to carry on when all he really wanted to do was settle down with his sweetheart...and good luck to him.

In my experiences, the age of discretion and responsibility at sea is reached at about twenty-four. If younger than that, unless the person has been actually raised throughout most of his or her childhood in an ocean-going vessel making long-distance voyages, there just has not been enough *time* for him or her to have absorbed the knowledge and experience that ought to be in hand, or rather, between the ears. And if that knowledge has been gained, then there hasn't been enough *time* to gain experience in the ways of this wicked world to, for example, deal with (sometimes) corrupt officialdom in many of the outlying parts of the globe, or to deal with some of the many vexing and serious emotional problems that crop up from time to time. Of course, as always, there are exceptions, but they are rare indeed.

Anyway, I think that anyone younger than twenty-four who goes off on his or her own sailing for months on end is completely wasting time, what with all the shore-side attractions.

There's only one thing worse than a sea boot too small for your feet, and that's having feet too small for your sea boots. If that doesn't make sense, then don't tackle the paradoxes encountered at sea!

On the occasions when I have sailed with Western youngsters, and especially Americans (and this is not a criticism, just an observation), I have been astonished at the change in their attitude toward age and experience when the shit hits the fan in contrast to the usual (by no means always) disdain, which sometimes almost amounts to a complete lack of communication that is shown in port. I don't blame the kids for this, at least not for all of it; I blame the older people for having let this happen. This "generation gap" is a load of cod's wallop artificially engendered by the marketplace hucksters. Don't get me wrong. I don't want to identify with youth in the matter of social preferences; although I think some of the stuff they like is excellent, a lot of it is so much ullage. It's just that I would like them to know a lot of what I learned from men who were sailing before I was a gleam in my old man's eye. Advice that is invaluable and that they will need one day, later if not sooner. The calculated risk, the known error, the time and place of caution, of patience, of perseverence, of a dashing audacity that would make the most stirring shore-side activity look like an Easter Sunday parade down Fifth Avenue. It's not only the numbers that come up in dice; it's the way you throw the dice.

The attitude of the older people to youngsters in some areas in America is interesting, too. I have seen skippers in the West Indies and the U.S. who are, or appear to be, almost afraid to kick someone's ass when he makes a stupid move, almost afraid to criticize, to cajole, to persuade, to lead and to advise. The hell with that. Angles of view may change, but true values never do, and in the main these values must be learned, mostly the hard way. At least that's what I've found. A small craft in the ocean is, or should be, a benevolent dictatorship. The skipper's brain is the vessel's brain and he must give up his soul to her, regardless of his own feelings or inclinations. If he cannot do that, then he has no business being in a skipper's position.

No one is more democratic-minded ashore than myself. Even though I am British, one of the men I most admire in history is Thomas Jefferson; but once at sea, in a crewed boat or no, I am in charge on behalf of the vessel—even with the boat's owner on board. If I am appointed captain, then by God and under God, captain I am. Don't imagine that I become a sort of mini-Hitler, though. That would be foolish in the extreme. Don't imagine I am hard on crew; but on myself always.

As skipper it is my duty to complete a passage with the vessel and crew in good order and to be aware of budding problems and be ready to cope with them. In someone else's boat at sea I list my responsibilities in the following order: first, to God and the vessel; second, to my crew, and to the people in any other boat in distress; third, to the owner of the vessel.

When I am single-handed, in my own boat, the order of responsibility remains the same.

Thus I have led you to realize, I hope, that the skipper of a crewed ocean-going vessel should have all the virtues (and, I hope, none of the vices) of the experienced single-hander. He should never ask anyone to do anything that he cannot, or would not, do himself.

A good skipper must be a good seaman. He must anticipate any emergency or defect that might arise, not only in his boat, but also in his crew. A small example: if heavy weather is expected, it is his responsibility to see that all the gear is sound and well lashed. It is his responsibility to see that his crew has a good hefty meal, that they are well cheered, that active crew members are safely secured with lifelines, and that the unneeded hands are sent down below to rest before the blow. If the worst happens, and the boat sustains heavy damage, it is his responsibility to prevent panic if it seems to be rising, and to take the decision to abandon ship or not. When the passage is completed—when the strange new world on the other side of the ocean is reached—it is his responsibility to see that the vessel and her crew are maintained in good order.

When it comes to crewmen, I have sailed with a lot. Some were very experienced, some complete greenhorns. I cannot say that I prefer either, except on a short passage where the greenhorn has no time to learn anything. In that case, the experienced hand is very welcome because on a short passage (and by that I mean up to say ten days) personalities do not matter much. But when it comes to an ocean crossing, where you're going to be confined together for maybe up to three months, then personality counts a great deal. In that case, I would far rather be with a beginner who may not know the sharp end from the blunt end—but who has a stable, balanced, nature—than with a shit-hot winner of the transatlantic single-handed race who was a loquacious know-it-all who never stopped talking.

But again, as with so many other things in ocean passage making, it is a matter of personal preferences. The two best mates I have had, out of any number, were Peter Kelly, a Manx fisherman, and Conrad Jelinek, a London candy-truck driver. In both cases they had an intense capacity for learning, in both cases they were highly intelligent, and in both cases we could at times go for days on end without more than a few words, to do with the running of the vessel, passing between us. I know that paragons like these two are rare, but that is the ideal to be aimed at not only by the skipper looking for a crew, but also by a crew looking for a boat.

The more disparate the backgrounds of the crew, the more the burden on the skipper in holding them together. If this is the case, then the less the skipper reveals of his own background, the better. Here the crew will be finding a new base, and the skipper should not influence it—that is until the time comes when the crew has found its points of contact, then in goes skip, feet first!

Women make good crew. Good women sailors are, I have found, physically more enduring than men, though they are not as strong. If a female takes to the sea she is very good for as long as her emotions will allow her to be; and in my experience this is for about eighteen months. I am also recalling female crews on other long-distance craft. Women's natural needs being what they are, it seems to me that most of them have a basic nesting instinct to stay in one place, if only for a while. The emotional strain of continually being on-the-move shows up either in the first three weeks, or between one year and eighteen months after departing the homeland.

Then there is a period when they seem to go to pieces emotionally, though a very few get over this. I would say that no woman should cruise continually for over a year without having a rest, even if it is only a couple of months in one port; just long enough to establish fresh roots, however tenuous, and make some friends among other people. Or she even might return to her country of origin for a spell. I know that the women's libbers will be after my guts for breakfast for saying this, but it seems to me that the female psyche, whether we like it or not, is at the hub of the wheel, right in the centermost molecule that does not revolve with the whole wheel moving round her—the spokes, the rim, the whole thing. The male psyche can be anywhere else but in that one central immovable molecule, anywhere from clinging on the outer hub, up and down the spokes, or right out on the outermost edge of the rim itself. I guess that small-craft ocean-passage makers are the outermost, or at least well among them. It's a hell of a strain for a female to be out there, and the ones that I have seen on the rim are among the people I most admire in this world.

I have seen any number of marriages and alliances broken up simply because the husband or whoever failed to see the innate female need for security above all things. They would talk to the girls until they were blue in the face about how fine the vessel was, about the attractions of warm winds, blue ocean, and sunny skies. But what most of them never understood was the very nature of femininity itself, which yearns and almost begs for security. Sure, it's easy and simple to be an independent, secure female in urban life, but once you get back to nature and contesting the elements both physically and mentally, then the deep longing of the female for security sticks out like a sore thumb—at least to me. And she can only take so much, unless she is a moron or a paragon.

My point is that the strength and security of a boat is more often apparent to the male and is by no means always so to the female. She has an affinity for earth, not water. You have only to see her after a long ocean passage, scrunching her bare toes in the sand, touching lingeringly stray flower blossoms, gazing at children, to know this. If

46

humans are descended from animals who left the sea, I'll bet that the first one to straggle out, wobbling on its flimsy fins, was a female! But bless 'em, what would we do without them? What is a wheel without a hub? Oh, sure, it'll turn, but it will be able to bear no load. Anyway, when the libbers have had their way and we're all supposed to be unisex, count me out; I'll head for Morocco and start a harem!

Lastly, children. In the past ten years or so, some ocean voyagers have raised families whilst on long passages. I have met some of these kids, and they are admirable. I think they will be very fine adults, but it's too early yet to know for certain. Wouldn't it be great if the first person to reach the stars was the child of an ocean roamer? I bet he or she will be!

THE DREAMING COAST

This piece, I feel, gives the essence of what it is like to cruise on a remote coast, far away from the usual yacht haunts, where time has stood still for a thousand years and more. If there is an ideal cruising ground on this Earth, it is surely the northwest coast of Madagascar, where the monsoon winds are always from the land, and there are a thousand insect-free, golden-beached islands to anchor behind. The locals are courteous, helpful and friendly, a mixture of African, Polynesian, French and Arab. This account appeared in Motor Boat and Yachting *in 1972.*

Madagascar . . . August 1971. As *Barbara* chugs on down to Cape St.Sebastien, through a mirror-flat sea, it's as if we are in a vast crystal bowl. Water and air seem to lose their properties and become mingled. The horizon has vanished; sea and sky are as one, so that the blue sky at our zenith curls round, comes under the boat, and stretches away to the east fading into a film of opacity. The coastline hovers above this, shimmering, with the headlands turning up out of the haze, like Polynesian prows. Gravity has gone, it appears, and with it the sense of location, which only returns to our numbed senses as we near the Cape, where the water shallows and we can see the weed ghosts, rock shadows, and the shadow of the boat sliding along the sand, distorted, fifty feet below the keel, restoring the sense of belonging on earth again.

Close to the shore the sea is glass-flat. The heat beats down, eased only by our hastily rigged awning, my floppy Seychelles straw hat and the slight breeze from the hills.

We anchor and the three of us row ashore dragging the dinghy onto a clean, sculptured, shady beach, and tramp

48

along the sea edge. I still have the feeling of floating. It's as if I am trying to walk on a rippling carpet in space. Again the sense of location leaves me; the mountains in the distance, the small islands nearer all merge into the sea and sky and it is only when we come to a creek, with its steep banks, that my earth-chain again drags on my feet.

I once emerged from a three-week binge in another place and I have been in love down to the joints of my toes, but never have I felt less earthbound than here. My two companions are lingering behind as we plod and slosh through the hot, muddy creek, chasing mercurial moving crabs as big as a cat.

"Watch it, Conrad . . . might be alligators here, this is just their kind of stomping ground . . . "

Finally, we arrive at a tiny settlement of straw huts, with a sliver of smoke ascending lazily between the close-knit trees around a clearing. We enter the compound, careful to make just enough noise to signal the hut folk that we come in peace, that we are strangers, and that we bear no malice. I round a clump of high, thorny bushes . . . and find . . . no one. I stand there feeling as if I have entered someone's house, foolishly staring around. Conrad joins me. I sing out, but not too loudly. "Hello there, anyone at home?" Silence. He looks at me and we grin at the sublime, cartoonlike situation. So funny and yet so potentially dangerous, for we know nothing of the people of this coast . . . for all we know they could be head-hunters or even cannibals. Alem's (our Ethiopian deck boy) eyes are as big as saucers now, as he warily looks around the compound.

He seems to sniff. He pokes around the ashes of a fire, he tastes the lukewarm water in a rusty pot, he even feels the ground with the flat palm of his hand. He goes to the door of the biggest hut and stands there, stock-still and tense for a few minutes. "They got man here, Skip . . . he ver' close . . . he no go from fire . . . he lookin' at us right now!" he says quietly.

"Where?"

"Dunno, but he here, Skip. *I feel him.*"

"Say something in Arabic, maybe he'll understand."

"What I say, Skip . . . he ver' frighten' he no come out."

"God is great, there is no god but God and there is peace in the land." I say the muezzin chant to Alem . . . and from the thorny bush, which we have passed on our way into the compound, comes the reply . . . "Peace unto you for truly God is great."

A rustling and crackling as he emerges . . . a young man of about twenty. He walks over the sizzling hot, bare ground towards me, the right hand held palm out, fingers up . . . I think, "Is this 1971 or 1871? Is this *really* happening, in a world of jets and moon flights?"

Alem has moved over, slowly and quietly, to my side. "Accursed be him who shall not welcome the true Believer, as Mahomet is the prophet . . ." he says in Eritrean coast Arabic. Back comes the reply, like a litany, "Even the fool is welcome here, if he believes."

He's not African: he's light, golden brown. He's not Asian. He must be Polynesian: his hair is straight, his features are almost Greek, and he does not have the jaguar litheness of the Arab of his age. He is stocky, barrel chested, and he has a clubfoot. This explains why he did not run away as all his friends have, he tells us. "Why do you run away? We are peaceful men of the sea, on a long pilgrimage. We seek only water and food, if there is food to buy."

"Where are you from? Are you Turks or Franks?" he asks. "We are Feringhi from beyond the White Sea (Mediterranean), where the land is cold and the folk, although rich with many goods, must light a fire such as you have here, every day inside their houses."

"And the son of the Feringhi?" He lifts his chin towards Alem. Alem replies, "A son of Tigrenea, above the coast of Massawa on the Red Sea, between the sea and the desert of Sudan . . ."

"I have heard tales of that land from the dhow sailors," he says. "I have heard that the people of that land are not true believers, but you say God is great ... "

"There is no god but God" says Alem quickly.

"You say this, and so I will give you water, coconuts, bananas, and two fish ... for we are poor people and have little to spare."

"We have no money of your country, but will bring ashore some cans of milk and fruit of the Black Coast (Zanzibar)" I say as we pile into the dinghy. He limps into the edge of the sea on his clubfoot.

"Go with God." He waits, a lone, poor man, on the long golden shore.

Alem tells me that "clubfoot" has told him, privately, that the men and women have all taken to the bush because they fear that we are Malagasy Government Tax Collectors! They are not fishermen, he says, and are probably just tolerated by the local, Arab, and African tribes, because they are such devout Moslems.

Alem returns to the beach and the waiting figure, with six cans of meat, milk, and fruit. The figure waves, then limps along the shore. He leaves a long trail of footprints, but the water washes them gently away, and in a few moments there is no trace of him.

We sleep, well fed in peace, and in the night keep anchor watch. I think of the timeless world of the Indian Ocean Moslem sea folk.

We do not shout or sing along this coast; no need, for the air has such a timbrous quality that a resonance is added to the ordinary speaking voice. It's as if a silver spoon is sharply tapped on a crystal wine glass. It's as if, if you shout loud, the whole world will fall apart, and the sculptured shoreline and islands will shatter in a million fragments.

As we weigh anchor we murmur to each other and the sound carries the length of the boat. We do not start the engine, except at night, when the blanket of darkness will hold this beautiful fragile world of pastel light and bind it securely, lest the noise destroy the dome of the sky.

We anchor at Mitsio Island, in a huge, deep lagoon, completely surrounded by fantasy islands of stark, bitter beauty. The people there are Arab with African strains of beloved slaves of long ago. Kind, gentle, and hospitable. They warn of the stingrays that haunt the bay and laugh at the distance I am anchored offshore of the village, but let them—they do not know how deep our keel is compared to their shallow-draft craft. We hear the throb of their drums in the night, shafts of sound in the clear air. And the voices of mothers comforting the babies. Half a mile away!

We sail away in the morning light, as pure as the taste of water, south, with a fair offshore breeze for forty miles, by Nosy Manghilo Island, over the Bay of Ambaro, the peaks of mountains a hundred miles away hardly moving the whole day, until we come into the haven of Helleville, on the island of Nossi Be. Back into the present with a bang, for there, at the head of the jetty, is a real, live fifty-foot yawl.

Here, in Helleville, with its soft mud tide flats, we lean *Barbara* drunkenly against a flat-bottomed harbor tug and clean the hull, well bearded on the waterline with bright green sea grass and the home, below, of a thousand clinging shells of a hundred hues. It seems unbelievable that this amount of growth has occurred in the two weeks since the lads last cleaned her off underwater at La Digue, or that these tiny bits of struggling life have managed to hold on to their temporary home through all the buffeting and pounding on our way south.

French guns in Helleville were arrayed under the shade of casuarina trees and bougainvillea on the lawn before the old government house, an interesting relic of the old colonial days. Only the French could construct a weapon of war in such elegantly traced lines of form. Stores in moderate variety are ranged along the tree-shaded main street. A French restaurant stands but six miles out of town. The taxi drivers seem to be the scions of the ill-famed Malagasy pirates. But a car can be hired reasonably enough, and the beaches of Nossi Be island are I think the best I have seen anywhere on the Indian Ocean islands, or anywhere south of them. Backed by deciduous woods and grass, with none of the alien, somehow menacing look of acres and acres of palm trees. Gentle trees, a breath of home.

September is soon. The official cyclone season will be upon the island's Crystal Coast in a month or so. South it is . . . out we go.

Fifty clear-aired miles, to Nosy Kalakjaro where *Barbara* anchors in a clean, wood-fringed, houseless bay. Up with the darting larklike birds skimming over the flat water . . . south again, all day and all night, in the gentle winds. Corned beef and rice, tea and French bread from Helleville, cocoa for the first and middle watches, then a stunning dawn over the massive Maramakotro Range.

Into Majunga. A bustling harbor, dirty and bad moorings for yachts, with the day wind and current straining the faithful fisherman anchor, chain protesting, to the limit. We clear immigration and harbor authorities (again, for Malagasy, like its sister, haunted Turkey, demands submission at each major port) and push off in search of a better, more comfortable spot outside the entrance to the harbor. Here we can imagine that we are in the Mediterranean, on the Riviera, perhaps, or in Catalonia, for there is a French holiday village, bikinis galore to disturb the past 300 miles of reverie. A nightclub, for somnambulists, and an airfield, with homing and departing planes daily. In the town, the Paris Restaurant . . . and "Madame Chapeau's Dance Hall and Refreshments of All Kinds for Weary Sailors." There are cinemas, good, well-stocked shops, souvenirs by the train-load, and a road to Tanarive, the capital, over 300 miles away.

The yacht club, not far from the holiday village, is simply and solely a dinghy sailing group, with no social facilities, but the members are helpful and interested in cruising boats of any description.

Formalities in Malagasy are not irksome, except, I believe, for South African boats, whose papers must be absolutely word perfect, or long and expensive delays will occur whilst Tanarive corresponds in long letters, Malagasy written, to Pretoria, where they must be translated into Afrikaans or English and vice versa.

We rest and exercise, swimming and walking round the town, elbows on the counter at friendly Madame Chapeau's, until the first of September; one month to go to the cyclones, so heave her up, me hearties, goodbyes all round, to everyone from the mayor to the sweeper in the Paris Restaurant. Then off we go, way out, off the shallows, thirty miles from the Dreaming Coast, headed for Inambane in Mozambique—a mere 1300 miles to the southeast on our way to the Cape of Good Hope, the "Cape of Storms."

SHERLOCK HOLMES AND THE MYSTERY OF THE *MARY CELESTE*

This, my personal favorite of my own short stories, is a typical example of the old, old technique of storytelling known to the ancient Welsh as crwn, *meaning, roughly, circular. The solution of the mystery is right there at the beginning and throughout the story. It is not until the very end of the tale, though, that the obvious is at last revealed. In order to write the story, I went through all the motions in Gibraltar and the Azores, which I made Holmes do. Except for Holmes, Doctor Watson (the narrator), and Mrs. Hudson, all the main characters actually existed. References to magazine articles and Gibraltar Admiralty Court records are verifiable as are all the circumstances mentioned in connection with the discovery of ship, crew and cargo. The story was published in SAIL in 1982.*

I t is with some feeling of trepidation that I put my pen to paper to write, at this late stage in my life, another story about my friend Sherlock Holmes. I write with some hesitation because the singularly strange events I am about to recall occurred over a quarter of a century ago, and have since been surrounded by such an air of mystery and legend as to lead anyone to conclude that this true account is, itself, so fantastic as to be fictional. It is perhaps meet that the true facts of this case, so far as they can be ascertained, should later come to light, for it is common knowledge that there are widespread rumors as to the fate of the crew of the brig *Mary Celeste,* which tend to make the matter even more terrible than the truth.

It was late in June in the year 1886 that upon going to breakfast I found Sherlock Holmes finishing his meal and Mrs. Hudson in a state of flusteration.

"Think it as well if you take your breakfast speedily, Watson" said Holmes, "things are astir at an early hour today."

"What? Have you then, at last, found the miscreant in the Bulgarian opal scandal?"

"No, a client," Holmes replied. "It seems that Mrs. Hudson, upon opening the door in answer to the milkman's knock, discovered a lady, in a considerable state of agitation, about to tug the doorbell. She insists on seeing me and is even now in the sitting room. Now, when a lady can hardly wait for the milkman to ladle out the day's order I presume that it is something of vital import that she has to communicate. As the evidence points to this perhaps proving to be an interesting case, you would, no doubt, wish to follow it from the outset. At any rate, I thought I would give you the opportunity."

"My dear fellow, I shall indeed take you up on your offer. I would not miss it for the world."

My experience of camp life in Afghanistan had at least had the effect of making me able, when the circumstances so warranted, to consume my victuals hurriedly. My breakfast eating habits were simple, and so in a matter of mere minutes I had cleared my bowl of porridge, my plate of eggs and bacon, and four pieces of toast with butter and marmalade.

There was no greater pleasure to me than in following Holmes in his professional investigations. There were no bounds to my admiration for his swift deductions, as rapid as intuitions and at the same time always well grounded in logic, with which he unravelled the sometimes insoluble-seeming problems that he encountered in the course of his endeavors. As soon as the teapot was empty and I had quaffed the last cup, I was ready to accompany my friend into the sitting room. A lady attired all in black and heavily veiled, who had been sitting by the fireplace, rose as we entered.

"Good morning, madam," said Holmes, brightly. "My name is Sherlock Holmes. This is my intimate friend and associate, Dr. Watson. Please feel as free to speak before him as before myself. Ha! I am glad to see that Mrs. Hudson has the fire drawing well. Pray do be seated, and I shall order you a cup of hot tea, for I observe that you are shivering."

"I am trembling, Mr. Holmes," said the lady. For a moment I was nonplused by her accent, until I realized that the lady was an American.

"What then?" asked Holmes of her.

"Excitement, Mr. Holmes, and to some extent fear and horror as to the fate of my husband." She lifted her veil as she spoke, and we could observe that she was, indeed, in a pitiable mood—her face drawn and gray, her eyes restless and frightened, like those of a startled deer. Her features and figure were those of a female of thirty-five, but her hair was streaked with premature gray and her expression was haggard and tired. Sherlock Holmes swiftly regarded her with one of his rapid, all-comprehensive glances.

"We shall soon find you refreshed," said he, soothingly. He bowed forward and patted her forearm. "No doubt we shall soon set matters right. You have very recently travelled by ship and train, I see."

The lady stared momentarily at Holmes, then dropped her glance. "You know me, then, Mr. Holmes?"

"No," said he, smiling, "but there is a simplicity in my deduction which I should convey to you. The right arm of your jacket has been spattered by salt in no less than five places, and the sleeve buttons of brass are slightly discolored with the green tinge of verdigris, but the coloring is too slight for it to have occurred more than a few days ago. That accounts for the sea travel. As for the train, well, madam, I observe that you have the second half of a return ticket tucked into the clasp of your reticule."

"Whatever the origin of your observations may be, you are perfectly correct," said she. "I have travelled all the way from Massachusetts in the United States of America. Sir, if this worry continues, I shall go mad. I have no one to turn to, none, save only my son, and he, poor young fellow, can be of little aid. I have heard of you, Mr. Holmes, from Miss Shaughnessy, the actress, whom you helped in her hour of sore need. She is, fortunately, I believe, a neighbor of mine in Boston since before the time that my dear husband Albert . . . " She dabbed her eyes with a tiny kerchief. Swiftly she recovered, "met with such a ghastly and untimely fate. Oh, my dear sir, do you not think that you could help me, or at least cast a little light on the dense mystery that surrounds the disappearance of my husband? At present it is beyond me to remunerate you for your services, but if it is at last proved that my husband is indeed dead, then I can remarry, with the control of my own income, derived from Mr. Richardson's life insurance benefit payment, and then at least you will not find me ungrateful."

Holmes walked over to his desk and unlocking it, withdrew a small case book, which he consulted.

"Miss Shaughnessy," said he, "Ah . . . Miss Shaughnessy. Yes. I do indeed recall the case, dear lady. It was concerned with a pearl necklace. It was before your time, Watson. I can only say that I shall be only too happy to devote to your case, madam, the same diligence as I did to that of your friend Miss Shaughnessy. As to reward, the pursuit of my profession is its own reward; but you are free to reimburse me for whatever expenses I may incur, at whatever occasion might in the future be most amenable to you. And now, madam, I beg of you that you lay before us all the facts that you know that may be of assistance to us in forming an opinion on this matter."

"Alas!" replied the lady, "the very misery of my situation lies in the fact that my fears are so vague, and my suspicions depend so entirely upon third-hand accounts of what may have transpired. But I have heard, Mr. Holmes, that you can see deeply into the manifold deviousness of the human heart. You may advise me how to walk amid the uncertainty and anxiety that now envelope me."

"I am all attention madam," said he, "and at this juncture allow me to assure you that it is always a pleasure to meet an American, for I am one of those who cannot believe that the foolhardiness of a monarch and the blunders of a government in far-gone years will prevent our children from being some day citizens of the same world-wide community of states under a flag of which the quarters shall be our Union Jack and your Stars and Stripes."

"My name is Mrs. Fanny Richardson, and I am the wife, or widow—for I know not which—of Albert Richardson."

"The name, I regret to say, is not familiar to me, madam."

"We are both of families who have been in North America for many generations; in fact my Albert's family is reputed to have arrived at Plymouth Rock with the *Mayflower*. My family now, so far as I know, consists of myself and my son, a bright young fellow, whom I hope later to send to West Point Military Academy."

"A worthy prospect, madam" said Holmes, rubbing his nervous hands together before the fire.

"My husband is . . . was . . . the first mate onboard the brig *Mary Celeste*, the mysterious abandonment of which you might, I dared to hope, be aware."

As Holmes knit his brows in silence for a moment I recalled to myself some of the facts connected with the loss of the British bark *Sophie Anderson*, of the singular adventures of Grice Patersons in the island of Uffa, and of the Camberwell poisoning case, upon the investigation of which, even at that moment, Holmes was engaged.

"I must confess, madam, that my knowledge of the matter is, like yours, of an extreme vagueness. But I seem to remember that it is a case of a vessel found at sea with some sail set and none of the ship's company in attendance; is that not so?"

"There you have the heart of the matter, Mr. Holmes." said Mrs. Richardson.

"Let me see, this was some years ago, was it not?" asked Holmes.

"Eighteen seventy-two. Fourteen heartbreaking years ago!" she cried. "Fourteen long years, and even now I am not certain as to whether or not my husband is deceased or taken prisoner by ill-intentioned persons, or a mutineer, or indeed perhaps even murdered by mutineers!" She burst into tears.

"These are strong words, madam" said Holmes, gently.

"Indeed they are, Mr. Holmes, for they emanate from emotions of despair just as strong, be assured of that."

There was silence for a minute or so, distributed only by the crackle and hiss of the anthracite coal in the fireplace. When she was again composed, Mrs. Richardson spoke. "I had become accustomed to my state as a widow, and last year a most respectable gentleman, a farmer of excellent reputation, asked me to marry him. But now I cannot, for I know not if I am in fact widowed, sir."

"Why then, madam, did you accept this gentleman's proposal of marriage last year?"

"Because there had been no news of Albert Richardson, or indeed of any of the crew of the *Mary Celeste*, for all the time since she had been discovered almost a derelict. A certain Captain Coffin, in January of this year, has written in the *New York World* that he has reason to believe that there is a mystery about the *Mary Celeste*, and I quote his own words here, sir, 'the solving of which would make anyone famous'."

Holmes glanced at me. There was a slight twitching of his aquiline nose. Gravely he said, "Madam, as my friend Dr. Watson will readily confirm, fame is of the least importance to me. Pray do carry on and tell me all you know."

"It seems that Captain Coffin has read the *Cornhill Magazine*..."

At this point Holmes held up one hand. He appeared somewhat perplexed.

"I beg your pardon, madam, would you remind repeating the name of the periodical to which you referred?"

"The *Cornhill Magazine*." She smiled. "Please excuse my accent."

"Ah, quite so, published here in London. And what was the date of issue of the particular data to which Captain Coffin referred?"

"January 1884. The story was an account by one of those who discovered the abandoned ship, and it was first published, according to the reporter, in a Gibraltar newspaper." Mrs. Richardson opened her reticule and from it extracted a small address book. She leafed through the pages, then suddenly, as we gazed at her, she said, "Yes, here it is, the *Gibraltar Gazette*."

"What was the name of the eyewitness whose account appeared in the *Cornhill Magazine*?" asked Holmes.

Again Mrs. Richardson consulted her address book. "J. Habakuk Jephson" she said.

"And the name of the reporter?"

"It was published anonymously." She reached into her attaché case and handed Holmes a copy of the *Cornhill Magazine*. Holmes rapidly, as was his wont, read through the story, then he closed the journal, looked up at Mrs. Richardson and said, "I take it to be understood, madam, that the crux of your query is whether or not your husband, Albert Richardson, is dead?"

"That is so."

"And if he is not dead, where can he be, as all the ship's boats seem, from this report at least, to have been found lashed down onboard the ship?"

"That is the case, sir."

"Whether or not this is a serious case, madam, I know not. It will necessitate communication with Gibraltar, to where the *Mary Celeste* was towed after her salvage. How long are you to stay in London?"

"As long as needed, if this problem can be solved once and for all."

"Are you at an hotel?"

"The Strand Palace."

"Capital!" exclaimed Holmes. "Then we can offer you a ride as far as the hotel." He turned to me. "Are you still willing to follow this case?" he half-cried.

"I can think of nothing I am more willing to do," I replied.

"Then we must be ready to depart for the Dover train within half-an-hour, my dear Watson. The train leaves in an hour. There is not a moment to lose!"

As I rose and passed Holmes to go to my room to change, he hissed in my ear "Meet me at Waterloo Station—the game's afoot!"

My experience of camp life in Afghanistan had at least had the effect of making me a prompt and ready traveler. My wants were few and of the simplest kind, so that in less than half-an-hour I was in a cab with my valise, rattling away to Waterloo. Sherlock Holmes was pacing up and down the platform, his tall, gaunt figure made even taller and gaunter by his long, gray travelling cloak and close-fitting cloth cap.

"It is really good of you to come, Watson," he said. "It makes a considerable difference to me, to have someone with me on whom I can thoroughly rely. Local aid is either worthless or else biased. If you will keep the two corner seats, I will get the tickets."

We had the carriage down to Dover to ourselves save for an immense bundle of papers. Among these he rummaged and read, with intervals of note taking and meditation, until we were past Canterbury. Then he suddenly rolled all the papers into a great bundle and tossed them onto the overhead rack.

"What we have to establish here, my dear Watson," he said, "is that a crime did *not* take place." He lit his pipe. "And that can be more difficult, according to the circumstances, than establishing that a crime *has* taken place."

"Have you discovered any more facts about the case?"

"I have, indeed. A most singular set of circumstances, Watson. Two ships were berthed alongside each other in

New York, the *Mary Celeste* and the *Dei Gratia*. The first ship to sail was the *Mary Celeste*, on November 7, 1872. The evening before she sailed the captains of the two ships dined with each other. Eight days later the second ship, the *Dei Gratia*, put out to sea, that is, on November 15. On December 5, twenty-nine days after the *Mary Celeste* sailed from New York and twenty-one days after the *Dei Gratia* had sailed, the latter sighted the former and hailed her. Receiving no reply from the brig, Captain Morehouse of the *Dei Gratia* ordered two of his officers, Deveau and Wright, to board the *Mary Celeste*. Having done so, these two officers, according to these reports, found the ship still slowly underway under headsails, everything in order, including warm meals still on the crew's table, and all the ship's boats in place and lashed down."

"Perhaps the *Mary Celeste* sighted a giant iceberg and her company deserted the ship as she was in danger of foundering?"

"Too far south, Watson. And as I have said, it is reported that the boats were all onboard."

"Perhaps the crew was stricken by plague?" As we both knew only too well from the case of Wilhelm Gottsreich Sigismond von Ormstein, Grand Duke of Cassel-Felstein, cholera and typhus were likely to strike anywhere abroad.

"No bodies."

"Perhaps a sea monster? Who knows what terrible denizens lurk in the murky depths of the ocean? Perhaps it was some giant octopus that appeared out of the blue ocean and swept the deck with its sinister tentacles?"

"No sign of struggle, Watson. It is reported that almost everything was in place, even to the harmonium that the captain's wife, Mrs. Briggs, had taken with her for the voyage."

Holmes sat, deep in thought, until the train arrived at Dover. There, while a porter carried our luggage to the ferry, Holmes purchased all the London newspapers that were on sale: the *Globe, Times, Telegraph, Star, Pall Mall, St.*

James' Evening News, Standard, and *Echo.* "Something to read on the train to Marseilles" he said cheerily. "Nothing on the other side, of course."

I followed my friend up the gangway and soon we were sitting in a first class cabin, watching the rough channel as the ship wallowed from side to side. Holmes lit his pipe and soon we were surrounded by the smoke from the Balkan Sobranie tobacco, just as if we were at home in foggy Baker Street. My experiences at sea on the way out to Afghanistan had at least had the effect of making me impervious to the discomfort of *mal de mer,* and so I was able to pay full attention to what Holmes said.

"We are lucky, my dear Watson. The S.S. *Duchess of Athlone* is meeting this train at Marseilles. She is on her way home from India, carrying the Berkshire Regiment. You recall Major Arbuthnot and the case of the one-eyed Buddha?"

"My dear fellow, I do indeed."

"We shall have the pleasure of the major's company. The ship is to call at Gibraltar for a day, and then proceed immediately home to England." He fell to scanning the newspapers.

Soon Holmes was again in reverie, his head fallen down onto his chest, his brows knit in deep thought. He remained thus, except for an altercation with a ruffianly French baggage handler at Boulogne docks, and for the instruction of a hansom-cab driver, in Paris, on the correct performance of his duties, for the remainder of the journey across France, which was accomplished in a wagon-lit's compartment and occupied most of two days and nights.

In Marseilles, after visiting a small house in a vile alley lurking behind the high wharves and emerging clutching a small package, Holmes brightened up somewhat. By the time we boarded the *Duchess of Athlone* he was positively brimming with cheer. Whether it was the cocaine or the thought of being once more under the British flag, which effected this change, I know not, nor dare I guess. We spent the first evening onboard the ship in the company of Major Arbuthnot. The next three days Holmes spent in our cabin, drowsy under the effects of his soporific drug, while I lounged on deck in a deck chair, or observed the soldiers, noting how a life far away from our own damp and foggy climate, remote from all the myriad temptations of urban life, has a most salutory effect on the health and well-being of our redcoats.

The day the ship was due to arrive at Gibraltar, Holmes was up bright and early. Indeed, when I awoke he was scolding the ship's steward at the lateness of the hour, which was 6:30 A.M. He was fully dressed, even to his cloth cap and coat, and indeed as I gazed at him he was even then placing his magnifying glass in his pocket.

"We are about to arrive in Gibraltar, my dear Watson, in an hour's time. There is not a moment to spare. The ship is sailing again on the evening tide. We must be prepared to step ashore immediately the gangway is lowered. Do not forget the letter of introduction from the King of Bohemia."

"Do you think there will be a clew as to this damnable deed?"

"It is not clews as to a deed for which we are searching, my dear Watson. Indeed, quite the reverse; it is clews to a non-deed, which we shall assiduously pursue, so that upon our return to England we might have information that will allow Mrs. Richardson to realistically presume her husband's death and so release her from her awful bondage to a long-dead man, and allow her to marry again and pursue the remainder of her life in marital bliss." Holmes opened the door. "I am going up on deck to observe the proceedings, shall you come quickly, Watson?"

"I shall, indeed, my dear fellow. There is nothing for which I should wish to be more precipitant."

Soon Holmes and I were striding up the main street of Gibraltar. All was in brilliant sunshine and only the shadows served to hide the sinister faces of Levantine merchants and their runners lurking there.

"I must say, Holmes, this has been a singularly swift investigation. It is only a week since Mrs. Richardson visited us."

"Swift enough. But we must be wary, Watson. A little overprecipitance may ruin all," he said as the Government House sentry came to a smart "present arms" and we entered the courtyard.

We were received civilly by a young subaltern, who welcomed me to sign the visitors' book, an invitation I deferred to my good friend, who, handing me his still-smoking pipe, scrawled his signature and our address across the page: Sherlock Holmes, H, Baker Street, London. Afterwards I proudly added my name just below that of a man of such extraordinary acumen and sagacity. We were then led by the subaltern into a waiting room hard by the entrance to the courthouse. We had hardly adjusted ourselves to the discomfort of the wickerwork seats when a gentleman burst into the room in a considerable state of agitation. It was a huge man who framed himself in the aperture. His costume was a peculiar mixture of the professional and the colonial, having a white pith helmet, a long, black frock coat, a pair of high gaiters, and a riding crop swinging in his hand. So tall was he that the pith helmet actually brushed the crossbar of the doorway, and his breadth seemed to span across from side to side. A large face, seared with a thousand wrinkles, burned yellow with the sun, and marked with every sign of impetuosity, was turned from one to the other of us. His deep-set, blue, bile-shot eyes and his high, thin, fleshless nose gave him somewhat the resemblance of a fierce old bird of prey.

"Which of you is Holmes?" asked this apparition.

"My name, sir; but you have the advantage of me," said my companion, quietly.

"I am Solly Flood, the attorney general and admiralty proctor for Gibraltar," said the intruder, in a loud voice. His accent was cultured, but with Irish undertones.

"Indeed, sir," said Holmes, blandly. "Pray take a seat."

"I will do nothing of the kind. I know you, sir. You are Holmes the busybody!"

My friend smiled.

"Holmes, the Scotland Yard Jack-in-office!"

Holmes chuckled heartily. "Your conversation is most entertaining," said he. "When you go out close the door, for there is a decided draught."

"I will go out when I have had my say, sir. Don't you dare meddle with the affairs of the Gibraltar Admiralty Court. I know you are here to pry into matters that are the concern only of the administrators of maritime jurisprudence. I am a dangerous man to fall foul of."

"I am here merely to inspect the court records of the Admiralty hearing on the discovery and salvage of the brig *Mary Celeste* in 1873, sir."

"Bah! Before my time. Pack of scoundrels. Piracy, sir, rank piracy. But I shall have them yet!" Solly Flood said as his face turned more sallow than when we had first seen it. "In the past year I have sent letters all over the world, sir, all over the world, from Vladivostok to Valparaiso, from Hong Kong to Harwich. I have instructed the admirals of all the far-flung stations to have their intelligence agents watch every port, every dock, every jetty, every ship arriving and departing, until the ruffians who perpetrated this terrible crime are finally brought to justice, and unless I am very mistaken, to the hangman's noose!" The attorney general crashed his riding crop against one knee. "There is no call for Scotland Yard landlubbers to interfere in the workings of the wheels of Royal Navy criminal investigation. We are dealing with a wide-flung plot to hide the nefarious machinations of a maritime criminal master mind. A monstrous plot to seize ships plying the high seas on their lawful occasions, to hypnotize their crews, arm the craft, and so construct a fleet of vessels capable of terrorizing the seas. It is an anarchist design, sir, and even now they are placing their infernal machines on their ships. But we shall have them, never fear."

"I am here on behalf of the wife of the first officer of the *Mary Celeste,* merely to inspect the records in order to ascertain whether or not her husband may be presumed dead, so that the lady may remarry. Fourteen years is surely, sir, a respectable period of mourning, is it not?" suggested Holmes.

"There were no British persons onboard the *Mary Celeste,* thank God!" said Solly Flood.

"The lady in question is American, sir."

"So, I believe, were the foul pirates who perpetrated this monstrous deed. Revolutionary rascals from the Carolinas, no doubt."

"She is from Boston."

"Indeed, sir." For the first time there was not a scowl on the attorney general's face. "A most respectable place, I believe. Many of my countrymen have made their homes there."

"I can assure you, Mr. Flood, that Mrs. Richardson is of good family and of impeccable character."

"In that case, Mr. Holmes, I shall afford you the opportunity of inspecting the records. Carson, the chief clerk, will show you into the court library. I never look at the things myself, poor eyesight, malaria, did twenty years in India, you know. Anyway, I'm off on the Algeciras hunt today. Are you here for long? You should ride with us. We cross the border over into Spain."

"Unfortunately Mr. Flood, my friend and associate, Dr. Watson, and I are merely here for one day, for our ship sails with the evening tide."

"For England, home and beauty? Lucky fellows. Have another five years to do out here. But let me wish you luck on your quest, sir. I shall make it my business to call upon you next time I am in London. Who knows, I may have need of your services?" Flood said, mysteriously. Little did we guess then that five years later Flood would involve us in the dangerous mission to retrieve the diamond cuff links of a certain royal personage from the clutches of a notorious Bohemian courtesan.

I have always been astounded by the rapidity of my friend's reading. In the library, Carson, the clerk of the court, placed before Holmes a tome almost a foot thick. Within half-an-hour, as I looked through the mullioned windows of the courthouse library at the great upward sweep of the mighty bastion of Empire Gibraltar, Holmes banged the file shut. I looked at him, expectantly.

"Just as I thought, my dear Watson."

"You have found a clew?"

"I have found a nonclew, my dear fellow. In fact I have found a number of nonclews."

I stared at Holmes, I must confess I was somewhat perplexed.

"I was led here, I must admit, by some clew, but I now have what we need to get to the heart of the matter."

"What is that?"

"The truth, so far as can be known in the circumstances. The most glaring truth about the *Mary Celeste*, my dear Watson, is that in fact *there was a boat missing from the ship when she was discovered.*"

"Indeed? Then the crew may still be alive?"

"Hardly a chance. Deveau and Wright, who were, you surely recall, two officers from the brig *Dei Gratia*, which had the single misfortune or fortune, according to the point of view, to fall in with the evidently abandoned *Mary Celeste*, gave evidence in Admiralty court that when they boarded the unfortunate vessel they found that two of her sails had been blown away. Only the fore topsail was hoisted, and that hung limply by its four corners. All the other sails were furled. The main-peak halyard, which as you probably know, Watson, is the rope used for hoisting the big mainsail, was found hanging over the side of the ship with its end frayed and broken. Now, in a ship so obviously well run and crewed by such a fine selection of first class seamen and officers, this is a very signal clew, and I assure you, Watson, that I intend no pun by that phrase."

We took our farewell of the ancient Mr. Carson and made our way once more out into the brilliant sunshine on Gibraltar's main street.

"Yet another signal clew" said my friend as we made our way along the narrow street, crowded with nefarious-looking Orientals, elegant Spanish ladies and gentlemen, and fine-looking, robust bluejackets in straw hats, "is the cargo the *Mary Celeste* was carrying and the fact that one of her cargo hatch covers was found removed from its proper place. You recall when we had occasion to visit Professor Clitheroe?"

"The case of the suspicious explosion in the Black Swan Inn at Silchester? When we proved that the death of Clothilde Fontaine was, in fact, an accident?"

"Yes. Ha! We discovered the effect of the violent movement of barrels of raw alcohol, which the landlord was illegally employing in order to manufacture his own distillation. There was, of course, a violent explosion." Holmes' eyebrows raised slightly at the memory.

"And the weird noises coming from the inn's cellar before the explosion, which the good Lady Yarborough, you recall, so tearfully imagined was the sound of the ghosts of souls who had died besotted with drink."

"Indeed, Watson, what we have here is an almost exactly parallel case. There were, we know from the court records and the cargo manifest of the *Mary Celeste*, 1701 barrels of raw alcohol stowed onboard. We also know from the ship's log, which was found in perfectly good order, that the ship had experienced foul weather for the greater part of her voyage. We also know, by the good offices of the meteorological services of the Azores, that there was a sudden calm in the area where the *Mary Celeste* found herself, south of the Azores, on November 24. So I deduce that when the loud noises of a sailing ship in hard winds had ceased, the rumbling was heard, Watson."

"The rumbling?"

"The rumbling of the raw alcohol in the process of spontaneous heating, preparatory to exploding. I then deduce that Captain Briggs, who, according to the United States Consul in Gibraltar at the time of these unfortunate occurrences, was a fine efficient ship's commander, upon hearing the rumbling from down in the cargo hold, ordered the hatch removed and all the sails except the headsails furled. As this was being done the low rumbling increased in volume, louder and louder. As you may imagine, Watson, this alarmed Captain Briggs and his crew. The good captain ordered everyone onboard, his wife, their little daughter, the two officers, the cook, also American, and the six stalwart German sailors, into the longboat. He took with him the end of the main-peak halyard, which was the rope he could most conveniently find quickly. Bear in mind, my dear Watson, that all the while the sinister rumble in the hold was growing louder and louder. They were apprehensive of a mighty explosion, which would shatter the vessel and themselves, at any minute." I followed Holmes through Her Majesty's dockyard gate.

"Why did the captain take the rope with him?" I asked.

"Simple, my dear Watson. He wanted a long line to which he could secure the longboat, yet well clear of the vessel if she exploded."

"But why did the crew leave the headsails hoisted?"

"There are two possibilities here. Either the captain wished to keep the ship moving, but slowly and steadily in the prevailing west wind east of the Azores, so taking the ship and the towed longboat all the while closer to their destination. I think this highly likely. Or they left the ship far too precipitantly to lower the headsails. But Captain Briggs was a fine seaman, a most experienced, steady, sober man. He was also, from the sworn evidence of those who were acquainted with him, a resourceful mariner. From this I deduce that he left the headsails set intentionally."

"Then why was no one found onboard? What happened to the longboat?"

"Again thanks to the clear evidence of the report from the meteorological service of the Azores, we find that on the morning of November 25, the day when the ship's log reports ceased, there was a sudden southwesterly storm. From this I deduce that the *Mary Celeste* was sailing before the light breezes, towing the longboat, when quite without warning to the poor souls in the boat she was struck by a strong wind and lunged ahead. The towing line, the main-peak halyard, was 300 feet long. It broke under the sudden strain of the ship's lunge. The ship then, with a heavy breeze playing on her headsails and on all her standing and running rigging, picked up speed and, untended by any helmsman, plowed on before the wind, increasing, with every slight wallow, the distance between her and the now-cast-away longboat." As we reached the gangway of the *Duchess of Athlone*, Holmes paused, his face creased in an expression of compassion. "We hardly dare guess, my dear Watson, the feelings of the poor souls in the longboat as the four American and four German men strained at their oars to catch up with their ship. Despair and terror, Watson, the despair of the damned. Faster and faster they pulled, until, who knows? Mercifully perhaps, the weather worsened as night fell, and as they prayed for deliverance from their cold, wet misery, the boat was swamped and foundered. Their end was probably swift, for the weather had got up into a full storm by the night of November 26."

"Then that was the same storm that blew away the two headsails?"

"A remarkable deduction, my dear Watson." Holmes gazed up at the passenger deck of the *Duchess of Athlone* to see Major Arbuthnot waiting to speak with him. Little did we guess that this occasion was the commencement of the mystery of the missing cavalry horse. "We must board the ship for England. The secret of the mystery of the *Mary Celeste* lies in England. It is there I shall seek it. The key factor of the matter is to find the anonymous writer of the report on this nonexistent crew member of the *Dei Gratia*, J. Habakuk Jephson, for he was absent from the court record." Holmes brought out from his raglan coat pocket the copy of the *Cornhill Magazine* and consulted a page he has already marked with a length of powder fuse. "Ah, yes, here it is. J. Habakuk Jephson" he read. "We must find the inventor of this legend, the writer of this tissue of fiction, who so assiduously enveloped a comparatively straight-forward sea mishap with all the verbal accoutrements of a supernatural occurrence, and thus, after fourteen long, solitary years of mourning, has caused a flood of anxiety to a respectable woman as to her future, and a resurrection of the sorrows in her past. I shall demand redress sir, have no fear of that, and if the fellow was ill-intentioned, I shall have him horsewhipped within an inch of his life!"

It was in a disturbed condition that I followed Holmes onboard the England-bound ship, for I had seldom seen my friend in such anger. But soon after Major Arbuthnot greeted us again, and told us of the alarming disappearance of a cavalry horse, Holmes was cheery again, as, magnifying glass in hand, he preceded me down to the depths of the ship to inspect the stables.

The voyage from Gibraltar to England occupied the space of five days, and immediately upon our arrival at Woolwich, where Major Arbuthnot and the Berkshire Regiment were to disembark, Holmes and I parted. He to pursue the trail of the mischievous author of the erroneous report in the *Cornhill Magazine.* I once again to continue my medical practice, which, owing to my absence from the country, had diminished considerably, three of my erstwhile regular patients having taken leave of this life during the two weeks that Holmes and I had been engaged in tracking down the mystery of the nonexistent mystery of the *Mary Celeste.*

It was three days later, when, as Mrs. Hudson was showing out my one remaining patient, Miss Golightly, that a hansom cab stopped at the door. From it, as I gazed through the window, I saw Holmes emerge, looking travel worn and somewhat pale. He was followed out of the cab by the figure of a man dressed in country clothes, with a wide-brimmed hat pulled down low over his face, which was further hidden by a large scarf muffled up around his neck and chin.

Without a word Holmes strode into the sitting room, leading by the elbow the muffled stranger. Quickly he drew out the tall Chinese screen and gently urged the stranger behind it. "I want your word of honor, sir" he said to the stranger, "that you will remain behind the screen until I say so."

"You have my word." said a muffled voice.

"Very good, please seat yourself comfortably. I shall, in a moment, order for you a cup of tea."

"That will be eminently acceptable" said the voice.

Holmes turned to me. His face was drawn and strained. "My dear Doctor Watson" he half-cried, "Please do forgive me for my somewhat brutal return."

"My dear fellow, your arrival can never be anything but welcome."

"Time is of the essence." Holmes said in a low voice. "Mrs. Richardson is on her way here at this moment by a hansom cab that I have sent around to her hotel. This gentleman who has accompanied me here and who, as you see, is at present sitting behind the screen, is none other than the author of J. Habakuk Jephson's statement, which was published in the *Cornhill Magazine* in January of this year, and which regrettably was the cause of all the furor, and the fount of the mystery of the *Mary Celeste!*"

Even as Holmes spoke, another cab arrived and Mrs. Richardson was in a moment at the sitting room door.

"Ah! Mrs. Richardson, pray, take a seat. I have ordered hot tea, which will be served directly."

"It is good to see you again, Mr. Holmes, do you have news for me?"

"I do indeed, madam, but first let me see that you are comfortable." He bent to stir the fire with the poker, while Mrs. Hudson served tea. Mrs. Richardson's face expressed curiosity as Mrs. Hudson took a cup behind the Chinese screen.

"At this juncture I must tell you, Mrs. Richardson," said Holmes, standing in front of the fire, "that besides your goodself, my dear friend Dr. Watson, and myself, there is another person in this room."

"Can he be trusted?" she asked.

"That remains to be seen. The fact is that the person behind the screen shall remain concealed, though he may hear what we have to say and we may hear what he has to say. I am certain that when you have heard his account you will be satisfied that your husband, Arthur Richardson, is in fact dead, and has been for fourteen years."

As Mrs. Richardson listened in silence, Holmes then recounted our expedition to Gibraltar and what transpired after our return to England.

"When I parted from my good friend and confidant, Dr. Watson," he said, "I immediately took a hansom cab around to the offices of *Cornhill Magazine*. The editor, a rather impertinent fellow, as indeed are many members of his profession, flatly refused to tell me the name of the author of the story. But even as he was showing me out of his office I had a flash of inspiration. The name of the supposed crew member of the *Dei Gratia* was given as J. Habakuk Jephson. The writer had changed the name of the abandoned ship to *Marie Celeste*. Here, I deduced, were two clews. First the name Jephson. A singular name, I think you will agree, madam?"

"Quite unusual, Mr. Holmes."

"Then, suddenly it came to me in a flash. I recalled that when Dr. Watson and I had been engaged in the adventure of the Copper Beeches, a black business indeed, madam, in which a person called Jephs was involved, we were accompanied for some of the time by a young gentleman who aspired to be a writer, but who was prevented from being so by the exigencies of his profession."

"Surely you don't mean . . . ?" I cried out, but before I had time to finish Holmes held up his hand. He turned to me and said solemnly, "I must have your word that this matter be kept secret."

"My dear fellow, you have it. My lips are sealed forever," I replied.

"I immediately took the train down to Brighton and there found the gentleman in question. Madam, I can assure you that this young man who now is sitting behind the screen before your very eyes is guilty of nothing more than youthful impetuosity, and that the pain he has caused you did not spring from any malice, but rather from the necessity to increment his earnings, by writing, in order to support himself until he can fully do so by the income from his profession as a doctor of medicine."

Mrs. Richardson nodded slightly. "I quite understand, sir."

"Further, after I had explained the ramifications of his action in submitting the story for publication, he immediately offered to give all his earnings, the substantial sum of thirty pounds, to you, madam, to support some of the costs that you have been subject to in your excursion. I might add here that thirty pounds will, I think, pay for your return passage to Massachusetts and also, no doubt, for your stay in the Strand Palace Hotel."

"The gentleman is most kind, but am I to be permitted to know him?"

"Only if you give me your solemn word, as my friend Dr. Watson has done already, that his name shall never escape from your lips or your pen so long as you shall live."

"That is a rather strange request."

"But not a harsh one, madam. I must explain that the gentleman behind the screen is in possession of information that, should it be aired in public at the wrong time, might lead to the toppling of half the thrones of Europe and untold misery to many innocent persons and children yet unborn. Failing your word that this gentleman's identity be kept by you for the remainder of your life a deadly secret, then I cannot permit you to communicate with him one word. Our lives depend on it."

"You have my word, sir, I promise, on the life of my son and the dear man who has expressed his attachment to me."

"Very good. Watson?"

"My dear fellow?"

"I want your solemn vow that not one word about this gentleman's identity will be heard or seen by anyone outside this room for a considerable period of time, for a hundred years since the finding of the *Mary Celeste*, until 1972."

"It shall be as you wish, my dear friend," I replied. "I shall wait thirty years to write the account. Then I shall lock it in a box marked 'not to be opened until 1972'."

"Capital. Then I shall introduce you both to the gentleman who invented the mystery of the *Marie Celeste* in January of 1884."

Holmes strode from the fireplace to the screen. He moved the ivory and ebony scrollwork to one side, to reveal the mysterious stranger. He still sat at the small card table, still muffled up to the ears by the scarf.

"Please stand up, sir," said Holmes. The stranger did as he was bid. "You may remove your scarf now, if you would be so good to do so."

The stranger unwound the scarf and let it fall to the floor. He was about my height, five feet nine inches tall, of ruddy complexion, and bright eye. His age was about twenty-six years.

Sherlock Holmes took the stranger's hand in his, as he turned to face us. "Mrs. Richardson," he said, quietly, "please meet the author of J. Habakuk Jephson's statement, the originator of the mystery of the *Marie Celeste*, Doctor Arthur Conan Doyle."

The End.

STORM CLOUDS OFF THE ANDES

This is one of the very few pieces that I actually wrote at sea on passage. Samuel Johnson once said, "It is wonderful how proximity to the hangman's noose will clear a man's mind." So it is with a man's writing. This piece has never been edited in any way whatsoever. It is exactly as it was written in my notebook off the coast of Peru in December of 1973. East West Journal first published this in 1981.

December 8, 1973. **7100 hours.** *Sea Dart* has been anchored in Salaverry Road since two this morning, having managed to get into the anchorage minutes before a thick fog came down like a cold blanket. Despite the violent rolling all day I catch a few hours' sleep and assemble a decent meal of rice and fish for lunchtime and supper.

Like most of the harbors on the west coast of South America, Salaverry is wide open to the swell and is protected from the wind only by a slightly protruding headland. It is crowded with fishing vessels at anchor, all rolling away, and the heavy surf beats on the shore all around the bay with a noise like thunder.

Cheered up by the hot meal at 4:30 P.M. I'm thinking, "Well, there's a good full moon and a breeze of about fifteen knots. I'd be better off rolling and banging out there, getting somewhere, than just sitting here in this discomfort. If I'm going to get over the Andes to Lake Titicaca before the wet season sets in, I'd better get cracking."

The sun has shone all afternoon, ever since the fog lifted at noon. The sea looks green and inviting, so off we go. Up main, up hook and away, clear the headland, up stays'l and genoa and here we are, *Sea Dart*, all twenty feet of her, bashing once more against the Humboldt Current. By this time we're both pretty well used to beating hard. From Panama to Salaverry we've beaten continuously for 2,225 miles through the water. Only another estimated thousand to go and we shall be in Callao, ready to haul up three miles across the Andes. Three miles straight up, that is.

On this part of the coast of Peru, this year at any rate, the Humboldt Current has approached the coast very closely, and the area around the Guanape Islands—twenty miles to the south of us—is notorious for a continual, strong, northerly going current and fogs; so the sooner we leave that little lot well astern, the better.

1900. Going like the clappers with everything up and the wind strong—about 20 knots. I have to keep the big genoa up much longer than is seamanlike, for with the heavy swell and *Sea Dart*'s short waterline, I must keep her moving forward at 3 knots in order to overcome the current, which always has an unknown rate (generally between 1½ knots to 2 knots), eternally heading north. To make things even more interesting, the wind generally blows along the coast from the south. If I stand out more than twenty miles, the current increases to about 2½ knots, so after sailing for twenty-four hours in the offing I would find myself north of where I started from.

To avoid the strong current I must stay inshore. But inshore, six nights out of seven, a heavy fog sweeps down and stays there, at least for the small hours of the morning, lightening to a haze at midforenoon. It is a strange fog, for it comes on the wind, and it can be blowing quite hard whilst you can't see the bowsprit.

I'm still a little concerned about the bowsprit, after *Sea Dart* collided with a whale off Colombia. It busted, and I fixed it, but the bolt that holds it down through the deck lifted on the last leg. I spent three hours this morning straightening and refixing it, but with the continual pounding I'm afraid that it might work loose again. If it does, I shall have some cold wet fun fixing it, that's for sure.

1915. I've just made myself some Bovril extract sandwiches with raw onion. I shall eat half of them at midnight and half at 4 A.M. when my resistance is lowest. I also have a special treat as it's Sunday: a bar of Cadbury's fruit and nut chocolate. My thermos flask is broken, so it will be cold tea with the sandwiches. I've no ready money until I reach Callao as the Peruvian immigration official in Piura would not let me travel overland to Lima to collect money from the bank there. So I must reach Callao as soon as possible.

I take a bearing on the North Island and find I am being set out to sea, so I come about two miles close to the shore before dark. There will be a fine moon, so I'm not too anxious about hitting the rocks to the north of the islands, and if I press sail I can be clear of the islands before our friend the nightly fog turns the night sinister.

1930. I jolt my way forward and inspect the bowsprit. It's holding well. My sea boots fill with water, cold Humboldt water, all the way from the Antarctic. I curse in good old-fashioned Liverpool fashion and put on my only dry socks. To ameliorate my hurt feelings, I steal one of my midnight sandwiches, then come about. This is a chore, as I have to lean right over the stern to alter the altitude of the wind vane to the wind. I get another "green'un," this time over my chest. I'm wearing "oilies," so I can laugh this time. All the while little *Sea Dart* and I are pounding up and down and the wind in the rigging and on the metal mast is howling a gale. "Blow it" I think and go into the doghouse to listen to the news from the BBC and adjust the chronometer to the time signal.

My Bulova wrist watch, which I normally use for navigation, has finally broken down after years of hard service, and I am using a century-old sailing-ship chronometer, which was bought in London as a curio years ago and which is still running at a loss rate of only one second every thirty-six hours. I'm treating it like the Holy Grail, for the conditions on this coast are such that one can be anywhere. I have to be ready for snap sights at any time since the overcast is general.

I cannot get my usual forty winks this evening because *Sea Dart* will be working her way between the islands and the coast. I can hear the breakers very clearly to the east. I can also make out the wicked looking rocks, shining white under the moon. Things always look bigger by moonlight, and rocks will always appear to be closer than they really are. I must not haul away too soon.

Apart from the direction of the wind, the heavy swell, the roar of the breakers, the cloud overcast, and the continual violent movement of *Sea Dart,* the night is fine. I think to myself, "It would be a damn-sight finer in some cozy warm little pub somewhere."

2200. It's getting hazy, and as the fog thickens it gets colder, so I crash below and put on another sweater, a Greek one this time, and recall sunny days in Mykonos. Ah well! Back on deck, we come about; this time I get one in the face. "Right, you bastard!" I think, "getting naughty, eh?"

At midnight I'm really keeping my ears and eyes open, for the haze is almost white now. We pound along, lonely and hopeful.

0130. I hear the beating of surf to starboard. Strain my eyes. There it is! Through a windy gap in the fog, shining white! The Middle Rock. It's not where it ought to be, but then if it were, or if I were, *Sea Dart* would be perched on top of a 5,000-foot mountain right now, that is, if dead reckoning could be trusted.

Here, on this coast, dead reckoning is about as useful as striking a match on a bar of soap. There's such a thing as "feel," and I am developing an uncanny instinct for knowing just about where I am. All my senses come into play, and I swear I can *smell* sand now. Rocks have a pungent, slightly bitter smell; sand has a dry, mouldy aroma. "Might get a job as a whiskey taster one of these days," I say to myself. I've come about and I'm shivering. Grab another sandwich. A maverick sea sends spray right onto it as I stagger up through the tiny companionway. "Salt and Bovril; tasty!" Still, better than nothing.

0230. I'm guessing like mad now. If the charts are right I should be sailing along a dried-up river bed about three miles inland by now. The sea "feels" shallow but not less than fifteen fathoms. I glance wistfully at my electronic depth sounder, which gave up the struggle with the sea atmosphere back in the West Indies. The fog is as thick as a London pea-souper is supposed to be but hardly ever is; it swirls away to the north, ghostly, like a death shroud. Get some music on the radio. Bad reception, but anything to stop me thinking like that. Must sew some buttons on this jacket.

The wind is still strong. I'm keeping a very wary eye open for the light on the South Island, but there's no hope of seeing it. I go into the doghouse every five minutes to stare at the stove lying at a crazy angle on its gimbals. Eat another sandwich; remember flat seas a thousand miles up the Amazon last year; broach the chocolate bar; try to figure out where the nuts and raisins come from. Back to staring at the chart; lost. Bloodywell hopelessly lost.

Turn back? Where to? In what direction?

Then I remember the still, calm voice of old Tansy Lee, when we had gone aground on the Hailsborough Sands in the North Sea, years ago: "Well, ol' son, we can't go nowhere, so might as well make a cuppa tea!" All the time the barometer had been dropping and there we were, high and dry, with a rising tide and the North Sea in a frenzy.

I laugh at the memory and feel fifty times better. I can keep a steady watch, thinking of Tansy and his funny stories.

0300. The wind is dropping and the swell "feels" deeper. I crawl forward and check the bowsprit. Holding. Allah be praised! As I move aft I trip over the plough anchor and it shifts. The lashing has come loose. I curse myself for a sloppy job. Back to the cockpit. I see a nice tear in the bottom of the genoa. Well, I'll fix that at dawn, with the blooming sail still up and pulling; my usual method on this hard beat, for I won't give the bloody Humboldt even the few yards it would steal from me whilst the genny was down.

0400. Ecstasy! Four whole sandwiches at one go. Two mugs of tea. I've been a good lad tonight, so I reward myself. Still no sign of anything, except the swirl of fog, the roar of the genoa as the tear flutters, and the lash of the sea under the hull aft, for *Sea Dart* is a hard chine. And the cold. The deep, damp, Humboldt cold. The air feels like a seal's nose. Whiskers and all.

0500. The false dawn. Everything is grey, including me. More tea.

0600. The wind is down to ten knots, southerly. The haze has lifted so I can see about a mile. This is difficult to estimate, but I have spent a lot of time watching birds and fishing boats in haze, so I have a good idea of the visibility. I keep the kerosene lamp brightly lit and snatch an hour on a cold, damp, sleeping bag which has seen better days—and nights, too.

0700. The movement has eased off. I light the stove and make coffee and burgoo (porridge and whiskey, only in this case, rum). That's better. Up forward I go with the sail-maker's housewife tied to my belt. Repair the genny. Great big one-inch stitches so as to spread the load away from the rip. Have a check round. The bowsprit is okay. All bottle-screws tight. Stays'l pretty fair. Mainsail working. Another sleep.

1000. The fishing lines are out. I've scrubbed the cockpit—amazing how *dirty* it gets in a fog—polished the kerosene lantern and come about, standing inshore. Then I see it! Through the haze—North Island! On the *port quarter* not more than two miles away! "Hmm," I think, "so you think you've got 'feel in a fog,' eh?" Look at the chart.

Well, well! All night, sailing like a blooming train; the taffrail log shows fifteen miles since 8 P.M. last night—and poor little *Sea Dart* has moved south, over the ground, *only five miles* . . . and there's a thousand to go to Callao! Well, it could have been worse; we could have met the White Jaws. Instead, here we are, with the fog lifting swiftly, the promise of sunshine all afternoon, the glow on the beautiful Andes and, who knows, perhaps less current further down, at Chimbote. Only another forty miles to an anchorage and sleeeeeeeeep.

THE LONGEST HAUL

The following article described part of the voyage of my twenty-foot Sea Dart *from the West Indies to Callao, Peru, and the subsequent hauling of the boat up the Andes to Lake Titicaca. At the time I wrote this story for* SAIL *in 1974, I was existing on my earnings from what I could publish and the piece was submitted while I was still on the lake. I had to be very careful about what I wrote. I couldn't say, for example, that I had a price of 1000 dollars on my head in Peru for having, in essence, smuggled the boat through, nor could I write about the repressive political conditions in Bolivia. That had to wait until my first book,* The Incredible Voyage.

On Saturday, January 4, at six in the evening local time, a battered 10-ton truck, leaking oil as it coughed along, pulled into the main plaza of Puno—a dusty Andes town on the shores of Lack Titicaca, more than two miles above sea level.

A crowd of locals, mainly Indians wearing ponchos, and their bowler-hatted wives, stared in amazement at what the truck had dragged into town. There sitting on the back was a 20-foot British sailing boat, complete with two Red Ensigns, worn fore and aft, fluttering in the breeze. Both truck and boat were covered in fine dust, while the boat's crew looked like ragged scarecrows. And felt like it.

Sea Dart had arrived at the place she set out for from the West Indies back in May of 1973 . . . and I had arrived at where I set out for three years ago from the Dead Sea Valley in Israel, 48,500 sailing miles ago.

I had attempted to take a sailing vessel to the lowest sea in the world and from there to the highest. I left Eilat, in

Israel, in the 38-foot yawl *Barbara,* in December of 1970 and made my way through the pirate-infested Red Sea to the Indian Ocean.

From the Seychelles Islands I originally had intended to make a passage east across the Pacific to Peru, but a friend in Lima had written saying it was impossible to haul a boat of that size from the coast across the Andes.

So I turned around and headed round the Cape of Good Hope in December 1971, destination Pucallpa, 3,800 miles up the Amazon River. Information had reached me that there was a 12-ton crane there and a rough track that just might take the load. But repairing damage caused during several storms off the Cape delayed me, so that when eventually I reached the Amazon, in February 1972, the river was already rising with the current reaching seven knots at times. I tried every way I knew to reach Pucallpa, even heaving the boat from tree to tree with hawsers, but the current, heat, malaria, and other factors eventually defeated me.

Again I turned around and headed for the West Indies, where I hoped to find a smaller craft that I would sail into the Pacific and tackle the job from the other side of South America. I rested for a few days at Devil's Island, which has a very healthy climate, and then headed for the islands, where, after an 1,800-mile search, I eventually found the boat I was looking for, *Sea Dart,* a really tough little nut, only 20 feet long on the waterline and two tons dead weight. Besides this, and most important of all, *she has three keels.* Theoretically she shouldn't go to windward at all, or at any rate hardly, but someone had fitted her with a bowsprit so she can fly a large genoa. That shifts her all right!

The three keels would save building a cradle to haul her in and would ensure that the jolts and bumps would be distributed as evenly as possible. Apart from this, she was very well rigged and had a load of sound gear. So I bought her, bent her mast to spill the wind early in the mountain squalls, nailed up my letter from Haile Selassie, and took off to try for the Lake again.

This time it was important to sail as hard as could be, for the alternative was to make my way round the Magellan Strait and so on up the west coast of South America. I did not fancy that very much as the route was too indirect and anyway I'd still have a contrary current as far as Recife, in Brazil. So the most direct (and I think the hardest) route it had to be—through the Panama Canal and straight into the fast-moving Humboldt Current, tooth and nail against continual headwinds.

Sea Dart made a good fast passage to Panama, almost two thousand miles, via the San Blas Islands, which I thought of as the shakedown cruise. Off the north coast of Venezuela the sea is very steep and the winds hard. In this area I tried my best to put her on her ear, but with the bent mainmast she was as stiff as a corpse, and it was impossible to lay her over more than 35 degrees. Fortunately, for I happen to be a nonswimmer!

Anyway, I purposely shook her up, to see what she would stand. Never once did she protest. Never once did I have to pump her out. Of course, she bounced around like hell. Her movement is similar to being on the top deck of a double-decker bus that is making 30 miles per hour and stopping dead every five yards. If you can imagine it.

After a refit at Taboga Island near Panama City (I can't afford boatyards and slipways), *Sea Dart* took off into the Pacific in September of 1973.

Seventy-five full sailing days later, *Sea Dart* and I arrived at Callao, having sailed 3,322 miles through the water. The distance direct is about 1,400 miles. Most of the time we were close-hauled and bashing away into the heaving Pacific coastal swells. I kept everything up all the way to keep moving; with her short waterline *Sea Dart* cannot make more than about two-and-a-half knots through the water when going to windward.

Navigation on the Pacific side of South America is a bit hazardous. Off the Colombian coast it is a continual rainy downpour with visibility down to a matter of yards, while farther south it is fog from the early hours of the morning until noon. There is also the ever-present risk of striking a whale, which would break *Sea Dart* up like matchwood in a matter of seconds.

Then on the Colombian coast there is the grave risk of piracy. Several yachts have been pirated in that area in the past few years. The only safe anchorages are Bahia Solano, where one has roaring jaguars in the jungle on either side; and Isla Gorgona, which is a prison island and where the guards keep you covered always with machine guns.

At Esmeraldas, in Ecuador, 40 days out of Panama with hardly any sleep, I met a young Dutchman, Ernst Kraft, who had been working in Peru and Bolivia for two years and knew the language and the customs. Ernst agreed to help me to the Lake. From then on, things got easier and I could sleep for a few hours during the day at least.

Sleep is the problem, for in the Humboldt we were literally between the devil and the deep blue sea. I had to stay near the coast in order to avoid the worst of the current, but then with low visibility much of the time it was a matter of forcing my eyes to stay open for days on end.

Towards the south, navigation is a matter of "by guess and by God," for the sky is overcast most of the time, which makes a sextant sight impossible. Just to keep things astir there's always an unknown rate and direction of current under the lee of one of the most inhospitable dry desert coasts of the world. I can tell you now, there's many a time I wished I was in a good pub somewhere knocking back a pint.

All this time there was nothing I could do in calms but wait, for my four-horsepower outboard motor had a broken crankshaft. Sometimes I would drop anchor on *40 fathoms* of line 15 miles out to sea and we couldn't see the shore. There we would fish profitably.

On December 23, after busting a gut to do it, *Sea Dart* hauled into Callao, where we celebrated Christmas and New Year, waded through a mountain of paperwork to pass through Peru, and met an adventurous truck driver who would haul *Sea Dart* 800 miles for 375 dollars.

"What size truck do you have, Salamon?"

"Oh, *muy grande*, very big."

"Can she lift three tons up two miles?"

"She very strong, and you *buena gente*, good people, we get there okay."

"Do you know the road?"

"No, but we can ask the *paisanos*, no?"

"Okay, Salamon, you're on."

Obviously, an adventurous spirit, it would be a shame to leave him behind. That's what I thought *then*. When the truck arrived, I had a few qualms, as most of the floorboards were broken, or missing. But Salamon kicked the tires, grinned and spat. "Good truck, hey? No?"

"Strong as a bull, *amigo*."

"*Bueno, vamanos?*"

"*Si, vamanos!*"

As *Sea Dart* was lowered onto the bed of the truck, both boat and truck seemed to groan. Salamon said *"Bueno matrimonio, no?"* Good marriage! It was more like lowering a coffin onto a hearse. But we took off, trailing two Christmas decoration electric wires behind us, through the streets of Lima and on south down the tarmacadam coastal road for 24 hours, crawling up steep mountain passes and twisting round narrow precipices with a 1,000-foot drop down into the angry-looking Pacific breakers on the shore far below.

We had shored up the boat inside the truck with sandbags but it was obvious, by the time we reached Arequipa, a beautiful city with spring-like weather, where the rough mountain ascent begins, that sandbags would not be enough. We needed to jam as many old tires as we could get in the spaces between the truck body and the boat. But where to find them?

As we entered the city center, a police motorcycle roared up and ordered our "circus" to the main plaza. The *Alcade*, or governor of the province, was waiting with a crowd of about 3,000 townsfolk.

"What do you need?" he asked me.

"Old tires."

"How many?"

"As many as we can fit in."

"Old tires!" he bawled at the policeman. And we had 20 in a minute!

At three the following morning we started off to cross the Andes with the first-ever ocean-going vessel even to attempt it. I stayed on board the whole time, for Salamon had his girlfriend in the cab and I didn't want to intrude on what seemed to be a very torrid love affair going on, with lots of tears and hands waving out the windows as we crawled upwards through the mountain passes and over very rickety-looking bridges that appeared to have been built by the Inca Atahualpa himself. I swear that one bridge we passed over, with a gorge of at least 1,000 feet below it, actually creaked and swayed as we bucketed over.

While Salamon sorted things out with his girlfriend in the cab, bouncing away like mad along the rough dirt road, doing 30 miles an hour on the downhill stretches and sometimes stopping with a jolt on the heart-wrenching bends of precipices, I sat in the cockpit and *worried*. The scenery was breathtakingly beautiful, the finest I had seen since the south coast of Turkey in autumn: snow on the high peaks, deep purple in the shadows, and gold where the sun struck the mountains. I felt like I was being reborn with one half of my soul and dying a thousand deaths with the other half as we narrowly shaved by another truck jam-packed with bundled Indians. This on a blind bend with a sheer cliff dropping down what seemed to be a mile on the near side.

We came across the first llamas at 8,000 feet and our first drunken Indian at 12,000 feet. He laughed like crazy at the sight of a boat up there. At 14,000 feet we were above the snow line and it was *cold* in the cockpit after almost seven years in hot tropical climes. So now, besides worrying, I turned blue in the wind. But there we were, with the Red Ensigns legally flying and by right, at an altitude of almost two-and-a-half miles above sea level.

As Salamon's girlfriend calmed down, so the truck motor groaned more and more and so the loss of oil increased. We crossed the Continental Divide in the late afternoon and coasted into Cabanillas about four in the afternoon, still bucking like a bronco. Here Salamon drove a piece of wood into where the oil sump plug should go, and in this fashion we reached the good road at last after 185 miles of what in the United States would be considered a poor farm track.

At 5:30 P.M. with the boat still bouncing about on the back of the groaning truck, I at last had my first sight of Lake Titicaca, after trying to reach it for three years almost to the day. It looks as I always imagined it would: beautiful, sort of smiling in the evening light. Welcoming.

A SEA TO MYSELF

Both this story and the previous one were sent from Sea Dart *by means of an Aymara Indian paddling a balsa canoe over Lake Titicaca. From the shores of the Lake they were transported by llama to the outskirts of La Paz, the capital of Bolivia, which is so high that it does not need a fire brigade—there is so little oxygen to support a fire . . . What I wrote about the beauty of the scenery around Lake Titicaca still applies. Along with the south coast of Turkey, Norway, and the northwest coast of Madagascar, it is without doubt one of the most eye-shattering places on God's earth. The air is so clear that you can see the peaks of mountains 300 miles away. Would I make that voyage again—yes!* SAIL *published this piece in 1974.*

Sunday, 17 February. The surface level of Lake Titicaca was rising still and was now almost up to the top of the mole in Puno. I had been moored at the far outer end of the mole, where the afternoon lake breeze sent small waves scuttling over the mole. This kept the crowds back and gave me some peace. I planned to sail to look at both sides of the Peninsula of Capachica.

No one in Puno could tell me very much about it. The local Indians, who come to Puno in their boats with produce, for the most part know only their own area. When I asked them about the eastern side of Capachica I might just as well have been talking about the moon. Huancane, which will be the farthest point on this cruise, is about 110 sailing miles from Puno. The locals talked of it as we talk about Tahiti.

For exploratory purposes this was the best time of the year to cruise in Lake Titicaca, for the level was rising at about one inch a day. This doesn't sound much compared to the ocean tides, but bear in mind that this was all rainfall over the vast inland area that drains into the Lake. The Lake itself is about 14,000 square miles in extent.

I purposely delayed sailing until late afternoon, for the off-Lake breeze is then the strongest, blowing straight into Puno from the canal that leads through the reed islands out into the open Lake. The local sailing craft are all off-the-wind gaffers. The sailors have no idea of going to windward at all. The nearest they can get is about 75 degrees off. The Indians, Quechuas, and Aymara, all in intricately patched rags and grinning faces, were intrigued indeed. They told me they could hardly believe their eyes when they saw *Sea Dart* sailing almost into the direct eye of the wind—or so it seemed to them.

I had been invited by some of the Indian sailing skippers to visit their villages and islands, so I was not exactly sailing off into a void. And I had already completed one 200-mile voyage to the remote northeast part of Titicaca. After almost six weeks on the Lake I seemed to have become a sort of legend among the Indians. They called me *Macchu Cuito . . . Old Barbed Wire.*

At five in the afternoon *Sea Dart* slipped her mooring and headed out under main and genoa. My idea was to anchor in the actual canal itself, in one of the off-channels between the islands, where the llamas graze. Poor llamas, they were only six inches above water level. Juan, a Quechua Indian of about 20 years, accompanied me.

We reached the canal at 6:30, after beating eight miles from Puno. The bottom there was soft clay. I found a spot well protected from the wind all round and dropped the light Danforth anchor. The llamas stared indignantly. Dozens of wild duck scuttled with their feet amongst the reeds.

We set to making supper: potatoes and fish stew. At 7:00 it started to rain; it usually does about sunset, but tonight we were lucky and only got light showers until 8:00. The ferry for Bolivia passed close to us on her way through the canal, but raised little wake. We were left alone among the reeds with the lights of Puno glowing away in the distance. At 9:00 the clouds unveiled the moon. A cup of chocolate and we turned in.

Monday, 18 February. I woke up early with anticipation as my sleep-breaker. Then I remembered—I needed color film. Rather than return to Puno, Juan said, the best thing was to call at Chucuito, about eight miles to the southwest, which is one place where the Puno-Bolivia road touches the Lake. There is a small, very expensive hotel there, and a mole.

So *Sea Dart* motored and sailed over in the fluky early morning winds, with the high mountains of the Sierra Occidental of the Andes gleaming bright snowy silver away to the west. I slid the keels, literally slid them, grating over the rocks on the entrance to the passage through the reeds at Chucuito. We lay alongside with an anchor out abeam to keep us off the mole.

I walked up the new steps recently constructed by the government, part of a trout breeding and fishing complex. This is one of the few places on the Peruvian part of the Lake where the 20th century impinges on the ancient ways of the Quechuas and Aymaras. Even here it is merely in the form of a small jetty, not much bigger in area than the average living room with steps leading up the bank to the highway, above, which is busy with traffic. At least one car an hour passes. And buses. And gaudily painted trucks full of country Indians on their way to market.

I went to the only shop: an earthen floor and the usual collection of empty cola bottles. Dirt.

"Any eggs?" I asked the bowler-hatted lady.

"?" She looked at me quizzically.

Juan rattled something off in Aymara. Then turned to me: "No eggs," he said in Spanish.

"Bread?" Another conference.

"No bread."

We walked to the hotel, through the wire gates, to the single-story structure. Juan was nervous. We were surrounded by what to him was unimaginable luxury. He had seen things like this only in the films. I saw the chefs through the kitchen window. They both smiled broadly and wished us good day.

"Have you films? Color films?"

"Yes, but the manager has gone to Puno with the keys to the souvenir cabinet and will not be back until tomorrow."

I had a quick look around the tastefully decorated hotel. It was neat and clean. The bar was furnished in the style of hotels the world over, except this was Peru and morning, so all was chaos.

"You wait for film, *Capitan?*" Juan was feeling his land legs again.

"No, let's sail to Capachica, Juan; it's only nine o'clock and soon the Lake breeze will put itself in march."

So *Sea Dart* slid out onto the calm Lake over the stones. A week earlier she wouldn't have been able to get alongside the mole.

As we hoisted the main the breeze sprang up. The genoa went up with it. We sailed through the *tortoras* or reeds, which, where we were heading, are the basis of one of the strangest economies in the world.

The sun shone. The Lake gleamed. To the north, rain hammered down on Julliaca from a black cloud. The Sierras shone white with snow far to the west. The air was clean, morning-young and so clear we could see all the way to the island of Taquile, almost 22 miles away.

A morning like this, a steady 15-knot breeze, the boat heeling over and dancing over the tiny wavelets...on a broad reach, *two miles* above sea level! The highest yacht in the world.

I sang to myself as we zoomed past Chucuito Peninsula, dotted with tiny adobe houses, roofed with reeds. We passed cows only yards away. Dogs barked at the *gringo* boat, so strange in these parts. Women, working in the fields, straightened themselves to stand, staring. Some of the men waved and called out to us. The Red Duster fluttered bravely.

The Lake water in Puno Bay at this time of year, in the height of the rainy season, is a khaki color. It reminded me of the Amazon, two years ago, and so far away. And yet the nearest headwaters of the Amazon system were only over there; I looked at the far Sierra Oriente, hazy grey in the east a hundred miles away.

Juan was fascinated with this speed, and later, when we rounded the point, with actually *going into the wind*. The breeze stiffened after noon, and soon we were lying over at a regular 25-degree heel. It took Juan time to get used to this, for on the Lake the sailing craft all have hardly any keel, and not much ballast. If they heel over, they keep on going.

There's a reason for their lack of keel. In many parts of the Lake, off the shore and in the creeks, grows the *llacho*. This is something like a bushy tree, 20 to 30 feet high, which grows under water in thick groves. It has the texture of rubber, very tough. The top-most foliage lies just below the surface of the Lake—just right for seizing the keel (in *Sea Dart*'s case three keels and a skeg) in an octopuslike grip. I have sailed into groves of this *llacho* several times. It brings the boat to a dead stop, no matter how strong the wind—a shock when we were bowling along under main, genoa, and staysail in a 30-knot wind. Some of the groves extend for miles. The boat just stopped. Within feet. Then it was let go all sheets, fast.

Getting out of the *llacho* groves was not easy. We pushed our way out with a long oar borrowed in Puno. Once out, it took a while to clear all the clinging foliage from the keels, rudder, and propeller. Now this all sounds fairly normal for sailing in uncharted, weed- and reed-strewn waters. But bear in mind we are two miles high. There is 40 percent less oxygen up here. By the time we hauled ourselves out of the *llachos* against a stiff breeze my rib cage felt as though it would burst with pain. The only thing to do was to open my mouth wide, wide and breathe as hard as ever I could.

I think that the nearest experience to sailing at full speed into unsuspected *llachos* must be planing a glider onto the top of an orchard.

One advantage it has, though. If I find *llachos* in a protected spot I can sail gently into it and stay there for the night, without dropping the anchor. The bushy stuff holds *Sea Dart* like a mailed fist in a velvet glove, all night long.

But this afternoon we were in deep, deep water. Titicaca is very deep, and in parts no bottom has been found at 6500 feet. We made four knots. Sometimes the wind increased furiously within seconds to speeds of 40 knots or more, measured on the anemometer. These gusts swept down in cold blasts, but we were warmly wrapped up and my tank-driver's hat was ideal. Better still would have been one of the old-fashioned airplane-pilot's helmets. When these gusts came, *Sea Dart* fought to get up and sit in the wind and it took all my strength on the tiller to keep her on the rails.

At 4:00 P.M. we were off the tiny harbor of Llachon. The whole harbor is only 30 feet square and full of *balsas*. These are the famous reed boats of Titicaca.

The Indians filtered down the mountainside to the jetty to welcome us. These are the most pleasant-natured folk I have come across in over 20 years sailing in over 70 different countries. One of the lads, in his strange woolen headgear, the only unpatched thing about him, took our bow line and we made a tight turn inside the tiny refuge to face the night wind and rain. And there we were, safe and snug. We put the big oar over the side, horizontally, outside the fenders, so it would take any knocks from the stony jetty.

I looked around. On the beach (one of the few sandy shores on the Lake) three men were constructing a *balsa*. The reeds are cut out in the Lake and the roots eaten. The reeds are gathered into tight bundles and pounded with a wooden mallet into the shape of a lashed hammock. These bundles are then lashed very tightly with a cord made from *pala*, a tough grass that grows on the spot, only yards from the beach. Into each *balsa* goes a surprising amount of reeds: something like half-a-ton weight. It takes three men one week to make one *balsa* complete.

While the hull is being made, another *maestro* or master is making the nets for catching *cachara*, the small freshwater fish which is a staple food here. The women make the reed shelter that protects the fisherman from the wind and rain, while others make mooring lines and anchor rode from *pacha*, another tough grass. In every case the lines are three-stranded plait.

Each *balsa* has a life of about six months. Then it gradually gets waterlogged. The cords used are saved, but the rest is discarded and a new *balsa* is made. The old reed craft is left to rot as fertilizer.

Propulsion is by a single oar, which is set in a wooden rowlock. A good oarsman can reach surprising speeds, and I have seen them making three knots, in bursts, sitting under the shelter and weaving away. The *balsas* are very stable, as about two-thirds of the hull is under water.

In some remote parts of the Lake *balsas* are also propelled by sail, square sail, also made of reeds. Off the wind, of course, all the way.

Monday, 25, February 1974. *Sea Dart* returned to Puno on a dead run. Force 3 or 4 and a beautiful, clear sunny day. As we passed by the farmsteads on Chucuito Peninsula, we heard the weird-sounding Indian music of flutes and drums. They were celebrating carnival. All the fields were deserted, for this is their one great holiday—their annual break from the eternal toil in all weathers.

As we neared the Puno channel entrance, through the reed islands, several ferry boats turned towards us to get a closer look at the *mad gringo*. They were packed with Indians. By their different styles of dress we could see where they hail from: Capachica, Chucuito, Amantani, Acora,

Siscati, Llave. They all cheered and waved, laughing and shouting.

The mole at Puno was an inch under water, but we managed to tie up securely. I suspended the oar, weighted down with stones, horizontally on a level with the top of the jetty. Between it and the hull I hung two fenders, also weighted down.

On the way to the Lago Restaurant for a blow-out of steak, egg, and chips, quite a few people stopped me and asked how the voyage was. It made me feel a bit like a returned astronaut. But then, a lot of Titicaca is about as remote as the moon, only a million times more beautiful. And you can sail on it!

THE GREEN HELL

The following excerpt from The Incredible Voyage *begins after I was summarily dumped onto the desert by the Bolivian railways, sixteen miles from the River Paraguay, my only route to the sea. The river was rapidly dropping. My companion, Huanapaco, was a Quechua Indian who had sailed with me on Lake Titicaca. All my previous sea-going career, and the hard lessons I'd learned since 1938, had readied me for the tremendous effort I would need to make. Once I was through, I was a changed man. I believed there had to be a reason for my doing what I did. Later years showed me what it was. I have received many letters from people who thought they were at the end of their tether until they read of my Calvary in the backwoods of Brazil and Paraguay in 1974.*

On September eleventh we commenced hauling the boat to the River Paraguay, which we ultimately reached on the second of October. For over sixteen miles we sweated, heaved, hauled, pushed, and shoved until it seemed that we had never done anything else but this. For twenty-one days the two of us hacked and slashed at the thorny creepers that barred our passage along the railroad cuttings and embankments. How many men, I wondered, had died here to drive this forlorn hope from Bolivia to a waterway which finally might, or might not, lead to the sea? Before we were allowed to leave, the *aduanero*, in cahoots with the station-master, charged us twenty dollars in exchange for a worthless permit to pass over the border. The way we were going there was no border, and he knew it! The bloody bastard sent us into the Green Hell of the world with only fifteen dollars and enough food to last a month! For my twenty dollars I got no receipt, no acknowledgment, just a wave of a fat, sweaty hand to send us on our way. It is quite possible that a desire to tell the world of the *aduanero's* action was one of the main motivations for carrying on during the next few weeks.

Once out from the station, heaving the keels over the greasy sleepers (railroad ties), we came to the scrub. First we would hack a clear way about eight feet wide for a hundred yards or so, then run a long mooring line, my old storm-running line, to a thick scrub bush ahead, then haul in with the handy-billy rig. At the same time the brush and grass had to be beaten continually to guard against snakes. We saw many cascabels, deadly giant rattlers, and frailesca, poisonous little vipers which live in the long grass. We wrapped our legs and feet, over shoes and trousers, with torn strips of blanket to guard against possible bites. The agony of being wrapped up in thick blanket material in that temperature can hardly be imagined, but we dared not to take it off until we were safely inside the stifling cabin with all the exits, hatch, and ventilators tightly closed against entry by serpents or vampire bats, which were numerous.

We hacked away, Huanapaco and I, with cutlass and ax, from dawn until about two in the afternoon in the thicker growth. Then we hauled forward, always watching for snakes. Compared to them, the insects, *biting through several layers of cloth,* were a mere nuisance.

Sometimes we would come to a comparatively clear patch, and we would think we were doing extraordinarily well. I dared not empty the water tanks to lighten the load until we were nearer to the river, for I didn't know if there was an alternative supply. On the uphill stretch, of which, thank God, there was only one, about two miles long, we went at a snail's pace. It was all we could do, even with a four-purchase block, to heave her up inch by inch, slight though the old railroad gradient was. But eventually, after rounding a curve on this uphill Calvary, we came within sight of the river. There it was, in the distance, about five miles away as the crow flies, gleaming silver in the misty green of the Mato Grosso! It seemed to be so wide as to stretch beyond the horizon, but I realized that, in fact, we were looking at a number of small streams running parallel. We redoubled our efforts as well as our watch against snakes. As we neared the river, I was concerned about jaguars and anacondas for they, too, like a drink of water; but we saw none, though we did hear, three or four times, a distant roar and many screams of terror.

Going downhill was as hard as, if not harder than, going up; we had to rig not only the forward hauling gear, but another block astern in order to check her when she started to slide.

The heat was suffocating from about ten in the morning until around four in the afternoon. We once tried working after dusk, but without any lamps it was hazardous work. So we suffered the heat in preference to stumbling onto an anaconda or falling prey to a hungry jaguar looking for a tasty morsel. Besides, Huanapaco didn't like to work after dark. The mountain Indian is very superstitious and hates the dark: unless he's asleep his mind is full of evil demons.

By the thirtieth of September we were within easy walking distance of the river. The brush had thinned out somewhat. *Sea Dart* was in more or less clear country, with only a few bushes scattered around on each side of the old railroad embankment. Leaving Huanapaco to dig in the anchor and rig up blocks, I made my way to the river to spy out the land, or rather, the water. It took me about four hours to get to the bank, for we had both been on a meager diet for days, each eating only a handful of rice and half of a seven-ounce can of corned beef per day. Huanapaco found some white grubs under a rotting tree and mixed these, fried, with his corned beef. He pronounced them delicious. For a day I was wary of eating them, but when he didn't die or fall writhing to the ground, my hunger overcame my squeamishness, and after that we had grubs daily. They were about an inch or so long and half-an-inch round. They tasted, when fried, something like scampi (at least they did to me then). At any rate, they added tremendously to our protein intake.

What I found at the river almost broke my heart. For the first time in many years I was tempted to sit down and cry. The jetty was completely rotted through, eaten away by ants! Balanced on the end of it was an old British steam crane, built at Gateshead on Tyne, with the date "1878" on the door. It was a solid block of red rust! Inside the boiler generations of birds had built nests. In the eerie silence of the jungle afternoon, I carefully made my way back, trying to avoid the rotten planks that might give way and drop me forty feet into the swirling brown waters below.

If I could have sat down, I would have. Whether I would have cried or not is a moot point, for the hordes of ants crawling around, billions of them, discouraged any sitting and probably made the act of crying superfluous anyway. As I made my way back to the boat, I worked out a plan to get her down the steep riverbank. When I arrived, Huana-paco lifted his sweaty head, his almond eyes dull and listless with exhaustion.

"*Buenas, Capitán,*" he puffed. Nothing if not polite, the Quechua.

"*Buenas, amigo,* good news; I'm pretty sure there's enough water for *Sea Dart* to be able to navigate, at least in the stretch we're aiming for."

His face lit up, his white teeth flashed.

"Now the bad news, *amigo;* the jetty is useless, so is the crane; we have to get there fast, and then we have to carve a track down the bank to launch the boat."

"How far is that, *mi Capitán?*"

"Forty feet." I didn't have the heart to tell him yet that we couldn't go straight down the bank, that we would have to slash, beat, and dig our way at an angle down the bank for *2600 feet!*

It took us another three days to reach the riverbank. On the morning of the second of October, *Sea Dart* was separated from the Atlantic only by 2,000 miles of wild river and a forty-foot drop. Down below, the swirling waters flowed rapidly on their way to the Plate estuary, that great brown scar through which flow the waters of half a continent.

I considered dropping the boat down the bank directly, on her side, controlling her by blocks and tackles, but the risk of straining the hull was too great. I considered erecting a sheer-legs, a sort of crane made from straight tree trunks, and trying to lever her out over the waters and lower her in, but this would take several days to construct, and I wasn't absolutely sure that the rope blocks, severely strained by now after all the heaving they had done, could do the job. There was only one course—dig at an angle down the riverbank!

We slashed, cut, burned, dug, beat, and lowered for eight days, sometimes with the boat leaning at so acute an angle over the river I felt sure she would capsize. I safeguarded against this by taking a complete turn with a heavy rope around her hull and digging in the anchor to secure it.

For eight days we worked like maniacs, watching the river level drop. We had no time to spare; I had learned, back in Santa Cruz, that 700 miles downstream, on the southern edge of the Mato Grosso, the river rushed over a shallow rock ledge—the Paso de Moros! If we could not get past·the Paso de Moros, we would be trapped in the Mato Grosso. There we would have three choices—die of disease, die of hunger, or be eaten alive by the insects.

Little by little we forced her down the bank, transforming it as we went from a mass of scrub into a scarred slipway. We threw the soil as hard as we could into the bushes to save beating them with a stick to scare away serpents and other dangers.

At the bottom of the slope, keeping a wary eye out for alligators, we eased her in. I went out in the dinghy and dropped both anchors. Over the wet sleepers she slid inch by inch, and finally she floated. The swirling current grabbed her and sent her downstream, but the anchors held. And would you believe it? She didn't leak one single drop of water!

"*Maravilla!*" said Huanapaco.

"Bloody marvelous!" said I.

Since *Sea Dart* had arrived on the banks of the River Paraguay, or rather on the bank of one of the numerous streams that comprise the so-called river—a maze of winding, twisting, muddy canals, stinking like a midden with the smell of rotting jungle—we had not gone short of protein. Now we had *fish!* True, it was mainly piranha fish, but it was meat, for all that. From my Amazon days I knew just how to catch them; each morning Huanapaco and I performed the drop-of-blood-and-bucket trick. The piranhas on the River Paraguay are smaller, skinnier, and bonier than their Amazon cousins, but to our hungry eyes they looked like succulent salmon. They were a lot fiercer, too, and jumped ten feet in the air for five minutes before they grew still enough for us to poleax them.

As we hauled up the mast and rigged the sails, I realized that the variety of life here was even more prolific than in Amazonia. In the high trees at day time hung huge bats, called *andiras* by the Guaicuru Indians. Some of these bats were up to eighteen inches across with their clawed wings extended: evil-looking monsters, vampire bloodsuckers. At night we heard the clicking of their little feet and the sound of their wings trailing on the deck above the stuffy little cabin as they tried to find a way through the hatchboards and windows. Through the tiny windows in *Sea Dart*'s doghouse, by the light of the tiny oil lamp, we saw their beady eyes and watched them scratch at the Perspex window screens.

There were birds, too, by the thousands: the hornero-bird, which builds a hanging nest, something like a wasp's nest, that dangles from the branches; and the uratau, which sings the most plaintive song I have ever heard from a bird, a sort of low, infant whisper of complaint. Cutting through the brush ashore, we had noticed the strange habits of the macagua, an inveterate snake fighter. The macagua attacks ferociously any snake it sees, rushing at it with one wing covering its head and its long beak poking through like a bayonet. If the snake bites it, the macagua rushes over to the bushes and pecks away at berries also called macagua, which are a snakebite antidote!

The trees along the banks were generally not as tall as those on the Amazon, but the tall ones, few though they were, grew much higher than anything I had seen on the northern river. The lapacho is immense, anything up to 250 feet high, and 50 or 60 feet around the base. There were wild pineapples in the undergrowth, and great bunches of passion flowers, the plant whose beautiful blooms reminded the old conquistadors, when they first saw them, of the crucifixion. They have a blood red flower with a golden stamen in the form of a cross. Along the banks of the streams grew the izpa tree, something like a weeping willow, which gives off a misty, pine-smelling vapor.

The rest of the flora was unknown to me, mostly dead or half-dead trees strangled by creepers. The branches of the trees would often overhang the narrow streams, and we would have to either shin up the mast and cut a way through or lower the mast to pass them. The distance to Paso de Moros and the main stream was only some 200 miles from Ladário, our miserable embarkation point, but by the winding course of the stream it came to nearly 600 miles! Often we would follow a stream around an immense bend, maybe for an entire day, and after we had completed the circle, would find ourselves looking over a narrow peninsula, a few yards wide, at the spot we had passed early in the morning!

The heat was intense, suffocating; and yet the sunshine was not strong, for the vegetation gave off a continual mist, day and night, forming rainclouds overhead that blew away to the west to break over the Andes. But hidden away in the narrow channels between thick clumps of high trees or grass fourteen feet high, crawling with snakes, we hardly felt the breeze. In the upper reaches, where we started sailing, or rather drifting, downstream, caimans were numerous, and we would often see hundreds of them sliding through the water. When they lashed into a shoal of fish, the water would boil and then ugly snouts would open and their loathsome eyes rise about the surface. Some were about twelve feet long from the tip of the tail to the snout.

Many a time (and this we dreaded more than anything), the stream would divide into two or three channels. If we chose the wrong one, we might not realize it until we had drifted some miles and found ourselves at a dead end, with solid brushwood and thick branches denying further passage. Then we had to jump over the side, into water about 4½ feet deep, sometimes deeper, sometimes too deep to stand up in, and take turns, one of us beating the water to scare off lurking piranhas, water snakes, and caimans, while the other pushed and dragged the boat back upstream. Periodically, we would climb onboard and run a kerosene-soaked, lighted rope over our bodies to burn off the great, black, shiny leeches, some of them five inches long. I do not know how much blood we lost in this manner, as well as to the piúm flies, mosquitoes, and bichus, but it must have been plenty, for by the time we emerged at Paso de Moros we were both as weak as children. I weighed 80 pounds against my normal 120, while Huanapaco weighed 100 against his normal 180!

As the awful days went on, we got yellower and yellower. We had now found, by testing, which leaves we could chew safely, hoping for vitamin C, but I don't think they did us any good. At the end of a day, swept up against a bank of tall swamp grass, we were too exhausted to do anything but shut all the inlets to the cabin, fall back on our berths, and sweat all night. By the end of the second week, the fresh water in *Sea Dart*'s tanks was running very low, and we had to resort to river water, much muddier than in the Amazon, strained, as before, through fine cotton wool. We must have ingested a whole laboratory of biological specimens that would have been of great interest to the London School of Tropical Medicine.

The whole period of the passage up to Paso de Moros merges together in my memory; each day for three weeks we fought tooth and nail for our lives. Each second of every minute we struggled forward—if we stopped, we were dead men. There was no doubt in our minds about that. We could not go upstream against the four-knot current, we could only drift down with it, barely maintaining steerageway with the sails; there was no fuel for the engine. Even if we'd had fuel it would not have done us any good, for the little four-horsepower outboard could never have bucked the swift current when we were forced back upstream. Moreover, we would have used up a ton in a week, and where could we put a ton of highly explosive gasoline in a twenty-foot boat with an inside temperature of *130 degrees?*

Again, writing about this more than a year-and-a-half later in the safety and comfort of Manhattan, it is difficult to sort out the days. My log is very terse on the period; there was no time, no energy to write anything but the estimated distance "sailed" on any particular day. All my thoughts, all my will, all my deteriorating energy went into moving the boat downstream. I explained to Huanapaco that we had to keep going as hard as we could, and that if we did not we would certainly die. Fortunately, as well as being very strong to start with, as well as having grown up in one of the toughest environments on earth, the pitiless Altiplano, Huanapaco was also a stoic. He would keep going until he dropped. In addition to a sense of humor, he had the patience of Job—*he had never known anything else but the eternal struggle against nature.* He'd been at it all his life. If I'd had with me a young man of Huanapaco's age from a so-called advanced society, I am sure he would have given up long before we finally broke through.

Time and again, day in, day out—wet, sweaty, stinking, miserable, hungry, hot beyond explanation—I wished I was back in the arctic ice, even in a force-ten storm, even on a lee shore. The sea could never be as cruel as this rotting, evil, malignant inferno, with its millions of insects descending on us at every hour. I even, God help me, wished I was back in the Amazon, pulling from tree to tree! Compared with this, the Amazon was like a weekend on Coney Island!

Anacondas dangled from trees to the river's surface. Their evil heads dove under the water and swallowed fish without even chewing them. We saw one big brute whose belly wriggled with live fish still kicking as they were being digested! Another time we saw a dying anaconda. It had eaten a mass of flesh, probably a capybara, a big rodent similar to a water rat that swims in the streams. The snake had lain on the bank in the sun to digest the animal and had stayed there so long that maggots were still eating the belly with the half-digested rotting flesh of the capybara still inside. The anaconda was feebly thrashing.

Inside the Mato Grosso for three weeks we saw no sign of any human life. It was only nature gone wild—a mad biological riot. We could have been on some faraway planet in another universe, or on earth five billion years ago. Awful in the true sense of the word, and very, very frightening. It was as if every malignant spirit on earth was pitting its evil intelligence against us. The plant life was so thick we could not see more than six inches away from the river's edge! Even now, almost two years later, I can hardly bear to go near a green plant in someone's apartment. I cannot even look into a florist's window and see an array of household plants without a shudder passing through me. I can hardly bear to look at grass or a tree, unless it is surrounded by all the impediments of urban civilization. A zoo, if I could find the courage to visit one, would shock me rigid.

Day after day we hacked our way along the river. Times out of number we dropped the mast to pass under some impossibly thick overhanging branch. Twice a day we would gulp down raw piranha fish and tree leaves, along with maggoty flour from the emergency stock. Once a week we would drool over the special Sunday treat of cold corned beef, of which we had four cans when we left Ladário. We could not cook, for we have to save the kerosene for the ropes and for painting the anchor or mooring lines to keep the snakes off and to stop the ants from marching onboard to eat the marine-ply hull from under our feet. The kerosene was vaporizing with the heat, too. When we finally arrived at Forte Coimbra we were down to the last dregs. We used to lay the piranha fish out on a metal tray and try to heat them up in the pale sun. The idea was to dry them out, but we both got severe cases of tapeworm anyway. The one taken out of me in Buenos Aires was four feet long and waxing roundly.

By the time we joined the main stream of the Paraguay, we were near the state of wild animals. The veneer imposed on us by our respective upbringings was practically gone. I would grab a piranha and start chewing it, head, eyes, tail, everything. We would scoop up maggoty flour and swallow it in handfuls. Huanapaco eyed everything that moved, including me. If it moved, it was food! We did, in fact, make an agreement that if one of us died, the other would eat as much of him as he could stomach. At that moment even the thigh muscle of a dead Quechua would have been acceptable fare. Starvation knows no morals!

One of the main difficulties in the Mato Grosso lay in finding out where we were. By the compass and the sun I could tell that we were drifting in a more or less southerly direction; but there were several occasions when *Sea Dart* headed north and kept going in that direction with the flow of the stream. In our hunger and desperation this was terribly discouraging. I couldn't trust the compass too much, in case there were iron deposits under the river or some other magnetic aberration. Instead, I watched the sun, pale above the ever-rising swamp-steam, as it swung over us high in the heavens.

As we hacked and slashed at yet another obstacle, I remembered that the same sun, as it rose to noon over us, could be seen back home in Wales. There, in another life, another world, people were getting to go home after a day's work, life was easy and comfortable, the threat of death by nature was hardly ever thought of. Mankind had, many millions of years ago, hacked and slashed, struggled and fought, dreamed and wept its way out of the primeval swamp, just as we were doing. They started from nothing; they had no previous experience to guide them, nothing to go back to.

"Why?" I asked myself as I attacked another tangle of creepers hanging over the river. "Why bother? Why pit ourselves against the torments that cruel nature piles up against us? Why not just lie down and accept the inevitable?" For days I racked my being with this question, in real hunger now, for the piranha had completely disappeared at the end of the second week. Our worm-ridden flour, too, was gone. We had eaten the last of the rice, soaked in muddy river water to soften it. Every edible thing onboard was gone, even the olive oil, the sailmaker's wax, the linseed oil, the candles! In desperation, we soaked the skull of a llama, which I had hung in the cabin as a souvenir, and drank the "stock."

Why did we carry on against such impossible odds?

The answer, when it came at last, was simple. By *not* struggling we would simply be going against nature! We were *made* to fight against nature by the very thing we were fighting, *nature itself!* Here was Man's destiny. To strive, to seek, to find; and *not* to yield! Not to give way to sentimental claptrap, insidious temptations, not to retreat into ourselves, hoping to find a reason. *Nature knows no reason!* Not to be content to sit in a mental or spiritual cave, while all around us nature, the very reflection of ourselves, runs riot! We are *here*. This is our situation. If we don't like it, then Jesus Christ almighty, let's claw and struggle and *bite* our way out of it, because it will not change itself! That is the game, and we must play or go under!

I looked at Huanapaco as he patiently, steadily hacked away, determined to survive. He was in a bad way, haggard, his Indian eyes dull, seeing nothing but the blockage ahead. Only when he raised the cutlass or the ax to *attack* did his eyes come alive! As we drifted down a comparatively clear stretch, I dismantled the galley, searching for something edible. Behind the stove I found a treasure—a handful of beans resting on one of the stringers. Hard, black, sprouting. I staggered along the deck to where Huanapaco was resting, exhausted, awaiting the next onslaught of creepers. The boat was bows to the current, drifting stern first. Clapping him weakly on the shoulder, I passed him the beans. *"Vamos a comer, hombre!* Let's eat, man!"

He looked up, the sweat pouring off him, his *unku* shirt a tattered rag, stripped down to his *kuana,* the long scarf which the Quechua wrap around their loins. He grinned wanly, then extended his fist in the thumbs-up sign!

Five minutes later we saw the caiman. He was floating in midstream, about a hundred yards ahead of us; floating, not swimming. He must have left the banks because of the lack of fish. In this open stretch there was enough breeze to steer the boat. Dropping into the cockpit, I grabbed the sheets and tiller and brought *Sea Dart* around until the breeze filled the mainsail. Huanapaco grabbed the ax. The hammer, a fourteen-pound sledge, he laid beside him along with the cutlass. I bore straight down on the caiman, still lying there, drifting with the current. As we drew closer we could see he was about nine feet long. Then *Sea Dart* hit him full on, with her bows, broadside. He spun around, lashing with his tail and wicked jaws. The shock to the boat was enough to jerk the knife drawer out of the galley cupboard! From the bow, Huanapaco smashed the ax right into the middle of the caiman's belly, so hard the ax stuck! The caiman twisted over onto his belly, blood and guts trailing away from his underside. Moving fast, for one in such puny condition, Huanapaco fumbled for a moment, got his brown hands on the sledge, and, taking careful aim, crashed it down on the caiman's skull. In the cockpit, steering the tiller carefully, peering over the side to keep the animal hard against the bow, I heard the crunch as the alligator's skull was smashed to a pulp in one blow. After one last, mighty lash of his whole body, he went completely dead in the water.

I threw the grappling hook to Huanapaco, who, with some difficulty, finally stuck it into the caiman's belly. We dropped the anchor right away. With a jerk the boat came up all standing and swung quickly around to face the current and the wind.

We pulled the caiman up alongside, turned him over, and hacked the ax out with a knife. Inside the belly we found four small fish only half-digested; these we made short work of. The caiman's blood was cold and tasted fishy. Our knives could not penetrate his armor scales, so we slashed away from the inside of his belly, delving down towards the tail, and extracted a good four or five pounds of very stringy meat, which we first soaked in water, then hung up to dry in the sun. We were now in a fairly open spot, and we carefully scanned the banks for a tiny clear space in which we might start a fire to cook the meat. After several hours of drifting, we found one—on top of a huge tree trunk which had fallen into the stream. It was crawling with ants, but we didn't care. Keeping an eye out for snakes, we built a fire and feasted on alligator meat. It was like eating tarred rope and with sore gums was very hard going; but it was one of the best meals I have ever had in my life, and it gave us enough protein to crash, smash, and bash our way for another few days.

At the end of the third week, we were nearing the end of the hellish maze, although we did not know it. Little by little, the banks cleared of overhanging trees and creepers. Little by little the streams got wider, the current slower. On the last night in the jungle, before we emerged into the swamplands, we had one of the most frightening experiences I have ever known. With the river fairly clear, we anchored midstream, away from the vegetation, for the night. In order to sleep we covered the hatch, not with the boards, which we left lying in the cockpit, but with the old British army mosquito net I had brought along from the West Indies. The idea was to try to get more air into the sweltering cabin. In the early hours of the morning, as a full moon swung pale and wan above the jungle mist, I woke to a loud noise. It was as if a large outboard motor or a motorcycle was running in the cockpit! I jumped up, shaking Huanapaco. Shuffling back to the companionway, I was aghast to see that the mosquito net was being eaten! It was actually collapsing into the boat under the weight of hundreds of moths, each about ten inches wide. As I watched, horrified, paralyzed at first, I could see their mouths chewing away at the *plastic* net! Coming to my senses, I grabbed the frying pan out of the galley rack and started to bang them away. Huanapaco, stupefied with sleep and terror, grabbed the cricket bat. We beat and beat the net for four hours, until the light of dawn brought the strange onslaught to an end. In the morning, with only a few of these monstrous insects left, we saw, to our astonishment, that the whole topsides of the boat was carpeted with their corpses to a depth of four inches!

On the twenty-second of October we sighted smoke away in the distance. There was no chance of its being a forest fire, for the jungle is much too humid and dank to burn. Smoke meant fire; fire meant humans. Now, the question was, what kind of humans? I knew that the southern Mato Grosso was the home of the Guaicurus, aboriginal primitives, very savage, very aggressive, and very, very dangerous—probably the most dangerous savages in the whole of the Americas. Warriors to a man. Well, we could understand that, all right, so long as we were not the intended victims! Even so, at the sight of smoke our spirits rose. We were near humans! Even though they might be the most dangerous animals of all! They ate together, they slept in groups, they talked, they sang, they made music, even if only by banging two human jawbones together, they had the spark of an idea about superior spirits, they loved in their fashion, and they *dreamed!* They were our kind, our kindred!

Keeping the Very flare-pistol and the harpoon gun handy in the cockpit, we pushed on downstream. Apart from the ax, cutlass, sledgehammer, and our knives, they were our only weapons, and we were determined to use them should the need arise. We had discussed this thoroughly. There was no doubt, no hesitation on our part. The first savage to come within yards of *Sea Dart* would get a harpoon straight through his chest. If that did not stop him, he would find a distress flare, a great blob of flaming phosphorescence, right in his face, a sledgehammer crashing down on his skull, and a cutlass slitting him up the gizzard! We had fought too hard for our own lives not to respect other men's right to life, no matter how savage they were. On the other hand, we were determined to survive. We had fought tooth and nail for our lives and we were damned if somebody was going to deprive us of our *earned* right to live!

Rounding a bend in the 200-yard-wide stream, we saw the first human we had sighted since leaving Puerto Suárez, five weeks before. At least almost human! He was standing in a dugout canoe about twelve feet long. He was poised over the river, looking like the statue of Eros in Piccadilly Circus, with an arrow in his bow pointing down at the water. The surprise on both sides was complete. We had passed him and shot out of sight round the next bend before Huanapaco could get the harpoon gun in his hand or I the Very pistol. The savage, too, went bone rigid. He stood there, in a state of utter astonishment. His head was smothered in what looked like red clay. He seemed hair-less, even around his loins, for he was stark naked, although around his thighs he wore a bracelet of yellow feathers.

The red clay, I found out later, was actually blood, animal or human, mixed with earth and dung. The grown men smear it over themselves. The Guaicuru *pluck* all their hair out, even their eyelashes. Before the age of fourteen, they paint themselves completely with blue dye. From fourteen to sixteen, or until they kill their first human, they paint themselves red, after which they smear blood and earth over their heads. When not engaged in killing something or someone, they spend their time plucking each other's hair out.

They have always been feared, they have always been a terror to a vast area stretching from the eastern side of the Mato Grosso for a thousand miles and more over to the western edge of the great Chaco Desert. I was told later that long before the Spanish penetration into the Chaco, these savages had crossed the burning, waterless Chaco for a thousand miles to attack Tahuantinsuyu, the mighty Inca empire itself, and in the Bolivian province of Chuquisaca had inflicted a severe defeat on the (until then) invincible armies of that far-flung civilization. Now here they were, in 1974, in the same state of utter savagery, still unconquered, fighting tooth and nail for every inch of their fetid swamp, for their right to bash others over the head.

After seeing the Guaicuru brave, we kept an even sharp-er lookout until finally we emerged into the main stream of the Paraguay River, a half-mile wide and deep. But we still had to negotiate the rapids at Paso de Moros. With bleeding gums and loose teeth, we pressed on until, on the twenty-fifth of October, we saw white water through the rising heat-mist ahead.

It stretched clear across the river. As we drifted closer we could see the river humping over the great rock shelf, then breaking into foam as it rushed over, boiling, spuming, spitting in a mighty cataract, the water of half a continent squeezing inexorably over one of the ribs of the spine of South America! We headed straight for the seething cauldron.

I scanned the white wall of foaming water ahead. Three hundred yards upstream from the rapids I sighted, to one side, off the bank, a passage of less disturbed water. Shoving the tiller over, I headed for it, hoping we had enough speed over the current to reach the gap in time. Out of one corner of my eye, I saw a great lone hump covered with greenery, like a mountain in an old Chinese painting, the mist from the cataracts hovering around its base. This was the Pão de Azucar, the Sugar Loaf, and it looked like one too. All alone, with only a small cluster of foothills to keep it company, it sticks out of the Brazilian Mato Grosso like a sore thumb. This is the only landmark, the only high ground in millions of square miles of flat, dreary swamp and low scrub. It marks the utmost point, or very nearly, of Portuguese penetration into the southwest hinterland of Brazil.

We rushed into the rapids and suddenly were in the gap. It all happened in less than a minute, yet it seemed to take a year. One minute we were in calm yet swift-running water; the next, in the middle of a roaring cloud of foam so thick we couldn't see anything. The eddies, brutal and determined, gripped the rudder as if trying to turn the boat sideways to the fifteen-knot current. Wet through with spray and sweat, Huanapaco and I strained against the tiller to keep little *Sea Dart* on her course. I prayed the rudder would not break loose from the pintles, the hinges that hold it to the rudder post. If it did we were dead men, for in that fierce, savage maelstrom there would be no chance for either of us, both nonswimmers. Besides, in the state we were in, at three-quarters of our normal weight, and with nothing left to go on but will power, we would have gone straight down. If she turned broadside on to that wall of rushing spume, thousands of tons of water would lift her up as if she were a paper boat in a rain gutter and throw her in the air, right over.

In the 200 yards or so of rapids we *hit the bottom* with the three keels at least twenty times. We didn't float, we were *pushed* over the flat stone bottom, sliding on the keels with a terrible jarring shudder. Each time she banged the bottom the shock passed right through my feet, up my legs and spine, to my already loose teeth.

The last three bumps were the worst—Slam! Bang! Crash! The whole boat shivered and shuddered, the hull, the mast, the keels, the deck—if anyone had told me that a boat of her size and construction could withstand this encounter, I would not have believed it. But *Sea Dart* did! As we roared over the rapids, I didn't think of anything at all. All I remember is *willing* her over with every fiber of my mind, heart, soul, spirit, and body. I do not recall having any thought of death or drowning or being battered to pieces on the rocks; all I thought about was beating this last bastard of a barrier.

Then, we were through! As if by magic. One second we were in a wet hell of mad, murderous movement, the next we were in calm, deepening waters, moving sedately down to the southern edge of the Green Hell of the Mato Grosso.

With only a few minutes to go before nightfall, we rounded a narrow, swift-running bend and sighted the Brazilian army fort of Coimbra, old and white, looking just as it had when the hardy Portuguese *bandeiras* built it 200 years ago!

The Brazilian soldiers thought they were seeing a mirage. They could not believe their senses as a filthy, bedraggled, blistered sailing yacht, wearing the British Union Jack from the masthead, sailed into their riverfront as smartly as two ragged, yellow, haggard half-skeletons could manage her.

Quickly, a boat loaded with soldiers and officers came out to us. We were helped ashore, where we were bathed and disinfected, fed a little, and put to bed under sedatives.

When we woke up next day, the Brazilians had debugged the boat with a gas exterminator and their soldiers were, even as we talked with the *commandante*, scrubbing her inside and out.

"Where in the name of God have you come from?" asked the *commandante*.

"Bolivia, from the north. We hauled to the river from Ladário."

"Good God Almighty!" He spoke Portuguese slowly enough for me to understand. "The way you came—our army has been trying to penetrate that area for forty years! We've only gotten into the outer fringe of it! The Guaicurus, we've been fighting them off and on ever since Brazil was first brought out here! But *Senhor* Tristan, when you feel better, you must tell us your story. Feel free to go anywhere you wish in the fort. Stay in bed if you care to. You both have open house, and you will dine with myself and my officers as soon as you feel well enough to do so."

The few days we spent at Forte Coimbra seemed like a dream. Even though we were still surrounded by the Mato Grosso, we had reached safety! Even though we had almost 1,500 miles to go downstream to the sea, it looked like child's play compared to what we had been through.

At Coimbra we were cosseted in the sickbay for three days; then, as soon as we could hold down solid food, we messed with the army officers. Out of his own scant supplies, the medical officer gave me mosquito repellent. The little outboard motor was taken ashore and tested. Five gallons of gasoline were put onboard, along with a gunnysack full of jerked beef.

After another two days I was itching to continue south. Even though we were still shitting green liquid, we pushed off, because the river was still dropping and soon there might not be enough depth for *Sea Dart* to navigate. In a small gesture of gratitude for the Brazilians' hospitality before we left, I managed to shin up the eighty-foot flagpole in front of the gates and repair a broken sheave.

Fifty miles downstream from Forte Coimbra, a hot, sticky finger of Bolivia pokes through a Godforsaken stretch of putrid swamp and humming jungle for a hundred miles, to touch the River Paraguay at Puerto General Busch. Trust the Bolivians to name their only viable outlet to waters leading to the sea—a tiny, insect-ridden, primitive, ramshackle camp of rotting wood grouped around a raft—after a president who blew his brains out after an all-night orgy in the palace of La Paz! Here we stayed one night, tied up alongside the raft. There were only two Bolivian soldiers. They were dressed exactly the same as the sailors who had arrested me on Lake Titicaca in the freezing cold of the Altiplano—rough, dirty, blue uniforms, trousers tied up with string, shaven heads, filthy bare feet—and they had the same charm, the same courtesy to the traveler, the same curiosity, the same *simpatía*. This place was Bolivia's last outpost, and it looked it! From here we finally took our last farewell of the one country that in all my travels stands out most clearly in my mind. I wore the Bolivian maritime ensign, the only one, all the way to the ocean.

A few miles downstream, on the swampy riverbank, a lone monument pokes up into the sky. This is the point where three countries meet—Bolivia, Brazil, and Paraguay. Nothing else marks the frontier. No customs post, no tanktraps or barbed wire; only the jungle and the cement post. It is probably the only place on earth where you can sail between three countries without challenge, without paper inspections or tax impositions, or any of the rest of the legalized extortion that has crept into international travel. In my grandfather's day you could sail around the world, showing nothing more than a five-pound note or a gold sovereign! But of course that was in the days before the "little Hitlers of the filing cabinets," with their proliferating piles of paper and the Himmlers, with their beady eyes behind rimless glasses, started creeping around in the shadows behind their ever-thickening barriers of bull.

Within a day's sail of the frontier monument lies the first outpost of Paraguay, a row of neat, clean, wooden buildings perched on top of stone columns. The reason for this is to allow a breath of cool air to come up from the river and ventilate the houses through grilled holes in the floors. Also, of course, to keep out ants, snakes, jaguars, and all the rest of the crawling life of the Chaco.

There was no bull here, in Bahía Negra. No papers to riffle and stamp, no mean minions sitting behind desks, no rubber stamps, none of the paraphernalia of the potbellied, bullet-headed, myopic pen-pushers. This particular place was too hot, too remote, too bloody dangerous; piles of forms don't mean a *thing* to a hungry jaguar!

The man in charge of the place was a naval commander. When he had recovered from his astonishment, he treated us royally. All the people in the tiny settlement of about five hundred turned up on the toy jetty. The first thing I noticed about the Paraguayans was how very *handsome* they are. So different from the poor Bolivians. It was a pleasant change to be surrounded by pretty women and good-looking men. The mixture of Guarani Indian, Spanish, German, and other assorted European strains through centuries of miscegenation has resulted in what is probably, along with the Madagascan Polynesian, the best-looking race of folk on earth. Also the happiest, friendliest, and most hospitable, as well as the jolliest and most musical, always ready to play the guitars and dance.

The whole population of the town made merry at sunset—the young men played guitars and the girls, in long petticoats, danced intricate steps. The *commandante*, Huanapaco, and I ate wild duck shot that day, washed down with warm, sweet, Paraguayan beer. We were still out of range not only of bureaucratic bull, but also of refrigeration.

While the dancing and other festivities went on, the older people walked up and down on the grassy sward of the river's edge, flicking themselves with huge handkerchiefs to keep the pests away. To save our precious mosquito repellent, we adopted this idea and it became an unthinking habit, so much so that when I finally returned to England I would involuntarily grope for my mosquito-flicker as the sun went down.

By midevening the *commandante*'s house was choked with people, old, young, men, women, children, dogs, chickens. At one stage even a horse wandered in!

In the morning, amidst cheerful farewells and handshakes from the men and wistful looks from the women (for Paraguay has a great excess of females), we slipped the moorings and headed downstream. We used our four-horsepower outboard motor for the first time since I had bought it in Panama, ten months and over 7,000 miles ago. We used it infrequently because the noise and fumes from the motor, added to the intense heat of the Chaco, made life a misery. We made four knots on the current, to which we added perhaps two knots with the sails; in this way, now we were out in a clear, wide river with few hazards, we made our way downstream.

TRISTAN JONES GOES SOUTH

This is a different account from all the others in this book, for it is about a cruise to Antarctica in a big ship. Originally, the article contained a warning about Argentinean designs on the Falkland and South Georgia Islands. This was edited out as being "too political and of no interest to mariners." I believe that in any future world conflicts, the Panama Canal will be shut down within hours. Then the Falkland Islands will be more valuable to the West than anyone dreams now. One look at the globe will show why. This article was published in Seacraft in Australia in 1978.

I joined the *Lindblad Explorer* as guest lecturer on November 28, 1977, at Puerto Montt, on the west coast of South America, in Chile. I had originally been invited to join her in New Guinea, but the press of getting my 20-foot sloop *Sea Dart* to Seattle on the northwest coast of the U.S.A. prevented this.

The situation, as our bus trundled through the small fishing port of Montt from the airfield, was no worse nor better than I had expected in South America; Lan-Chile Airlines had lost my baggage and there had been a long delay in Santiago, the capitol, caused by a bomb scare. But I had learned to accept such matters with calm and equanimity during my passage over the continent in 1974 and my mind dwelled more on the prospects of the first "big" ship voyage I was to make since 1952, when I left the Royal Navy.

A couple of hours after the 70 or so passengers had boarded the ship, she got underway, heading south through the Gulf of Corcovado, with the island of Chiloe to starboard and the great massive Andes rising straight up from the shores to port.

As we ate dinner in the sparkling luxurious dining room I told Captain Hasse Neillsen and his wife Ami of the previous time I had encountered his ship. This had been at the port of Moroni in the Comoro Islands of the Indian Ocean in 1972. I had been heading for the Cape of Good Hope, on my way to the Amazon, and the *Explorer*'s crew had swapped some books with me, for the library of the 38-foot yawl *Barbara*.

Lindblad Explorer is more like a very large power yacht than a ship; being around 213 feet long but with Scandinavian ingenuity, her Finnish builders have managed to accommodate 80 passengers in first class comfort and 60 crew, all in double cabins. Her twin diesels of 2000 horsepower each drive her along at 13 knots cruising speed and the ship has bowthrusters, with a double hull and watertight doors throughout, very necessary considering the unusual areas in which *Explorer* operates world-wide. One striking thing about her is the eight 18-foot Zodiac rubber boats she carries for landing passengers on remote shores. There are two boat derricks and the crew are able to sling out all eight boats in a matter of minutes. The Zodiacs are powered by 20-horsepower Johnsons, which have been found to be the most dependable outboards for the job.

Another striking thing is the number of different nationalities represented in the crew. All the officers are Swedish but the hands are Spanish, Dutch, German, American, British, and Portuguese with three very popular Tongan seamen; pleasant guys but extremely tough.

On this occasion *Explorer* was heading south, to base herself on Ushuaia, on the south coast of Tierra del Fuego, the most southerly town in the world, to make five voyages to the Antarctic Peninsula during the southern summer. The vessel is operated by Swedish-American lines, on charter to the Lindblad Travel Co., which specializes in visiting remote areas—the Antarctic, the Arctic, the Amazon, Indonesia, the remoter South Pacific Islands, mainly with wildlife observation as the objective.

Many famous people accompany her, for instance on the Antarctic trips she had onboard Prince Bernhard of the Netherlands; Sir Peter Scott, founder of the world wildlife trust and son of the immortal Antarctic explorer Robert Falcon Scott; Peter Shackleton, wildlife painter and nephew of another famous man, Sir Ernest Shackleton.

One of the passengers on the first trip was Alan Gurney, designer of ocean sailing yachts, including Chay Blythe's *Great Britain II* and the Italian *B & B Italia*, which took part in a Whitbread Round-the-World Race. Alan is also an enthusiastic birdwatcher. We had many an interesting conversation on such topics as to why the wandering albatross's system of salt water filtration (which reduces the salt content of the sea water he drinks on his year-long continuous spells over and on the ocean from 4 percent to a manageable 2.5) could not be adapted and perhaps improved upon for small ocean sailing vessels. We have much, very much, to learn from the ocean birds, such as the frigate-bird, the fulmars and the albatrosses.

By the time my two voyages were over I realized how little I knew of the wildlife in the ocean—the birds, the fish, the mammals. I had seen thousands upon thousands of them. How much more interesting my own voyages would have been if I had studied at least some of their habits before setting out. By the time I had absorbed as much as I could of the knowledge broadcast onboard *Explorer* I felt humbled indeed, like a great oaf who has been wandering blindly through a whole world of miraculous natural phenomena. Ah, well, live and learn . . . one thing's for sure, on my next voyage my eyes will be open much wider, my curiosity renewed and sharpened and with my curiosity, my wits.

These thoughts were already upon me as I met my companions during the run down through the Chilean Islands, down south, under the lee of a long, long chain of islands protecting the leads from the great Pacific swell.

The only rough part of the voyage down to Ushuaia was when *Explorer* had to pass outside the Tairtao Heads. This severely curtailed attendance in the second evening out. But the roughish sea, driven by a good 30-knot wind, did not prevent the naturalists from going topside to observe the first of the giant petrels, the sooty shearwater, the fulmars, the cormorants and the diving petrels which zinged around the ship.

On the third day *Explorer* entered the Fuegian Channels and we were again in protected waters, sailing (or is it steaming?) among scenery even more splendid. One Swiss lady told me that she felt she was sailing among the Alps! I told her that I hoped one day to do that.

At Puerto Eden, on Wellington Island, the local shell fishermen crowded alongside the ship, bartering huge king crabs for cigarettes and other ship supplies. The school-teacher allowed the young scholars out of their tiny school-house to sing for us as we went ashore to look for unusual life, such as the bog plants which eat insects. The local policeman, resplendent in his best uniform, proudly preened himself on the broken-down jetty; we were well away from the jack-boot ambiance of Santiago.

Small vessels navigating in these parts have no problem with fresh water supplies in the summer, for all the way down through the thousand miles of the Chilean leads the snow on the heights melts, causing waterfalls at very frequent intervals along the shore.

At Puerto Natales, which *Explorer* fetched on December 1, all of the passengers and quite a few of the crew set off by bus to visit the spectacular Torres del Paine National Park, observing enroute and in the Park Andean condor guanacos (a sort of llama) and rheas, a type of ostrich. On the way back to the port we visited the Milodon Cave, where the remains of a huge extinct sloth, about 26 feet long, have recently been turned up.

Next day, as we were underway heading for the Magellan Strait, Cape Horn weather descended with a vengeance, lashing rain and screeching wind. As we steadily plodded through the extremely narrow Kirke Nárrows, hardly much wider than the ship, we were reminded of the dangers in this area by the many wrecks strewn about the coast and I wondered at the skill and courage of the first explorers and surveyors in this forbidding scene, during the days of square-rigged sailing ships. These had been mainly Royal Navy men, during the early 1800s and their names, bestowed on islands and fiords, lakes and mountains, are scattered everywhere. But the one who will always be remembered, as long as ships sail around these waters, with their fast flowing tides and currents, their high winds and sudden murderous squalls, is Fitzroy, the captain of the *Beagle* (he later became governor of New Zealand).

Without Fitzroy, Charles Darwin would, I believe, never have been able to make the voyage which led to his theory of evolution; and the history of the world would have been very different indeed.

On through the tortuous channels *Explorer* glided, smoothly, eventually emerging through the eastern end of the Beagle channel, with its frowning cliffs and ice-falls glittering in the sunshine, sighting many different bird species; plumbeous rail, dark-bellied cinclodes, ground tyrants, rock shags, Magellanic oyster catchers, kelp geese and flightless steamer ducks by the thousand, whilst in the water several hourglass-dolphins gambolled in the wake of the bow.

During the passage over the open ocean to the Falkland Islands the weather was kind until we got into the lee of the colony. Then a northeaster blew up and by the time we were alongside in Port Stanley it was blowing a storm. The intrepid passengers did not let the weather prevent them from touring the island, however, whilst some of the crew, myself included, found our refuge in the two pubs of the town, the Upland Goose and the Bell Hotel, where we comforted ourselves with good English ale for an hour or two, noting how very, very British the place is. Only in two places in the South Atlantic is this so, here at the Falklands and in St Helena, an island even more remote than the Falklands, about 3700 miles to the northeast. Around the harbor of Port Stanley, the hulks of a half-dozen condemned square-riggers lie, old Cape-Horners passing their old age in fairly calm waters. On the town foreshore sits the mizzenmast of the Brunel-designed *Great Britain*, whose hull was towed to Britain some years ago and which is now a museum ship in Bristol.

Following our short stay in Port Stanley, *Explorer* visited several offlying islands on the western side of the archipelago, landing people to see the king penguin colonies in the Zodiacs, which were escorted all the way to the beaches by the black and white Commerson's dolphins. Besides the king penguins there were great numbers of gentoo and Magellanic penguins and the scavengers of the beaches, the brown skua.

On Carcasse Island we met the McGill family, which had just completed shearing 2000 sheep. Rod McGill showed us the black-crowned night herons that nest under the gorse bushes and we watched the kelp geese, tussock birds, and black-chinned sisking. That night, a short night, for dusk did not fall until 10:30, swarms of tiny prion birds flew chattering around the ship.

On December 9 *Explorer* weighed anchor at New Island and headed south for the Antarctic. Overhead, on the wing, were the great black-browed albatrosses gliding in the blue, calm sky. The crossing of the Scotia Sea was the calmest I have ever seen in a dozen voyages in this area in ships of different sizes. The sea was calm, with only a gentle swell from the northeast. On the three days it took for *Lindblad Explorer* to cross to Elephant Island from the Falklands the passage around the Horn could have been made in one of her Zodiacs.

The crossing of the Antarctic convergence, where the cold water of the Southern ocean wells up against the warmer waters of the South Atlantic, was of great interest to me and I was up at midnight, watching the temperature being taken by the navigation staff.

Sure enough at 1 A.M. on December 11, the sea temperature dropped very quickly to 35 degrees Fahrenheit; and from then on we knew it was only a matter of hours before we would sight our first iceberg, which loomed up on the southern horizon at 8 A.M. As we inspected its mile-long tabular shape we were welcomed to Antarctica by white-headed petrels and Antarctic fulmars overhead, whilst down near the ocean surface the pintados screeched and a single light-mantled sooty albatross swooped across the bow.

It was foggy approaching Elephant Island, which was a pity, for I was keeping a lookout with my binoculars to see Shackleton's camp, on the northeast end. This is where that magnificent explorer—perhaps the finest leader of men the world has seen—after bringing his shipwrecked party 300 nautical miles over the ice from the *Endurance*, in 1915, had camped. From Elephant Island, after seeing his 24-man crew safely refuged, he left with Frank Worsley and two others, in a 20-foot lifeboat, *James Caird*, for an 800-nautical-mile run to the Norwegian whalers in South Georgia Island.

Along with Bligh's open-boat voyage after the *Bounty* mutiny to Timor, over 3,000 nautical miles in an 18-foot boat with 20-odd men, Shackleton's voyage in the *James Caird* crossed over some of the roughest waters on the face of the earth, then, having been wrecked on the coast of remote South Georgia, with two men exhausted, Shackleton and Worsley made the first-ever crossing of that savage blizzard-swept island, over heights of 9800 feet, with only a 65-foot length of rope and an axe, in 38 hours, to find succour and rescue for the men left behind at Elephant Island.

In the whole history of Antarctic exploration three men stand out—Shackleton, Scott and Mawson.

When my Zodiac arrived at the rocky sea-swept landing on Explorer Point on Elephant Island I found myself pocketing bits of rock to take home to remind my young friends of true courage, of superhuman efforts against all odds to help others. Whilst the naturalists clambered away to see the chinstrap penguin colonies and the nesting snowy shearwaters, I chipped away with my hammer at the rock.

By "evening" we were underway again for King George Island to see the giant petrels and to visit the Elephant and Weddel seals, the Antarctic terns and the Adelie penguins, and by the following evening, December 12, anchored off the Soviet scientific station Bellingshausen. This is named after the admiral of the Imperial Russian Fleet ships, which in 1821 made a complete circumnavigation of Antarctica and which may have been the first to sight the actual continent.

The *may* is because when the fog lifted to reveal the mountains of the peninsula momentarily, it also revealed, quite close to the Russian ships, an American whaler, captained by Nathanial Palmer, which is why the Americans call the Antarctic Peninsula 'Palmer land'.

Next to the Soviet base, only a couple of hundred feet or so away, across a flat ice field, is the Chilean Base Presidente Frei. Since the fall of Allende in 1975 the personnel of the two bases have completely ignored each other! Even when invited onboard the ship that evening, the Russians and Chileans maintained a frosty silence towards each other. But our passengers were a merry enough crowd and somehow we all got through the evening.

I was lucky to dine with a Russian scientist who spoke fair English, so we were able to converse on matters such as the recent discovery that bacteria and algae and fungi in the few ice-free areas of Antarctica survive by actually penetrating *into rocks* so that they gain shelter and yet receive sunlight through the quartz crystal and mica of the rock's surface, thus turning the actual rocks into a sort of green-house.

It was from Alexander that I first heard of the discovery of active volcanos in Antarctica on the Pacific Ocean side, on Mount Berlin in Marie Byrd Land, southeast of New Zealand, and also of the first successful penetration of the Ross Ice Shelf's 1400-foot thickness and how cameras and fish traps had been lowered into a sea about the size of the North Sea to which sunlight has never penetrated ever since the ice shelf formed millions of years ago. He told me that crustaceans had been trapped and a five-inch-long fish was photographed in that icy gloomy depth!

From King George Island *Explorer* made her course south, down through the Lemaire Channel, dropping people off in the Zodiacs to explore one of the most beautiful places in the world—Paradise Bay, with its thousands of colored icebergs, glaciers and clouded mountain peaks, its floes, with the leopard, crab-eater and Weddel seals lazing around between hunting expeditions in the icy-cold water. Then a visit to the abandoned British scientific station at Port Lockroy, which we reached by breaking through several miles of ice fields in the Peltier Channel.

At Port Lockroy, which, before the Second World War was a whaling station, we were reminded of the relentless slaughter of the great Leviathan over the past two centuries. Staring at the huge bones on the beach, miles and miles of them, and comparing them to the few whales, humpback and finwhales, we had seen in the Antarctic, we realized the urgency of stopping the holocaust which was being pursued, day and night, in all the waters of the world, mainly by the Japanese and the Russians. We cannot afford to risk the loss of these irreplaceable animals, these vital links in the natural chain of life in the sea. And that's from a man who has lost a boat to a sperm, and collided with two other whales. As far as the danger to small sailing craft from whales is concerned, surely it is not beyond the ingenuity of man to develop some kind of signal to warn the whale of the approach of the vessel?

Piled ice prevented *Explorer* from approaching the American base at Palmer station, so she headed north for Deception Island, through the grey Neumayer Channel, with dark clouds scudding overhead and icebergs, some of them monsters of five-mile length, all around the ship on every horizon.

The entrance to Whaler's Bay, in Deception Island, which is shaped like a horseshoe, a sort of volcanic "coral atoll" is very narrow, with a shallow rock sitting right in the middle of Neptunes Bellows, as the old whalers had christened the entrance. Once inside, with volcanic peaks surrounding the ship on all sides, and hot-water fumaroles steaming away around the shore, we dropped off the Zodiacs and headed in to visit the old British station, once a whaling factory.

The harbor of Deception Island is probably one of the most strategically important places in the whole of Antarctica. The huge bay, protected on all sides, has only one snag. Sometimes, during periods of volcanic activity, the water in the bay boils. Many times whalers had to evacuate the port because the bottom paint was blistering off and the plates beginning to buckle! This would make a beautiful old-salt's yarn, except that it is absolutely true.

The port of Deception Island is so useful to potential belligerents that in 1941 the Royal Navy blew up the whaling station to prevent its use by German submarines which could have based there for attacks on shipping in the South Atlantic. A big earthquake in 1969 completed the job of destruction and the base was abandoned.

Now the only signs left of the weather stations are several bottles of Major Gray's Military Chutney, still in good order on the only uncollapsed shelf in Biscoe House. All the canned food had blown; probably the result of a warm spell years ago. On the beach are a couple of old whaling boats, which had, at some time, been converted into shelters for personnel, probably during the volcanic period.

At Deception Island all is either black or white. The volcanic ash on the shore and in patches up the hills, is set off by the gleaming ice and snow of the ice falls and snow drifts. On the beaches Elephant seals scratch themselves as they stare at intruders with mournful eyes, whilst around the rock crevices Wilson's storm petrels (Mother Cary's Chickens) flutter around under gray, wind-driven clouds.

On December 17, at Telegraph Bay, in Deception Island, Mike McDowell had a brief swim in a warm fumarole, thus becoming the most southerly swimmer in the world. The air temperature was 30 degrees Fahrenheit, the water temperature 68 degrees Fahrenheit. Seeing as it was Mike's birthday, we celebrated by sharing a bottle of champagne as he splashed around in the stream by the beach.

The next port of call after Deception Island was Hope Bay, or Esperanza, as it is known by the Argentineans, who maintain there a full-blown military base, even though this is specifically forbidden by the terms of the Antarctic Treaty. Argentina also is establishing at Hope Bay a civilian settlement. The first baby born in Antarctica arrived there in December. All the soldiers at the base that I talked to clammed up as soon as I mentioned the birth. But one soldier did confide to me that it was true.

Of course, when the sort-out of territorial claims starts in the 1980s, then Argentina will have a lever. So she thinks. For that reason visitors' passports are stamped by the Argentine Army at Hope Bay with immigration stamps into Argentine territory. This is the only place in all Antarctica where this is enforced.

Hope Bay is a beautiful place, doubly so when the sun shines, which it often does in the southern summertime, Hope Bay being on the northernmost end of the Antarctic Peninsula. The bay is dominated by the towering mass of Mount Flora.

It is a pity to see the Argentine Army still keeping a dog team, though. It is, from what I could see, completely unnecessary, as there are motor-sleds at the base. Evidently the dog team is kept only for display to visitors, yet it involves the slaughter of hundreds of penguins every week for dog food.

It took *Explorer* three days to reach Ushuaia, across the Drake Passage. Again, the weather south of the Horn was moderate except for the last 50 nautical miles or so, as we approached Cape Horn. As we passed the surprisingly unimpressive Cape-islet and entered the narrows between the disputed islands of Lennoz and Nueva and the Argentinean pilot came onboard, I again reflected on how different my own small craft voyages would have been if I had made a trip like this years ago, with knowledgeable naturalists. But then, I reflected, even merely reading about wildlife would have made a lot of difference. Instead I had to find out about what little I knew the hard way, by experience. But what's the good of watching birds or fish or mammals if you don't know anything about their habits and the reason for them?

I've learned more about birds and fish, dolphins and whales, all the things I have lived so close to over the past 25 years; I've learned more about them on this one voyage than I've learned during the whole time I've been sailing!

I made one more Antarctic voyage with the *Lindblad Explorer*, with more or less the same itinerary as the first, with the exception of the trip through the Chilean leads, of course. The smoothness of the ship's operation has my profound respect. The friendliness of the passengers, the scrumptious food, the fantastic service, the almost unworldly comfort of the quarters . . . all this I will remember, along with the expertise of the other lecturers.

But as a small-boat man, there's something I missed . . . and when I looked around Ushuaia harbor and saw the 53-foot Swedish ketch *North Wind* anchored off, I knew what it was . . . The three-man crew was bound from Buenos Aires to Valparaiso on their way around the world. They had not been able to obtain charts of the Chilean leads on the Pacific side, so I introduced them to Captain Neillsen of *Lindblad*

Explorer and arranged for them to have tracings of the ship's charts. Over schnapps in the captain's cabin we discussed the best time for them to pass through the Magellan Straits . . . early February.

It was snowing heavily when I flew back into New York. During December there were three gales in the area south of Cape Horn. The first and the third from the west, wind around 40 to 50 knots, and the second, in the ocean between Tierra del Fuego and the Falkland Islands, from the northeast. The third gale was observed in the area extending 150 nautical miles south of Cape Horn. The seas were long and high but regular and there was little rain in each case.

South of latitude 60, approximately where the Antarctic Convergence occurs, there are phenomena which should be noted by anyone making the passage around Cape Horn.

First, the frequency of heavy weather is *much less* than north of latitude 60.

Second, there is far less cloud, therefore less precipitation, although both air and sea temperature drop drastically.

Third, there are ice floes and icebergs in irregular progression. There is also, when the wind is slight, fairly frequent fog, which can reduce visibility down to 150 feet or so but generally visibility in fog is about a quarter mile.

Fourth, as the Antarctic Peninsula is neared, so the winds, when they do (infrequently in summer) increase, tend to be from the east. The direction of moderate winds, however, is from the west.

Fifth, the Bransfield Sound, protected in the west by the South Shetland Islands and in the east by the Antarctic Peninsula, affords good shelter. There are a number of scientific stations in the area where craft in distress could obtain assistance and/or supplies. All the abandoned bases are left fully stocked with food for such emergencies. Anyone contemplating a voyage through the Drake Passage should bear the above points in mind. Before setting out he should obtain information on the Antarctic bases south of the Horn from The British Antarctic Survey, Cambridge, England.

The average temperature offshore and on the coasts, in the Antarctic Peninsula, during my two visits (December and January) was around 30 degrees Fahrenheit but this greatly decreased with the wind chill factor. On several occasions, when the wind dropped, in brilliant sunshine the temperature rose to as much as 50 degrees.

Twilight lasted from around 11:30 P.M. to 3:30 A.M. but there was no real darkness.

The amount of fog depends on wind conditions, of course. It was around eight percent of the period.

Ever since the days of the great lumbering square-riggers, sailing vessels have rounded the Horn in both directions as if they were balancing on the black edge of the world. We must become accustomed to bearing in mind that to the south of the stormy Drake Passage there are many safe havens and that the area is becoming more and more populated and trafficked year by year.

Take plenty of warm clothes and keep a good look out!

THE YANKEE

In one's life, certain people stand out in one's memory. They may have been known over a number of years—or perhaps merely over a few hours. I only knew the man in this story for a few days, but he stuck in my memory. This tale first appeared in Sailing *magazine in 1981.*

The sight of the Statue of Liberty in New York Harbor must conjure up many different emotions in different people. For the past couple of years I have seen it almost every morning on my daily exercise walk down the West Side Highway. Every time, I am reminded of an early morning eleven years ago in, of all places, Venice, Italy, and of one of nature's gentlemen.

It was dawn as our thirty-eight-foot yawl *Barbara* crept into the shelter of the long breakwaters that protect the low city from rapid subsidence into the Adriatic. The sun was still behind the low black clouds on the eastern horizon. My shipmate, Conrad Jelinek, and I slowly nursed the boat under power (our engine was defective) into the City Club Marina, on the very bows of the ship-shaped city. All around us the Grand Canal, the palaces, and the ancient houses were pale and colorless. There was no one around at that early hour to receive us into port. I decided to tie up alongside a long, blue, new-looking ketch. The ketch was moored stern-in to the jetty, so I could not see what her name or her nationality were. It was too early yet for national ensigns to be hoisted, and anyway, we were not much interested. We'd had a weary passage from Yugoslavia. There had been no wind at all and *Barbara's* engine, as I said, was malfunctioning because of water in the diesel fuel, and we had taken the fuel system apart time and time again. In short, we were tired.

Soon we had *Barbara* tied up alongside the ketch. Wordlessly, Conrad went down below to make breakfast before he turned in to sleep, while I finished some small chores on deck and waited for the harbor authorities' office to open at 8 A.M. As I was so engaged, a troupe of small boys wandered along the jetty, six of them, all ragged, all incredibly dirty, shoeless, and all carrying shoe-shine boxes. Their ages must have been between five and seven. Without saying a word, they stood there and stared at the yachts with big brown eyes.

Barbara was much smaller than the big blue ketch, and so my cockpit well was four or five feet below the ketch's deck level. As I sat in the cockpit, greasing the sheet winches, it was impossible for me to see anyone on the ketch, or for them to see me. But of course in the still morning air I could hear everything.

I heard the sound of a companionway door open. Then I heard feet walking along the ketch's deck. Then I heard him speak to the boys in very slow, rusty-sounding Italian, *"Buon giorno,* I see you are looking at my boat," said the male voice.

"Si signor, it is very beautiful," said the eldest of the tykes.

"Would you like to come onboard and look around?" said the man.

"Is it possible, *signor?"*

"If you are very quiet; my *signora* is still asleep."

"No, I'm up now" called a female voice in American English.

"Okay if they come onboard?" said the man.

"Who is it?" called the woman.

"Some local kids. Maybe we could fix them something for breakfast."

"Why, sure," said the woman.

I sat quietly, watching Conrad make tea and porridge below, and heard the youngsters patter onboard one by one. If I craned my neck I could just see the two smallest ones, bringing up the rear of the line, carefully stepping on the gangway with their grubby bare feet. Then, as I sat there, silently, listening, I heard the man slowly and carefully explain everything on his deck and how it worked. He showed them the wheel, and the sails, and the shrouds, and the dinghy. He went as carefully through the function of each item of equipment as many of the usual yachtsmen would with their peers. Then I heard the woman invite him and "the boys" to breakfast. There were a few low murmurs from the boys as they went down the companionway evidently, for I could not see them, then there was silence again.

I sat for a moment or two thinking of all the harbors *Barbara* had called in during the past year's voyages in America, Europe, and Africa, and of all the sleek yachts we had been in company with in those ports. Never once had I ever witnessed such an invitation. Just as Conrad called me down to breakfast the sun rose above the line of dark clouds in the east and fingers of gold touched the sky and all around the beauty of Venice exploded as the colors sprang from the buildings and the gondolas out in the Grand Canal. I looked around me for a moment, amazed, then I went below and thought no more about it. There were technical questions about the engine to discuss with Conrad.

An hour later I went back topsides to clamber over the stern onto the jetty. The man on the ketch was seeing the boys onshore, standing at the foot of his gangway as they trouped past. The boys were all still barefoot, but were now all scrubbed clean and bright-eyed. Each one was clutching a small parcel, which I presume was food. Hesitatingly each little lad picked up his shoe-shine box from the jetty, then, after a soft *"molto grazie signor,"* one by one, they trouped off again to the city, the tourists, and the dustbins. The man suddenly noticed me.

"Oh hi!" he said, smiling. "My, you must have come in like a mouse! I've only just noticed your craft."

"Sorry about taking a liberty" I said. "There was no one around to allot us a berth."

"No, think nothing of it. You stay there until you get fixed up," he replied.

I held out my hand. "Happy to meet you" I said. "My name's Tristan Jones."

"Well..." he grinned widely. "Say, I've heard of you...my name's Irving Johnson."

In my Welsh way I kept a straight face. Of course I'd heard of the famous, the fabulous Irving Johnson, who had made so many world passages in the twenties and thirties on the immortal *Yankee*, a schooner school-ship, and who was known to millions of Americans for his wonderful sailing accounts in *National Geographic* and other periodicals.

"Nice craft you have there, Irving," I said.

"Yes, this is the new *Yankee*. As you can see, she's an old-folk's boat, Tristan, and much simpler than the old *Yankee*..."

"She's the same boat to me, Irving," I said. "Once a *Yankee*, always a *Yankee*." I nodded my head at the small boys just disappearing along the jetty. "Thanks...Irving ...for them," I said, and he laughed.

I learned a lot about the *idea* of the United States that morning eleven years ago, and when I hear Americans express doubts about their country I remember Irving Johnson that morning—but I say nothing.

THE TRUTH ABOUT THE TRIANGLE

This is an exercise in writing about a routine voyage from New York to St. Thomas. There is nothing unusual in the trip—it has been made by thousands of sailing craft. The point of the tale is that if you write about a voyage, no matter of what duration, always have something to say, and say it plainly and clearly. Your enjoyment or otherwise is of much less import to the reader than is helping him or her to clear up questions in his or her own mind. The time of day that your anchor is weighed, or the number of the jib you had hoisted, is interesting to some pedantic souls, but the vast majority want to know "how did it feel?" The article appeared in SAIL *in 1976.*

Every year in the autumn a massive migration of pleasure craft takes place. They head south from the northeastern United States and Canada, to follow the sun's warmth. Some make for Florida, some carry on to the almost-tropical islands of the Bahamas, whilst others go even farther afield, to the West Indies.

The craft bound for Florida and the Bahamas mainly use a route that leads them through almost completely protected waters, a system of rivers and canals almost 1,000 miles long, running through five states, Virginia, North Carolina, South Carolina, Georgia, and Florida—the renowned (and rightly so) Intracoastal Waterway.

Those boats bound for the Caribbean Islands have a choice of three main routes. (1) You can follow the Intracoastal Waterway down to Florida, then strike east through the Bahamas and so on to the Virgin Islands. The main problem with this route for sailboats is that it entails your using the engine a great deal whilst in the Waterway, and then, once you emerge from Florida you have a long, long beat to windward of about 1,000 miles to the Islands. (2) You can head out from New York direct to Bermuda, then south on a reach to the Islands. This is the most direct route, but calls for accurate navigation and preparedness for heavy weather. This route keeps the vessel out of the so-called Devil's Triangle. (3) You can sail offshore south from New York to the entrance of the great Chesapeake Bay, enter the Intracoastal Waterway at Norfolk, Virginia, then can go down the Waterway, bypassing stormy Cape Hatteras, 350 miles or so south to Morehead City. At that time you can emerge into the ocean, then head out east for 300 miles or so, and bear south for the Virgins. Apart from avoiding Cape Hatteras, plus a shorter time out in the open ocean, this latter route has the added interest of enabling you to travel through some delightful countryside. On the debit side, enroute from Morehead City to the Islands one must pass through at least a section of the Triangle.

Aboard the 44-foot yawl *Sundowner*, bound for charter in the Virgin Islands, we decided to take the latter route and to head *straight through* the Triangle, on a direct course from Morehead to San Juan, Puerto Rico. I would keep a sharp eye out during the 1,300-mile or so passage to see what conclusions could be made from all the tales of mysterious disappearances of ships and planes in this vast area, tales of an "underwater UFO base," where extraterrestrial beings are quite seriously (in some quarters) supposed to ascend from the depths to seize yacht and plane crews . . . for what purpose it is, at least for me, difficult to imagine; tales of voyages and overflights across the area by psychics and their side-kicks; enough tales to have given rise to a full-fledged industry of publishing books on the subject by the millions to feed the paranoia of a supposedly gullible public.

After some years of sailing in many parts of the world, including some odd places indeed, I had my own ideas on the truth of the Triangle, but in order to prove them I would have to cruise the area in all its moods. The best way was to tackle it tooth and nail and beat hard right across it. This is what *Sundowner* did, in a cruise containing great contrasts, from the wintery weather of New York, through the placid waters of the Intracoastal, across the rough Gulf Stream and then a continuous beat of 1,000 miles through the squally Triangle, to finish in the comparatively steady winds of the trades, among the palm-strewn sandy beaches of the Antilles.

I was lucky in the way of a crew, though they were a fairly mixed bag: Ray, 28, some experience of offshore sailing off Long Island; John, 19, of Korean-Swedish descent, hospital orderly, no experience; Terry, 32, signed on as cook, ex-photographer in the U.S. Air Force, no previous experience; and Peter, 45, restaurant owner from New York, some experience. At least the galley would be well looked after, for Terry had a cast-iron stomach whilst Peter had the recipes and the cooking know how.

The boat herself is an interesting amalgam of Tahiti ketch and Colin Archer, very solid timbers, built in Nova Scotia by old-timers, using all British fittings, including an 86-horsepower Perkins diesel, and obviously built to take the weather. Considering her displacement for length, she goes surprisingly well to windward, though she must be driven hard with plenty of canvas aloft, to push her through the seas.

For myself, after single-handing a small craft like my own 20-foot sloop *Sea Dart* for several years on a most arduous voyage of many thousands of miles in some of the most remote places on earth, this passage was in the nature of a recuperation, a return to civilization.

On the fine, clear, cold night of October 25 *Sundowner* slipped quietly out of East Rockaway Inlet, on the south shore of Long Island, with the big road bridge opening to our radio call. No delay, no hassle. I recalled the time in Uruguay only three months back, when it took a full 38 hours to open up the road bridge over the River Santa

Lucia, just West of Montevideo. None of that here; we were in the land of super-efficiency, where *things work*. Ray's girlfriend was on the bridge to wave us a final farewell from New York. Soon *Sundowner* was lifting to the ocean swell and we were off on the 300-mile passage offshore to Chesapeake Bay.

Standing about 28 miles offshore, we missed the contrary Gulf Stream current and were outside the main tidal influences. Navigation was easy, with lighthouses and buoys flashing friendly and on time. What a contrast to the west coast of South America, where the lights that *are* there may or may not work, where the overcast is continuous, and the Humboldt current cold and vicious, with a desert shore somewhere under the lee, instead of these well-lit entrances all along a friendly shore.

A fresh to strong easterly sang in the rigging and we hoisted the mizzen staysail, whizzing along until, in an extra-strong gust, it parted at the tack with a crack they must have heard all the way to Philadelphia. But *Sundowner* and we laughed as we handed the staysail, for on this, the second day out, we had our sea legs, whilst she had her crew and a fair wind and she knew it.

We arrived off the Chesapeake Inlet on the third night and, guided by the easy-to-follow buoyed fairway, ran free straight under the gigantic road bridge which carries one of America's throbbing arteries straight across the 12-mile gap. And so into the harbor of Norfolk, past a fleet of warships far bigger than most of the world's navies combined, to sleep at anchor and peace at the first anchorage inside the Waterway.

By the dawn's early light (to coin a phrase) we weighed the anchor and wore over to the Holiday Inn Marina, one of the many. In a jiffy we were fueled and watered, showered and iced, Coca-Cola'd and hot-dogged, then off south down the Intracoastal Waterway, for *Sundowner* is a charter boat, an American charter boat, heading for business, and tarries not.

Once past the naval base, past huge carriers, menacing cruisers and fussy destroyers, suddenly we were in the southern countryside, chugging along at six knots, accompanied by a continuous procession of small craft of all shapes, sorts and conditions, from the most luxurious huge motorcruisers to tiny sailcraft. One or two vessels were heading north, but these were rare indeed. On the whole, manners were good, with the bigger, faster power craft slowing down as they passed us, but on one particular occasion I noted the worst display of ignorant boorishness it has ever been my misfortune to encounter. This was a powerboat all of 70 feet long, which, in one of the narrowest parts of the Waterway, roared past *Sundowner* at 20 knots. I had pulled over to the side of the canal to let her pass, but he kept on full speed, little heeding the fact that in the steep swell he left behind I could, with my six-foot draft, easily touch bottom in an eight- to nine-foot depth, or worse, bounce onto a tree stump. I had signalled him, with downstrokes of my hand, to slow down, but was answered only with shouted abuse and obscene gestures.

The variety of craft using the Waterway is amazing, including many commercial craft and fishing vessels. On one notable occasion we even passed two houses being shifted bodily to a new site . . . by barge!

The Intracoastal Waterway is impressive in many ways. Not so much from the scenic point of view, I suppose, because after the passages up the Amazon and down through the Mato Grosso, anything else is bound to suffer in comparison, but it is impressive by the really excellent state of repair of the canals, the banks and levees, the buoys and markers. Also impressive is the efficient, prompt, clockwork alacrity of the bridgekeepers, borne up by the fact that *Sundowner* never once had to sound her horn to get the bridge or lock opened. In my own Celtic contrary way I sometimes found myself wishing that one of the bridgekeepers, *just one*, would be asleep, or drunk, or off gallivanting, but no, everyone was on the ball. The nearest thing I can think of in Europe is the Dutch Canal system.

So we pass on, just one almost anonymous pilgrim in the yearly Hegira heading south with the wild geese. Past a British power vessel heading north and (naughty, naughty) wearing aft the British Union Jack instead of the Ensign . . . the Queen's prerogative only . . . on through the low swampy bayous full of wildlife, across wide bays under (joy at last!) full sail . . . past jolly-looking little marinas and boat sheds, and starkly antiseptic Coast Guard stations, with their crewcutted grass lawns and boatshow condition launches, not a soul to be seen, and great monstrous cars parked on the spotless gravel . . . and so on, over the state line into North Carolina, where you can buy a beer in a grocery store on condition that you step outside the property line to drink it! Most strange and a far cry from another inland waterway I recall so well, the Grand Canal in Venice, where the waiters take delight in bringing a beer on a tray right to the boat's cockpit, but "different ships, different longsplices," so, like the three wise monkeys we "hear all, see all and say naught" as we drink our bottle of beer on the roadside.

Out we sailed into Albemarle Sound and over to quiet, sleepy Belhaven, anti-mosquito-screened in the evening twilight, to order more fuel at the marina and wrestle with the "gas jockey's" broad Southern Rebel drawl, looking round for my companions though I was alone, every time he addressed me as "you-all." Hominy grits for breakfast, southern fried chicken for dinner; in accordance with time-honored tradition, the "yachties" were "going native."

We reached the last stop on the Waterway, Morehead City, after three days of steady chugging through an old-salt's heaven and made ready to tackle the ocean passage to Puerto Rico . . . through the Devil's Triangle.

We moored off the aptly named Sanitary Restaurant, a famous seafood establishment which does a roaring trade and does not have a piece of bread in the house, as the owner proudly informed me; instead they serve only corn fritters and strictly seafood.

After cruising in the more primitive parts of the globe, it is a shock to shop in a U.S. supermarket. Everything is packed and canned; and simple, nutritious food is conspicuous by its absence. Everything or nearly everything that is not canned must be refrigerated. It is difficult to get a selection of such things as dried fish, dried beans, nuts, dried fruit or even a good selection of canned meat; but perhaps I was just unlucky in the places I could go in the time available. One thing is certain; I could cruise South America or Africa for years eating quite sufficiently for healthy activity without the use of a fridge or an icebox. This would be difficult in the United States, at least in places with which I was not very familiar. Apart from this, cruising in the United States is far easier in every respect than in most parts of the world, with the exception, perhaps, of Western Europe. There is one simple reason for this last observation: in the United States a car is almost a must in most towns visited. They are spaced out, whereas the average European town is compact, with shopping centers within walking distance of the harbors.

A check-up around the rigging, seacocks, engine and stores, a last minute "pier-head-jump" for Peter who was just joining, and we were off, heading out into the Gulf Stream, which here passes within a few miles of the coast. The weather was sunny, but cold, for here the Gulf Stream separates the temperate continental weather from the semi-tropical weather on the ocean side of the current; and that, in a nutshell, is what all the tales of the Devil's Triangle *are all about*, or at least most of them.

On the landward side of the Gulf Stream is the fairly steady, sometimes rough, weather of the temperate climes. On the ocean side is the balmy, warm, sunny, blue-watered, *highly temperamental*, suddenly changeable, squally weather of the tropics which always occurs whenever trade winds meet a warm current passing along a continental landmass, witness the southeast monsoon of the Indian Ocean's meeting the Mozambique Current off Southern Africa, or the southeast trade's meeting the Brazil Current in the South Atlantic, or the northeast trade's meeting the Kuro Siwo current south of Japan (where, incidentally, there is another notorious area also known as the Devil Sea). But follow *Sundowner* and see what happens, and imagine what might have happened if we had all been unaccustomed entirely to tropical conditions, if we had all been solely temperate climate sailors, no matter how experienced in the cold northern latitudes. And there, in another nutshell, is another reason for the bad name of the so-called Devil's Triangle; there is a lot of traffic and *much of it is by people who have not experienced the catspite nature of the areas where tropical weather meets the land masses over a warm current.*

By the end of the second day out, in latitude 33.40 north, longitude 74.40 west, we were at last across the Gulf Stream, with a weak east-northeast wind pushing us along slow but steady on a broad reach, with blue seas and blue skies. In the evening the clouds increased somewhat and now and again, far out on the horizon there would be a small shower. *Sundowner* was a happy ship again, with everyone well rested and a good supper of chili and salad, washed down with a bottle of Cote du Rhone from the far-off French valley south of Lyons . . . and so on, through the night, with a waxing moon, into next day's dawn, just as ideal, the same conditions, but a bit more wind. All the third day, we bowled along, warm and free, with the off-watch hands sun bathing on the poop deck and a feeling of utter contentment. Into the fourth day, and by now *almost* everyone is lulled into a state approaching nirvana, a condition of unwary bliss. Only the wind veering slightly in the afternoon to disturb the timeless day, by forcing us to close-haul the sheets a little more; and more, and more, until by nightfall we were as close to the wind as *Sundowner* will go and keep moving. But still we had utter peace and confidence, right into the fifth day.

Then it happened. I was below, taking my off-watch afternoon zeez, when, for some inexplicable reason I woke with a feeling of tremendous foreboding. Up through the hatch for a quiet, calm look round; all well, steady wind, bit of cloud ahead, in fact lots of cloud, all piled up, and, that looks strange . . . a very disturbed sea over on the port bow, it's . . . no, wait a minute, look carefully, yes, by crikey! It's a white squall, or as near as dammit to one! "Bring her about! Fast! Come on, all hands, up and out, ready about!" Over she went, onto the port tack, pots sliding around in the galley, everyone rubbing his eyes . . . the wind increased and veered.

Before the squall, which showed very little rain, there was a patch of sea showing white with wind. It would be impossible to guess the speed of the wind over that patch with any accuracy, but I would say at least 65 to 70 knots. Ahead of that was an area of flat calm. Any boat overtaken by that with all working sail up would have been floundering around for some minutes before she was knocked completely flat, unless the crew was lively enough to douse all sail.

The light rain behind the squall was about eight miles in extent, and we stayed on the port tack until it had passed, then came about and carried on course, as if the squall had never passed, except for a patch of very smooth sea to windward of the squall, over which we scooted like a bat out of hell. *Sundowner* emerged again into sunny blue skies and sea.

It's difficult to say, but my guess is that if we had been overtaken by that wind with our genoa up and flogging around we would probably have lost at least the sail, if not the forestay or the mast.

On the sixth and seventh day we sighted many squalls, black and gray, by day and by night, but particularly up to two hours after sunset and from two hours before sunrise.

In every case we would head for the windward side of the squall. The wind would increase and veer, the sea would flatten, but we would keep moving and fast. We would never get to leeward of any squall, no matter how harmless it looked.

Altogether *Sundowner* beat close-hauled for almost 600 miles, until the wind barely backed around again to the east-northeast. This occurred somewhere around 200 miles due north of San Juan. On the night of the run in to that port we were involved in a U.S. Coast Guard search for a yacht which had supposedly lost her way, and another vessel reported to be sending flares up. Peter had accidentally picked up the Mayday on the VHF radio. Immediately afterwards, Ray sighted what he thought was a flare away on the horizon over our port bow. These I reported to the Coast Guard, along with our position. Within minutes a helicopter was over our mast, taking a bearing on the reported flares, which by now were ascending regularly away in the southeast.

The helicopter took off towards the supposed action, only to advise us that what we had sighted were, in fact, practice star-shells from the U.S. Navy proving grounds over Vielques Island, over 150 miles away from us. Nevertheless, as the helicopter pilot told us in his thank you message, if we were not sure what we had seen we were quite right to report it, as the chances were that quite possibly they *could* have been flares. My mind went back to the South American coasts, where you could radio a distress call until you were blue in the face and never get a peep in reply, even if there was anyone ashore who *did* care.

At midnight on the 10th day out of Morehead City we entered the moonlit harbor of San Juan, past the frowning old Spanish fortress of El Morro, with its ghostly palms waving in the silvery light, tied up on the Old Town jetty and went ashore into the narrow streets of charming Old San Juan for a nice cold beer.

Next morning we met a "chummy ship," *Yankee Pasha*, which had also left Morehead City on the same day. She is about 60 feet in length and so faster than *Sundowner*. She had stood out farther east to avoid close-hauling. Nevertheless, she had been caught in the lee of a squall and had sustained a knockdown which had carried away her stem-fitting, together with the forestay, and sustained damage to her hydraulic steering caused by, I understood, a very heavy freak sea which had smashed into her rudder. At the same time we were informed of the fate of a 40-foot ketch, *Tumbleweed*, which had been run down by a tanker somewhere near Puerto Rico, fortunately without loss of life.

On the whole we had cause to congratulate ourselves quietly, for *Sundowner* had sustained no damage of any kind on a very hard beat, mostly against winds of Force 5 and 6 and fairly boisterous seas. In fact, if anything, she was probably in better shape than when she left New York. Which, after all, is as it should be.

After a day's rest in San Juan, during which Peter took off back to his restaurant in New York, we had a 24-hour beat to the east and reached St. Thomas, U. S. Virgin Islands, in apple-pie order, fresh and raring to paint the topsides to get ready for the charter season.

Entering St. Thomas brought me back a flood of memories, for it was exactly 3½ years since I had sailed in with the yawl *Barbara* after a 38,000-mile voyage which included a circumnavigation of Africa. But the yacht harbor has changed completely from being a mere jumble of sheds into a modern complex of super-duper condominiums. Let's hope it's a change for the better.

A final word on the so-called Devil's Traingle; first with regard to all the small planes which have been reported missing. It stands to reason that a squall of several miles in extent must have a very low pressure in its center. This would affect the reading of the plane's altimeter, and with the low visibility would cause the pilot to shape a course which would lead into a dive into the sea.

As far as magnetic anomalies are concerned, I kept a close eye on the compass and took azimuths often. I did not once detect, all through the middle of the Triangle, anything amiss. The normal magnetic variation, as noted on the chart, was evident, but nothing more.

The weather phenomena were nothing extraordinary, given the geographical situation of the area. There was no hazard which could not be avoided by keeping a good lookout and applying the time-honored rules of good seamanship.

THE VOYAGE OF *QUIBERON*

Since the early fifties and, in a number of cases, earlier, there has been a growing number of true ocean gypsies. Unheralded, and for the most part unsung, they have sailed other people's small craft wherever they were needed to be sailed, winter and summer. Whilst this story, being part of an autobiography, is perforce about myself and a French crewman, it is also a tribute to the men who, long before sponsored ocean voyages became fashionable, contributed more to the advance of safety and security in small ocean-going vessels than most others. I last saw Jean-Pierre in Amsterdam in late 1982. He was then owner and captain of an oil rig supply vessel plying the North Sea, and had four rosy-cheeked children by his Dutch wife. The story originally appeared as part of Saga of a Wayward Sailor *published by Andrews & McMeel in Kansas City.*

"**D**id you find anyone?" Jean-Pierre asked as I went below into the humid, hot cabin, the oil lamp flickering fitfully.

I shook my head. "There's no one around who wants to go back east, except an old English biddy."

"*Quoi?*"

"*Une grande dame Anglaise.* Trouble, my friend: bloody chatter about Wimbledon day and night, brassiers in the sail locker, stockings in the porridge. Jesus Christ!" I threw my cap onto its hook.

"Then we must go on—just the pair of us, *hein?*" He set out the supper plates.

"Yep. But look, Jean-Pierre, once we get to the turning point, 65 degrees west, 30 degrees north, we won't be on a close reach anymore. We can turn her off the wind and belt off to the east on a run. Once we get past 50 degrees west, we should be fairly safe. Out of range of anything really dangerous."

"You're sure, Tristan?"

"Oh, come on, Jean-Pierre; you know as well as I do that in a small craft you can never be absolutely sure of anything, especially weather. And you should know, too, there are four kinds of seafarers under sail."

"What are they, Tristan?"

"Dead, retired, novices, and pessimists!"

Jean-Pierre grinned.

I went on. "The thing for us to do is load the dice, and the only way we can do that is to get out of here as soon as possible. Tomorrow night, after we've got fresh water and stores onboard. And shoot off north, as close to the wind as we can manage and still keep up a good speed." I tapped the salt cellar on the table.

"How long do you think it will take us to reach 65-30? What do you call it, the 'turning point'?"

"Well, if the winds are as steady getting us away from here as they were fetching us here, I'd say . . . let's see . . . If we can keep a speed average of four knots . . . say 1,100 miles . . . Say 12 to 13 days. Two weeks . . . " I reached for my fork.

"And it's now the eighteenth of July. That takes us to the thirty-first of July."

"Yes, that means we can just slide out of harm's way by the skin of our teeth, and be well clear of the hurricane tracks by the time the really serious stuff is due to start, say the second week in August."

Jean-Pierre looked serious as he leaned to his dinner. "Then we have a margin of seven days?"

"Now you know damned well, Jean-Pierre, nature doesn't run to a fixed timetable. There's always a chance that the first hurricane of the season might come a week— even two weeks, even a month—before it's expected. We can only go on the averages over the years since records were kept, which indicate that the first blow can reasonably be expected about the middle of the second week in August. Anyway, we've found that *Quiberon*, although she leaks and is cranky as the devil, will stand up to a reasonable blow. There's a thousand dollars each for us waiting in France—and hell, after all, we *did* contract to bring her back. And we *are* a delivery crew, are we not?"

"*Oui, mais . . .* "

"*Oui mais* nothing! *Mon ami,* Pinet wants her delivered to Cherbourg for a winter refit. If we wait until after the hurricane season, it means we'll hit bad weather on the European side in November. If we wait for spring, for February, it means we'll get to Europe in April, and Pinet will miss his sailing next year. And you and I, Jean-Pierre, will lose our reputations as deliverers. We'd be lucky if we could find a job scraping and painting, once that happens. You know the yachting world—how small it is, and especially in France. And how the word gets around."

"Okay, Tristan. You're the skipper. If you think we can do it—just the pair of us—then I'm willing to try. Now, what fresh food will we need?"

"Two days' fresh beef—but check the fishing tackle—20 days' apples, 60 days' onions, two weeks' cabbages, three months' potatoes . . . " I started reeling off a list, which he scribbled on his pad. "And three months' kerosene. And better buy another storm lantern; the one we have is very rusty. It's the only lamp we've got, so better make sure."

So on July 19 we weighed anchor, secured a tow from a friendly English yachtsman with his outboard dinghy, and, after he slipped our line outside the narrow harbor entrance, made course for the northeast. The routine was much as it had been on the way from Cayenne to Antigua: four hours on the tiller, four hours off, with the boat again on the reach but a bit closer to the wind. I did not want to lose ground to the west. The aim was to stay in as easterly a position as we could. This meant that the boat was pounding down off the seas continually—close-hauled, as we say.

On the twenty-fifth of July, about 600 miles north of Antigua, the wind began to rise. The sky in the southeast darkened, until by midafternoon, a full gale was blowing and we reefed the main down four hands and shortened the headsail down to the No. 3 working jib (the second smallest). By midnight the seas were in a frenzy, with ghostly white horses sending lashing spray over *Quiberon* as she heaved and groaned from one huge sea to the next. Jean-Pierre hung on to the tiller, despite the regular crashing of seas into the cockpit (which, thank God, had been converted to self-draining).

By dawn—a gray dawn, full of black scudding storm clouds and heaving, crashing, monstrous gray seas 20 feet from trough to crest—the banshee wind was screaming at storm force. I reckoned it was blowing at least 50 knots. I had handed the mainsail entirely, and we were down to storm jib and mizzen only, wallowing and weaving, twisting and squirming like a stuck pig. With all the working, *Quiberon* started to take water into her hull at an alarming rate, and whoever was not on the tiller was on the bilge pump, when he was not tending sail or trying to heat something to drink or eat.

By midday on the twenty-sixth the storm was up to hurricane force. We were forced to bring down the storm jib and let her ride bows on to the storm, with the mizzensail weather-cocking her. The movement now was much easier, but she was still leaking, not only through the hull but through the sides, where her planking had opened with too much exposure to the sun in the tropics. The decks, with the seas crashing over them, were also leaking, and everything below—everything except what was canned or tightly wrapped in plastic bags and sheeting—was soon wet through. Hove to, at least we were free of the tiller, and after making sure everything on deck was snugged down, we went below to continue pumping and to wait out the storm.

By the night of the twenty-sixth, all hell was let loose on the world. It was as if the devil himself were having a fit. The seas were so huge and steep that their size alone, even without the sheets of spume whistling off the crests, was frightening. Not merely from the threat of death—immediate, absolute, contained in each one as it loomed, black and gleaming out of a dark, noisy nothingness—but from the realization of the mighty forces at violent play, forces that make anything that man can muster look like the feeble waving of a baby's fist.

"*Merde!*" said Jean-Pierre, patiently pumping. "How long do you think this will last?"

"Don't know, but we seem to be riding out well enough. It's just a matter of patience," I said, balancing myself in the plunging cabin. "Here, have some biscuits." I handed him a soggy packet of damp cheese crackers.

For three days, until the twenty-ninth, we were hove to, bouncing and crashing in the hurricane, until early on the thirtieth of July the sky to the southeast brightened and the wind dropped to gale force, around 35 knots. Struggling, I hoisted the storm jib. By midday I knew our position by sun sights, the clouds now being scrappy, allowing the sun to peep through fitfully.

We had lost 120 miles to the west! Our position was now approximately 400 miles due south of Bermuda.

"What do we do now, Tristan? Make for Bermuda?" Jean-Pierre asked as we pored over our small-scale chart of the Atlantic.

"No. If we do, we'll be stuck until October. We clean up for an hour, then set the main, reefed, and claw our way northeast. We'll still try for 65-30, or as damn near as we can get to it. If the winds are still southeast when we get there, we'll carry on northeast, until we meet up with the west wind, then run for the Azores."

Jean-Pierre balanced himself in the cockpit, holding onto the wheel, sunburned, his eyes squinting against the glare from the glistening sea, the salt shining on his hair and cheeks.

"What about food, Tristan? Do you think we have enough?"

"Sure." I leaned down into the galley and grabbed the food-account notebook from its shelf. This was where we kept track of all foods consumed. Just as a housewife pays for food in the shops, we entered details of the food we used into the notebook. In this way, by comparing what we had used with what we had originally taken onboard, we could tell at a glance what stocks we had remaining. I leafed through the dog-eared pages.

"Sure, Jean-Pierre, enough for at least another two months. Anyway, if we *do* go into Bermuda, the chances of finding anyone to go with us without pay are slender. All the posh yachts will have sailed weeks ago and anyone with any brains will have gone with them. Only an inexperienced amateur would want to trust his life to a bloody old tub like this!"

Jean-Pierre nodded. "The last thing we need is a passenger."

"And if we took on a paid hand, it's going to bite into our delivery dues. Let's see—say two months; he's going to need at least 80 bucks a week, if he's any good to us. That's $640 off our dues. Only leaves 680 bucks apiece for us when we get to France."

"Yes, it makes sense. It would mean we'd be working— June to September—for 160 a month, 40 a week. *Nom de Dieu!* Six dollars a day!"

"Right. And that, *mon ami*, is exactly 50 cents an hour! If we take it that we each work 12 hours a day. Obviously, we're not. We're working about 18 hours a day each, and often more. No, Jean-Pierre, to go into Bermuda would be a waste of time, and the chances are if we did go in we'd be stuck there until October, with no pay for the waiting weeks. The only thing is to push on."

All that day, the thirtieth of July, the wind gradually lessened though the seas carried on, one after the other, heaving bulges of gray green water out of the southeast. As the wind diminished we eased out the mainsail, until by midnight we were back to full working rig. The night was clear, with millions of stars shining benignly at us from a black, velvet sky, sending reflections from thousands of wave crests on the tired, sighing ocean.

In the morning, the seas had smoothed enough for us to set the sails for self-steering, and Jean-Pierre and I were able to sleep the whole forenoon, until it was time for me to shoot the equal altitudes of the sun over the noon period. With starsights the previous dusk and at dawn, this gave me a very accurate fix. We were doing well: an average of three knots, northeast.

For the next 10 days the wind was down to about 25 knots and we steadily pounded our way northeast, until on the ninth of August we were at longitude 60 degrees west, 35 degrees north—farther east and farther north than the intended turning point.

Here, at last, we met the west wind. It came in the form of a full storm, suddenly screeching out of the evening twilight—with a weak, anemic-looking sun, pale and watery, sliding down behind coal-black hammerheads to the west. From the semi-tropical 70 or so, the temperature dropped to less than 50 degrees in an hour, while our barometer, the old-fashioned long-stemmed glass-tube variety, which miraculously still worked, plunged.

Our radio, a small transistor receiver, was playing music from Radio ZBM in Bermuda. If there had been a storm warning we had missed it among all the commercials for soft drinks and king-sized beds. We had listened carefully as the wind whistled overhead and the seas roared by, but we were 250 miles east of Bermuda and the radio emissions were fading at regular intervals to a very weak signal. We donned our woolen jerseys.

By dawn on the tenth of August, we were again hove to, under mizzen only, slowly drifting west, with the wind, up to storm-plus force, raging over a flaying sea. We had tried to run before the storm with a spitfire jib hoisted, a tiny pocket handkerchief of a sail, but the sea movement was so violent, that the twisting, wrenching movement of the hull would cause her to open up even more, that we dared not. Instead we hove to. To this day I am sure I was right to do this, for already the hull was weakening seriously.

The rate of drift to the east I reckoned to be about two knots, around 50 miles a day; and this went on for *11 days!* For 11 days the sea rushed and battered and crashed against the fragile hull of *Quiberon*. For 11 days and nights the wind roared and screeched and tore at the rigging, while Jean-Pierre and I, taking six-hour spells, worked away at the bilge pump—steadily, like a human heart pumping the blood of life.

By the time the wind eased off we were on longitude 51 degrees west. We had drifted 540 miles, but this time the right way—east. We were about 800 miles east of Bermuda, with clearing skies and a rapidly diminishing wind.

Jean-Pierre unlashed the tiller while I prepared to hoist the working jib on the wildly plunging foredeck, holding onto the shrouds like I was welded to them. I dared not trust the guardrails, for *Quiberon*'s gunnels (where the deck joins the sides) were rotten. Already, three guardrail stanchions had collapsed under the weight of seas crashing onboard. I hanked the working jib onto the forestay, all the time with the wind blowing hard around my ears, and half the time up to my knees in cold sea water, whenever the bow plunged into the head seas. Suddenly, through the roar of the wind, I heard Jean-Pierre calling me.

I looked around. He was braced in the cockpit, feet apart, holding his arms out wide with wide-open palms and horror on his face. I lashed the jib to the foot of the forestay, clambered aft, and fell into the cockpit, wet through.

"The rudder, Tristan. The rudder. It's gone!"

"Gone? What the hell are you talking about?" I seized the tiller. It was true. There was no resistance to the movement of the tiller. The violent movement of the hull in the tremendous seas over the past 10 days had worked the rudder loose of its shaft, and it had dropped off.

There we were, in mid-Atlantic, 800 miles from the nearest land, with the wind blowing us away from it, and no rudder!

"*Merde . . . merde!*" wailed Jean-Pierre.

Oh, suffering Christ! said I, quietly, to myself.

Quiberon's rudder was the inboard type; that is, it did not hang over the stern. The rudder shaft went through the bottom of the hull through a gland about four feet forward of the stern and the rudder hung down below the hull. I had never liked this type of rudder because of this very reason: if anything goes wrong with it at sea, it is almost impossible to get at it to effect repairs. I have always, *always* preferred the outboard-hung rudder; that is, one which is connected directly to the stern of the boat. It can be removed, repaired, and replaced at will, and you can always see the state of the rudder and its fittings.

At any rate, a sudden lurch of the boat had sent me flying onto the starboard cockpit seat with a rib-jolting thump.

"*Qu'est-ce que nous faisons maintenant?*" Jean-Pierre shouted over the soughing of the wind and the crash of the seas, the whine of the shrouds and the groans of the tortured hull.

"We *make* a bloody rudder, *mon ami!* We're reasonably safe from the full strength of any maverick hurricanes going east."

"*Comment? Nom de Dieu!*" Jean-Pierre threw his hands out in wild despair. "*Comment nous faisons une nouvelle barre?*"

"There's plenty of wood in the boat. We've got tools, even though they're rusty, and there are enough screws and bolts to build a blasted sports arena. We'll dismantle the berths forward; there's some good mahogany there and plenty of screws. I'll do that while you take the engine to bits and get as many long bolts out of it as you can. Once we've got the berths and the engine in bits we'll see what we can build from that. We can expect a few days of steady weather, so we'll leave her hove to, bows to seas, and just plug away steadily."

"But suppose a strong storm comes up? How will we hold her head to the wind? Is the mizzen enough?"

"If a blow rises we'll put out a sea anchor. Knock out the bottom of that bucket, string it out on all the mooring lines we have, tied together, and that should do the trick. But we won't do that until the blow comes. The mizzen will hold her up to the wind in any reasonable weather."

We set to, working like navvies to dismantle the forward berths and the engine. We were fortunate, for all the while we were doing this the weather was moderating. We worked all that night and until noon the following day, when I found that we had drifted yet another 40 miles to the east. At least we were heading in the direction of Europe, even if it was stern first.

The main cabin was a shambles, with bits of wood and oily engine parts jammed onto the sole (floor) of the compartment. Soon I had two big pieces of fine mahogany, each six feet by two-and-a-half by one inch thick, together with sufficient battens to bolt them together, while Jean-Pierre had several four-inch bolts and the inboard part of the propellor shaft, together with its bearings.

"*Bon*, Jean-Pierre; we'll use the propellor shaft as a rudder post. We'll use the shaft bearings to fix it onto the stern."

Jean-Pierre grabbed the midships stanchion as the boat lurched yet again. "But how do we fix the rudder to the shaft?"

"We'll have to drill right through the shaft, four holes; then bolt two metal plates to it and bolt the metal plates to the wooden jury rudder."

"Plates? What plates?"

"The sides of one of the steel jerry cans will do. Come on, I'll rig the shaft; you saw up the jerry can. We need two plates, eight inches by six."

For two more days, with the boat rocking and yawing, we sawed and drilled, until at last we had the semblance of a rudder hanging from the stern, with the propellor shaft bearings bolted through the transom, the shaft's upper end projecting above the transom just far enough so we could seize it with a large pipe wrench, to use as a tiller. Because the mizzenmast was in the way, it was impossible to lengthen the "tiller" so we could steer from the cockpit. Instead we rigged a system of pulleys on the stern, through which I rove lines each side from the pipe wrench, and by this means, by pulling on the lines, the tiller could be worked from the comparative safety of the cockpit.

As we finished the building of our jury rudder the weather was fine and sunny, with a fresh breeze out of the northwest. I tested the rudder all that afternoon, gradually increasing sail, while Jean-Pierre cleared up the mess below as best he could. We could spare no fresh water for cleaning, and sea water is useless against grease.

Soon we had all working sail up and were going well at four knots on a broad reach. The new rudder, roughly built though it was, steered the boat better than the original. There was now less weather helm; that is, the boat did not continually try to turn her head into the wind. I soon found that she steered herself better with the helm lashed and the main reefed down a touch. We plodded on, resting and eating, trying to recover the strength we had expended in the past few days.

Three good days of moderate, sunny weather followed, and by August 26 I found that we were at 44 degrees west, 35 degrees north. The Azores were almost exactly 1,000 miles due east of us. All we had to do was keep pressing eastward, hopefully afloat.

On the twenty-eighth of August the sky in the northwest

darkened; thunderheads swelled in the ever blackening sky, and soon lightning and the roar of thunder accompanied our curses as we reefed down for yet another gale. This one came out of the north. Due north! A very rare occurrence in mid-Atlantic, if the Maury weather charts, calculated since the 1830s, are anything to go by. A 110 to 1 chance. But down it came: sheet rain, lightning, fierce wind, steepening seas lashing themselves into lunatic rage—and poor old *Quiberon*, again surrendering herself to the gods of the weather, hove to, this time under a *reefed* mizzen, in the brutish wind.

For four days we were bashed and belted, the wind and seas ever increasing in their fury. We were pushed, jolted, pelted, and pummeled *south*. This was of grave concern to me. We were drifting into an area affected by the Azores High: an area where generally there is little wind. The area the square-riggers in the old days avoided like the plague—the Sargasso Sea.

Legend had it ships were seized by the clinging fronds of Sargasso weed, miles long, and—with the crews thirsting and starving to death—rotted away, until they finally sank, dragged to the depths by monsters unimaginable.

But these legends were not the cause for my concern. When this unusual northerly wind dropped, we were liable to be stuck in an area with very slight or no wind at all; and already our food and water stocks were depleted by half. I decided to go onto short rations. The fresh water would be consumed at half a pint each per 12 hours. All cooking was to be done with sea water, not as before: half fresh and half salt.

Dawn of the first of August revealed a sea of slashing white-fanged mad frenzy, with the wind howling down from the north, tearing at the rigging, plucking at every frap of canvas. Jean-Pierre and I, wet through, crawled on all fours over the crazily heaving deck, wrapping extra lines around the sails, clutching onto the guardrails and handholds, the wind seizing us, trying to push us over the side, lifelines tied around our shoulders, each working with one hand, one elbow, and our teeth.

It took us about two hours to wrap a line around the mainsail and lower the boom to reduce top hamper. All the while *Quiberon* writhed and tossed, bucked and bounced, laid over and sprang back before the ever advancing, un-numbered, immeasurable, glowering mighty seas, with the hurricane blasting the gray spume off the crests. A watery blizzard—with cannonades of windspit battering our oil-skins, stabbing our squinting eyes, and ricocheting off the throbbing drum-tight mizzensail—now reefed down to a mere rag. With our feet braced hard against the lee toerail and our bodies splayed low over the coachroof, hanging onto any firm handhold as if we were begging for mercy, we threw the line to each other time and again, gradually wrapping it aft along the boom to safeguard the mainsail against the mighty wind's tearing and clutching.

After what seemed forever, we slithered into the drunk-en cabin and, with the stove rocking on its gimbals like a crazed devil dog, shut the hatch and collapsed, half onto the berths, half on the sole, still clutching onto the midship stanchion, the least frenetic place in the boat.

Jean-Pierre grinned grimly. *"Et maintenant?"* he panted. "What now?"

"Rien, mon ami. Maintenant nous sommes dans les mains du Bon Dieu!" I gasped. "Nothing, my friend; now we're in the hands of God!"

Jean-Pierre grunted. He was a good son of the French Republic, a spiritual descendant of Marat and Robespierre, a confirmed atheist. Somehow he hauled himself onto his feet in that violence and hand-hauled himself to the wildly swinging stove. *"Bon. Donc, moi je vais faire du thé!* Good. Then I'll make some tea!"

I had to smile to myself at this.

Even as he managed to light the stove, after a seeming hour of struggle with damp matches and flaring alcohol primer, suddenly, with a lurch that seemed to stop the world, *Quiberon* lifted up in the air and was thrown sideways with a teeth-jarring crash. Jean-Pierre was slammed across the boat, landing in a heap on the quarter berth. For a few seconds, which seemed to my numbed senses like a century, there was a deathly stillness after the boat lurched upright, a quiet pause, a ghastly lull.

Jean-Pierre and I stared into each other's eyes. We both knew what was happening. We both felt like condemned criminals the moment before the switch is pulled, the second before the trap door is opened, the breath-stopping eternity before the triggers are squeezed. *Quiberon* had broached! She had slid sideways to the mighty seas.

With a mighty roar, sounding to our paralyzed ears and frozen minds as if all the wild animals on earth were about to spring on us, *our* sea, the one that had waited for us all these years, after all these thousands of miles, was upon us! I remember thinking to myself, lying spread-eagled on the cabin deck: *This is it. What a pity I can't see it!* Then, it seemed, the boat tore asunder.

There was a rumble under the roar, a hiss under the rumble, a screech under the hiss, a scream under the screech, and overall an explosion of the wrath of all the forces in the universe. It was like being in the vortex of an implosion. It was as if all the energy in the world was concentrated on *Quiberon* and, through her, passed into my spine, my heart, my soul and mind. It was the essence of destruction shooting into my very being. Here was death, naked and pure. Then came the shock of bare-fanged pandemonium.

With a mighty roar the boat drove downward, downward, *downward*—slowed, juddered, jolted, shivered, halted—rose, was *rising*. Then the coachroof side gave way before the ever ranting roar of monstrous power and I was staring up at the Atlantic Ocean as it gushed through a gap between the sidedeck and the edge of the coachroof, a gap fully a foot wide! The next few eons of time were utter chaos, as the boat filled with cold sea water.

I remember hauling myself onto my knees in that swirling vat of wet, rushing turmoil, then forcing myself upright, to find that Jean-Pierre also had stumbled toward the midship stanchion. In the deafening blasts and blares, the thunder of hell, he grabbed my shoulder.

"*Ca va?*" His voice was rock, steady.

"Okay," I sputtered.

The water was up to our waists. Then we both came to our sailor-senses. At the same moment, we dove toward the bilge pump. Jean-Pierre made it first. It was underwater, but he fumbled for it and started pumping. I made for the hatch and scrabbled it open. Then I slid back into the freezing water and groped in the galley for a bucket.

There followed an effort, a wild reach for the right to *live*, of which the memory is blurred. I know that Jean-Pierre stuck to the pump while I bailed water out of the cabin through the hatch like a madman for several minutes, until I realized that I would have to deal with the hole in the deck.

I staggered through the cabin and, after heaving a ton of jumbled gear out of the way, dragged the mattresses out of the forward cabin, one at a time—hauling them out, tying a lifeline around me as I clambered up the ladder, hefting a mattress with me out onto the pounding deck, the wind screeching. Somehow, I rammed the two mattresses into the gap, beating at them like a maniac until they were jammed in. Then, as best I could, I surveyed the scene on deck.

Quiberon was a shambles but, thank God, the rigging had held, except that the starboard mainmast spreader had collapsed. The deckhouse, doghouse, or coachroof (call it what you will) had been smashed in on the port side, but the starboard side had held. The hurricane was still raging, but now it was of secondary importance. What mattered now was to survive!

The first thing was to secure the top half of the mast, which was whipping around like a crazed conductor's baton. Somehow I hauled myself against the ramming wind to the mainmast and, hardly able to command my shaking finger, untied the main halyard. This I hastily yet carefully led to the starboard chainplates, where the rigging wires were fixed to the deck. This was dangerous, for the loose upper shroud was flogging around like the flaying hind hoof of a dying steer, but I managed to get to windward of it, then secured the main halyard as taut as I could to the forward-shroud deckfitting. I captured the loose shroud with a short length of line and, with a struggle, secured it.

Next I scrambled to the after end of the boom, which had been lowered onto the coachroof before the disaster, and with a herculean effort unshackled the topping lift, all the while clinging to the handrail, with the wind and spray slashing like a million rapiers. I crawled forward to the starboard chain plates and secured the topping lift, again as taut as I could. Thus the masthead was reasonably anchored on the starboard side. I squinted aloft against the flogging, flailing spreader. Time to deal with that when the weather eases off, I thought.

Through some miracle, the mizzen had survived the battering and was still holding the boat up to the wind.

Satisfied that I had given God as much help as I could aloft, I crawled back down below. Jean-Pierre was keeping a steady, agonizing, panting pace at the bilge pump, and the level had dropped about six inches. In the violence below I set to with the bucket again, steadily throwing oily sea water into the cockpit, where it would drain away.

Later, I reckoned that the stove-in happened at 9 A.M. By the time we got the boat reasonably clear of water it was 4 P.M., and obvious that the storm had done its worst. The wind was easing off, though the seas were still like restless mountains.

Jean-Pierre had kept a steady stroke at the pump for seven hours solid when I relieved him at four o'clock. Then I stayed at the pump for four hours, and so it continued for the two of us all that night: four hours pumping, four hours repairing damage. The following morning, exhausted, with the wind at a comparatively mild 40 knots and the boat riding safely though violently, we both collapsed for three hours, to sleep.

"What about the spreader?" asked Jean-Pierre, before closing his drooping eyelids. "When are we going to fix it?"

"Later," I mumbled. "Our first need is sleep, then some grub when we wake. Then we'll tackle the spreader, Okay?"

"You're the boss," he murmured, half asleep.

By the evening of the second, when we woke, the weather was moderating even more, and by the morning of the third, after another night of pumping, sleeping, pumping, sleeping, it was down to 20 knots and the seas had flattened out enough so we could tackle the spreader.

"Who's going up?" asked Jean-Pierre, staring at the wildly weaving mast.

"We'll toss a coin; that's the only fair way."

I flicked a coin, retrieved from the odds and sods box in the navigation locker, and, hoping it would turn up tails (heads is always the skipper's side), watched it bounce onto the hatch coaming. Tails!

"Your privilege, Jean-Pierre."

"*Phut!*"

He tied the safety harness around the mast, secured the canvas pouch for tools around his waist, and started to clamber up the weaving mast with a new spreader, which we had cut and shaped the previous day, tied around his neck. It took him six hours to fix the new spreader in place, but by late afternoon the mast was safe again and we gingerly hoisted the mainsail to try it out.

While this was going on, I had nailed down six yards of heavy canvas over the mattress-filled gap in the deck and shored up the mattresses from below with a plank of wood cut from the cabin shelves and most of the cabin floor-

169

boards. Then I bolted three floorboards across the deckhouse coamings to add rigidity to the hull, normally afforded by the deckhouse.

Topsides and below, *Quiberon* was a devastated ruin. In any yacht basin or marina in the world she would have been beached and burned out for her metal fittings. But we were in mid-Atlantic and, wreck or no, must get her to her destination. She was our lives!

Jean-Pierre put the last bolt in place on the spreader and tightened the last rigging screw on the starboard shrouds. His face flushed with effort and pride in a difficult, arduous, dangerous job well done, he announced as I handed him a mug of soup: *"Moi, je ne crois pas ce miracle!"*

He sat in the cockpit, with a wan sun at long last shining in the west, and stared around at the floating, patched-up shipwreck of the crippled *Quiberon*, then squinted up at the sails which were pulling her at long last toward the east again.

"Don't believe what?" I asked as I spooned the hot soup.

"I don't believe we are still alive." He trailed off, dipping a hardtack biscuit into the steaming ox-tail bouillon.

"Jean-Pierre, the gods love those who die young. You'll be all right; you've got the Devil on your side."

He laughed, gripped his cup between his knees, and gave the jib sheet another few inches of easing.

Quiberon lurched on. East.

Quiberon was at 43 degrees west, 30 degrees north. Steadily she pounded over the moderating ocean seas, east-northeast for five days, with either Jean-Pierre or me pumping away for 30 minutes out of the hour right around the clock. Then, on the eleventh of September, the wind shifted around to the west, its normal direction, and we made good time due east for another five days.

On the fifteenth of September, to our utter surprise, we got a blow out of the *south*. In the area of the Azores this is about as rare as a snowstorm in San Diego. I was thankful, for it put the damaged deck away from the weather. This gale, however, was short lived and soon the wind veered again to the west, so that on the eighteenth of September, exactly two months after we left Antigua, we clawed our way into the narrow entrance of the tiny harbor of Fayal, on the island of Horta in the Azores.

It was midnight when we tied up at the broken-down jetty, weary to the bone but thanking all the gods for our safe arrival. After the police had entered the boat into Portuguese territory, we collapsed and slept the sleep of honest toil and utter relief, though the boat bumped the stone jetty all night.

Next day, bright and early, I went around the small harbor, called on my old friend, Don Enrique, at the Bar Sport, and explained our plight. Don Enrique was happy to see me and gave me all the news of the boats that had passed through during the previous five years. (The numbers were increasing steadily year by year, as transatlantic sailing became more and more popular among a growing number of ocean sailors.)

Soon, arrangements were made to careen *Quiberon* (that is, take her out of the water) by dragging her up the ramp at the Horta whale-fletching station. We handled her just like they handled a whale, which hand-harpooners hunt in those waters. The fletching crew shackled a cable around *Quiberon*, then I dangled both her anchors and all her chain from the masthead to heel her over to starboard, an angle of 50 degrees from the vertical. The steam winch whirred, the cable tautened, and within five minutes she was high and dry on her side on the whale-fletching ramp, which was reeking with the blood and guts of the last great sperm, caught three days previously. The whole area stank to high heaven.

All day we toiled, strengthening the makeshift rudder, recaulking the garboard seam (where the keel joins the hull). All day and most of the night I caulked, while Jean-Pierre scraped off our two-month collection of barnacles and other marine life from the bottom planking.

On the morning of the twentieth we lowered *Quiberon* back down the ramp. A dead whale, a monster well over 100 feet long, was moored offshore, waiting to be hauled up the ramp as we slid down.

The next day we spent repairing the side of the cabin coachroof with the aid of two whalers. It was a rough job, but strong. Jean-Pierre made a quick tour of the local shops for a week's supply of fresh food. A hurried topping of the water tanks, two beers apiece in the Bar Sport, and we were off again, headed direct for Ushant, an island off the northwest corner of France.

On the eastern side of the Azores we got mainly fine weather all the way, with no winds over 30 knots and very few below 20. The distance direct from Horta to Ushant is 1,500 miles. *Quiberon* logged only 1,650, which shows how steady the wind direction was. We made the distance in 18 days, picking up the mighty, welcome flash of the Ushant light (one of the most powerful lighthouses in the world) on the evening of October 8.

With the wind still blowing steadily from the southwest, I decided to make straight for Cherbourg. We had good stocks of food and a third of our water supply still in the tanks. I headed east-northeast. Within sight of Guernsey, in the Channel Islands, the wind dropped to a flat calm! The gods still played with *Quiberon*.

For eight days we sat there, drifting back and forth on the strong Channel tides, as much as 25 miles east and west, as the tide flowed and ebbed into and out of the English Channel. At last, 10 miles north of Alderney, we found ourselves within hailing distance of a French trawler out of Cherbourg.

"Bonjour, M'sieurs!" shouted the skipper, leaning out of the wheelhouse, as his crew of four (two young boys and two old men) stared at us, bemused. I left the talking to Jean-Pierre.

"*Bonjour, Capitaine!* Where are you going? Can you give us a tow toward Cherbourg?"

"Where have you come from?" the skipper shouted through his cupped hands, as he gazed at the ravaged hull of *Quiberon*.

"Cayenne, Guiana, by way of the Azores!" Jean-Pierre hollered.

I heard it plainly over the calm, mirrorlike water from all five fishermen: "*Alors!*"

They threw a line over but it fell into the sea. "*Putain!*" they cursed in unison.

Jean-Pierre fell on deck to grab it over the side, out of the water.

"*Leave* it, Jean-Pierre." I called. "Leave his line; don't touch it! I want no claims for salvage. Throw him our line, but first fix a price with him."

"How much will you charge to haul us into Cherbourg, *M'sieur?*" shouted Jean-Pierre.

"Ah, nothing. I'll tell you what, *mes amis*—do you have any whisky on board?"

"I have two bottles of rum," I said (the only two unbroken bottles onboard).

"Okay, I'll tow you in at five knots for one bottle. It's only 18 miles." (French sailors use the *mile*, not the *kilometer*, which goes to show how unnatural the metric system is.)

"Done!" I gave him the thumbs-up sign. "Jean-Pierre, cast him the line!"

"*Bien sûr!*" he called as he heaved the line away.

And so we were pulled into Cherbourg on October 17, 1964—104 days after setting out from Cayenne. We had spent 99 days at sea, in a craft hardly fit for an afternoon's sail, with no engine and more than three weeks of wind over gale force. Our rate of pay, including the refit time in Cayenne, was $7 a day! With food, say $10 a day.

The name of the fishing boat that towed us in was *La Vie C'est Dure* (Life Is Hard). Very fitting, I thought.

We were met at the yacht club jetty by my old friend

Marcel Bardiaux. Then, I telegraphed M. Pinet, the owner of *Quiberon*, news of our arrival, made arrangements for the yacht club attendants to pump his boat out every day, and accompanied Jean-Pierre to the railway station to see him off for Brest.

"You'll get your money in the mail this week, Jean-Pierre. If you don't, telegraph me at the yacht club and I'll make sure you do. If that bastard Pinet doesn't cough up, I'll come back to Cherbourg and personally sink that bloody floating death trap!"

Jean-Pierre laughed. "Tristan, you are absolutely crazy, but . . . " He didn't finish, just grinned.

"So long, Jean-Pierre; I couldn't have done it without you. I'd sail with you anywhere, anytime, but as sure as hell not in bloody *Quiberon!*"

The train left, headed for Brittany, and I returned to the yacht club, where Marcel had arranged a small room for me to sleep in while I waited for the local boatyard to take charge of *Quiberon*. M. Pinet made arrangements to pay me in Spanish pesetas on my arrival in Barcelona. It seemed to be, after all, only a currency "fiddle."

Marcel Bardiaux, about 13 years before, had made a west-about circumnavigation of the world in a home-built 31-footer, the famous *Les 4 Vents*, by way of the Horn—the "wrong way" around the Horn, against winds and currents. His sloop capsized twice when approaching that lonely, wild cape-island. His adventures are described in his excellent book, *4 Winds of Adventure*, which he had published four years earlier, in '61. Marcel was a dark, broody-looking man, with a hungry stare but with a great sense of humor.

Next day, as we sat in the Cherbourg Yacht Club, gazing through the wide windows at the rain whistling in a high wind across the gray, cold harbor, he described how he had smashed into an uncharted reef 65 miles out to sea from Nouméa, New Caledonia, in the South Pacific, and how he had kedged *Les 4 Vents* off the cruel, jagged reef by walking out with his anchor over the smashing surf for days on end. When he finally got her off, by the strength of his arms, he had sailed the boat to Nouméa, passing 27 wrecked craft on the way in! When he arrived in the tiny, hot, tropical port, it was with his decks awash and the boat almost sunk.

I stayed with Marcel for a week or so, exchanging yarns and looking over the new ketch he was building, a large, comfortable 60-footer, and meeting his friends. I was so anxious to get back to *Cresswell* and Nelson that I decided against a quick trip to England. I bade *adieu* to Marcel and made my way back to Toulouse.

As I got out of the taxi on the bridge of the boat basin, Nelson saw me and, throwing his head in the air, woofing, hobbled slowly up to me. I dropped my seabag and fondled his neck while he wagged his tail like a young puppy. I took Nelson into an *estaminet* for some bock beer, which he loved, but I could see by the way he was bumping into things that his one good eye was not so good anymore.

The barman, a cocky sod, said to me: "That dog's a nuisance. I don't want him in here."

"*A ton face, crapaud!* Up your arse, Jack!"

We turned round and walked out, slamming the door. Nelson looked up at me, his black ears twitching, and I could see that his good eye was much duller than it had been. He wagged his tail as we walked back onboard in the rain.

"Don't you take any notice, old son. We'll soon be in the sun and sailing the sea again." I tickled his ear. "Want some burgoo, boy?"

As soon as he heard the word "burgoo," he brightened up. I unlocked the companionway hatch and in a few minutes had a good pot of the gooey mess steaming away. All the while his tail waved and wagged, bumping the ladder and the stove, and I cursed the barman, thinking of the time Nelson had saved my life on the trip to Iceland, and how he had stuck by me through thick and thin, and guarded *Cresswell* so faithfully while I was away.

"Well, my old mooch," I said to him, as he scoffed the burgoo eagerly, "it looks like you haven't got long to go." I tickled his ear again. There was a scab on the back of his head and he was drooling. "But by Christ we'll have another sail before you pack off—and get some of the Mediterranean sunshine." Again, his tail wagged.

That evening I went to M. DuPont's house. Dod Osborne was ill and in the hospital in England; Joe had completed the repairs to DuPont's boat and had returned home to the Isle of Man; and *Cresswell* was the only non-French boat in Toulouse. During November I delivered M. DuPont's boat now more shipshape than ever, to Marseilles, along with Nelson, then returned to *Cresswell*.

After Christmas I started the slow voyage down the rest of the Canal du Midi, so as to arrive on the Mediterranean coast in the spring of '65. From there I would sail to Barcelona and pick up the money due for the *Quiberon* delivery. There was no rush, so I took my time getting *Cresswell* ready.

The first stage of the tedious canal trip was to Villefranche, a small town about 25 miles south of the city. It was tedious because, after the first novelty of chugging along the narrow, poplar-tree-lined waterway, as straight as an arrow, it became monotonous. However, even in February the weather was fine and sunny, and I looked over the fields and low, vine-planted hills to the east and saw the snow-covered Pyrenees in the far distance.

On the second day, after an evening at the canalside *estaminet* at Villefranche, I headed for Castelnaudary, a town on the main road route from Paris to Spain. Just outside the town is a wide basin in the canal and set in the middle of the basin is a little green island. As *Cresswell* chugged into this basin, with wild ducks flitting across the water, and the Pyrenees shining to the southwest, in sunshine and warmth, I made up my mind to stay for a week or so.

I walked into town, met some of the people in the bars, and found the place crowded with lasses from all over

Europe, studying French at the local college. What with the friendly, hospitable people, their good sense of humor, their superlative cooking, their fine wines, and the peculiarities of the sex ratio, I decided to stay moored up to the island and let the canal world pass me by (at the rate of one or two barges per day). I heard the song of the sirens and *loved* it.

One good thing about being in paradise: you don't see, or even think of, snags until they crop up. So it was with me, and for two whole months I worked desultorily onboard during the day, making good the ravages of twelve months' neglect. In the evening I wallowed in the fleshpots of a fair-sized French provincial town. It was one of the happiest, most carefree periods I have known. There was no indication at all that doomsday was near.

The only *navigateur* I met at Castelnaudary was an English naturalist who was canoeing through the canal system of France. Except for some imported nuts, he was actually living off the land—collecting different kinds of grasses and leaves and making very good salads. The diet seemed to have done a good job because this gentleman was one of the toughest, fittest men I ever clapped eyes on. He was an excellent raconteur and hated Freud and Hegel, so we're birds of a feather.

During the day I worked on the boat, the sails, or the engine, taking Nelson with me for a sedate walk to the pub at the main crossroads in the evening. There I chatted with the locals for an hour or two over Pernod, then went to the restaurant for a fine meal, rendered with the simple elegance found only in that part of the world. On Saturdays and Sundays some local acquaintances came out to visit us. There were a couple of lads who sailed small dinghies on the canal basin, and I helped them repair their boats and tried to improve their sailing. Twice I took trips on the fast train to Paris, to look up friends, but always I longed to be back in Castelnaudary, amid the peace and quiet, with the fish leaping in the evening and the ducks' dawn flapping, the tall trees rustling overhead in the gentle breezes, the church bell tolling on the quiet evenings, and the massive Pyrenees gleaming—silver in the dawn, gold in the evening—across the clear-air vineyards of the Aude. So the quiet spring passed.

Suddenly and irrevocably, this crystal-pure Nirvana, this sailor's dream, this hard-earned oasis of peace was shattered into a thousand fragments.

It was early, early. Outside the fields and the grassy canalside walk were soggy with dew like tiny diamonds, scattered over green baize, and rain clouds broke now and then to let the sun touch the Pyrenees. *Cresswell* rocked gently as a slow barge pushed through the calm waters of the basin, toting her cargo of Algerian wine from the bustling jetties of Marseilles.

Down below, all was quiet. Nelson was sleeping in his usual place, just forward of the saloon table. I was embraced with a cozy little friend, in hot sweet breath and blankets, while on the cabin table the bottom inch of the wine in last night's bottle shimmered in the pale-dawn light.

"I say there! *Cresswell!* Ahoy! Come along, Tristan, shake a leg. Shake a jolly old leg there!"

I stirred heavily.

"Come *along*, theah!" A loud bang on the doghouse roof. "Wakey-wakey!" Thump! Thump!

I opened one eye. Nelson was balanced with his forefoot against the companionway ladder, growling.

"Come along, my jolly hearty!" The voice was piercing.

"*Qu'est-ce qu'il y a?*" I asked my friend.

"*C'est rien, mon petit chou, c'est rien. Dors-tu!*" I nestled close.

"Hullo theah, h'loo theah! Tristan! Tristaaaaaan!" Another bang on the doghouse.

I woke and shouted: "*Qu'est-ce qu'il y a?*"

"Tristan, old bean, it's *me*. Cecilia St. John. You know . . . I met you in Antigua, back in July lawst yeah!"

"*Nom de Dieu!*" whispered the little cabbage.

"Oh shit!" said I, clambering out of bed and donning my trousers. "Bloody, flaming, satanic, bleeding, goddam, hell!"

"*Quoi?*" my little rose asked.

"*C'est rien du tout. Attends!* It's nothing. Wait!"

I clambered up the ladder, opened the hatch door, and peered out, eyes full of sleep, into the gray drizzle of the morning, with the trees of France weeping at my fate. Standing there with brogued feet thrust apart, a dirty gray raincoat over a herringbone tweed skirt well down to her calves, her ginger hair drooping and dripping under a soggy English district nurse's brimmed hat, complete with bedraggled partridge feather at halfmast, her crabapple cheeks shining with the threat of rosy health, was Sissie, the bishop of Southchester's sister. In one hand she was holding a great leather explorer's traveling bag and in the other, streaming with rain, a tennis racket, a folded umbrella, and a hockey stick.

"Hello, Sissie. *Comment ça va?*" My surprise was so complete that I could not think of the English greeting.

"What-o, old chap, lovely day *what?* Had a *ghastly* ride down. Got a lift with a little Frenchman, *terribly* boring. He couldn't speak a *blawsted* word of English and he couldn't understand my French. But then I'm not surprised, neither can I—what, old chap? But Tristan, my deah, how *are* you?"

She was coming onboard! Those great brown brogue boots were actually on *Cresswell*'s deck. She was dripping her way down the ladder. I fell or staggered back, into the cabin, as her beige-stockinged legs clomped into the cabin, like a medieval baron descending dank stone stairs to visit deep dungeons. Sissie slammed her great leather bag on the cabin deck, where it subsided like a tired, wet rhinoceros, then slung her racket and hockey stick down on my berth.

Ma petite choute jumped up with a cry of astonishment at the violence of Sissie's throw. Her fragile, doll-like, silky-smooth arms, her golden hair, her canto shoulders, her dove-feather throat, her kitten-cuddling breasts, her Dresden tummy, the winking eye of her delicious delicate navel —all revealed as she threw her hands in the air and grabbed at me, shouting *"Au secours, mon amour!"* Then she turned around, terrified, to stare at Sissie, the British country woman compleat, looking like Florence Nightingale at the storming of the Alma Redoubt, like Mrs. Gladstone receiving one of the Grand Old Man's Piccadilly stragglers, like Britannia, the terrible Queen of the Sea herself, awful in the majesty of wrath, the revenge of Boadicea in her dagger-steel blue eyes—to see Sissie gazing at her as Queen Victoria would have gazed at a loose toilet roll in the Windsor Castle music room.

I cringed in the tiny space between the kerosene stove and the potato locker, upsetting the pan of bacon-burgoo, which slithered down the bulkhead. Nelson, petrified, stared dimly through his good eye, while the underwear of *ma petite choute,* like the drooping shirts of the defeated, abject Burghers of Calais, dangled in disgrace from the top of the navigation table. In the awful silence, even *Cresswell* seemed to tremble with shame before the accusing eye of the Dragon of Devon.

Sissie broke the silence, her bayonet-sharp tones cutting the calm morning of the Aude clear to the Pyrenees.

"Tristan, I think this little expedition needs some *moral support,* so I'm joining you." Her teeth looked as strong and white as the Cliffs of Dover gleaming through a Channel fog.

"Awfter awl!" she continued, eyeing my companion, who stood shivering naked, "Awfter awl, you *did* invaite me, you know!" She plonked herself on the berth, heavily, her umbrella at shoulder arms.

The honeymoon was over. Paradise was lost. Irretrievably, immutably, irrevocably. The English had arrived all right and with a vengeance!

Nelson whimpered.

BREAKDOWN

This is one of the few stories I have written about powered vessels, in this case a tramp steamer bringing a load of mutton from New Zealand to England. It is based on a true incident that was briefly described in the Sea-Going Engineer's Handbook *for 1889. Do not let the Victorian language put you off. That is the way that ships' officers actually spoke in those days. I am sure of that because I was brought up among them. "Breakdown" is another example of the Welsh storytelling technique known as* crwn. *There are no prizes for guessing who the narrator is in the first few pages, but if you can guess correctly, then you surely know something about maritime literature. The story was published in* Sea Breezes *in England in 1980.*

I am tempted to tell this story in the form of a novel, but I am wary that the notion might get around that I had been bolted away with. Some reviewers might maintain that a work starting as a short story had got beyond the writer's control. So this story, of a man who was tested by the dark vindictiveness of fate—and who failed the test—I shall tell as briefly as many years' practice of making entries into ships' log books enables me to do.

There is nothing more enticing, disenchanting, and enslaving than the life at sea, not even for an engineer on ships steadily plying, year after year, on the "mutton run" —from damp fogs of England out to the bright islands of New Zealand with general goods, and home again with 50,000 frozen sheep carcasses. The hopes and dreams of a new nation must be sustained, and the toiling masses at home must be fed with good, cheap meat.

The usual route of the voyage was out and back around the Horn. But in mid-1892 the ship owners had contracted for *Rangapui* to haul 10,000 mutton carcasses to Singapore for the British army garrison, on her way home. Besides, the owner's chairman's newly married son and his bride were at Singapore and wished to return home. I had made the newlywed couple's acquaintance in the Raffles Hotel, and accepted their invitation to accompany them back to England. I had been in the islands for some years, "knocking about" in tramp-ships; I had made many voyages. I knew the magic monotony of existence between sky and water. I had had to bear the criticisms of men, the exactations of the sea, and the prosaic severity of the daily task that gives bread—but whose only reward is in the absolute love of the work. That reward had eluded me, even though I had reached for, and gained, chief mate's certificate some years before. I had never been, nor witnessed others, tested by those events of the sea that show in the light of day the inner worth of a man, the fitness of his temper, the fiber of his being; that reveal the worth of his resistance and the secret truth of his pretenses, not only to others but also to himself.

In steamships that truth is not made apparent so often as people might think. There are many degrees to the danger of adventures and storms, and it is only now and then that there appears to be a sinister violence of intention—that indefinable something that forces itself upon the mind and the heart of a man as furies coming at him with malice, with a strength beyond control, with an unbridled cruelty that means to tear out of him his hope and pride, the pain of his fatigue and his longing to rest. Only once in all my years at sea did I glimpse a storm meant to smash, to destroy, to annihilate all a man had seen, known, loved or hated; all that was priceless and necessary, the joys, the memories, the future, his pride in his work—which means to tear the whole precious world away from him by the simple act of taking away from him his reason to live.

The *Rangapui's* cargo for Singapore was soon off-loaded. The Chinese and Malay coolies, each with their own two gangways, streamed aboard with a continuous shuffle of bare feet, without a word, a murmur, or a look around. They picked up their two carcasses each, and plodded back down their own gangways to the great go-downs on the quay. Together with their two mutton carcasses, they were each swallowed, one by one, by the black gaping door of the shed.

The captain and crew of the *Rangapui* looked upon the coolies with sympathetic eyes, it seemed to me, and yet there was an undefinable hardness about them. The other white men in port, who sailed the islands, had, in the main, been thrown there by accident, and had remained as officers on local ships owned by natives, Chinese, Sumatran, Javanese, and Malayan. They now, mostly, had a horror of home service with its harder conditions, severer view of duty, and the hazard of stormy oceans. They were attuned to the eternal peace of the island skies and seas. They loved short passages, good deck chairs, large native crews, and the distinction of being white. They shuddered at the thought of hard work and led precariously easy lives, always on the point of dismissal, always on the point of engagement by local owners. They would have served the devil himself if he had made it easy enough. The *Rangapui's* captain and crew had none of this about them. Duty hovered about them like the ghost of an ironmaster.

Captain McTaggart of the *Rangapui* was a tall, thin, ascetic man of about sixty, who spoke mainly in words of one or two syllables. After a lifetime at sea, thirty of them under sail, this was his last voyage. He was as gloomy and cold as his native Clydeside at some times, and at others as brusque and coldly witty as the winds that whip the Horn.

"Ye'll have your meals with us, mister." He said to me soon after I first boarded in Singapore. "The chief mate, the chief engineer, the two . . . lovebirds" here he glanced at the owner's son, who sat, with his bride beside him, on the two deck chairs under the shade of the midships bridge, "and myself. The second engineer is sick. We're having to leave him here; can't find a replacement."

Conversation at the captain's table was stilted—some would say dull. The presence of the bride may have had a bearing on this, but I doubt it. The chief mate, when he was not on duty during mealtime, was a saturnine man, self-educated and morose. The chief engineer, Briggs, was mostly engrossed in his work, and brightened up only when the technicalities of steam were mentioned, which was seldom. The owner's son was engaged mainly in criticizing what he saw as wasteful practices onboard, while his young wife was for the most part silent, though pleasantly so. I myself did what I thought might brighten up the conversation around the table by recounting my various adventures and misadventures during my years sailing among the islands. The woman's presence, at least before she retired to her cabin, precluded my telling the more scandalous tales. With the protagonists well disguised, of course, for the sake of discretion, I told of piracy on the China coast, of warfare in the islands among the native rulers, and of the various breakdowns of machinery in some of the rusty hulks in which I had served—fallen-off rudders, sheared-off propellor shafts, exploded boilers and the like—and of how repairs had been effected using the brute physical strength of the native seamen, of whom we always shipped a crowd, and the ingenuity of the white officers, those who were not already ruined by idleness and drink. These stories served as entertainment, I like to think, for most of the passage up the Straits of Malacca and across the Bay of Bengal. The chief engineer, Briggs, in particular, always cocked his ears and brightened up when the subject of one of my yarns was a mechanical jury-rig on some stopped and floundering old hulk of a vessel that, years before, should have, by rights, ended her days in a breaker's yard.

About the voyage home until the breakdown I will say little. It was an average twixt-monsoon run. The Arabian

Sea lay like a leaden sheet under a blazing sun by day, and glistened like a million scimitars below a billion shivering stars at night. In a local ship there would have been awnings covering the deck with a white roof for protection from the sun. *Rangapui*, though, was fitted out only for the cold Southern Ocean and the breezier tropics of the Atlantic, and so the three passengers and the crew sheltered as best they could, while the days—still, hot, heavy—disappeared one by one into the past, as if they were descending into an abyss forever open in the wake of the ship. The ship, lonely under a wisp of smoke, held on her way, black and smouldering in a luminous vastness, as if she were scorched by a brazier reflected at her from a heaven without compassion.

The nights descended on her like a cool blessing.

We had just passed through the Bab-El-Mandeb, into the Red Sea.

Briggs, the chief engineer, was an inch, perhaps two, under six feet. He was powerfully built, and as I sat with the newlyweds in the cool of the deck under the bridge wings, he advanced at me like a charging bull. His voice was quiet, urgent, and strained.

"Will you come down below and give me a hand? I've a spot of bother with one of the refrigerator compressors. There's a boiler suit behind the door in my cabin. The third engineer's too young..."

"Of course I will, old chap," I replied as he, with a hurried "thank you" rushed off again to the engine room companionway.

As I donned the boiler suit in the tossed disorder of the engineer's cabin I reflected on what I had seen of the engineers routine, on how the chief and third engineers—there were now only two of them—kept six-hour watches, watch on and watch off, for the whole time the ship had frozen cargo onboard. The smooth running of the three ammonia compressors was essential if the tens of thousands of frozen sheep carcasses were to survive the two months' voyage through the tropics safely. And with mutton at five pounds a carcass (I did a quick calculation in my head) that was 40,000 carcasses remaining onboard—a quarter of a million pounds worth of meat. (American readers note: at the then current rate of exchange, this was the equivalent of *one-and-an-eighth million dollars*!) All in the hands of two persons—one a man whose only education had been five years of rote-repeating in the village church school and a three-year apprenticeship in the local blacksmith's shop, and the other, a pimply youth of eighteen now on his first voyage.

Within a matter of minutes I was down at the bottom of the engine room ladder. All around was the smell of steam and oil. The great gleaming main engines thudded up and down, up and down. Beyond them, through the stoke-hold doorway, I caught a glimpse of a scene from the inferno—a momentary impression of sweating bodies wielding coal-laden shovels into the open doors of the boiler furnace. Briggs was pacing the engine room plates. He seemed calm enough, only he stumbled several times; and once as I stood listening to him over the roar of the machinery he walked right into me as though he had been stone blind.

"What shall I do?" he shouted. "There's three compressors down here, as you see, all steam driven. Number one compressor has broken down. I saw a crack in the crank web, and the key sheared off the other driving eccentric, blinded one steam-entry port, and got a full blast of steam on the other end of the piston. The piston went with a bang, and completely broke the fractured crank web, causing a complete breakdown."

"Where's the third engineer?" I asked him. Even as I spoke a small, thin boy, dressed in a boiler suit, reached the bottom of the ladder. His hair was in disarray and he was rubbing his sleep-laden eyes. I had noticed him hurrying around the deck on a few occasions, silently, like a grubby wraith.

"This is Craig" the engineer said, hurriedly. "What shall we do? Will you assist me to start up number three compressor?"

As we opened up steam to number three, the middle compressor, number two, was working smoothly, even though it was now having to do the work of two machines. We soon shut all the steam connections to number one compressor, and the rest, such as the injection, the feeds, and suctions, and the freezing pipes, to the meat-holds, while all the pipes to number two compressor were open everywhere. Carefully, we examined all around and thoroughly oiled every part of number three compressor, then opened all the connections except the throttle, which was just eased off by Briggs, just eased off to allow enough steam to pass through to warm up number three's cylinders before starting the compressor. Briggs started the engine slowly, the perspiration streaming down his face. The engine turned on its centers for a few minutes, at the same time as Briggs's face brightened. Then, with a grin he opened the throttle full and number three took half of the load from the panting number two compressor.

"Good, looks alright," Briggs shouted in my ear. "Now, how shall we fix the broken crank of number one?"

"Perhaps we can forge a strap or belt around the bottom crank?"

Briggs looked at me with tired eyes. "That should do the trick" he said. "I'll be off to look for a suitable piece of iron. He turned to Craig, "You keep a steady eye out 'til I get back, now laddie."

"Aye aye," replied Craig.

"I'll start work on a rekey on the eccentric if you like, chief" I offered.

"Yes, I'll appreciate that," said Briggs as he headed up the ladder.

Minutes later he was back. "I've looked all over the ship," he shouted. "The only iron I can find that might do the job is this hatchway crossbar." He laid the heavy bar down on the deck plates.

"Craig!" the chief engineer shouted.

"Chief?"

"Nip up to the bridge and tell the skipper we need some hands down here."

Craig did as he was bidden, and was soon back in the hellishly hot engine room, shortly followed by the six ship's apprentices—"my boys" as the captain called them. Very shortly, we were ready to commence operations. The first job was to force the broken crank boss off the shaft end; but as the boss was keyed flush we could not draw the key, so we tried to wedge it off. All our wedging was to no avail, try as we might; the shaft was too cold.

"We'll have to warm the shaft" I said to Briggs.

"How can we do that?" Briggs almost sobbed.

"Get an old can and put some oily waste rags in it and paraffin."

"That's a good idea ... Craig!"

"Chief?"

"Do as the gentleman says," Briggs could hardly get the words out.

"Aye aye."

After the shaft had been heated up amid stabs of flame and clouds of greasy smoke, and two of the sturdier apprentices had clouted the boss with hammers, it started to come off the shaft. All the while this went on we all, although nothing about it was said, had in our mind's eye the vision of what would happen, in this heat, to the 40,000 frozen carcasses in the cargo hold, should the other compressors, for any reason, fail. Both the chief engineer and I glanced at the two pounding machines at frequent intervals, to reassure ourselves that they were running well enough to provide enough refrigerant to the mountain of meat.

Finally, after much sweaty persuasion, the boss came off the shaft, and we then started to take the eccentric strap and rod apart. With the aid of luff-blocks and spanners we soon got the huge eccentric rod off the sheave, and the pin out from the valve double eye (or fork end, as the British call it). Now the next job was to get the sheave off. This was a difficult task, with the gear that was available to us, and we stood around it, all nine of us, discussing how it would be done. The chief engineer was now much less agitated than he had been, for he could see that there was a good possibility that the defective compressor would soon be back "on the line." He sat down, wearily, on the bottom step of the engine room ladder.

Now, as I write slowly about what happened in the next few minutes, I remember swiftly and with extreme vividness; I could try to reproduce, like echoes, the sharp clang of the machine and the moan of the engineer for the better information of those of my readers who want the facts, but after my first feeling of revolt I have come round to the view that only a meticulous precision of statement would bring out the true horror behind the apalling face of things. The facts, my reader might be so eager to know, had been visible to me, tangible, open to my senses, occupying their place in space and time, requiring for their existence an 1800-ton steamer and twenty-five minutes by the watch. They made a whole that had features, shades of expression, a complicated aspect that could be remembered by the eye, and something else besides, something invisible, a directing spirit of perdition that dwelt within, like a malevolent soul in a detestable body. I am anxious to make this clear. This was not a common affair, everything in it was of importance, and fortunately I remember everything. I want to go on writing about the matter for truth's sake, perhaps for my own sake also. While my writing is slow and deliberate, my mind positively flies round and round the serried circle of facts that surge up all about me to cut me off from the rest of my kind. I am like a creature that, finding itself imprisoned, within an enclosure of high stakes, dashes round and round, distracted in the night, trying to find a weak spot, a crevice, a place to scale, some opening through which it may squeeze itself and escape. This awful activity of mind makes me hesitate at times as I write . . .

On the bare face of the matter, the facts were plain. As the rest of us stood around perspiring, number three compressor made the sort of noise that a spring might make when it would break and, as we watched, amazed, it seized up with a bang. The chief engineer's moan could be heard clearly, even above the noise of the thudding main engine.

The third engineer and myself immediately sprang over to the stopped machine. Nothing had overheated. I told Craig to shut the steam-stop-valve, and as he did so we heard Briggs shout, "The meat . . . *the meat.*" We looked around to see him flailing his arms around, his eyes staring wildly about. Then he staggered over to the stopped compressor and, gibbering, pointed one shaking, quivering finger at the cause of the mishap—the crank-boss had cracked fore and aft on its shaft.

As Briggs stood there, jabbering and howling, all the load was shifted onto number two compressor, and with a grinding wheeze, it halted. Now there was only the steady thud of the main engine, the roar of the boiler on the far side of the bulkhead, the excess steam blowing off loudly, and Brigg's screaming about the spoiled cargo, until, quite suddenly, he dropped to the floor plates and lay there, squirming like an epileptic.

I quickly told Craig to watch that Briggs did not hurt himself, scrambled up the ladder, along the deck, and up to the bridge chart house. I had hardly time enough to notice that it was now nighttime, until I found the captain, in the chart house, in his pajamas and with his jacket flung wide open. Pale of face, only half-awake, the right eye partly closed, the left staring cold and glassy, he hung his head over the chart and scratched his ribs sleepily. There was something obscene in the sight of his naked flesh. His thin bared chest glistened soft and greasy as though he had sweated out whatever fat he had in his sleep.

"What's the matter, mister?" he asked in a voice harsh and dead, resembling the rasping sound of a file on steel.

"All three refrigerating machines have stopped, sir" I answered with deference; but the thin, stark figure, as though seen for the first time in a revealing moment, fixed itself in my memory for ever as the incarnation of everything cold and uncaring that lurks in the world we love. In our own hearts we trust for our salvation in the people that we are among, in the sights that we see, in the sounds that we hear, and in the air that we breathe.

"Where's the chief?" he asked, looking past my shoulder.

"He's . . . ill sir."

McTaggart pushed his way past me and looked at the night sky. The thin gold shaving of the moon had floated slowly downward and lost itself on the darkened surface of the waters, and the eternity beyond the sky seemed to descend closer to the earth, with the brightened glitter of the stars, with the deeper sombreness in the luster of the opaque dome covering the flat disc of the half-transparent sea.

The ship moved so smoothly that her onward motion was imperceptible to my senses, as though she had been a crowded planet speeding through the dark spaces of the ether in the appalling calm silences awaiting the spark of creation.

"What do you mean . . . ill?" McTaggart opened the wheelhouse door.

"He's having a breakdown, sir."

"Half-speed ahead—sixty revolutions." The captain ordered the helmsman, whose face was underlit by the compass light, like a devil incarnate. "Half-ahead it is sir," the helmsman replied, sing-song.

"What do you mean, a breakdown? The man's either sick or he's well, and there's an end to it. Now, which is he?"

"Sick, sir. I think you'd better come down to the engine room."

"Right mister, lead the way" said McTaggart.

"I think you ought to put on some shoes or slippers, sir. Hot is no name for it down below."

We clambered down the bridge ladder and scrambled on down the wheelhouse ladder below, on to the main deck, myself first, McTaggart shuffling down in two minutes with carpet slippers on his feet. I waited for him at the bottom of the ladder, until his cadaverous form was beside me. He mumbled to himself at first. All I heard were a few words that sounded like "confounded steam" and "infernal steam."

A draught of air, fanned from forward by the speed of the ship, even as she slowed down, passed steadily along the upper deck between the high bulwarks. A few lamps cast blurred circles of light thrown down and trembling slightly to the unceasing vibrations of the ship. On the stern, the patent log periodically rang a single tinkling stroke for every mile traversed on our Empire-binding errand. We waited a few minutes, while McTaggart calmed down.

"What'll I do?" he said. "What'll I do, mister?"

"I think the first thing is to see to Briggs." I replied.

"What about the cargo? What about the damned cargo?"

"It will take several hours for it to thaw out. We have the rest of the night before the sun comes up and warms the side plates. I can, if you wish, captain, work with young Craig. We may be able, at least, to get one compressor working."

"Will you do it?"

"If that is your wish, sir."

"I cannot thank you . . . " McTaggart never finished what he was saying. As we walked toward the engine room companionway a figure rushed out of the blazing light. As we stood there, stock still in our astonishment, Briggs, for in a flash we saw that it was he, his eyes still staring wildly, his lips frothing, collided with the captain, almost knocking him against the bulkhead. In a second both men recovered their balance. Nothing was said. Nothing, until Briggs had

staggered five yards further aft. Then he stopped, suddenly, turned around, and we saw his face, distorted as if in an
agony of pain. He stood with both feet apart, his arms
stretched downward and outward, his palms wide open, as
if he were imploring not to have ever been born. We saw in
the dim lamp of the trembling deck lamps that his mouth
was twisted in an awful, bestial distortion. Then he opened
it and screamed. It was a piercing howl, as though he had
been a wild animal caught in a steel clamp trap. The sound
he made was so desperate, so unholy, as to paralyze us as
we stared at him. Then, he grinned a maniacal smile of utter
madness. He caught hold of the bulwark and swung himself up to sit on it. Briggs stared at us again, his eyes like
fiery coals. From the depths of the ship came the harsh
noise of a scraped shovel, the violent slam of a furnace
door, exploding brutally, as if the men handling the mysterious things below were consumed with a fierce anger,
while the slim, high hull of the steamer went on, evenly
now, ahead, cleaving continuously the great calm of the
waters under the inaccessible serenity of the night sky.

I started to walk slowly toward Briggs. There was in my
mind some vague idea that I might catch hold of him.

"Stop where you are!" he shouted. "Stop. Come no
nearer. I am a sinner. Do you hear me? I am a sinner! I have
betrayed the lamb. I have betrayed the flesh of the lamb—
the flesh, the blood, the blood of the lamb!" With that, he flung
himself backward and was gone.

I ran to the ship's side and caught a glimpse, no more
than a fleeting impression, of Briggs's bald head in the side-
slip of the hull. In a second it was gone, disappeared into
the white wash of the propellor wake, and there was only
the water stars of phosphorescence below me. I turned
quickly even as Craig came running out of the engine room
companionway. The captain moved for the first time since
we had seen Briggs dash on deck. He caught hold of Craig's
arm and said in a low, tired voice, "Up to the wheelhouse,
Craig. Order the helm to heave-to right away. Then help

the chief mate roust the hands. Get a boat away and search for the poor soul."

Soon the cry was ringing through the ship as she lay dead in the water. "Man the cutter!" A mob of men clambered on the bulwarks, clustered around the davits.

"Man overboard! Just astern of us, about half a mile" shouted the chief mate. "Lower away!" Then moments later, "Let go the falls!" Craig was crying, sniffling, beside the captain, who in the lamplight looked like a standing corpse. We stood by the bulwarks, the three of us, staring into the calm velvet night, for an hour, until we saw the steadily repeated gleam of the cutter's oars as it returned from its search. We knew from the cutter crew's silence that Briggs had not been found, and watched, saying nothing, until the cutter was almost alongside.

"Well, that's that," said Captain McTaggart. "Now, mister, what about the meat? Do you think anything can be done?"

"Craig and I will do our best" I said, as McTaggart slowly climbed the ladder back up to the bridge.

I waited until the cutter was once again lashed to the falls. The boatswain looked up at me as I stared down. He shook his head slowly, in silence. The fall blocks squeaked and the boat rose in jerks. As the ship started to get under way and gathered speed the sharp hull seemed to rise a few inches in succession through its whole length, as though it had become pliable, and settled down again stiffly to its job of cleaving the smooth surface of the sea. As it reached full speed its quivering stopped, and the ship steamed along smoothly, as though on vibrating water and in humming air.

I turned to Craig, gently took him by the arm, and led him to the engine room.

I will not tire my readers by a long account of how we repaired all three compressors. Suffice it to say that after a careful examination of the problems and a muster of the crew, we found a deck-seaman who had served his time in a blacksmith's shop. With his able assistance over two days and nights' continual effort, we did it, and by the time we reached Port Said all three compressors were running as smoothly as could be expected under the circumstances, although under reduced speed. At Suez the *Rangapui* engaged a Greek, certified second engineer. As the chairman's son and his bride were in a hurry to get home the cargo was not transferred, and we reached Tilbury docks in London a month later. Unfortunately, when the cargo was discharged it was found that *only one carcass* was preserved and fit for consumption. The rest, 39,999 stinking, mouldy, green, slimy sheep corpses, were off-loaded midstream at Gravesend, by men desperate for work, muffled up against the unbearable stench, into barges that took them to Canvey Island to be burned on the beach.

Of course I attended the inquiry, at Captain McTaggart's beseeching, and told the nautical assessors in the court, in as plain words as I could, of what had transpired. The captain and the ship owners were exonerated of all blame. Outside the court, in the wan Greenwich autumn light, Craig approached me. He looked brighter now, and certainly cleaner, than I had seen him before.

"The company sent you this letter, sir" he said.

Quickly, for I had a ship to join that very day, I opened it. The letter was one of gratitude and praise for my assistance onboard the S.S. *Rangapui* "during and after the unfortunate occurrences which took place in the Red Sea." I placed it back in its envelope and put it in my pea-jacket pocket. Craig was still standing there.

"Thank you Craig," I said.

He smiled at me shyly. "No, sir, it's me that should be thanking you. The company have put my name on the top of the list for examination for second engineer, and I sit for it next week."

"Then I certainly wish you luck at it," I said.

"All the men said how they thought that for a foreign gentleman like yourself you did very well, sir, very well indeed, and they said for me to get an address because they would like to send you a small token of their regards.''

I searched in my wallet for one of my few remaining cards and gave it to him.

''Thank you sir,'' he said. He read the card. ''Thank you very much, *Mr. Joseph Conrad.*''

''Think nothing of it, Craig,'' I said, and walked off through the docks, under the looming cranes, beside the muddy water.

Much later, I was told that there was loud complaint about the temporary rise in the price of lamb—a penny-farthing a pound.

TROPICAL CRUISING IN MOSLEM COUNTRIES

I wrote this because more and more Westerners who sail for a pastime are finding themselves employed in Arab countries, and more and more yachts, now that the Suez Canal has reopened, may find themselves wandering down through the Red Sea. If they are not careful more and more of them will find themselves in trouble simply because they are not aware of local customs and beliefs. This is true, too, in Indonesia and the Indian Ocean. Never scoff at local taboos or superstitions. Your life or freedom might depend on your courtesy. This appears here for the first time.

"T he Owl and the Pussy Cat went to sea in a beautiful pea-green boat..." Edward Lear was much wiser than we guess when he wrote that; a few years ago naval psychologists conducted habitability tests in small ships and found that the color least conducive to seasickness *above decks* was, in fact, green.

Below decks they found that white-painted bulkheads tended to induce insecurity and, if my memory serves me right, people living in white-painted messes over a period of time were more prone to get into trouble ashore. The best color, they found, was pale, pastel blue.

I am sure that many "environmentalists" would agree with me that the surroundings, which we make for ourselves in small craft, are of the utmost importance on long voyages, and especially in extreme climates and perhaps in difficult weather conditions. We must be able to find relief, and the only place we have is down below, in a confined, mostly crowded space, at times moving violently.

Too much varnish is unwise, especially above shoulder level. After a few months it becomes very depressing and confining. It makes the boat darker inside, without reducing the temperature. Much better to have a good hard washable paint and either small coachroof windows or tinted plastic sheets, which would be fitted on outside the windows to keep out harmful sun rays. I would personally prefer smaller windows, or ports if possible. So small that to look out of the boat would require a conscious physical effort. The aim, in a long-distance cruiser, as in a house, should be to keep the weather *out*, visually as well as physically. Curtains won't do it; nothing is so calculated to accentuate the movements of a boat in a seaway as curtains swinging to and fro, or the meanderings of a sunbeam, let in through a gap in the curtains, as it swings about the cabin.

A bit of brass here and there is a good thing, especially in a fiberglass boat, where maintenance of the hull is minimal. Humans, and especially youngsters, seem to need a constant reminder that manmade materials need keeping up, and that they can be beautiful, cheering, and comforting. I'm not proposing bright metal all over the cabin, just a touch here and there. Maybe a clock, a barometer, a couple of brass strips, in odd places, perhaps on the edging of the companionway steps.

All drawers and cupboards should, of course, be well ventilated, especially in high humidity areas. Ventilation is very important, not only for drying out the boat, but also for cooling. In many well-protected places a wind scoop simply isn't enough. If you carry batteries, it is worthwhile fitting a twelve-volt car fan. These are quite small and use hardly any power. They are sold with a plastic dashboard fitting, and if several of these fittings are obtained, they can be screwed into places in the boat where the fan will be most employed. With a long electric lead the fan can be moved about at will.

Plenty of silica gel should be carried, in small cotton or canvas bags, to place in the clothes lockers or navigation locker as an antihumidity precaution. But in areas like the Red Sea, or the Amazon, everything will have to be aired at least once a week and the silica placed in a warm dry place to give up accumulated damp. Tools should, if possible, be of stainless steel. But if not, they should be well protected: the oft-used ones with grease, little-used ones with a good hard anti-rust paint. Books must only be stowed where plenty of air can get at them, yet in a dry place.

On deck, for coolness in harbor, an awning is a great help. But be wary of Dacron. I believe it lets through harmful rays and if you fall asleep in its shade you may still be burned or may still develop a skin rash. I don't know enough about this; only that on three occasions people with me who did this complained afterwards of a burning sensation, something like prickly heat. Nevertheless, Dacron will last much longer than canvas or cotton in humid areas.

Of course, when actually under way, no awning is really suitable. Even if you adjust it every half-hour, the sun will move too fast in the midday period and you can go barmy untying little lanyards on the rigging to shift the small awning. The answer to this problem is to carry a couple of big, cheap umbrellas, such as those carried by little old men in Mediterranean countries. These are obtainable in any sizeable town in the tropics. They are Greek-made and cost no more than one U.S. dollar each—probably less if you bargain or make the shopkeeper laugh.

If you have a wind-vane steering apparatus and avoid long hours at the wheel, the sun will not bother you too much; the remarks above are addressed to the hardy souls not so fitted. Autopilots of the electronically controlled variety also let you avoid the wheel. We had one in *Barbara* —and it continually failed. The reason it would not perform was that the transistors were not man enough to stand up to the heat, until we found an electronics expert in

Durban who fitted transistors capable of withstanding temperatures up to 200 degrees Fahrenheit. Since then we have had no failure with the autopilot, although it was not powerful enough to steer against the Amazon current. Personally, I think if an electric autopilot is preferred (and there is much to be said for them, especially when becalmed), then the "whisker" variety should be fitted. These are much simpler, working through two tiny wire brushes that touch studs set in a compass, so passing a signal to a two-way electric motor, which turns the wheel. But for pure ocean sailing, by the usual routes, I wouldn't give an autopilot houseroom. A wind-vane steerer every time—and the simpler the better.

When you are hand steering, the two areas that will catch the sun most will be your knees and the tops of your feet. So you should wear sandals, with a canvas flap over the instep, and long trousers, at least until people bronze off. Hands, too, should be protected at first, but sunburn lotion can be used. If you put lotion on your legs and feet, for some reason it seems to get everywhere—even on the charts.

There should be at least two water tanks on board, each one with a valve on the outlet to isolate it from the other. Then, water should also be carried in five-gallon containers. Have at least two, which should be kept in the shade and should be kept full, emptying and replenishing at each watering point. In areas north of the Kenya-Somali border, fresh water is a matter of life and death. In many parts of the Gulf of Aden and the Red Sea it is possible to be at anchor, offshore, and yet a hundred miles or more from the nearest fresh water.

In boats with plastic water supply pipes rats should be fanatically guarded against. Food is so short onshore in these areas that if they can find no loose food (and they shouldn't, in a properly run boat) they will gnaw plastic materials. The first thing they go for is a hose, perhaps with a droplet of water seeping out of a connection. Rats are extremely difficult to catch in a loaded cruising boat with all its nooks and crannies.

Care must be taken when bathing in the tropics. One way to treat sea-urchin spikes left in the flesh is to soak a rag in olive oil, burn it until it is a hot, black char and slap it straight on the part affected. I don't know why, but the cure for the pain and festering caused is immediate and is 100 percent certain. The flesh will not be burned if the rag is merely smouldering and there are no sparks left on it. But the best remedy is prevention, and sandals or deck shoes should always be worn whenever you leave the boat, even to go swimming. There's many a bad cut caused on the soles of feet through scraping on barnacles whilst trying to clamber onboard out of the water and those scrapes can fester, too. Other menaces are sharks and stingrays. Here it's a question of common sense and always having some-one watch out from the yacht whilst there are people swimming, ready to sound a loud and continuous alarm at any suspicious shapes in the offing. Usually, it's safer to swim near a reef, especially where there are plenty of small fish, for the shark is well fed here. But farther out to sea he will probably be a bit peckish and so more liable to attack. *Never, anywhere* in the tropics, wear anything that flashes, such as a bracelet or a wristwatch. It will attract predators from many yards away.

Generally speaking, it is fairly safe to swim near the main towns. Great care must be exercised, though, especially in the Red Sea and Gulf of Aden. I have heard it said that if a shark is about, the best thing to do is to slowly make for the boat, making as little disturbance as possible. But if he does come for you, then you should hit him on the nose as hard as you can, as sharks are, essentially, cowardly beasts. They do run away from small porpoise when butted like this. But the best thing is to take no chances. If you need to cool off so badly, then a bucket and a sluice down is the answer. Then, always wipe down with fresh water after-wards, for salt water in the hot humid climate, can cause bad sores, which take weeks to heal up. This is especially the case where clothing might rub, such as the collar, the crotch (very prone; a sarong-type garment is the answer, short, down to the knees), and also the tops of the feet if deck shoes are worn. That's why I recommend sandals. The best sandals I've ever come across are the Australian navy-issue sandals, which are infinitely adjustable every way, thick soled, and they last for years.

For the rest of clothing, each person needs two or three pairs of hardy shorts and several sets of tee-shirts and pants for use at sea. Clothing rots very quickly in the tropics with the help of salt water. For shore, some old long trousers and shirts, with a best pair and perhaps a light jacket for the main towns and social occasions. The old clothes are for anywhere but the main ports. There, your oldest, scruffiest, meanest rags will be ten times better than what is worn by the locals. Should you throw them away as beyond any hope of repair they will be seized on avidly and made to last perhaps another ten years.

Alcohol should never, under any circumstances, be offered unless specifically asked for, not even in Coptic Christian areas. There is no more certain way to make mortal enemies. Neither should booze be consumed whilst locals are onboard, unless they have asked for some for themselves. Nothing should ever be offered with the *left hand*, under any circumstances in Moslem communities in the remoter areas. Neither should anyone ever be stared at for longer than is civil, lest they fear the Evil Eye, which is still very much believed in. Medicines are like diamonds on the African and Red Sea shores, but if you find someone in need of medicine, even if it's only an aspirin, try to find the local chief or headman and offer the remedy through him. Bear in mind that there are certain periods when, for a Moslem to put anything to his lips between sunrise and sunset (even if he were in extremity for lack of a medicine) would be the gravest sin he could ever commit.

The headman of a village or settlement should always be

called upon, anywhere on the mainland and in most of the island areas mentioned. Regardless of the religion, in most places the pleasure you give by this courtesy will only be outmatched by the help you will receive. Women, in Moslem areas especially, should keep well in the background, especially in the remoter coasts and islands. This is unfortunate but necessary.

Cigarettes are very acceptable to the headman. It is customary for them to call in all the senior male members of the community to share the cigarettes on the spot. Sweets and chocolates for children are, I suppose, appreciated by the children. But I think that, in Moslem countries, this gesture is looked upon as being something of an eccentricity. After all, they think, "what can the children give back?" Gifts should never be offered to women, not even through their husbands, until you've been in the anchorage at least ten years. Though if you are lucky and ladies are on board, it could probably be done through them. Of course, Western women should be very careful what they wear in remote Moslem districts, and leave as little skin exposed as possible to avoid offending the locals.

Boys are considered to be men at about nine years of age and they are, from what I could see, at their brightest and most able between the ages of fourteen and eighteen. So if you are offered a pilot who looks like a schoolboy, don't be surprised. He's probably very good. But never take a pilot from strangers, unless in extremity.

If possible, in these remote areas (which in many ways are still in the tenth century), never, if you can help it, wear spectacles when addressing any locals. They have a deadly fear of the Evil Eye. Anything that aids the eye, such as binoculars or even a camera (though there are also deep religious reasons for cameraphobia), is looked upon with almost murderous suspicion and a violent distrust.

Whilst on the subject of glasses, eyesight is, of course, the most important physical sense on a cruising boat. Have at least two pairs of polarized sunglasses. Not only will they prevent you from being half-blinded by the sun's cruel, needlelike reflections off the surface of the sea, but they will also help you a great deal in seeing the reefs, which will show up quite clearly when you are between the sun and the reefs. I don't know much about optics, but it seems to me that it doesn't do to wear polarized glasses too long at a stretch. Other people have agreed with me that they tend to cause headaches and/or loss of night sight to a noticeable degree if they are worn for more than a couple of hours a day and especially if worn down below, out of the sun.

You need plenty of tea towels. These are used as sweat rags; for instance to rest the arm on when working on the charts, Irish linen is best, and Thomas Foulkes of London sells an admirable range in many designs, mainly to do with yachting.

With Europeans in the Red Sea and Gulf of Aden, Scotch is by far the favorite tipple. A highly prized commodity in Zanzibar is chewing gum. For antimalaria pills, much known and sought after amongst the dhow skippers of Massawa and Assab, the going rate for 100 pills is a fair-sized pearl, about an eighth-of-an-inch in diameter, or five Maria Teresa thalers (the silver coin used in the Red Sea).

In the islands to the northwest of Madagascar, a worn, but perhaps patiently repairable white shirt with tail and no collar is worth two fowl, a cock and a hen. Forty cigarettes are worth one small goat. Two cans of green beans are worth a good-sized hen. Canned foods in the Seychelles are much more expensive than in Mombasa, and are practically unavailable in most other East African countries.

On the coasts of Tanzania and Kenya, many of the Moslem schoolteachers speak and understand English. A couple of paperback books, in English, of any description, will be received with grace and delight. You will have a school full of children to carry water to the boat, plus probable gifts of fruit or a chicken.

On books, if you are at all a reader (and what cruising man or woman isn't?), then take plenty of paperbacks with you. They needn't be new. Chances are that somewhere along the line you'll come across a British or American merchant ship with a library. Generally they are very pleased at the chance to swap. You'll find other yachts, too, but in these areas, except for the Seychelles, they are extremely rare. In the Red Sea and Gulf of Aden, there are usually none at all.

In Tanzania and Kenya, the port pilots are sometimes British. In Djibouti, Madagascar and also the Comoros, the port authorities are French.

In Mozambique and South African ports, always take your log along when you call on the port captain.

A letter to the tourist office, or consulate, of the country to be visited, written in your own country, helps to a varying degree on arrival in some ports.

Apart from all this, it's all a bit like Long Island Sound—only warmer and much more rewarding.

RENDEZVOUS IN MOMBASA

This story took place during the six-year-long venture described in
The Incredible Voyage. *The problem with that book was not
what to put in, but what to leave out! Otherwise, it would have
been 1000 pages long. By the time of this story,* Barbara *had made
the passage from Israel down the Red Sea to Massawa and
Djibouti, a voyage even more perilous than normal because of
draconian Arabian laws regarding boats that have been to Israel.
By the time we reached Mombasa after the Indian Ocean and Gulf
of Aden, we'd made a total voyage of around 7000 miles, more
than half of it to windward. My mate, Conrad Jelinek, had joined
me in Malta. Before our meeting, he had never been to sea. By the
time this was written, he was a first class deckhand and, at age
twenty-three, was also one of nature's gentlemen. The story was
published in* East West Journal *in May 1980.*

S teering the thirty-eight foot yawl *Barbara* into a setting moon, our sails pregnant with anticipation and
the Indian Ocean breeze, Mombasa was now a hundred miles away. We were no longer voyaging to Mombasa. We were *fetching Mombasa to us*.

The way in which land is discovered from the deck or
rigging of a small craft has a curious, dreamlike quality to it.
The land does not reveal itself gently out of the horizon, nor
does it suddenly stand into view. Rather, it appears almost
as a figment of the imagination at first; it is there and yet it is
not there, a mirage revealing itself out of the vastness of the
surface of the world and the sky of the universe, a coy
wraith ascending reluctantly from the curve of the ocean
edge. Suddenly, with heart-stopping charm, for one
moment the land is there, then it is shyly gone again, like a

promise of spring in the North when the sun breaks for the first time through the March clouds. For long anxious moments to every eye onboard it is there—it is not; it is a cloud—it is not; it is a darker haze—it is not; and then, triumphantly the cry is raised "Land Ho!" and we know that humanity is all around us, once again.

Dawn is the best time to enter a tropical harbor from the east so that the low sun is behind the vessel and the helmsman can see and avoid the reefs, pale creamy-green, in the azure ocean water.

Of all the sacramental sights in the Indian Ocean, the chief, to my mind, was the landfall of Mombasa after only momentary sights of the barren desert wastes of Somaliland and the Red Sea. Until the vessel was about three miles offshore, there was only a low, dark gray, hazy line on the horizon with a couple of lighter gray humps to mark the town. Then, quite suddenly, like a bride appearing for her wedding, the whole of that green, luscious coastline, crowned by the white silver glory of Mombasa Old Town, stepped out to meet us; Conrad and I were back among other human beings, the ship became a different thing, and the surface skin of the world, which had been without end and simple, once again took on the veins of her global complexity.

We entered Mombasa with *elan*. Once to leeward of the harbor entrance our splendid craft rounded to the wind, rolled sometimes over so far as to show our centerboard to the startled Kenyan onlookers in their harbor craft, then righted and headed forward fast again, like a humming bird chasing butterflies. Then we were off the wind again and running free to the Mombasa Yacht Club mooring, where we again rounded smartly to the wind, full of pride and swank. At my signal Conrad let go of the jib halyard. Down the sail came with a crash just as, on my next signal, he threw the fifty-pound anchor overboard. Another dart into the wind on the close-hauled mainsail, then, as the mainsail fluttered like a startled widgeon Conrad heaved the second, thirty-pound anchor overboard, far from the first. He looked aft at me, eyebrows raised. Then I nodded my head and down came the mainsail on the run. Conrad had the mainsail lashed, as shipshape in its tiers as a trussed bullock, before the rattle, roar and screech of thirty fathoms of anchor chain and cable had ceased and the boat, grabbing on dearly once more to Mother Earth, tightened to her double hawsers.

The first passage in twelve years from Djibouti to Mombasa by a Western sailing vessel, over four thousand miles, mostly against the wind and the currents, and almost wholly with hostile shores all around, was completed.

We had said nothing coming into harbor. We had said nothing sailing to anchor. Now Conrad grinned at me as he made his way aft. "Cuppa tea, Skip?" His torso swaggered.

I grinned, looking up at him as I untied my seaman's knife from the base of the port headsail sheet winch.

"Ah, that'll be nice, mate."

"Up in a jiffy," was all Conrad said as he swung agilely down the companionway.

There must be something about a hot and humid climate that affects one's sense of humor. Perhaps it's that we ocean sailors meet quite a few oddball characters. In East Africa, especially, it might be that the stranger is uncomfortably made aware of being an intruder by the honeyvinegar spirit that eventually pervades everything that enters, and everyone who touches, that ancient shore.

By 1971 the countries of Kenya and Tanzania had been independent for a few years. The scenery was about the same as it had been in colonial days. Even yet the coolies hauled the huge sacks of freight onboard the drawn-up dhows in the Old Harbor. Still the Indian merchants supervised the cargoes, still the ancient Arab dhow skippers dozed or smoked their hookahs on the poops of their vessels and watched the glistening black bodies as they staggered up the narrow, sagging gangplanks under the loads that in any Western country would be the subject of an

S.P.C.A. inquiry if they were piled onto a donkey's back. Over on the other side of the hill on which the glistening white Old Arab Town sits, still the *bwanas* sat on the verandah of the yacht club, sipping iced drinks as they watched the blue Indian Ocean through the entrance of the New Port. There were fewer of them now than in the old days. They were almost all getting on in years and underlying their bravado was a note of anxiety. A schoolmaster, years out, who was worried about his government retirement pension; a harbor pilot, his work curtailed now that Kenyan pilots had been trained. Yet the old shibboleths were still maintained, still the waiters bowed as they took orders in gleaming white jackets buttoned tightly around the black necks, and still the club member's eyebrows raised—ever so slightly, as English eyebrows do, when Conrad and I inquired as to places to go in the city: a good bar, a cheap cinema. One still simply did not "go native." In two words, it was all still "somewhat stuffy." But Conrad and I, after checking over the moorings of *Barbara*, managed to escape from the club grounds and found a fan-cooled bar owned by a Kikuyu ex-Royal Naval steward where we could play darts, drink beer, and for an hour or two forget the boring reminiscences about "the good old days," the depressing complaints, the references to "jungle bunnies," back at the club.

Later that night we sat with two tall, beautiful Masai ladies-of-the-night and watched the dancing displays at a very large, very crowded, very noisy establishment only yards from the moon-gleaming waters of the New Port. For Conrad, who was twenty-three, this was exciting and new. For me it was exciting and memory-laden. By the early hours of the morning, merry and chatting, we made our way back to the boat, talking in the dark shadows of the low hills all around the glistening harbor, the big ships lit up like diadems under a star-crowded sky.

As we crossed the railway lines by the port entrance Conrad found a hedgehog, a tiny spiky creature, cowering in the lamplight; his dark gypsy face, as he picked up the animal, looked like that of a small boy opening a birthday gift package. I said nothing as we strolled on under the quivering palms into the dockyard grounds.

Back onboard, having paid off the boatman, Conrad set the little hedgehog down so as to get the companionway keys out of his pocket. In the dark shadows of the cockpit, quick as a flash, the hedgehog darted for the nearest hole—a cockpit drain, an orifice of about an inch-and-a-half diameter, and down he went, down the pipe, safe again.

"Damn!" said Conrad, his face piqued in the flashlight glare.

"Bloody hell!" said I. The boat rocked slightly.

"Can you reach it?"

"No," I replied, "but we'll have to get him out in the morning, mate. We can't chance going to sea in the monsoon season with a blocked cockpit drain, can we?"

"S'pose not, Skip." Conrad's face dropped as he climbed down into the close, humid cabin. "Do you reckon he'll live?"

"Sure he will—that's home away from home for a hedgehog. Let's get some sleep. We'll dismantle the drain tomorrow before we sail."

"Right Skip. G'night."

"Night mate."

Conrad gathered up his blanket and mosquito net and clambered topside to sleep the sleep of the gentle and brave under the stars and the moon and the harbor breeze whispering in the shrouds.

Dismantling a cockpit drain in a thirty-eight footer at midforenoon, as the African sun climbs higher and higher overhead, is no joke. The engine compartment was a tiny space under the cockpit, jampacked with machinery and pipes. The ideal yacht mechanic would be a cross between a Cunard Line stoker, a conjurer, Harry Houdini, and a Methodist preacher. Not being any of these, by the time I had disconnected the offending clear plastic pipe, extracted the hedgehog, placed it safely in Conrad's waiting hands, and rebuttoned everything up again, I was covered in oil and grease, sweating like a pig, aching from contorted limbs, and swearing like a duke.

"Got the little bugger—here, take him and keep him safe—put him in a box." I groaned, puffing my way out from over the top of the engine, bleeding slightly from God knows how many scratches on my torso.

"We can't do that, Skip . . . it's a wild animal," Conrad said quietly.

"Then take him ashore. If you don't he'll disappear into some other hole and we'll never find him and he'll starve and rot and stink the bloody boat out—even worse than it is now," I added for good measure, just to keep him on his toes at the cleaning chores. (It's very easy to let things slide in the tropics.)

"Aw . . . oh, well, alright Skip."

"And don't be too long, Conrad, we sail at noon, re-member, and we've a long beat ahead down the coast."

"Where're we bound? Did you decide yet?"

"Yeah . . ." I wiped my filthy body down with a damp rag and put my shirt back on. "Kilwa Kisiwani," I said.

"Kill what?"

"Kilwa Kisiwani. It's about 150 miles this side of the Mozambique border, down in Tanzania. Good harbor, a sort of fiord. Nothing much there, but that'll perhaps save a lot of this bureaucratic baloney we get in these bigger Afri-can ports . . ."

"Great. I'll take Marmaduke ashore then."

"Right," I said. I bent over the chart table to make my calculations, then I grinned to myself. "So he's named the little sod Marmaduke, eh?" I said to myself. "Typical . . . typical." Then I forgot about the hedgehog and reached for the dividers.

The passage from Mombasa to Kilwa Kisiwani was not easy. We had to beat against currents, ocean, and wind all the way, but after almost two weeks of persistence we

211

eventually reached Kilwa Kisiwani, where the first Europeans to reach the Indian Ocean around the Cape of Good
Hope had established their first base around five hundred
years before.

We passed under the walls of Vasco da Gama's castle,
staring with wonder at the state of preservation of the
building. There was not a soul to be seen, only the wrecks
of two large dhows at the Kilwa fiord entrance, which was
as narrow as a linnet's throat. We hove to (that is, stopped
the boat) and peered around at the jungle foreshore that
tumbled down over the gray rock-littered beach. I took a
quick glance over to the northern side of the fiord. There,
about two miles away, was a jetty, the wind-whipped
waters from the ocean side creaming at its seaward base.

Conrad had sighted the jetty at the same time as I.

"Jetty over there, Skip," he cried from the bow.

"Whereaway, mate?" said I, squinting my eyes so as to
give him the honor, prestige, and importance which sharp
eyesight can bestow on a lad with only a year at sea. I did
this even though I could see plainly a ship's name painted
red on the jetty head.

"Over there, Tris." He thrust out an arm and finger
urgently.

"You sure?" I squinted again.

"Sure, see it?" The burgee at the masthead whipped
away in the wind.

"Oh yes. Right. Hoist the jib. Keep your eye on the jetty
and tell me when I'm on course."

"Right, Skip," he replied, feeling pleased that he was of
service to his ship. And so we crossed the brown grey,
wind-lashed waters of Kilwa Kisiwani, one of the most
ancient havens in the world, wild, silent, and deserted
now, and very, very beautiful.

The jetty was in a state of disintegration. What the wind
and the ocean had mercifully spared so far, the teredo
worms were gratefully, it seemed, devouring. We managed to get a line onto the jetty ruin, laid out an anchor to

hold the boat off, and, after the "squaring up chores"—a ritual of sail-tending and line shipshaping as old as navigation itself, a litany of care as loving as the folding of a priest's cassock—we clambered ashore.

"What a strange place," observed Conrad. "Look, Skip, what do you think those railway lines were, all overgrown —and that road, with the grass breaking it up all over the place, and those ruined old sheds? What do you think it was, a wartime base or something?"

"No, lad. What you're looking at is the ruins of one of the world's most forlorn hopes."

Conrad stared at me, puzzled.

"The Great British Groundnut Scheme, Conrad, me old son."

He looked at me again, as if he thought that the sun, at last, had got to me.

"It's a fact, mate. After the Second World War the bright boys back in London thought they would establish here a farming industry—the growing of vast plantations of groundnuts, that's peanuts, see?"

"Mmm—so what went wrong?" Conrad swiped at a small snake with his rope's end (always carry a rope's end in wild places). The snake, untouched but frightened, slithered away smartly.

"Nothing went wrong. I mean with the place. It was already wrong with the people who planned it all. Bloody nincompoops. They lavished almost a *billion* pounds on the scheme . . . that's a *billion* pounds, Conrad, a billion pounds from the people of a war-torn country up to its ears in debt. They sent a British work force out here that would have made the Pyramid builders look like a domino tournament —thousands of 'em. They sent thousands of trucks and enough stores to have put Britain back on her feet in six months—this was right after World War Two, in 1946, remember—and they sent railway lines and engines, and a hospital and bevies of beautiful nurses and a regiment of doctors and agronomists and dentists and drainage engineers. Everything from ocean liners to safety pins . . . "

Conrad sat down in the shade of one of the ruined sheds. "So what went wrong, then? I mean there can't be any harm in trying to develop a Godforsaken hole like this, can there? And anyway, there was still the British mandate of Tanganyika in those days, wasn't there?" No flies on Conrad when it came to modern history.

"Well, mate, like I said, nothing went wrong. It was already wrong, at least for peanuts. You see, the blummin' bureaucrats had not taken into account the monsoon rain season. They planted a million acres and the whole lot rotted in the ground as soon as the Indian Ocean wind changed from northwest to southeast. The place was like a quagmire. Mud up to your shoulders after two continual days of rain."

"Blimey," said Conrad. "What a stupid balls-up."

"Yes, not enough sailors among them, was there?"

"How d'you mean, Skip?"

"Well, the first rule of a sailor. They'd never heard of it, it seems."

"Wazzat?" said Conrad, tired.

"Look before you leap, me old son, look before you leap."

We wandered back to the broken-down jetty on its sad pilings, as our mooring ropes groaned slightly, the boat heaved in the swell and the dusk rose from the jungle to accept and comfort the dying sun, and not another human soul near us, so it seemed, only the rustle of the trees and the howls of monkeys fading to a distant chattering murmur as another mote of the eternity of Africa crept away into infinity.

In a small craft at anchor in the tropics, one is usually woken up by the heat of the sun soon after it rises over the horizon. We were woken by a call. A very British call.

"Hullo theah!" Silence for a moment as both Conrad and

I, me down below, he topsides, opened each one eye.

"Ai say!" Another short silence. "AI SAY!"

Below, now with both eyes open, I heard Conrad say "Oh...good morning!" I listened to him gather himself out from under his mosquito netting.

"Good morning, old chep..." said a high, quivering voice, then, after a moment, "British?"

"*Blimey*," I said to myself as I started to climb out of my berth. "*A right one here, that's for sure*," I looked at my watch. "*Five thirty in the morning. There we left the blessed ensign on the flagstaff all night, a great big British ensign—big as a Ganges blanket—and he asks us if we're...*" I emerged from the companionway and peered with sleep-besotted eyes almost directly into the sun at a figure standing on the ruined Peanut Jetty. I could not as yet make out the appearance of the figure. He was almost directly between me and the sun.

"Cuppa tea?" I chanted my particle of a rite honored by time and geography from the blood-soaked ramparts of Sebastopol to the freezing polar steppes at the top and bottom of the darling World.

"Ah, yes...good, British," said the voice, rising with justification, satisfaction, and a threatening touch of anticipation.

"*Oh, God*," thought I, as I put the kettle on the stove and Conrad, with masterly understatement, welcomed the figure onboard. "You're just in time for breakfast," I heard him say as I donned my pants.

"Ai say," said the voice. "Thanks awl the same, old chep, but ectually, I hed mine about an hahr ago, beck et the mission."

I heard his feet step lightly onto the deck overhead. Then, as the canned kippers sizzled in the pan I lost track of the conversation going on topsides. I did a mental double-take as soon as the kippers were settled and frizzling. "*Mission?*" I said to myself. Then again. "*MISSION? DID HE SAY BLOODY MISSION? Holy Christ, I hope he's not or-*"

dained!'' The thought raced through my mind of the bad
luck that can enter a sailing vessel along with a round collar.
At least in Celtic waters. Then, as the kippers browned off
nicely and the kettle sang I decided that the Gods of Fortune
would forgive us this occasion, in these circumstances, in
this place. I set to passing breakfast up to Conrad, who by
this time was cozily seated with our visitor in the cockpit.

When I finally emerged from the galley (we took turns in
the harbor making breakfast) I inspected our guest as we
shook hands. He was about thirty-five at a guess, with
sandy hair, as I could see now that he had doffed his bush
hat. He had pale blue eyes and a wispy mustache, which
at first sight reminded me of the floor sweepings in a rope
loft. He seemed to be all protuberances at first, until I
became accustomed to his appearance. All his extremities
—the ones I could see, at least, seemed to stick out from
his sandy body and head. Even his bush outfit of jacket
and shorts was sandy-colored, even his boots and socks.
His pale blue eyes were like cool oasis pools at the northern edge of the Sahara, seen from an airplane high up in
the sky. Everything stuck out. His ears, his nose (a beauty,
that one), his chin, his hands and feet, his knees, they all
seemed to be much too big for the man's elfin core. It was as
if the Lord had taken a fourteen-year-old boy and stuck a
man's extremities onto him. The high-pitched voice only
served to accentuate this impression. I introduced myself.

"Ffoulkes-Fleming, old chep," he responded. "Roger,
ectually." I knew he was a little puzzled by my accent. The
"ectually" was not for nothing. As Kipling said, "What do
they know of England, who only England know?"

"Aim over at the mission, weah just over the jolly old hill
beck theah . . . " He trailed off as the aroma of fried kipper
reached his nostrils. (I will not try to report his torture of the
English language, but to translate it, instead, for the sake of
my American readers.)

"Mission?" I said to Roger. "You a preacher, then?"
Conrad almost grinned at me as he raised one eyebrow. He

knew my fondness for Voltaire. (He used to say that Voltaire was the only Frenchman I ever had time for.)

"Lay preacher, old chap. Doing a two-year stint out here in the jolly old jungle, you know. We have a doctor and a dentist, run a hospital, all that sort of stuff, and, well, we try to keep the locals happy, treat the tsetse fly fever, dose the trachoma, keep the rotten old yaws at bay, all that sort of thing."

"Must be interesting. Quite a change from Blighty (Britain)," I observed.

"Yes, but we still manage to muster up a game of cricket, you know. Got a few of the locals trained. Actually some of them do quite well. Particularly as bowlers. Not too good on the jolly old bat and a teeny-weeny bit scared" (Conrad's mouth twitched with the ache to grin), "a teeny-weeny bit scared of catching the jolly old ball." He was silent for a moment as he watched us mop up the kipper juice with our bread. Then he said, "But after all, it keeps us in practice, you know."

"Yes," said I, after another moment of silence. "Practice, important, that. Very important, the old practice. Can't be perfect if we don't practice, can we?"

"That's what I always say," agreed Roger, dead serious, as Conrad dashed down below, unable by now to contain his mirth. I heard him spluttering as he splashed the breakfast dishes around in the sink. Roger invited us to dinner that night at the mission, which invitation I accepted gracefully and gratefully. Then he left us and bounced jauntily along the destroyed jetty and the ruined road and I watched him, a cheery *hurrah!* in a world of tears and hopelessness.

Dinner at the mission was like a scene from a Somerset Maugham novel. Everyone was dressed up, cheerful and deadly serious at the same time. There were six British staff at the mission. Conrad and I enjoyed the simple meals while the two *ladies* (there is no other word) regaled us with stories of the lions prowling around outside the compound at night and of their being stranded in the jungle in their jeep, unable to go forward or back because of the monsoon rains, and how Roger had sloshed and muddied his way through to their rescue. It was all entertaining and at the end of the evening, after some sprightly tunes on the piano from one of the ladies and *Abide with Me* from a Reverend Doctor, I was pleased to accept Roger's invitation to ride with him in the mission jeep to the nearest town, Kilwa Kivinge, about twenty-five miles to the north.

"You can buy some fresh fruit there, and perhaps even some fresh turtle meat. Indian traders, you know, so watch the jolly old prices, old chap," Roger said. When he spoke, all his protuberances seemed to flap, like a suddenly vacated tent in a high wind.

We finished the evening early, about 8 P.M. while the moon was still out, so we could see our way back to the boat and watch for prowling animals. The wise old African moon guided us safely; Conrad with a full belly and me with my story, back to our boat *Barbara*. She, now that the blow was over, rocked gently to her own melody in the night, until she, too, was fast asleep and dreaming of the gray Atlantic waters, our own true loves.

The jeep trip to Kilwa Kivinge was—bumpy. The rough jungle road was, to a simple seaman like myself, much like any other rough jungle road anywhere in the world. The only thing that made it at all very interesting was the fact that we were racing against the monsoon rains, which were expected to start pouring down any day.

The town of Kilwa Kivinge was like most other small towns on the East African coast south of Somaliland. Small wooden structures, mostly gray and unpainted, mostly rotting away in the hot sun, their tin roofs shimmering with a heat haze by noon hot enough to fry eggs atop. On the unpaved dirt streets, small potbellied children and mangy, incredibly skinny dogs played in each other's excrement. Not to worry, they all fell fast asleep by early afternoon, in the street, in the shade, and the street then looked tidier.

The Indian merchant's shop was resplendent inside with a fly-spotted electric bulb and an electric fan. Both these amenities, whilst the town-generating station was in operation for (perhaps) three hours after dusk, were the wonders of all the country people who came down from the inland rises to shop at Kilwa. The townsfolk, as townsfolk do the world over, had become a bit blasé about the light and the fan, and one of them, a young man of twenty-five who had actually been to Dar Es Salaam, had a portable radio. This was a matter of grave concern to the Indian merchant, so much so that he even forebore to attempt to cheat us two *bwanas* and wished us a safe journey back to the Christian mission, for which Roger, in his turn, blessed the Parsee. I felt it was rather as if a praying mantis was blessing a cobra.

As Roger drove the loaded jeep down the coastal road out of Kilwa Kivinge, I noticed a memorial standing on the shore. It was in the form of a big cross, and stood about fifteen feet high, if I remember rightly. A stone cross on this wholly Moslem coastline is enough to rouse anyone's curiosity. I asked Roger about it. He at first said nothing, but drove up close to the monument and stopped. When the dust had settled a serious look clouded his usually cheery face. His pale blue eyes darkened.

"German war memorial, old chap," he said. Laconic, our Roger.

"German? . . . " I asked at first in surprise, until I recalled that Tanzania had once been the Imperial German colony of Tanganyika, and that a minor war campaign had been fought in this land and Kenya in 1914–15. The war had amounted to not much more than a few skirmishes between African troops on both the British and German sides and long forced marches through mountain and jungle. But still, I had read of the gallant voyage of the German Imperial Navy ship *Emden* and of the incredible way in which she had, although beyond hope of succor, gallantly avoided a vastly superior British squadron for months until she was finally sunk.

"Yes," said Roger. He thought for a moment as I stared at the memorial and the now withered dry bunch of flowers at its base.

"Funny thing," he continued. "Practically all the people in this town, in fact all of them, are Moslems..." He hesitated for a moment as I looked at him. "We Christians haven't been terribly successful around here, old chap. Not at all, only thirty conversions in the past ten years, and most of them revert sooner or later..." He trailed off into silence as my gaze followed the sweep of the mangrove-fringed bay. Then I looked back at him just as his face suddenly changed from gloom to light. "But as I was saying, Tristan, old chap, it's a funny thing, even though they're all Moslems, they turned up... at least their head men did, at the mission insisting that someone come down and hold a service here on Armistice Day a couple of years ago. Of course, everyone was a bit shy of the thing at first..."

"Shy? What do you mean, shy, Roger?" I swatted a mosquito off my arm.

"After all, they *were Germans*, you see..." He gestured at the cross.

Astonished as I was I kept my face poker-grim, determined not to move a muscle. After a moment's nothing I asked him, "So what happened?"

"Well," Roger replied, almost nonchalantly, his face absolutely set calm. "We discussed it between us at the mission for a while, then we decided that I would come down with two of the African staff and hold the service."

"And did you?"

"Oh, yes. We couldn't make it for November 11. That was a Friday, you see, and the stores here were closed. Moslem holy day and all that, and there wasn't much point coming in if we couldn't pick up a few of the jolly old stores, what?"

"I suppose not," I said.

"So we came in the next day."

"How many people turned up at the memorial service?"

"Oh, just the three of us, myself and the two mission groundsmen. They sing a few hymns, you know." He sighed, then said, "Of course, there were some Moslems watching us from a distance, kids and old men . . ."

"Well," said I, brightly, "that was nice. How did the service go?"

"Oh, we didn't hold a full service, I mean not like we do at home for *our chaps*, of course, I mean after all . . ."

I looked at him. His eyes had dropped. I waited, not believing my ears. Then his face brightened. His elfin eyes crinkled.

"We did give *The Old Hundredth Hymn**, though. I mean after all, even if they were Germans they weren't like that lot in the Second War, were they?"

> All people that on earth do dwell
> Come to the Lord with cheerful voice . . .

We were back at Kilwa Kisiwani by dusk, and I recounted the day's stories to Conrad. We sat there like two madmen and laughed and laughed our way into, through, and out of the heart of darkness.

Next morning we sailed for the Comoro Islands, still laughing.

**Mark Twain mentions* The Old Hundredth Hymn *in* Huckleberry Finn *where Huck and Tom are rescued from the cave and the townspeople give thanks.*

THE SAGA OF *DREADNAUGHT*

The following story is based on events that occurred in 1965 when Cresswell *was anchored in Ibiza. Sissie St. John, the bishop's sister, who had joined me in France, was still cruising with me and my one-eyed, three-legged Labrador retriever, Nelson, was still alive. When the story commences, I was recovering from the pulling of a molar tooth, without anesthetics, of course, at the local dentist. On my way to the dentist's, I had noticed my neighbor, a rusty old steel lifeboat, which had been very amateurishly converted to a schooner-type rig. Her name was* Dreadnaught *and on her stern she wore a ragged, oily, British Red Ensign. Although I've changed some names in the story, it is a true tale. This is the first time it has been published.*

Sundays are what you make of them. They can be days of holiness and gloom if you go to chapel, sacrifice and misery if you go to visit your in-laws, a sports day if you think that chasing a ball around, or watching it being done, is the acme of human endeavour — or you can rest and read. Not being Scottish, Irish, English or continental I decided to do the latter the day following my visit to the diabolical dentist.

That Sunday was to be, I thought, ambrosial. Despite the cavernous hole on the starboard side of my upper jaw, when I awoke, I was elated. It was the first time in months that *Cresswell*, Nelson and I were alone, to do as we pleased; I could lounge around in my underpants, without the necessity of sluicing my face in the water bucket, I could burn the bacon and eat an egg raw in milk and throw my pillow playfully at Nelson and he could jump around as best he could on his three legs, with his tongue hanging out, and pant and grin at me, and not worry if his tail brushed a damned china cup off the table. By the time breakfast was over we had, both of us, sloughed off, in half-an-hour, months of weary fair manners-at-table and "Oh-deah-we-reahlly-jolly-well-ought-to-buy-a-decent-bally-tea-towel!" which was Sissie's plaint every breakfast time. Now Nelson could hop onto the starboard berth, which had been his favorite lounging place in the happy days before Nemesis, in the shape of the bishop's sister, had overtaken us in the midst of the vineyards of France. Now he could lie there, with his head on his paw, grinning at me, until I gave him my tin bacon plate to clean with his eager tongue before I restowed it, by throwing it at the stove and letting it find its own resting place, just like the good old days.

After breakfast and the daily exercise just described, and as it was yet cool topsides, I chose a book to enjoy. Shake-speare isn't for the morning, and Boswell's *Life of Johnson* I decided to save for the next day. Conrad's *Nostromo* temp-ted me, but in the end I settled for my old friend *The Oxford Book of English Verse*. I made another pot of tea and subsided onto my berth, with my head on piled pillow and oil-skin jacket, my back to the hatchway, from whence came the daylight. Now, after I lit a cigarette, I was in my own version of *paradise*. Here was bliss, a quiet ecstasy, perfect contentment, supreme happiness; now I was as near to Avalon or the Fortunate Isles as I could ever expect to be in this life — and probably after. No one had ever told me, in those days, that a "man of action" was not supposed to enjoy poetry. No one had ever tried to insinuate into my consciousness that poetry and action were completely inimical, one to the other. In my Welsh innocence it never occurred to me that poetry was anything else but the ex-pression of action, nor that action could be other than the expression of poetry. True, years before, in my navy days, when Hollywood films had been shown on deck to the lads in the less-cold Arctic nights of Heflavik fiord, I had sometimes wondered why none of the heroes ever seemed to look at a book, unless it was a cattle-baron totting up his profits and losses; but this I had put down to an ignorance on the part of the film makers.

As for real life and as for sailors, I never met a real sailor yet who wasn't, at heart at least, a poet, and as a general rule, the more of a rough-and-tumble scallywag he was, the more of a poet. They must have been poets-at-heart; none of them ever had any *justification* for doing what they were doing. I'm not saying that sailors are all working poets — God saved us from that debacle by making most of them mute; but I never met one of them, no matter how roguish he was, who did not have a sense of the rhythms of the ocean, of life; the mystery, the ineffable surging song that is born wherever and whenever a boat meets the water of the sea. No one could live the life we live without being a poet at heart, at least not for long, and certainly not happily. Those who try to, exist like aliens in a strange land, trying to speak and understand an incomprehensible tongue, an insane babble. They cannot fathom that the very act of sailing is an act of pure poetry; that the sanity of sail is not, cannot be, *presumed*, as is the sanity of the land. At sea it either *is* or it *isn't*, and there's nothing in between—and nothing can be saner than that.

That morning, turning the pages of Wyatt and Spenser, Byron and Donne; tasting and savoring each spicy morsel, in between winks at Nelson and sips of tea, I imagined the shadow of a landsman on my shoulder, asking the eternal question that landsmen have always asked of voyagers — *Why*? I looked around the cabin again, all gray paint and smoky from the stove-smuts. I saw the shining brass oil lamps jiggling in their gimbals every time a fishing boat rumbled past, entering port from her night labors, with the crew (I knew in my mind's eye) already changed into their best black suits for church. I gazed at the pictures on the bulkheads—Nansen and Scott, Shackleton and the Queen, they stern and intrepid, she smiling. I felt the warmth of the sun as it slowly climbed into the sky and the rays streaming into the cabin, and their angle, without my even looking at them, telling me the time as precisely as any clock ever made, even as I read. I heard the low groan of the mooring lines and the anchor rode every time the boat was disturbed, and I heard a voice . . . from the direction of *Dreadnaught*, a junk-piled lifeboat.

"*Cresswell*! Hello there!" It was a high-pitched halloo. Nelson started. He jerked his head up and stared at the companionway, his tongue hanging out. Again the voice, "Anyone home?"

I stuck a teaspoon in the page I was reading and quickly donned my pants. It was a man's voice, but you never knew if there were women around at that late hour of the morning—or any hour, come to that, especially on Ibiza Outer Mole. I made my way up the companionway ladder, and gazed around and saw him.

"Morning," said I.

He was a stocky set man with a round, red face which was decorated with one of the biggest mustaches seen around since General Kitchener was a lad. It was black-gray and *huge*. It was so big and droopy and magnificent, with its ends curled up, that the first impression I had was that the mustache was wearing *him*. At each end of the mustache were ears which stuck out from his head as if they were about to flap as soon as the mustache whirled into a propelling motion. Under the mustache, so far as I could see, all he wore was a pair of overalls, so begrimed that it seemed if he doffed them they would stand up on their own. His feet, black and grimy, were bare. On his head he wore a white-covered peaked yachting cap. It was the only clean thing about him. That cap was *pristine*. Its gold badge gleamed in the morning sun. He looked like a cross between an admiral, a British army sergeant (Boer War vintage) and an unshod, overworked omnibus-workshop mechanic. I scanned his face and guessed he was about sixty-five.

"Ah, yes, 'morning old chap," he said in a Midlands accent. "I was just making a cup of tea, as it were, and I wondered if you'd like a drop? I saw your boat yesterday over the way, there . . . " He threatened the old-hulk berth, far way on the other side of the harbor, with his mustache. The mustache appeared to resent being pointed at the hulks and trembled in seeming anger, " . . . lovely old girl, isn't she?" The mustache subdued it's annoyance as it was pointed again at *Cresswell*. "Royal National Lifeboat Institute?"

I nodded, both to the mustache and the man. He was standing on a once-blue-and-white-striped mattress, which was now gray and black and sodden with rain and damp, and which lay thrown across the foredeck of the tiny *Dreadnaught*.

"Must introduce myself, as it were . . . Amyas Cupling."

"Tristan Jones."

"Yes, I know . . . I met your mate Peter Kelly in Monaco."

He gets around, I thought to myself, in a flash.

Amyas Cupling looked up at *Cresswell*'s masthead, then as he spoke he slowly took in every inch of her rig and hull. "Beach-launched heavy weather rescue vessel. Lovely jobs . . . real engineering, put them together like steamers, like battleships, as it were." Both he and the mustache smiled with genuine pleasure. "Let's see, let me guess her year . . . " He frowned. The mustache drooped in deep contemplation as it followed the line of *Cresswell*'s forestay. Suddenly his blue eyes smiled. The mustache lagged a little behind the eyes, as if waiting for an order over a ship's telegraph. Then it, too, curled its ends up even further, an order was somehow passed and the ears wiggled. I fully expected to hear the tinkle of a telegraph bell, and the roar of an accelerated forced-draught fan, followed by the whine of whizzing steam-turbines. "Hmm . . . let's see, couldn't be before oh-five . . . they had the thirty-footers until then . . . I'd say oh-seven or oh-eight."

"Dead right," said I. "Spot on, Amyas." I would have congratulated the mustache, too, had I known its name.

"Thames Ironworks?"

"Absolutely hundred-aye-one," said I, truly impressed with his knowledge of small craft.

"Marvelous craftsmen," said Amyas Cupling, "really knew their stuff, eh?" Without waiting for my comment he went on, "double-diagonal mahogany on grown oak frames? Goodness me, they really took their time, as it were. Do you realize that if you take into consideration the years it took to grow the oak frames into the exact shapes needed for . . . " Amyas checked my boat's name again. *Cresswell*, as he leaned over to read the name on the lifebelt hanging on her port shroud, seemed to purr. By now Nelson was at the top of the companionway, staring at the mustache. He looked as if he'd at first imagined it was some kind of tomcat perched on Amyas's upper lip.

Mister Cupling went on, " . . . ah, yes, *Cresswell* . . . named after a place in Northumberland, eh? Yes, it took them about eighty years to grow those oak frames into shape, as it were. They had plantations in Portugal, you know, and that means . . . let's see . . . she really started building in about 1828! That's when they planted the oaks for the frames, as it were."

"Amazing, isn't it?" I said. I already knew what he was telling me, but I didn't want to be impolite. He was evidently enjoying himself and his view of *Cresswell*.

Amyas Cupling and his mustache both looked at Nelson. My dog shook his shoulders for a second in consternation, as if he expected the mustache to leap onto the jetty and race away toward the town. "Your mutt?" said Amyas.

I introduced Nelson. Amyas approached close to *Dreadnaught*'s guardrail, which consisted of one rusty wire that undulated around the ship as it passed through stanchions which leaned this way and that, like drunken derelicts around a hostel door.

"Lovely boy," said Amyas. Nelson wagged his tail in pleasure at the wagging of the mustache. "Had a dog myself until a few months ago — of course not a thorough-bred like yours, just a little old sort of cross between a wire-haired terrier and a King Charles spaniel, as it were. Found him in an alley in Tangier, and those blessed brutes were kicking him and throwing stones. 'Course, couldn't let them get away with that, could I? Boxed their ears, as it were, and brought the poor old thing home to *Dreadnaught*. Had him for a year ... nice little chap, Teddy I called him ..." Amyas meditated for a moment, until a high-pitched whistle broke into our requiem for Teddy. Amyas Cupling and his mustache immediately perked up. "Ah, there's the kettle singing. Do come onboard, I'll have tea made in a jiffy as it were. No need to remove your shoes ... I'm refitting as it were ... bring the dog if you wish ..." he called as he lowered himself down through a rusting steel hatchway at the after end of *Dreadnaught*'s rusting steel coachroof.

Nelson, of course, would not accompany me. He was very jealous of his duty to guard *Cresswell* whenever I left her. It would have taken a whole panzer division to have shifted him once I was off my boat. How the police sergeant had gone onboard the previous day was still a wonder to me, except that Nelson must have known that I was ill and incapable. But he must have had an ugly attitude to the sergeant, else why would he have been tied up?

As I scrambled over *Cresswell*'s taut, shining guardrails and *Dreadnaught*'s rusty, drooping wire, I inspected the one sail that was still bent to the rusty steel lifeboat's black, unpainted, half-rotten, stubby mainmast. The mainsail was in the same state as it, and half its parrel clews had been ripped away from the canvas. It looked as if it had been savaged by a drunken pterodactyl. I gingerly danced over the damp mattress on deck, scrambled across and through a jumble of rusty one-inch wire cable, picked my way through a collection of oily cans and barrels, all rusting, and finally reached the hatchway.

The scene below was almost indescribable. It was as if I had been hiking on the Yorkshire moors, and had come across the wrecked relics, abandoned decades ago, of some early-Victorian underground workings—a tin or copper mine, which had petered out long, long ago.

Down in the gloom, in the dim yellowish light of one small electric bulb, was a mass of dismantled machinery— eccentrics and connecting rods, valves and tappets, old batteries, engine casing, pistons, nuts, bolts, oil pumps, water pumps—all dead bone dry and rusty; electric wires sprawled every which way, all ancient and discolored; batteries, a battery of them, all dirty black and dusty; and tools—spanners, socket wrenches, drills, pliers, screwdrivers—scattered everywhere, mostly corroded. In the center of the rust-streaked steel cabin, with condensation sweat gleaming on all sides and dripping from the roof, was Amyas' obvious pride and joy — a gray, rust-patchy box with great thick black cables spouting from it and disappearing into the dark gloom of the forward end of the boat. I stared at the box until, just as my foot slipped off a rusty cylinder-head lying at the bottom of the rusty steel ladder, I figured out that it was, in fact, a portable welding set.

Recovering my balance, I peered around. Apart from the engine bits, tools, batteries and electric cables, welding set, the steaming kettle that Amyas, beaming, held in his hand, and Amyas himself, everything in the cabin seemed to be *welded*. Everything seemed to be rusty steel: the cabin table, a steel plate welded onto two bent steel pipes that were welded onto the steel hull frames; the berths, one piled with rusty engine pieces and tools, steel plate welded together and to the boat; the shelves, all quarter-inch steel plates welded to the damp steel ship's sides, everything seemed to be welded. I spotted the library shelf. Fully expecting to find rusting steel books welded to the shelf, I clambered my way over to it. I inspected the titles. *The Sea*

Engineer's Manual, Emergency Repairs at Sea, Marine Engines and their Maintenance, The Marine Engineer's Practical Handbook, and so on.

I turned from reading the book spines, to see both Amyas and the mustache smiling at me. The whole scene, in the dim glow of one tiny lamp bulb — there were no port holes — was as if the manacles-workshop in some gloomy corner of Dante's inferno had gone on strike some five years before, and was now in the custody of a benevolent Victorian ironmaster. If Isambard Kingdom Brunel had come aboard that moment, I imagined, he would have doffed his top hat and for once in his life smiled.

Amyas was now pouring tea into two rust-spotted metal mugs on the steel table. He cocked one bushy eyebrow and the mustache at me. "Like it, eh?" he said. Without waiting for my response he went on. "Of course, I'm refitting at the moment, as it were. I started this one in Gibraltar. Of course I don't stay in one place while I refit, sort of sail around anyway, as it were. Been to Sardinia, Corsica, Malta, Greece, Yugoslavia, Italy, South of France, and Majorca while this refit's going on. Can't stand to be in one place for too long. I was in the merchant service for forty-seven years . . . got to second engineer. Then Suez came along and the old Line folded up and sort of left me high and dry, as it were." As he spoke he doffed his immaculate white-topped peak cap and hung it on a rusty steel bolt over his berth. His graying hair, rather long and lanky, fell all around his head, making him look like a happy walrus who has just surfaced from below a patch of long-stranded seaweed.

"That must have been quite a wrench?" I punned.

"Worst of it was, I lost my missus in the same year . . . " he said. The mustache drooped for a moment, then picked up again. "But anyway, we can't mope around, as it were, can we? So I decided to go to sea for a change. The Line was now defunct and the brokers had sold my old ship *Princess of India*—good old girl she was, made the London-Bombay run four times a year, rain or shine, for sixty years—and I managed to get hold of one of her lifeboats, sort of rescue it, as it were. This is it."

"What, *Dreadnaught*?"

"Of course, old chap. She was the forward lifeboat, starb'd side. Officers only. I used to take her round Bombay harbor for trials in the old days. Great fun. Used to take the lads for a spin, as it were."

"So how did you get here, then?" I asked him, fascinated.

"Oh, I bought her in Inverkeithing, in Scotland, three years ago. But she was in a terrible state. They'd let all the lifeboats go to wrack and ruin, as it were."

"Did you refit her there, in Inverkeithing? I know it well . . ."

"Oh, no. It was autumn you see, and what with the weather and the Scotch mist, as it were, it would have meant a longish delay, so I slapped the masts in and sailed her direct to Gibraltar and started the refit there. A bit warmer, as it were."

"But that's well over a thousand miles!"

"Yes, she was a bit sluggish at first, but the wind picked up off the Bay of Biscay. Only took us six weeks . . . well, just under seven, as it were."

"How did it go in Gib? I mean the refit?"

"Oh, I couldn't stay there long enough to finish it. The harbor mooring fees were too steep for us, so we took off on a little bimble into the Mediterranean, as it were. Went to Malta, first, but it was cheaper in Greece, so we went there."

"But that's another thousand miles . . . more?"

"Only took eighteen months. Of course we didn't hurry. I mean the Med's too interesting for that, so varied, as it were."

"When did you get the refit done then, Amyas?"

"Well, as you can see, I'm still at it. There's no point in hurrying, unless, of course, it's an emergency, as it were.

No engineer that's worth his salt wants to bodge a job, you see. I know it might seem a little slow to some people ashore, as it were, but three years is not such a terribly long time, especially when you're alone on a job, is it? She sails quite well, even if she's a bit slow compared to *Princess of India* for example, so I haven't missed much of the Mediterranean. Been in Spain, Italy, France, Malta, Morocco, Greece, Yugoslavia . . . no, little old *Dreadnaught* and me, we've been refitting all over the place. Fixed quite a few other boats' engines, too. Of course I always help the local fishermen out before the yachts. I mean they're working. They've their families to feed, as it were."

"Do they pay you?"

"Oh no, I wouldn't dream of asking for money. After all I'm a professional ship's engineer, and the golden rule . . . if someone's in a fix . . . as it were."

Amyas and I finished our tea. I had looked around his galley. It was such an incredible mess—rusty steel pans hanging over a rusty steel stove; an ancient Colman's mustard can, so patchy with rusty brown that it would have given Escoffier a fainting fit. I invited my engineer friend over to *Cresswell* for fish stew.

"That sounds jolly good," he said, accepting my invitation. "After all, it is Sunday. One really shouldn't do too much work on the Sabbath, as it were."

We finished our fish stew. Nelson avidly cleaned our bowls. Replete, Amyas and I adjourned to *Cresswell*'s cockpit. There he talked of refits and gudgeon pins as I watched the Sunday afternoon parade, a procession of Ibizan locals out for their weekly *paseo* along the seawall. It was always a spectacle. Whole families, all together, from grandpas and grandmas down to minute week-old babies in costly perambulators resplendent with silk tassels and sunshades and shiny chromium wheels, and all the mature adults soberly dressed in black suits and black dresses with black shawls. The older women wore their best jewelry and the older men tried their best not to follow the younger women with their eyes. All the younger women, the single ones, promenaded in tight-knit groups of five or six, all flashing eyes and white smiles for each other. The younger men also trooped in tight-knit groups until they were within a few feet of the knots of nubile women. Then the young men's groups dissolved into a file, and a straggle of unspoken questions were shot at the women as they were passed. The young women duly giggled and some even turned their heads to follow the youths, but you could always tell which young woman really fancied one of the men. That one kept her head still as she walked on, straight-faced, eyes front.

It was fun, watching the oldest game in the world. The West End and Broadway could do no better when it came to a show. The locals never seemed to notice the foreign boats or the people on them. This game had been played before the first boat floated. It was as if we did not exist. Which was as well, for Amyas Cupling and I had front stall seats and I could enjoy the sights and sounds of the promenade without any embarrassment. Amyas dealt with compression ratios and propeller pitches and a lot of other engineering esoterica, most of which was, and still is, a complete mystery to me. It was poetic, all the same. What could sound more helpful than "camshaft?" What could ring more solid than "block-lining?" Amyas, when he murmured words like "induction," "compression," "ignition," and "exhaust," sounded so much more romantic than my terms for the same things — "suck," "squeeze," "bang," "blow." Amyas was an engineering poet, a poet-engineer, *as it were.*

Toward three o'clock the little converted Spanish fishing boat, on the other side of *Cresswell* from *Dreadnaught*, moved slightly toward the jetty. I turned round to see if someone was playing with the mooring lines, and saw that it was a little old man in a black suit, just like a hundred other little old men who passed along the jetty that Sunday, on their after-church promenade. As I looked up in his direction, the little old man bowed toward me slightly, with true Castillian courtesy. Somehow I knew he was the boat's owner.

I jumped up, just as Amyas was explaining some intricacy of third-stage expansion, and I scrambled over *Cresswell*'s stern onto the jetty. I heaved the little old man's mooring line, to bring his boat closer, and helped him to cross safely over the narrow gap between the mole-wall and the stern of his little craft. Safely onboard and down in his cockpit, he turned and smiled at me, and bowed again. *"Muchas gracias, senor,"* he said. "Alfredo Ramero Gonzales Rodriquez de Valdez y Compostella" (or some such name; it sounded more like the Real Madrid soccer team than one person, to me). "Please accept my deepest thanks, on behalf of myself and of my vessel, *Estrellita del Mar!"* His Castillian was of the purity of a mountain stream.

I introduced myself and Amyas Cupling to the little old man. *"Little Star of the Sea!* What a beautiful name, *senor!"* I said.

The little old man bowed again. "Thank you so much," he said, now in perfect English, Oxford accent and all, but with slight Spanish undertones. "If you have any need of me, please accept my invitation to come onboard and I shall make my best endeavours to be of assistance to you gentlemen." He turned and unlocked the tiny main hatch of his boat, and went below.

I smiled at Amyas, who raised an eyebrow. We said nothing until I was back onboard *Cresswell*. Then I spoke in a low voice. Sound carries much more between boats than anywhere else.

"Funny little fellow," I commented.

"Looks quite well educated, as it were," replied Amyas, also in hushed tones.

"Nice little boat, though. Looks converted at first, when you see her."

"But she's not . . . " whispered Amyas.

"No, she's been constructed like that. Copy of a Majorcan fishing vessel, built as a yacht. Nice job they've done of her, and she's very well kept, Jesus . . . " I remembered Amyas did not blaspheme. "Sorry Amyas," I said.

"That's all right, old chap. I know you're not taking the Lord's name in vain. Don't forget I was at sea for thirty-eight years . . ."

"I mean," I continued, "just look at that paintwork. You can see they took their time with it, whoever painted her. And look at that goldleaf trimming around the coachroof coaming. Holy smoke, it must have taken them a whole month to get that line around her alone!"

"Yes," said Amyas Cupling, "actually I intend to do *Dreadnaught* much the same way." He meditated for a minute. "When the refit's finished, as it were."

"Yes, it wouldn't really make sense to paint her before you get her shipshape, would it?" I said, as I glanced around and over at the saddest-looking, dirtiest, scruffiest, rustiest tin-pot of a vessel I had ever clapped eyes on outside of a coaling depot. Under my glance poor old *Dreadnaught* seemed to flinch, and move as if she were protesting that it wasn't *her* fault. What did Amyas Cupling expect after the glories of *Princess of India*? . . . Tommy Lipton's *Endeavour*?

We went down into *Cresswell*'s cabin again for me to show Amyas my library, so he could borrow one of my books. As he browsed through the titles, there was a low rumble from out in the harbor. Amyas turned to me, questioningly. "It's alright, Amyas; it's a powerboat coming in. Plenty of people up there to give him a hand. Take your time. I'll put the kettle on for another cuppa. Take whatever book you fancy."

A minute or two later Amyas commented, "Well . . . I think I've read all of these, as it were."

"Shakespeare?" I asked.

"Oh, years ago. I used to read him in the night watches, when I was third engineer on the old *Princess of Burma*." Amyas dismissed the Bard. "But I'll tell you what, old man, as long as you're not using it today or tomorrow . . . "

"No, I've got my book for tomorrow. Verse. It's over on my bunk. You can borrow any book in the library . . . " I offered.

"Well, it's not in the library. Look, it's on this berth." He held up my oil-stained engine handbook. He read the title *Volvo-Penta MD2 Owner's Manual of Operation and Maintenance*. "I'd really like to read through this, if I may borrow it, as it were."

I was just on the point of saying "By all means," when *Cresswell* lurched so violently that the steaming kettle was jerked out of my hands and clanged into the after cabin bulkhead. Amyas froze. I shot up the companionway ladder. Angrily I glared around. In the split second it had taken me to reach open air, I already knew what the cause of the shock was. Now I saw I was right.

A great monstrous powerboat eighty feet long, all gleaming white and silver, had backed right into the little old man's converted fishing boat, *Estrellita del Mar*. As the monster had bashed stern-first into her the tiny boat's anchor chain, a thin quarter-inch one, had snapped and the fishing yacht had smashed into *Cresswell*'s starboard side. Now, *Cresswell*'s sides, being constructed like the walls of Durham cathedral, would not give way as the motor yacht continued backing into the small fishing boat, crushing her against *Cresswell*. Something had to give. The laws of force and motion demanded it. *Cresswell*'s anchor chain obeyed the laws and, although it was three-quarter-inch galvanized steel, it snapped like a piece of knitting wool, even as, horrified, I watched. Then, as the big bruising bastard from Barcelona continued racing his engines at full speed astern, *Cresswell* smashed into *Dreadnaught*. It was no good yelling; the roar of the eighty-footer was far too loud for any voice to be heard. Then I saw the line.

The eighty-foot monster had secured a long thick nylon mooring line from her port stern right across all three bows of *Estrellita*, *Cresswell*, and *Dreadnaught*, onto the jetty bollard, and was now, as well as shoving with all the might of a thousand horses with his engines, hauling in the nylon line with his after capstan! It was as if a great big bully was not only pushing his way into a line of little old ladies, but was crushing them to death with his stomach as he drew himself to the wall behind them with hawserlike arms. Aghast, I glanced up at the bridge of the killer. There were three figures up there. One in a flowered shirt with dark glasses. The owner, I told myself swiftly. One in a white hat and dark glasses. The guest. One in a white cap and jacket and dark glasses and toothbrush mustache. The "captain." Not a trace of expression on any of the faces, except that of haughty might and right.

It all took place in seconds. I shot up the ladder, took in the scene, bent down . . . and then I did something that I had never done before, and which I sincerely hope I shall never have to do again.

I grabbed my double-bladed Royal Navy deep-sea diver's knife — it was more like a Roman short-sword—from it's brass "Siebe Gorman" sheath just inside the companionway, and I flew ashore. I don't remember leaping, or scrambling, or clambering, or climbing. The next thing I knew I was ashore, with my diver's knife at the throat of a large, dark, white-jerseyed seaman who was standing by the straining killer-hawser. He ran, wild eyed. I sawed through the thick nylon line, with the wicked edge of the knife. The line twanged and shot back into the harbor water with a *zuzz*, just as *Dreadnaught* smashed her stern against the cruel stones of the quay. Something went bang even over the roar of the killer-craft's engines and *Dreadnaught*, as Amyas, now on *Cresswell*'s deck, stared aghast, started to sink by the stern. We both shot wild looks at one another. In a flash we both knew that poor *Dreadnaught*'s propeller had smashed against a rock, that her propeller shaft had been bent so badly, that her stern gland had been ripped open, and that filthy harbor water was now pouring into the wretched little boat just as Amyas's lifeblood was pumping wildly through his heart.

I tore down the jetty, knife at the charge, toward another gin-palace crewman who was standing, flustered, at her starboard mooring rope. As I raced for him, I saw out of the corner of my eye, that the powerboat's stern was swinging clear now of Cresswell, but it had taken my bowsprit with her. I lunged at the crewman, a small, dark man. I must have been screaming my head off, but if I did I didn't hear it. The noise of the killer's engines was too high. A moment before I reached him the little crewman, his eyes bulging at me, threw himself into the harbor. I slashed the other rope just as the killer's engines died. Then, as he swung round slowly to face the east wind, I shouted up at the men on the monster, "You great clumsy bastards! You come ashore and I'll cut your bloody balls off!"

Then I came to my senses just as quickly, it seemed, as I had lost them. To this day I think I did the right thing. If I had not cut the lines all three small craft would eventually have been crushed against the wall and probably sunk.

The little old man on the converted fishing boat was now on the deck. He was staring, calmly, sternly, wordlessly at the ruin and carnage about him. Amyas was still on *Cresswell*'s deck, holding on to her guardrail as he wept and sobbed silently and stared down at the filthy harbor water, below into which *Dreadnaught* with a gurgle, had completely disappeared. I, too, looked down, to see the last of her air bubbles reach the oil surface and pop. For a minute I looked silently at Amyas. He was like a broken man.

A voice came from the killer ship. It boomed out tinnily across the harbor. They were using their loud-hailer. "I have reported you to the local harbormaster and the chief of police on my radio. Do not move from where you are . . . "

I cupped my hands around my mouth. The voice hesitated. "Get stuffed!" I shouted. "GET STUFFED YOU SODDIN' GREAT OAF!"

"YOU ARE TO REMAIN WHERE YOU ARE—POLICE ORDERS" roared the voice.

"POLICE BULLSHIT!" I roared at him and climbed back onboard *Cresswell*. At least if I were to be arrested it would now be onboard a British Registered Vessel, I thought. Let them pick the bones out of *that* bastard!

Amyas threw me a look of abject misery. He slumped down onto *Cresswell's* side-deck, his head in his hands. I put my hand on his shoulder. "Bugger 'em, Amyas . . . oh, sorry mate, I got a bit excited."

"It's alright, Tristan," his voice sobbed. "I understand . . ."

"You can stay onboard *Cresswell* if you like, mate, until we figure out how to raise *Dreadnaught*," I said.

I looked around me again. The haughty figures on the bridge of the killer ship were all three gazing in my direction, the two civilians with their arms over the bulwarks, folded, and the skipper inspecting me through a huge pair of binoculars. Still enraged, I threw him a British two-finger sign, then an Italian three-finger sign, then a French four. I turned to see the little old man, but he had gone below again, probably, I thought, to check the hull of his tiny fishing boat, to make sure she wasn't leaking. That reminded me to do the same, even though I knew that *Cresswell* was as tough a nut as ever there was.

Leaving Amyas, his head still in his hand, on deck, I hurried through my boat, inspecting her frames, checking the bilge water level to ensure that her keelson had not been strained, and her coachroof beam knees, her futtocks and her ribs, to see that they had not shifted. Even if I was headed for the jail, I thought, I'd make sure that *Cresswell* was alright, and Amyas could look after her for me until Sissie got back from Majorca . . .

As I set my plans, a harsh, imperative voice yelled out from the jetty. "*Cresswell*," it shouted, then in Spanish "come on deck with your hands up. You are under arrest!"

That's it, I thought. I stretched my hands up in good old Texas style and headed up the companionway, calling Nelson softly to stay where he was. As I ascended the ladder I saw, crowded all around *Cresswell's* stern on the Old Mole, about twenty Spanish navy seamen and their young officers, and a dozen Guardia Civil in their black leather hats and gray uniforms. Every one of them, except the officers, had a rifle or an automatic gun of one kind or another, and every one of these pieces of armament was pointed directly at my heart. I froze on the weather deck, silent.

"You are to come with us, you are under arrest!" A naval lieutenant addressed me, glowering as darkly as his twenty years or so would allow. Behind him all the sailors and policemen stared sullenly, threateningly. The lieutenant then waved his pistol at Amyas. "You, too!" he ordered.

Amyas had just started to rise from the deck, when suddenly there was a commotion among the four officers on the jetty. As if startled, the young naval lieutenant who was doing all the arresting, was arrested himself. As if rammed stiff by an electric shock he jolted upright and saluted. As he did he hollered "*Marineros atten . . . cion!* Seamen atten . . . tion!" All his uniformed minions sprang to attention and saluted as their guns clattered to their sides. All the Guardia Civil were now heels-together and eyes-front, all facing toward the little fishing boat. I turned to look at what had caused this transformation. It was . . . astounding. You could have feathered me down with a knock!

The little old man was now in the *full dress uniform of a general of the Spanish Army!* It was complete with sword and a great sash thrown across his shoulder! Around his hat was a red band under a badge so big and so golden it looked like a pride of lions. The little general's Spanish was far too rapid for me to understand exactly, but I caught the gist of them, in effect: "Lieutenant, you will arrest that offender," he languidly gestured with a white gloved hand across his shoulder at the drifting powerboat . . . "that offender against the laws of God, the dignity of man and the rules of common decency, place an armed guard onboard his boat, and you will hold him here for as much time as it takes to salvage the vessel of this *cabellero*," he gestured, again languidly, at Amyas, who, surprised as I was, gaped at him. The little general continued, "You will attend all three of us, tomorrow, early, to ascertain our estimations of the damage sustained by our craft and ourselves by the actions of that *moron*." Again he flicked a white glove at the power boat, " . . . and you will multiply that sum by three. That will be the amount of the fine which you will levy against that *animal*. After our repairs and the salvage of this gentleman's boat have been effected, you will then ensure that the surplus of money is donated to the local orphanage! Is that clear?"

"*Si, Senor Gobernador-General* . . . " the lieutenant hesitated, nervously, still rigidly at attention.

"Well, there are problems?" the little general snapped.

"There is no salvage firm on the island . . . it will take a long time for them to come from Barcelona."

"Time is essential. That boat must be raised tomorrow or the day after!"

"But . . . ?" The lieutenant was shaking by now. I turned and addressed the general. "*Perdoneme, Senor General* . . . "

The general turned to me. His face softened. "Yes, my friend?"

"Er . . . there is a salvage firm on the island . . . but it's foreign-owned."

The general smiled. "I don't care if it's owned by Russians! I want this thing cleared up before I leave Ibiza! Anyway, where is this firm and who owns it?"

"It's right here," I reached over and slapped my hand on Amyas's shoulder. "Cupling and Jones, Limited, Marine Engineering and Salvage Company, British, *senor*," I told the general as his dark eyes gleamed with amusement, "branches in Chatham, Portsmouth, Plymouth, Hong Kong and Singapore!" I missed out Gibraltar; it was a touchy subject at that time in Spain.

The little general threw his head back and laughed. On the jetty all the sailors and policemen's faces relaxed, and they started to grin. Then the general's face turned serious. "Do you think you can do it? Do you think you can raise Senor Cupling's boat?"

"Yes, sir, but we'll need the Port Captain's permission to use certain pieces of equipment and property which are lying in the harbor . . . "

The general gave an impatient wave of his hand. "No problem," he said. "He's having dinner with me tonight. Write me a list of whatever you need. This young man here . . . " he flicked a hand at the navy lieutenant, "will be responsible that whatever it is, it is provided for you and that you are afforded whatever other assistance our marine authorities can give you."

"Thank you, *senor*."

He bowed slightly. "*No hay de que*. No need. It is I who is in your debt after you helped me onboard earlier today, *Senor* Jones. You see, courtesy is not merely it's own reward . . . and by the way."

"Senor?" I grinned at him.

"When you proffer that estimate for repairs and salvage, bear in mind that the orphanage here is not very rich. I was there before I came onboard this morning. I think you may as well make sure that at least some little good comes out of the evil events of this afternoon . . . " As the little general said this, one of his dark eyes flickered just a tiny bit . . . or was it a wink?

From my dinghy, I recovered *Cresswell*'s anchor chain with a grapnel and secured her well again.

Over supper of beef kidney and chips, Amyas cheered up. We now had a plan. Tomorrow we would set to and raise *Dreadnaught* from her grave.

"What was it that officer called him? It wasn't just general as it were?" Mister Cupling asked me. Nelson whooped. He loved kidney.

"No, Amyas, it was governor-general. He's the boss of all the bosses in all the Balearic Islands! It just goes to show, you never know who it is you're meeting, do you, as it were?"

For the first time since *Dreadnaught* had gone down, Amyas smiled, and I knew that the difficult salvage job was already half done.

The little general was up and about very early next day. I heard him padding about over onboard *Estrellita del Mar* before dawn. He accepted an invitation to join Amyas Cupling and me for breakfast in *Cresswell*. Eggs and kipper, scrumptiously fried to a turn by Amyas, who was now rigged out in my spare pair of working jeans and one of my tee-shirts, and had washed his feet.

After discussing with the general his little boat for a while I asked him how long he had been cruising about alone.

"Ah, *Senor* Tristan, I have been sailing much more ever since I fell off a horse . . . had a bad injury you see . . . I used to love horses, still do in fact, but I can't manage it any more. I'm seventy-three now. So I sail around in my little boat. I don't do too much sailing; she has a good engine and I only sail on the calmest of days. I love it." The general thought for a moment, as if dredging words from his subconsciousness. "It's the . . . very antithesis of army life in a lot of ways; the informality, the camaraderie with all differing types of people. And yet in some other ways it's very similar to the military—the need for order and some kinds of regulations to keep the vessel in good . . . ?" he looked as if he were searching for a word. He was again dressed in a black suit.

"Fettle," I prompted.

"What's that word?" The little old man screwed up his eyes.

"Good fettle. It's the Saxon equivalent of the opposite of chaos, of anarchy. It's having things shipshape, the way a sailor likes it; the way it has to be, for the sea to let him survive. What do you think Amyas?" I looked at Mister Cupling, offering him a share in the conversation.

Amyas looked serious. "Order? I should think that sums

it up in one word, as it were? After all, can't sail a boat around for long that's not in good order, can we?"

A vision of *Dreadnaught* hobbling from Scotland to Greece under a continual refit, passed through my mind. "No, you're right about that, Amyas," I replied.

The young naval lieutenant, along with a burly petty officer and two ratings, arrived just after 6:30. The lieutenant seemed at first obviously flustered and disappointed to see all we old men up, about, alive, and awake before he arrived. Then he perked up and dashed onboard *Cresswell*, like a lad arriving at a fairground, all pink cheeks, gray green eyes and, enthusiasm. "Must be from Galicia," the general muttered, "—and anxious to succeed." Then, down in *Cresswell*'s cabin, he caught sight of the general's face. He froze to attention; so did his men.

The general looked up, stern-faced, but with a twinkle. "Well, lad . . . don't just stand there! Say something! What's your name?"

"Francisco Alvarez Dominguez etc. etc. etc. etc. . . . " The lieutenant's name went on for about a minute, like a ship's passenger list.

"Well, lieutenant, *Senores* Cupling and Jones . . . *Limited* . . . have worked out what they need for the repairs and salvage operation. They've discussed it with me, and I've approved the plan and the charges for the work to be done and the equipment to be employed. Now, I'm flying to Barcelona today, and I'll be back in three days. When I get back I expect to see *Senor* Cupling's boat afloat again!"

"*Senor!*" Lieutenant Francisco's head jerked upright.

The general languidly strolled to the companionway ladder, and handed Francisco a piece of paper. "Now when you relieve your armed sentry on that floating *pigsty* out there, you give him this. Tell him to pass it on to the *animal* who drives that *thing* around, and to inform him, *from me*, that he has exactly forty-eight hours to get hold of this amount and to hand it over to *Senores* Cupling and Jones here. If he doesn't, you can tell him I'll have his boat taken to Palma cavalry barracks and mashed up with the horse bran!"

"*Senor!*"

"Good. Now, get together with these two *cabelleros* and see that they get whatever they need!"

"*Senor!*"

The general mounted the ladder and passed over to his own boat. Before he went below he turned again to the young lieutenant, who was still standing at attention. "Oh, and one other thing, my son . . . make a good *Spanish* job of it, eh?"

"*Senor!*" shouted the young man. When the general disappeared he looked down at the piece of paper. Softly, he whistled. He looked at me. "My men are ready, *Senor*; all ready. What do we need for this operation?"

I introduced Amyas and myself, to put the lad at ease. He introduced himself again. Then, after Amyas handed him a cup of tea, and a flaskful for his men on the jetty ("Cheer them up a bit, as it were, eh?") I clapped my hand on the lieutenant's shoulder and started reading off the list that Amyas and I had worked out the evening before, over supper. When I started reading the list and describing our intentions, Lieutenant Francisco's face had been clouded; then as I rambled on, and made swift sketches on the back of an old chart, his expression lightened, became intrigued, enthusiastic, and finally amused; so much so that he at last laughed.

"Marvelous!" he said. He looked at me in my Breton smock, tea mug in hand, a mischievous gleam in my eye. Then he stared for a moment at Amyas and his mustache, twitching and grinning, as they hovered over our shoulders. Suddenly the lieutenant straightened. "*Senores*," he intoned gravely, "you know I'm beginning to think you really *are* professional salvaging experts!"

"Actually for salvaging spirits, as it were." Amyas murmured, with a wink at me. The mustache twitched in agreement.

"Yeah, *Johnny Walker, Black Label*," I muttered, "preferably. Come on, let's clear *Cresswell* and *Estrellita* out of the
way . . ."

I suppose some people must think of sailing vessels as
mere collections of inanimate objects, like planks of wood
and bits of iron and nails, wire and canvas. They may be
right, but if they are, then the old, dying hulk *Rosalinda* and
her next-door neighbor, which had no name, must have
been the most deliciously excited bits of inanimate matter
that ever existed when they felt Amyas and I jump onboard
them.

As we had walked along the town quay toward the hulks
they had looked sulkily depressed, as gloomily miserable
as ever, like old ladies with migraine, too pained to bother
to fix their hair, too old and worn-out to have it done for
them.

As soon as my feet hit *Rosalinda*'s deck, and Amyas's
directly afterward, I felt a transformation in the old derelict.
Some people will say that it was only the vibrations as our
weights descended onto her rotting decks that made her
tattered halyard wires jiggle and tremble, and that it was
merely an odd squally gust which fluttered the ragged
tatters of her mouldy mainsail as Amyas and I headed for
her cargo-hatch coaming and gazed down into the murky
water, still and scummy, in her hold. Others will say that
the voices I heard, as we discussed getting the water out of
her, were only the echoes of our own words bouncing back
at us from the great oak frames in the ghostly shadows of
the side-decks. Others will say that sailors are superstitious
creatures and anyway, all small boat voyagers are a bit
dotty and liable to let their imaginations run away with
them.

But I say . . . I swear . . . that as Amyas and I leaped onboard that old derelict her pulse leapt; it seemed that the
spirits of every man who ever sailed in her jumped for
inexpressible joy. We had not lowered ourselves down on

her deck like curious sightseers. We had no cameras slung around our necks. We were not looking for quaintness or bizarre curiosities from the distant past. We had little thought in our heads about the "romance" of sail; we were not dreaming of her past voyages, *and she knew it*. The moment we bowled onboard her that old girl's fainting blood *raced*. She knew that we were gauging her remaining strength. She knew we *wanted* her. She knew that, in some way, she was still useful. As we stared down into her hold she heaved and sighed, welcoming us — but it was only a passing fishing boat's bow wave that did that, of course.

Her next-door neighbor, an even more ancient, stump-masted ruin, which had been merely fidgeting as we inspected *Rosalinda*, seemed to almost faint entirely away with anticipation and excitement as Amyas clambered over her decayed bulwark. Amyas first walked back to her stern and peered over the counter.

"This one has no name, Tristan. Sort of nameless, as it were!" he called. I plunged my knife into *Rosalinda*'s mainmast. It was sound enough.

"Good, then we'll call her *Bloody Neverbudge*!" I sang back.

Amyas grinned as I hopped onto the nameless wreck. "*Bloody Neverbudge*—she certainly looks it," he said. "Hasn't moved in years, I'd say, but she must be built like Gibraltar, as it were. Hardly a drop of water in her—about a foot, probably rainwater."

"That's a wonder, Amyas, 'cus she's got dropsy," I replied. I meant that her keel was hogged, that is that it dropped down from the horizontal forward and aft. *Bloody Neverbudge* seemed to take that as a compliment. Her rotten gaff boom, which was swinging loosely over my head, suddenly moaned as if in pleasure.

After Amyas and I had prodded around the hulk's mooring posts and their bulwarks with our knives, seeking out the rot and marking the sound wood with great chalked crosses, for about an hour or so, the Spanish navy turned up. It brought two commandeered fishing boats. One of these belonged to Joselito, a local fisherman friend. I waved at José as his boat slowly chugged up to the hulks. He grinned back hugely at me. He was obviously pleased. He would be paid well for his labor, and it seemed he was remembering the Halloween visit to the graveyard with Rory O'Boggarty, Ireland's Hope and England's Dread. I winked at him.

Both fishing boats had portable diesel water pumps on their decks. Both had twenty fathoms of two-inch chain laid out. Both had a Spanish navy scuba diver who were already both donning their rubber suits in a welter of joking about how they were going to manage to make it with the mermaids dressed so.

By the time *Rosalinda* and *Bloody Neverbudge* (even the Spaniards were calling the ancient ruin by her new name now) were pumped out, Amyas and I, with the help of a couple of seamen, had one end of each long chain secured around the bases of both mainmasts, and the fishing boats were securely lashed alongside both of our hulks. With the amount of water taken out of *Rosalinda*, her hull had risen a couple of feet out of the harbor. Now both the old ladies drew less than three feet under their bows.

Soon our little squadron was ready to get underway. Before we cast off the shackles of the hulks' imprisoning mooring lines, Francisco, as I had requested, planted two staffs, with Spanish ensigns bent to them, on the stern of each hulk. The old ladies shivered with delight and seemed to be charmed at being invited out by a young, good-looking officer of their very own navy—but of course it was only the vibrations of the fishing boats' engines . . . let no one ever think that they were thrilled almost out of their keels, to be stepping out again, pretty new red and yellow shawls over their shoulders . . .

With a great roar as the fishing boat engines accelerated, and a mighty swirl and churn of mucky harbor water, the hulks moved off, shy and reluctant at first, then, as the fishing boats gently, courteously, insisted, and as the lash-ing lines took up the strain, and after the old ladies and we had glanced around nervously, to make sure their slips weren't showing, the whole fleet moved steadily in the forenoon sunshine across the dead-flat water of the harbor. *Rosalinda* and *Bloody Neverbudge* felt the wind in their hair — what was left of it, the jagged, torn, rotted bits of sail still aloft. They sighed in pleasure and delight. I was in *Rosa-linda*, Amyas was in the more ancient ship. There was no point in us trying to steer the hulks — their rudders had dropped off, or been removed, long before.

"See you in Miami, Amyas!" I shouted, joking of course.

"After I've had a look around the Bahamas, as it were!" he sang back over the yards of passing water between us. Both the old ladies jolted at this, as if they imagined we were serious, but of course it was only our passing over the bow wave of a passing ferry from Formentera. Of course boats don't imagine; of course they don't dream; of course they don't *know*; any sensible landsperson knows that! What do these sailors, these wandering fools, think the folks of the towns and cities are? Idiots? Romantics?

By the time we got both the hulks' bows alongside the sunken *Dreadnaught*, both of the long chains into her main hatch and out through her forward hatch and back to the hulks, and both hulks' cargo holds so full of water that their keels both rested on the harbor bottom, both chains tautened up around the masts, and the portable pumps again sucking water from the sunken old ladies, it was time for lunch.

Amyas, Francisco, and I, all three of us filthy shipmates, strolled over to Antonio's bodega. We took one of the seamen with us to collect sandwiches for his mates, who stayed and watched the water gush from the diesel pumps, and the two hulks' hulls slowly, slowly rise again, and the cables from the sunken *Dreadnaught* slowly, slowly tauten. Francisco ordered the petty officer to stop the pumps as soon as the cables were dead taut, and to await our return.

Such is the life of the owners of a salvage company and a naval officer.

It was obvious, when we reached Antonio's that the events of the day before and of the morning were now common knowledge, but of course distorted out of all proportion. From the loitering ancients outside the door we were told that "communist swine" had "made the attempt on the life of their governor-general and ought to be castrated." Antonio insisted that a bomb had been planted in *Dreadnaught*, which the foul murderers had mistaken for *El General's* boat. From Rory O'Boggarty who sat, as usual, in the back of Antonio's bar, in the gloomy shadows, a customary bottle of beer in front of him, we received a quote from W.B. Yeats: "Sure, *the center cannot hold . . . and the ceremony of innocence is drowned . . .*"

"Oh, for Christ's sake, Rory . . . stop getting on my soddin' *wick!* . . . Is it nothing better you have to do but spout bloody poetry at hard-working poor sailors?" I retorted. "Here we are, only come in for a quick beer and a bite, and you're covering us with your damned Bloomsbury gloom . . ."

"It's an old Keltic tradishun," he slurred, "for the bard to be welcoming the warriors."

"Along with the women," said I. That shut him up. Very conscious of sexual roles, they are, in County Limerick.

A half-hour later, when we arrived back at the salvage site, the pumps were still running, but soon the chains tautened, and, as the stumps and masts of the two hulks took the strain of *Dreadnaught's* ten tons, the mooring wires and anchor holding them in place strained and squealed, moaned and groaned. This was the crucial moment. We stared down into the murky harbor water, at the spot below which *Dreadnaught* lived out her agony. There had been a fresh southerly wind during the night. Whilst it had not blown the oily muck away from the Outer Mole wall, it had piled the harbor water on the northern shore of the bay, and this had drawn a lot of the gunge with it, so we could just see *Dreadnaught,* the mere shadow of her, as she lay with her deck five feet underwater.

Suddenly, as we peered down, as if we were gazing on some exotic sea monster, the shadow moved. Only a short jerk, but it moved. The chains jerked, and slumped slack again. The seamen on the hulks' deck again tautened them up with their chain-rachet-tauteners, their "bit-nippers." The pumps roared on.

José was sitting on the steps of his wheelhouse, eagerly consuming a fish pie his wife and brood had brought for him. As his eldest son, the pig-sticker, waited for José to finish with his lunch pail I turned and saw the fat baby. It was waving that damned rattle and frowning at me. It looked like Churchill in 1940, even though it was being drooled over by Amyas, Francisco, the petty officer and its mother.

I stared down again at the shadow of *Dreadnaught.* Suddenly, with a grating and grinding, a cracking and straining, the shadow disappeared, the hulks heaved and groaned and all the positioning cables brought up rigid, like the holding wires of a circus Big Top tent. The fat baby was forgotten now, except by its mother, of course. Every other eye was now watching the wires and the hulks. Francisco and Amyas were at my side. The *swine* on the arrested killer boat glared at us.

"We got the bugger!" I said. "Look, the chains are almost vertical now. We pump out another few tons of water and she'll start to rise." By now the jetty was crowded with well-wishers.

"To come back to life, as it were," said Amyas.

"*Felicidades*" Francisco said. "Congratulations!"

"Not yet. It's too early," I told him. "Softlee, softlee, catchee monkee," I added in pidgin English.

Even as I spoke both *Rosalinda* and *Bloody Neverbudge* heaved upward slightly. Again the chains slackened off. Again they were tightened by the sweating seamen. Then as we watched like worshipers watching the Host being raised in slow motion, the two hulks rose, inch by inch. In silence, almost breathlessly everyone watched, everyone, that is, except the fat baby, who was now forgotten and howling it's fat head off behind us.

Slowly, inch by inch, the freeboard (the amount of hull above the water) of the two hulks increased. Inch by inch, . . . six inches. . . eight inches. . . foot by blessed foot, . . . one foot, two feet, three feet, four feet, six feet . . . until, at long last, to the rousing cheers and *olé's* of everyone present, the dirty gray top of *Dreadnaught's* rusty-steel coachroof broke the water surface , and soon her deck was awash. In minutes, Amyas was onboard his beloved boat, hanging over her stern, bashing a rag-enshrouded, wooden chock into the damaged stern gland. Soon when *Dreadnaught's* deck was a mere inch above water level, one of the pump hoses was dragged over and plopped into her. After a few more minutes she floated again. A hundred spectators of a dozen nationalities, all cheered.

Dreadnaught's exterior looked to me only a *little* sorrier than it had *before* she had been sunk. The mattress was only a little damper, the oily ensign dripped harbor water, but apart from that, and the busted stern gland, I couldn't see much difference at all on her exterior. Of course the crowd and the seamen, most of them, didn't realize that, and so there was a long spate of ooh's and aah's of commiseration and pity for Amyas, even though he himself was now grinning like a Cheshire cat, as the last mucky liquid came from *Dreadnaught's* insides, spurting out of the pump hose. When the last burbling gush was over, he hauled *Dread-naught* close to the wall and stood looking up at me. The mustache ends were again cocked.

I squatted down. "Okay, Amyas? Think she'll be alright now? We'll get you over to the hauling railway in a while, when the hulks have been returned." I said this quietly, in case the hulks should hear me. "Everything alright down below?"

"Oh, fine. Of course, there's a bit of a mess and everything will have to be dried out. The stove jets will need to be changed, but otherwise everything's about the same, as it were," he replied quieting his voice, for while he spoke I had lifted a finger to my lips. Spanish hearing is very acute.

Soon the crowd had melted away. Soon the hulks were sadly, but it seemed to me proudly, being escorted back across the harbor to the graveyard. They were still wearing their new ensigns as the fishing boats pushed and tugged them across the calm waters. Now there was something indefinably *different* about them. It was as if they now had a fresh story to tell to the other condemned hulks when the soft night breeze disturbed their broken rigging wires and the tatters of their ancient sails. They were like old folks going back to the home after a day out with the lads and lasses. They had a new lease on life. They knew they had been useful; they knew they had helped another of their kind; and they knew that they and others would remember the story and that they might be called upon again, to help their own little world keep turning. But of course they were only two rotten, mouldy, ruined hulks which had been used as pontoons for a few hours . . . that's all.

But not quite. Francisco had promised me that he would leave the ensigns rigged. One of his minions would raise and lower them every morning and evening. Amyas had painted, in big red lead letters, a new name on the oldest vessel . . . *Bloody Neverbudge*. It was daubed all across her stern, where passing people would see it plainly. And under her new name he had written, in white paint, "Rescuer of *Dreadnaught*—November 1965."

By dusk, *Dreadnaught* had been hauled up by the horse-driven capstan onto the schooner repair slipway, over by the road to Santa Eulalia. She was safe and drying out slowly.

After supper Francisco took Amyas and I to Antonio's for a couple of beers at the next table to where the slumped O'Boggarty was fast asleep in his corner.

"You might as well sleep onboard *Cresswell*," I told Amyas. "Sissie—she's my mate—won't be back for another day, and anyway she won't mind if you sleep onboard then; too bloody bad if she does."

"Oh, that won't be necessary. I'd be grateful if I can stay tonight," he said, "but tomorrow I'm going to go round *Dreadnaught* with a blowtorch . . . I'll soon have her dried out again, as it were."

"How about your welding set? Do you think it's knakered?"

"Oh, I can fiddle around with it, as it were, sort of fix it up. Give me something to do . . . " Amyas's mustache wiggled.

Then, at Francisco's prodding, we talked about the war, about the convoys and the battles in the Arctic. Amyas, it turned out, had been less fortunate than I. He'd had *six* ships sunk from under him. "Of course, now I suppose I can claim seven ships sunk?" he said, as young Francisco gazed at his face, fascinated, and I grinned.

The following day I accompanied Amyas over to the slipway and gave him a hand to get all his sopping gear — his blankets, books, tools, engine bits, cooking utensils, food and clothing — out of his boat, and we laid it all out to dry as best we could in the sunlight. It looked a sorry collection. A bit like a scrap-yard. In the afternoon, it started to rain, so we threw a great tarpaulin over the lot and retired to a little boatyard worker's bar across the road. That's one thing sailors learn . . . never fight the weather — always go along with it, especially onshore. If we didn't, we'd be drooling lunatics before you could say "nice weather for ducks."

"Of course I don't mind being on my own," said Amyas over our third beers, "but I do miss having the missus with me. We'd planned to cruise around together for years before I retired, only she wanted a wooden boat, so I suppose it's just as well, really. She never did understand metal . . .

and she hated engines. I used to fix up the neighbors' cars and lawn mowers and such while I was home on leave . . . well, if someone's in a jam, as it were . . . and she used to do her nut. Never wanted me to take her out, to the cinema and such . . . stay at home with my slippers on in front of the fire. She was a good girl, but a real homebody as it were. I don't know if she really would have liked *Dreadnaught* . . . what do you think?"

"Well, women are a bit funny. Some of 'em like steel boats, some of 'em don't, I suppose," I replied.

"Yes, they are strange creatures, I suppose you never really get to know them until you've been living with them for a while?"

"My old biddie's not too bad," I said. "I keep her in the for'd dodger when there's nothing for her to do, and when I've got something on, I send her ashore, shopping and all those things . . . gets her out of the way and keeps us happy. Bloody dog can't stand her, though. It's like he thinks she'll commit barratry any day; you know, pinch the boat while I'm ashore. But really she's alright, at least when she don't talk too much. . ."

Amyas laughed. "Oh, that's pretty usual. Seems they're mostly like that, I'm told, after they get to know you, as it were. Actually I find that type of thing sort of refreshing. At least it makes a change from the Old Man continually complaining about not getting enough revolutions . . . enough speed, or the steam-winch breaking down . . ." He was silent for a minute then he said, "Yes, I suppose the ladies are a bit like Scots captains, really. You just have to put up with 'em I suppose . . . still . . . "

He sighed.

Suddenly I had a bright idea, but it half-faded away again. "Anyway," I said, "I was going to offer to pass Sissie on to you. She's not a bad hand, she loves hauling in the anchor and heaving mooring lines, especially when there's a cold wind and it's raining . . . she laps it up!"

Above our heads, the pouring rain battered the tin roof of the shanty bar. Amyas looked at me, interested.

I continued. "Problem is, she's leaving for Morocco in a few months . . . " I paused for a moment. "Anyway, I'll put it to her, when she gets back from Majorca. See what she says."

Then our talk went back to boats , and Amyas wound up giving me a full hour's rundown on the workings of gas-turbine engines.

Lieutenant Francisco was onboard *Cresswell* early next day. In his hand he carried an envelope. He gestured over his shoulder as he slid down the ladder. "He's waiting on the jetty," said he, after he had sang out a greeting.

Amyas was frying cod's liver and chips for breakfast. With Sissie absent we could relish sailor's favorites again. None of your bloomin' sickly pale eggs and underdone bacon now. I sat on my berth scratching Nelson's ear. I looked up at Francisco. "Who? Who's waiting?"

"The powerboat owner. Look, he drew the money yesterday. All four banks had to pool together to raise it. He wants a receipt."

I stood up and looked over Francisco's shoulder. On the jetty was the man in the peaked cap, toothbrush mustache, and dark glasses. His face was expressionless as the glasses stared my way. I felt like charging ashore again with my diving knife. Instead I reached under the galley stove, grabbed a roll of toilet paper, Spanish — a bit like wrapping paper anywhere else—and ripped off a sheet or two. I scrawled a receipt over the paper and thrust it into Francisco's hand. He looked down at it and read "received money for salvage of *Dreadnaught* and repairs to *Cresswell* and *Estrellita del Mar*," then my signature.

"You haven't written the sum of money, *senor*."

"Oh, Christ . . . " I grabbed the paper again, with my hand still shaking in anger at the thought of that sod on the jetty. "How much is it?" I asked impatiently.

"One hundred thousand *pesetas* . . . I have it here," he replied.

"Right . . . one . . . *what?*" I almost collapsed against Amyas, who dropped his frying pan, fortunately onto the stove.

"One hundred thousand *pesetas, senor.* That's what the general wrote down on your estimation, after he'd seen what you needed and the work required . . . "

Quickly I scrawled in the sum on the receipt, as I reckoned to myself . . . 2,000 dollars . . . divide that by three . . . my hand shook even more . . . that's 660-odd dollars for *Dreadnaught,* and over 1300 bucks for the orphanage . . . and the whole operation had cost us only the price of a few beers . . . except for the fishing boats . . . two boats at twenty bucks . . . still left Amyas and me with more than 600 dollars . . .

I rammed the receipt into Francisco's hand. "What shall I tell him?" the lieutenant asked.

"Tell him to stick it up his nose," I retorted.

Francisco turned to mount the ladder, wordlessly. I looked at Amyas. He was in a seeming state of shock. His mustache twitched, his hands trembled. I called to the lieutenant. "No . . . tell him thank you and to call again soon!"

Francisco glanced over his shoulder and smiled before he clambered to the stern.

Amyas subsided onto my berth. He stared straight ahead of him, before he looked at me. Then his eyes crinkled up and the mustache and ears followed into the biggest grin imaginable.

"Tristan . . . do you know how much that is?" Amyas's voice was hoarse.

I waved the envelope that Francisco had handed me. I tore it open. Out slid a bundle of notes, two-inches thick, onto the biscuit tin lid that served as a chart table in *Cresswell.*

"Two thousand dollars, my old friend, and 600 of it for you! By Jesus . . . sorry, mate . . . by jumping Jiminy, you can have *Dreadnaught* looking like a bloody admiral's barge!"

"Oh, I couldn't take all our share, Tristan. You did more than half the work . . . and anyway, it was all your idea . . ."

"No . . . listen Amyas, you take what's over after we pay the fishing boats and the orphanage. It'll mean you can get your engine fixed ashore. I'll tell you what, if you like, you can take Sissie and me to dinner one evening next week when we return from Formentera, fair enough?"

Amyas stared into space for a minute, then he said, "Well, that's very generous of you, old chap, but I simply couldn't . . . I mean, after all, *what would I do while I'm sailing around if I didn't have my engine to fix, as it were?*"

That knocked the wind out of my sails for a few minutes, while I struggled not to laugh. Then I said, "Well, at any rate, Amyas, you can get the whole bloomin' boat painted and new sails and all, and still have enough left over to cruise for a few months . . . "

"Oh, I couldn't do that . . . it wouldn't be right . . . honest . . . "

I lost my patience. "Well, alright then, Amyas, as senior partner in the Cupling and Jones *Dreadnaught* Salvage Company, which hereafter will be considered dissolved, and as director in charge of finance, I'm paying you your fee for your advice in the firm's recent operations and also a bonus upon your retirement . . . okay?"

Amyas' face drew itself into a certain dignity. The mustache ends curled up. His eyes brightened. "That sounds reasonable enough, as it were, he said. "How much is it?"

"Thirty-one thousand three hundred pesetas . . . here, sign this receipt, please, then I can close the company books. I scrawled a receipt on another piece of toilet paper, Amyas signed it, and thus was dissolved the shortest lived salvage company ever.

Amyas said—"Don't forget, bring your lady friend to dinner next week."

"When we get back from Formentera, Amyas," I said.

Sissie was back in the late forenoon. "Yoo-hoo, Tristan, dahling!" I heard her voice from the otherwise deserted jetty. Nelson growled softly. I put down my book of verse — *Paradise Lost*.

I helped her onboard, still in her rose-bestrewn finery. Her eyes glowed like new Barlow sheet winches. "*Deah* Tristan!" she bellowed, as I grabbed her arm. "How *did* you manage without me?"

"Oh, it was a bit rough . . . but we managed it somehow." I took her parcels.

She was glowing, excited, as she passed down the companionway.

"Theah's a present for you, *dahling* Tristan!" she yelled, "and one for *deah* dahling Nelson . . . " Nelson glowered at her. Sissie turned around slightly, rocking the boat. Her eyes stabbed at the stove. Three pans, treacherously littered with remnants of kidney, liver, fish, and chips betrayed me. Her eyes followed them to mine. "Oh, you *poor* deah . . . just look at this bally old galley . . . simply awf'ly . . . mmm . . . well, I s'pose you've been terribly *busy* while Ai've been away, dahling?" She plonked her parcels on the spare berth.

"Bit of reading. Filled the water tanks," I replied.

"Heah . . . " Sissie handed me an envelope. "A month's chartah fee . . . three thousand five hundred pesetas, dahling (seventy dollars)."

"Thanks, Sissie. That'll keep us going until I get another delivery . . . By the way, Willie get away alright?"

"Oh, absolutely. He bumped into one of his curates in Palma airport. They travelled back togethah." She ripped my present open.

"How delightful for the curate," I said.

"Spiffing!" she said, as she handed me a red and blue striped tie.

"Just what I needed — thank you, Sissie!" I gasped as she pecked my cheek.

"I simply *knew* you'd like it," she murmured.

BY THE SKIN OF MY TEETH

This was one of the most difficult accounts to write that I ever tackled. Originally, this story, part of my book Ice!—*published by Andrews and McMeel—was as long as the entire book. It took me months, sitting in a freezing New York apartment, with the building boiler out of action and little money or food, to whittle it down to its bare essentials—and that is what it had to be.*

B eing underway was the most immense relief imaginable. Free at long, long last, after one year and a day locked in the ice field, 366 days—staring death right in its grisly skull sockets. Even though the chance of collision with a floe was possible if a heavy wind piped up, I felt so unburdened, for the first three or four days, that I found myself taking risks which normally I never would dream of, steering straight for a floe, missing its leeward side by a matter of feet, and crowding on sail in forceful gusts.

The boat leaked like a sieve. The whole line of the garboard strake, where the hull joined the keel, had had the caulking shaken almost completely out of it during the wicked battering by the ice in the Brittania-Berg capsize. I had to pump her out almost continuously, though in calm weather I could take a rest, letting the boat take in two feet of freezing cold water. Then I would don my sea boots, reaching up to my thighs, go below the cockpit floorboards, and bucket the water out. It was heavy work and left no time for desperation or fear.

As soon as the wind picked up, I inflated the rubber dinghy below in the cabin for extra flotation, just in case I fell asleep or was knocked unconscious. This made life below difficult, with a seven-foot dinghy stuck into the living space, but somehow I managed. It was cold, wet, miserable work, a great expenditure of my body's strength, meager as it was by this time. Mainly, it was will power that enabled me to start bucketing once again.

I looked up at Nelson sniffing around the horizon during one spell of backbreaking bucketing. "Yes, you old bugger," I yelled at him, "and if you had two bloody forelegs, you'd be down here, too." He frowned and again turned his snout to the far horizon, pretending to ignore me.

My position, when I broke out of the ice, was about 185 miles west-southwest of the main settlement of Svalbard, Kongsfjorden (King's Bay). As this was the nearest human abode, this is where I steered for, with a slight to moderate southwest wind pushing *Cresswell* before it over a kindly sea. On June thirteenth, four days after emerging from the ice trap, I obtained a position fix. I was only fifty miles from safety! The weather was much warmer now, some degrees above freezing for hours at a stretch. Becalmed from the thirteenth to the sixteenth, I managed to bail enough water out of the thawing tanks to wash three shirts, together with underwear and long sea-boot stockings. I used salt water to get the worst grime out, then rinsed them in fresh water. Then I trimmed my beard, which was all of nineteen inches long. It had served as a chest-warmer during the winter! Then my hair, which was down around my shoulders. It took me hours to unmat the hair and wash it before I could cut it, as the scissors were blunt and the whetstone was worn away entirely. The spare knife sharpener had gone to a watery grave with the other lost stores under the Brittania-Berg. This was the first time I had doffed the Eskimo-rig since entering the ice cap, except for the three times I had to remove it to peel off a sweat-frozen shirt. The fawn-skin underwear came off like it was my skin itself peeling from my body, and underneath I was lily-white, while my face, around the eyes, was almost black. Naked, I looked like something out of a nudist-camp harlequin party. My weight had diminished, of course, but what I had been eating must have been good, for I'd no sunken gums, loose teeth, or falling hair, all sure signs of scurvy. I was eliminating liquids about an hour after drinking and solids about twelve hours after eating, and my body muscles were like high-tensile steel wires. At first, my normal sea vision suffered. This ability always surprises landsmen (I can, after a day or two at sea, read a ship's name from four miles' distance). I knew this was the result of being in the dark cabin, straining my eyes with the seal-oil lamp, and, outside, wearing the snow goggles. But slowly my vision returned. My hearing was most acute. I was so accustomed to listening for the slightest boat noise or other unnatural sound, such as a possible airplane, that I could hear every one of the hundreds of separate wooden joints working in the hull. My sense of smell was almost as good as Nelson's. I was well rested, the boat steering herself, now clear of ice floes except for the odd maverick. I was warming up some porridge for peanut burgoo when I smelled fish. It could not have been from the shore, as the wind was still southwest. I hopped topsides and looked around. There was nothing but a lone ice floe to the north. But I clearly smelled fish! Nelson was straining his nose around the compass, and finally settled for a direction to the west-southwest-by west from our position. I stared hard, but, seeing nothing, went below to finish cooking the scrimpy meal.

By this time all the canned food had been eaten, with the exception of six cans of corned beef and six of sardines. We were down to porridge, peanuts, flour (I was out of yeast), and lard, together with the remnants of the seal blubber, about twelve pounds, stinking to high heaven. I fished diligently the whole time after leaving the ice, but caught only the cod on the way out and two small, poor-looking creatures the names of which I know not. They were so ugly that I was suspicious of them. I fed a boiled morsel of one to Nelson. He got sick, and I threw them back into the Arctic Ocean and gave him an extra helping of peanut burgoo.

Eating solids in the form of seal blubber, we both had the runs, but the color was not bad, and now that it was warmer, we could shit over the side, to leeward, without fear of frostbite, which was a great luxury.

One good thing about being alone in the Arctic, or out in the oceans anywhere, is that there are no cold germs, no lice, and no fleas. All the time I was up in cold latitudes I never had a headache. Nothing but my regular bouts of rheumatism when the weather gauge dropped and a stiff blow was on its way. Also "chinky toe-rot," as sailors call athlete's foot. How this came about I've no idea. It must have been from the previous owner of the sealskin boots, but the itch was murderous at first, until I finally ground up some chalk and cured it by that method.

But mentally and spiritually I had changed. The man who went into the ice was not the man who came out. Going in, I had not known the true nature of fear. I had not known, that is, the natural *animal* part of man, always lurking, waiting for the slightest chance to overcome his intelligence; always lurking in the shadows of man's mind, to spring upon him and drag him so easily, should he not purposefully resist, back into the murky dark cave from which he has so painfully, so slowly, so bloodily, so heroically, dragged himself over the millenia of human history.

When I went into the ice I had not known, either, the true nature of loneliness. Over the months of waiting for death, I had realized that the emotion we know as "loneliness" is, in fact, learned. *If there were no one to tell us we should be lonely, we would not be.*

Animals herd together for two main reasons: for protection and for procreation. Along with these two instincts man adds another: to try to hide from himself the fact that everyone, in the long run, is alone. *Absolutely alone.* In the whole vastness of the wastes of space, every human is on his own. To admit this, and to accept it, is the key to freedom from so-called loneliness. The more it is accepted, the more the company of other, likewise "alone" people can be appreciated, and the more they can be respected, liked, and even loved.

The intelligent man need never be "lonely." We can, if we are prepared to make the effort, keep the company of thousands of other intelligent men who have gone before us. We can learn from them, cry and laugh and hope with them, and recognize our places in the thrust of humanity from the corner of the cave to the outermost reaches of the firmament. Then we need never believe that any one of us is useless, disdained, or unwanted, for as long as there is blood in our veins, or a dream in our hearts, or a thought in our heads, we are, each one of us, an inescapable part of humanity, part of a whole. We are all a part of a spirit, a force, a *will*, which is irrepressible. A spirit that, even after inconceivable aeons of time, even after the whole universe collapses upon itself, will continue *to be.* A spirit the form of which is unknown to us; we have only an inkling, about which we can only guess.

It is towards this spirit, this unity, that we all strive. All humans, regardless of our faith or our political colorations, strive towards the eventual unity of the human spirit in eternity. We strive towards this, consciously or not. Some of us fail, some of us lean on others. Those of us who can perceive the paradox of our *aloneness* and yet at the same time our *unity* with the Whole can defeat fear. We can triumph over the worst death of all, the death of the human spirit!

As *Cresswell* neared the haze of land to the east, I reflected on all that had passed, and wondered if I could rejoin the human race.

On the sixteenth of June, anxious and hopeful, I saw land. Magic, wonderful, solid, faithful, eternal land. True, it was the silver white, snow-topped peaks of the Barentzburg, but under the sinister white there was a glimpse, a shivering smudge of darkness down on the horizon. Rock! Terra-bloody firma!

Excitedly, I trimmed the sheets and fussed about like a weekend racing man, even though the wind was very weak and the boat was hardly moving. I grabbed the bucket and the deck scrubber and went to it like a maniac, scrubbing the ice-gashed, torn canvas deck covering, wiping the spars, washing down the porthole lights, fussing and tidying the grubby, stinking blankets below, squaring up the oil-smeared books in the repaired library, nailing down the floorboards, a mass of broken wood, and running up the red ensign; hardly recognizable, just a pale pinkish yellow shaggy-edged rag. The treble-stitched cross and triangles of the Union Flag, now pure white, bleached out of their colors, were still whole and sound.

It took another thirty-six hours to reach the lee of Prins Karls Forland, even though the wind was up to gale force three hours after I sighted the land. I dared not push her too hard, for fear of opening the garboard strake even more. There was a serious risk that the amount of water leaking in would be more than I could get rid of, so I made my way into the channel between the Forland and the mainland of Spitsbergen under spitfire jib only. Of course this tiny sail would only move her very slowly, no more than two knots, but at least she was only pounding the seas, not dropping off them, as she would under the normal gale rig of mizzen, trysail, and spitfire.

On the evening of the eighteenth of June, I found myself in flat water, in the shallow sound east of the Forland. While I worked the boat through the fluky winds as they swept round the island, I stared about in wonder and delight. There were beaches, and rocks, seals, walruses, birds, and in the calm water by the shore of the island, hundreds of jumping fish. The temperature was just below freezing, and there was ice and snow to within yards of the beach. Above, the sky was black with storm clouds charging for Siberia. Rain stabbed down at intervals, but now and again sun rays slanted down through the gaps.

No tropical island with white sandy beaches shining beyond the dazzling surf under the high sun of Capricorn ever looked to me as sweet, as inviting, as beautiful, as did this Godforsaken hump of half-frozen primeval rock, sitting in the raging, ice-spume-blown Arctic Ocean. The sound of the anchor chain coming out of the hawsepipe for the first time in fourteen months was to me like all the trumpet blasts of the heavenly hosts; the wind-torn wisps of ice-laden clouds whistling over the high ground of the Forland seemed like the very banners of Caesar's triumph; the walruses snouting out of the knife-thin ice by the shore and the birds gliding up on high, like a vast crowd of welcome. As I gazed around the small bay through the sleety rain, waiting to see the anchor dug in properly, I could feel the life force in everything about me. Suddenly my eyes blurred and I lifted my gloved hand to wipe away the sleet from my wet cheeks. But it wasn't raining.

I staggered down below, to sleep on the makeshift shelf I had fixed six inches below the top of the cabin, so that the rising water would not reach me if I overslept. Pulling the blankets, still damp from the washing, over me, I cried myself to sleep like a baby. I was safe from the clutches of death. I was back among living things, that swam and flew and *dreamed*.

Two hours after I fell asleep I was awakened by a far-off noise. It was an engine. I scrambled out of the blankets and clambered aloft. There, away to the south, was a boat coming towards me. I delved into the after dodger for the siren and started to hoot. Then I realized that this was futile. They would not hear me at this distance, above the noise of the engine. Nelson jerked up and down on his foreleg, yelping a welcome. Sadly, I sunk down into the cockpit bilge to bail out two feet of icy water.

When the boat was only a mile away and I could sense the human presence, could feel the nearness of their souls, I hooted the siren, again and again. The answer came loud and clear through the now dying wind. I saw a figure waving from the small wheelhouse. It was a man! It was that wonder of all the wonders of a wonderful world—a human being!

I could not speak as they came onboard, and I could hardly see for the tears. The skipper sang out something, but I could not understand. In that state, at that moment, I would not have understood the Lord's Prayer in plain English. A crewman, a large, ruddy-faced, clean-shaven, blue-eyed giant, jumped onboard with a line, his heavy weight thudding on the deck. He looked at me and said quietly, "My God!"

He walked along the deck, to where I stood clutching the mizzen shrouds, tears streaming down my face, sobbing. He put his arm around my shoulder and spoke again. The sound of his voice, this rough fisherman on one of the most forlorn, remote, cold islands in the world, was overwhelming. He held me for a full minute, while I struggled to put a round turn and two half-hitches on my emotions.

It is said that when a man drowns he sees all his life flash through his mind's eye. The moment Olaf touched my shoulder, it seemed as if I could feel all of humanity—past, present, and future—pass, like an electric shock, through my whole being.

Then the skipper of the boat leaning through the wheelhouse noticed my ragged flag. He spoke to me in English— the first time I had heard it since Reykjavik, two years before. He called the time-honored words of welcome the world over.

"Hey, where you come from, friend?"

"Reykjavik, by way of Greenland!" I croaked.

The skipper repeated this in Norwegian to Olaf and the other two crewmen, who stared at the boat in disbelief. There was hardly a patch of paint left on her hull, she was all dirty gray wood where the ice had scraped and hammered her. Her wounds and gashes seemed to bleed.

"When you sail from Reykjavik?"

"July 1959!"

"Goddamn!" the skipper ejaculated, then turned and spoke rapidly to Olaf. Another crewman jumped onboard my boat. I was feeling claustrophobic with two other highly complex nervous systems observing, computing, and analyzing, so very close to me that their thoughts, as they silently poured out, almost seemed audible, touchable, and visible, like the balloons of speech in the cartoons of kids' comics. It was as if, all at once, I could feel every sensation, every emotion, that these men had felt all their waking lives, and see before me all the visions of their long-past dreams.

The voice of the skipper broke through. "I put Olaf and Gudar onboard your boat, and I tow you into King's Bay. You come onboard, come, eat, drink!"

"No, captain."

"It's okay. They good seamen, they bring her safe—come onboard, bring the dog!"

I shook my head. I wouldn't leave my boat until she was safe and sound at her destination. I wouldn't leave her, even if she sank under my feet. She was my vessel, she was my responsibility. That is the hard law of the sea, immutable and fixed. I came to, squaring my thin shoulders, and nodded to Olaf as he fixed the towing line around the tabernacle. I could see, as soon as he picked up the line, that he was a fine boatman. His mate looked horror-struck at the Arctic Ocean creeping up through the boat. Grabbing the pump, he worked away at clearing the bilge. I'd not been able to completely clear the boat of water for days. He did it in fifteen minutes flat.

I steered *Cresswell* in, with the fishing skipper taking it very slowly and easily, right down the deep fiord of King's Bay. There were all of twenty wooden structures! There were houses and buildings, and a church steeple even, and although it was lightly snowing, it seemed to me like we were going up under London Bridge, with the great city all around, or up the Hudson into New York Harbor.

Olaf anchored the boat, while I deflated the dinghy and dragged it out of the cabin. Then Olaf reinflated it for me. But I went ashore in the fishermen's jolly boat, which they drove straight up onto the pebble beach. I didn't weep for joy as Nelson and I stepped our five feet onto the scrunching pebbles, but I surely felt like it. Instead I glanced back at wounded *Cresswell*, which looked battered beyond belief.

All the inhabitants of the small outpost were on the beach to watch us go ashore. Within the hour I was sitting in Olaf's house with an electric light bulb shining miraculously over roast beef and creamed potatoes, cabbage and, the running gift of a breathless lady, Colman's Mustard! And the miracle of a hot bath with water from kettles boiling on the big potbellied stove.

During the three weeks in King's Bay I tried to explain what I'd been doing, but it came hard, because for the first days my mind simply refused to remember. I would try to recall a date, or the weather, and a curtain would drop, and then I could think of nothing but the immediate present and the future. Above all, I could think of little else besides getting away from the Arctic.

The Norwegians of Svalbard are quiet, sturdy, stolid folk, and they understood well enough how the long, long solitude had affected me. By instinct, for the first few days, they confined their solicitude for me to the needs of the moment. Did I sleep well enough? (I was sleeping dreams of relief.) Did I have enough to eat? (I was eating enough to feed a horse.) Was I warm enough? (I was warmer than I had been for many months.)

The rest of the time they left me to sit in a corner, silently drinking in the sights and sounds of human interplay, like a thirst-crazed man sipping cool water at an oasis. Then, little by little, I talked to Olaf and his mates, at first babbling away incoherently in basic English, about the Kalatdlits and the bear; about the stars and the ice; about escaping from the Arctic and the everlasting numbing cold, away from the ever-present threat of a soul-freezing death in the cold, cold darkness of glittering ice. I told them how I longed for warmth and the sunshine and gentle seas, and waving palm trees in the clear, starlit heavens of the tropics.

The Norwegian air force ran a weather station at King's Bay. Their doctor, when he examined me, was amazed at the complete absence of any fat on my body; yet, though skinny, I was very strong. He pronounced me fit and gave me some lotion for my rheumatism. Then he asked me what I was going to do.

"I'm sailing as soon as I can, before the weather closes in again, before there's any chance I might get stuck here for a whole winter."

"But you can winter safely here. You have your boat up on the beach. You can take off in the early summer next year. We can even arrange work for you here, if you are concerned about earning money."

"No, doctor, I have enough money to buy five weeks' food. With what I already have, there will be enough to reach Canada, or, if worse comes to worst, Iceland. At least I'll be out of the Arctic Circle. I can work there a season, then sail on for Canada."

"Why Canada?"

"Well," I said, "look at all that bloody marvelous boat-building timber, pitch pine, Douglas fir—"

He patted my shoulder. "I know your type. We've got them, too. I won't try to stop you. You sense your destiny and you follow it."

I bought food: potatoes, dried egg, canned milk, canned meat, flour, sugar, chocolate, and canned vegetables and fruit. The kind folk of King's Bay, together with the air force men, donated another six cases of canned goods, and Olaf, with Gudar, helped me paint the boat and test the engine. On July tenth all the good folks in King's Bay turned up at the jetty to wish *Cresswell*, Nelson, and me farewell and Godspeed for Canada.

"Send me a card!" cried Olaf.

"A card?" I called back. "I'll send you a book!"

"When?" He and all the crowd were laughing.

"When I've something to write about!"

I patted Nelson. The breeze picked up. *Cresswell* lurched to the first wavelets beyond the pier. The new, blood red ensign fluttered. We were off on the long trail again, across the ocean!

EPILOGUE

This translation is an extract from the book Vagabond *(Editions Maritimes et d'Outre Mer, Paris) by J. Kurbeil and J. M. Barrault, who made a voyage to the Arctic in 1979 from France.*

1830 hours. We arrived at the port of Reykjavik (Iceland). We moored alongside a trawler. The customs officials came onboard and the two of them helped us moor up.

After we had almost completed the traditional formalities, the oldest official demanded, "Are you searching for traces of other navigators who have passed through on their way to the Far North?"

"Yes," I replied, "but how do you know that?"

"I read it in the local paper."

"In fact, I am searching for my predecessors. There are tales and rumors of them here and there, but it's impossible to find their names."

"I remember," replied the customs official, "a British sailor who arrived here; it must have been twenty years ago. He was alone with a dog, wounded and blind. He was at the hospital here. His boat looked like a sort of converted canoe. He circumnavigated Iceland and afterwards he left for Greenland. No one saw him again."

"What was his name?"

"I'm sorry. I've forgotten, but I can find it in my papers at home. I made a note of it somewhere."

1952 hours. The customs man returned. "His name was Tristan Jones and his craft was called *Cresswell*."

(Then follows the account of Tristan Jones' voyage.)